Death On Delivery

By

Hannah Fairchild

[handwritten inscription and signature]

authorHOUSE™

All events and characters in this book are fictional and a product of the writer's imagination.

© 2005 Hannah Fairchild. All Rights Reserved.

No part of this book may be reproduced, stored in a retrieval system, or transmitted by any means without the written permission of the author.

First published by AuthorHouse 12/05/05

ISBN: 1-4208-8464-6 (sc)

*Printed in the United States of America
Bloomington, Indiana.*

This book is printed on acid-free paper.

To Mother.

With special thanks:

>To my editor, Ann Proud, whose Herculean efforts made the manuscript readable.

>To Jen Rogers for her technical expertise in translating the manuscript into usable form.

>To my two sons, for their support and encouragement.

>And, to my daughter and son-in-law for keeping me warm and fed in the interim.

PRIMARY CHARACTERS

Salome Jane Thaxton McKnight
    Now a Plainfield Police Dept. Lieutenant
Samuel John Thaxton
    Sal's twin brother
Plainfield Police Department
    Tom Warmkessell
        Police Chief
    Lt. Charlie O'Connell
        Sal's friend and champion
    Sgt. Eisenhard
        Succeeded Sal as Juvenile Officer
    Sal's Team:
        Sgt. Rick Masters
        Sgt. 'Fourth of July' Burger
        Cpl. Adam Adamson
        Cpl. Emily Haines
    Dolores Columbo   Sal's secretary

City of Plainfield
    Rueben Butz   Mayor & Sal's uncle
    Phyll Dayly   Evening Call Reporter

Plainfield County
    Earl Frey   Police Commissioner
    Warren Watland   District Attorney
    Madeline Grimm   Asst. DA & Sal's cousin
    Dr. West   County Psychiatrist

Hawk County
    The Corrigibles
        Theodore Reinhard/"Main Duke"
        Tommy Mudra/"Mechanic"
        Kit Gaumer/"Wheels"
        Shari McCutcheon/"Flirtie Gertie"
        Danny Dietrich/"Turt"
        Robey Robinson
        Jamie Truman
    Col. Peter Hammond-Youth At Risk Program
And Ernie Maddox   A delivery man

DEATH ON DELIVERY

A Pennsylvania Dutch Mystery
By Hannah Fairchild

PROLOGUE

Outside the door of 64D, Hardtack Williams inserted a key in the lock and turned. Nothing happened. He used some words not learned at his mother's knee, withdrew the key and tried again. It was a new key and sometimes new keys.... Still nothing. He used the unapproved words again.

What now? To search the key ring clipped to his belt for another key meant dropping his clipboard. That meant bending down to pick it up again and he doubted if he was up to it. Even at his best, robust energy had never been his thing. In fact it was generally conceded that, even at his best, HardTack Williams exhibited the trait known as 'laid back' to the fullest. And today he was feeling far from his best.

Fact is, he did not feel at all well. He had overslept this morning, a consequence of the 'meth' party he'd hosted the night before. He had finally nodded off just before dawn, only to be jarred awake by the raucous call of his alarm. A splash of water on his face, a clean tee shirt pulled on top of the pants in which he had slept, just so had he managed to drag himself down to his car.

The heat, having waited mercilessly in the bowl of the valley throughout the short summer night, had already discarded any pretense of relinquishing its hold on the baked city. Now, even in this young morning, it had turned his car into a steam bath.

He had driven lethargically through the humid morning, scarcely aware of the blistering sun, arriving at work nearly an hour late. It had taken him half an hour to repair the dripping faucet in 22D, which Jonesy had estimated would take ten minutes.

Now, his toolbox dangling heavily from one hand, he consulted the clipboard in the other, twisting his wrist to see his watch. Twenty-five past eight. He consulted the clipboard again. Three jobs to be done by the time the manager came at ten. If he did the easiest first, he would be half done. That was here at 64D. The "New Tenant" form on his clipboard meant checking all plumbing and electrical fixtures, the gas fireplace, the automatic drape pulls, the window locks, the paint on the woodwork and some other dozen minor items on the printed checklist. Housekeeping had already completed its portion and signed off, as had Security. Both had given the two bed, three bath apartment a clean bill.

He tried the key again. Still nothing. He withdrew it and looked at the attached tag. 84D. Shit! Wrong key! Damnall! Should've worn his glasses. He'd have to go all the way down to the office for the right key. He looked at his watch again. He'd never make it.

He glanced up and down the wide, heavily carpeted hall of the swank apartment complex, listening for the sounds of vacuum or floor polisher, for the opening of doors, the sound of the elevator. Nothing. It was quiet as a tomb.

Live a little, he encouraged himself. Heeding this side of his nature, he checked everything off as OK. He'd just have to take the chance that the new tenants would find something wrong.

Replacing the key ring in its clip, he noticed the grey carpet seemed scuffed. Housekeeping moving out its rug shampooing equipment? He noted this in the space for *Comments* at the bottom of the form, proof of his own dedication to duty. His boss was big on dedication.

One less job to do and no one the wiser. He was inordinately pleased with himself. In the column with the heading, *Time Job Completed,* he wrote the current time. 8:27. He grinned at the clipboard. That put him right on schedule. Get them before they get you. That, thought Hardtack Williams, was dead right.

This time though, Hardtack Williams was dead wrong.

* * * * *

Smiling to herself, the woman in the non-de-script car scuttled out of the parking space. As soon as her hand was free, she pushed a certain single digit on her cell-phone.

On the other end, the phone rang and rang. When the message giving instructions for the caller to leave a message, she hung up without a word.

She looked at her watch. Where was he? Not sleeping in. That would be very unlike him. On the way to work? If so, why was he not answering his phone? Perhaps he had forgotten to turn it on. Yes. That was it. He'd been forgetful lately without her there to remind him. Never mind. She'd be seeing him shortly.

She hummed as she turned onto the highway leading to Hamilton Circle.

CHAPTER 1 Warmkessel

Ve grow too soon old und too late smart.

West Side Tower Apartments. Tuesday. Noon.
Warmkessel surveyed the crime scene with a rising sense of panic. In the doorway of the plush dining room, he paused to steel himself against the anticipated sight. From this angle, only the back of the victim's head was visible over the high backed chair. Tall one this time he deduced. He drew nearer, stopping as he reached the body.

The dead man sat well back in the chair, his left arm resting on the table, his right dangling over the padded arm, as if he had merely dozed off after a particularly fine meal.

Warmkessel moved off, making a quick but thorough tour through the other rooms. The entire apartment was large, airy, finely furnished and neat as a pin. Reluctantly, he returned to the dining room.

The body was neat too. No messy blood spatters to analyze. No ugly bullet holes to measure.

"Positively dainty," Warmkessel muttered to himself.

Even the still body seemed, at first, curiously to be merely part of the decor, no more bizarre or incongruous than the horns of deer and elk adorning fireplaces in Plainfield's West End. At first. Until he saw that, like those tributes to virility, the corpse too, seemed to appraise the enigmatic doings of man with eyes wild with fright.

Man, or, he muttered, more likely in this case, woman.

This last grim reminder further jarred the policeman's already jaded system. As Plainfield's Chief of Police, Tom Warmkessel had learned to accept--police work will do that--that women were not always gentle, loving and unassuming, as the women in his pre-cop life had led him to expect. A big man, "Tiny Tom" had walked unflinching among Plainfield's criminal element for more than thirty years. But nothing, even organized crime's periodic attempts to infiltrate his city, had alarmed him as had these senseless deaths. Daunting because, but for subtle differences in furnishings and room layout, the view before him was eerily like all the others.

Eleven now! Eleven deliverymen dead! Eleven ordinary, hard working men persuaded to sit down and let themselves be murdered by a stranger!

He stared at the corpse. Surely this was one of those nightmares that endlessly repeats itself.

A sound behind him disabused him of that hope. "Man's name is Don Thurston." He snapped the information over his shoulder at the tall, elegant woman suddenly looming in his peripheral vision.

He couldn't help the snap. Neither expecting her nor hearing the footsteps muffled by the thick gold rug, her sudden appearance startled and annoyed him. Hell, he'd only been there a few minutes himself! He would have to have words with the officer at the door.

He fished in his shirt pocket for a toothpick and clamped down hard, waiting at the body for her to reach him. She drew within six feet before stopping.

"Chief Warmkessel?" The voice was low, throaty, authoritative.

"Counselor Grim?"

He tried to match her tone. He failed. Like all true Pennsylvania Dutch, he either said nothing or flat out what he thought. To be sure, he'd learned to recognize the artful, the superficially polite, but he was damned if he would be one of them.

The woman gave the dead man a brief, emotionless glance before moving on through the rest of the rooms, stopping briefly now and then to examine various objects. He scowled at her back. Had she forgotten this was a crime scene?

No. That was she all over. Madeline Grimm played by her own rules. Madeline Grimm, Assistant District Attorney, had antagonized pretty well everyone in his department and these murders had only made matters worse.

Officially, she had been named liaison between the DA's office and Warmkessel's own. But the title fooled no one. Most thought it a thinly disguised excuse for her to be near, if and when, anything even remotely newsworthy broke, and that her real function was to spy for a boss in need of a feather for his, up to now, rather unexciting political cap.

Lately, she'd begun to appear suddenly, as she had today, wherever the crime scene unit (Plainfield doesn't run to a Murder Squad,) happened to be working. There she would stand, hands clenching some file or paper or whatever had been the thin excuse for the interruption, to minimal breasts, like a dog begging a bone. Which, Warmkessel thought, she was. Although with her you could never call it begging. Ordering, more like, he told himself.

He'd advised his officers to ignore her and just do their jobs, but like most advice, it was a lot easier said than done. Her waspish prods, "I *believe* the District Attorney would want this" or "I *think* I speak for the District Attorney when I say *that*," had become the most mimicked phrases at the station since old Chief Shankweiler's, "Naw, chust vait vunce."

Those of Plainfield's finest, not directly involved with her, found it amusing. But to those assigned to investigate the murders, it was not funny. Three good investigators had already quit due to her interference. The PPD was running out of cops!

She made no effort to conceal her critical scrutiny of the police, busily engaged in their assigned tasks. Finally, inspection complete, she returned to join him beside the corpse.

Warmkessel continued to stare down at the body, thinking it only marginally less offensive than the live one hovering over him. At least, he told himself, the dead one would mind his own business!

He pulled himself up short. There was nothing amusing about the real thing. Eleven deaths now--and no evidence that this was the last. Warmkessel admitted to himself he was in over his head.

She spoke again, impatience seeping through the thin layer of professional courtesy. "What have we got?"

She looked at him, Warmkessel thought, like one of the statues guarding the hub in Hamilton Circle, no more than a hunk of matter using up space.

"I don't know what *you* got, Counselor. As for us, what you see is what we got." Warmkessel stifled the impulse to stand between the corpse and the woman, as if to protect it from further assault. "Same as all the others. This one works--worked--for Premier Electronics. Was sent to pick up a TV for repair. His boss," he referred to his notes, "man by the name of Carl Brainerd called us. He became alarmed about noon when customers began to phone him asking where the promised deliveries were. He called each of the stops Thurston was to make, starting with his last scheduled delivery and backtracking to his first. That was here. When he got no answer, he called the apartment manager."

Warmkessel withheld the most significant piece of information--that the maintenance man had, according to his worksheet, been in the apartment that morning. That would have been about the same time the coroner thinks

Death On Delivery
A Pennsylvania Dutch Mystery

the victim died. He wanted to interview the man on his own before letting the DA in.

He continued. "Brainard called us. Call came in at 12:20."

The officer working prints cocked an eye in the chief's direction. "Chief?"

"Yeah?"

"You okay? You sound irritated."

"Hell," he thought. "I *am* irritated. Finding the killer ought to have been duck soup. Hadn't they already had ten chances to identify the 'perp'? Hadn't the MO been exactly the same in each case? Sometimes he felt the killer was patronizing them--keeping everything the same so as not to confuse them, tax their intelligence.

One thing he knew for sure. Between the worldwide media and the late night talk shows, the Plainfield murders had been the hot topic for far too long. And now the unwanted attention had gone well beyond embarrassing, and the DA's office was threatening a grand jury investigation of his department. And, he thought, to be honest, it *should* have been easy.

He turned a page on his clipboard. "According to Brainerd, this was a new customer. Said she left for work at 8:30 and could they pick up her set first. Usually they deliver the new sets first before they pick up the sets for repair. That way they don't have to move them around in the truck. But they are trying to develop their service department, and they figured, from the address, they could probably sell a service contract to the lady. That's why they sent Thurston here. Apparently, he's the--he was the number one charmer."

"Have your men found anything this time?"

Warmkessel felt the urge to snap to attention, click his heels, and give her the old 'Sig Heil.' He restrained himself. "As you see," he seethed, "what they always do. Their best. But you know how this 'perp' is. She leaves nothing behind.

Damned those forensic cop shows!" He ground his teeth on the toothpick. "Hell! She's not here long enough to leave a clue!"

"She?"

He ignored that, removing what was left of the toothpick and dropping it in his pocket.

"No witnesses?"

Her tone implied there were probably thousands of eyewitnesses standing about, just clamoring to testify if only given a chance.

"None so far. We've just begun here, of course."

"What poison was used this time--assuming it was poison?"

"Need the tests of course. The ME thinks strychnine. Same kind used before. If it is, the lab will run tests to determine if the poison is from the same batch."

"Oh. Can they tell?"

Hell, he thought, you're the one who knows everything. "Sometimes. Chemicals may be affected by age, light and so on."

She started to leave then. At the foyer she stopped and turned, addressing him from the doorway. "Who is in charge?"

"I am for the moment."

"Oh?" Again the single word required a response.

"Yes. Lieutenant Gorgoli, who handled the last couple has left us for the state police."

"I see." The tone again. "Well, I must leave. I have a prelim at three o'clock. I'd like to see the reports as soon as possible. Will you see to it?"

"Yes, ma'am. I'll have someone run them over as soon as I get them." Have someone run *you* over too, while I'm at it. No end of volunteers for *that* job.

If she heard the venom behind the words, she gave no notice. "The lab report, too."

"I *said* everything."

Relieved that she was finally gone, but bereft of the wisdom to know what to do, he returned to the spotless kitchen. It was useless. The Crime Scene Unit had been assiduous in checking everything conceivable. There was simply nothing there.

He returned to contemplate the body. It seemed slightly less horrible this time, perhaps proving the philosophy that you could get used to hanging if you hung long enough.

"Manager's back, sir. Want him now?"

"Yeah. All... No, wait. I'll go there."

* * * * *

Asked what he could tell them about the tenant, the apartment manager protested he had already told the police what little he could.

"Good. Then it should be easy."

He said he'd gotten a letter from Plainfield Hospital a week or so ago, saying they had hired a Nurse Supervisor who wished to rent one of his apartments. "Asked me to give her every courtesy. A couple of days ago she showed up in uniform, looked the apartment over and paid the security deposit in cash. She asked for a key. She wanted to replace the curtains and she wanted to bring her mother in to get her approval. Said she would be back the next day--that would have been yesterday--to sign the lease. Yesterday she telephoned just before noon to say she had to work late. Wanted to know if she could come today. I already gave the letter to the officer there."

Warmkessel pointed to the police warnings someone had pinned on the bulletin board. "Why the hell d'ya think we went to the trouble of sending out these warnings?"

The man shrugged. "You know how it is. Anyway, they had fixed four o'clock, the end of her regular shift, for her mother to come along in and sign the lease. Both leasers have to sign. We're very strict about that," he said virtuously.

"Today?"

"Yes. Of course today. Apparently," here he had enough sense to look embarrassed, "she came early."

"So you have nothing with her signature on it?"

"No." In answer to the next question, he said there was nothing distinguishable about the woman. "Middle age. Grey hair. Thinnish. Soft voice, a bit on the high side but other than that just ordinary." No. He had never spoken to the mother.

Of course not! There wasn't any mother. Warmkessel doubted this murdering hyena ever *had* a mother. The description would be useless, but his men would check it out. At this point, he could not afford to leave any stone, however small, unturned.

He gave instructions to the officer on the door to get the APB started, then returned to the interview. "I'd like you to come down to headquarters. Meet with an artist. You do that?"

The manager made a face. "Now?"

"Certainly now. Soon's I'm finished with you."

The manager heaved a sigh. Asked about the maintenance man, he had little to contribute. His employee had gone to the office just before noon and turned in his worksheet with a note stating that he was ill and was going home. So far, his secretary had not been able to reach the man on the phone. Later he could drive over there, but...

Warmkessel assured him that he needn't bother, they were taking care of it. He told the manager to leave the man's worksheet for the day with him, then he was free to go on down to headquarters. In answer to the man's question, he said they were finished with the elevator but would need the apartment sealed off for the time being.

Death On Delivery
A Pennsylvania Dutch Mystery

He left the scene-of-crime officers to complete their work, instructing them to leave the apartment the way they found it, seal it, work up their reports and get them to him yesterday. If they heard from the officer tracking down the missing maintenance man, they should send her right to him.

Glumly, Warmkessel headed back to the car he'd left baking in the one hundred degree sun. In his hurry to get to the crime scene, he had not thought to park in the shade. He pulled off his uniform jacket and covered the door handle with the sleeve before opening it. Once inside, he did the same with the steering wheel. He turned the air conditioner on as soon as the motor turned over, though he knew he would reach his destination before the air was sufficiently cooled. He cranked down the window. Maybe the air, hot as it was, would dry some of the sweat already dripping off him. God! This was going to be one royal mess!

CHAPTER 2 Sal

Vunn goot laff iss vorth two good lickins.

Wednesday morning. 27 Longmeadow.

Sal dragged herself from sleep to swat at the fly buzzing around her head. Apparently, she thought grumpily, the amenities of the dorm at Atlanta's "Y" did not extend to.... Another buzz, another swat. She struck herself.

Two bits of reality seeped into her sleep drugged brain. One: she was no longer in Atlanta but home in her own bed. And two: the buzzing source was neither small nor so readily dislodged.

She pushed the tiny button on her watch and growled into it. "I hope this is important."

"Oh! You're alive! I was trying to remember if I still have a black suit." Sam sounded testy.

"I hope you do. You'll be needing it if I get many more of these ungodly early calls!" She tacked on a mumbled comment, something about it being a good morning.

"Is now," he rejoined, "now you're finally back home."

"I take it that means you missed me. What time is it anyway?"

"Five minutes past five. And, you bet I missed you. Haven't I been doing your chores?"

"Oh. Right. So you have. Thanks. Are you calling to say you can do them one more day?"

"Nope. I'm calling to remind you I'm *not* doing them one more day. I'm leaving, remember?"

"Oh right," she said again. "Taiwan. About the pigs. I'm beginning to wake up."

"Good! Then I've done my good deed for the day. You going to work today?"

"Of course. I'm on the three o'clock shift. You coming to breakfast?"

"Of course. See you then."

Muttering compliance, she began the onerous task of hauling herself out of bed. Her watch buzzed again.

"Something else? I forget something?"

"No. I did. Welcome home."

Her turn at the chores meant forgoing her early morning walk, but she accepted it willingly. Nothing restored her to home and hearth as well as these humble, but necessary tasks. A quick brush of the teeth, an even quicker pass at the hair, a grab for tee shirt and jeans, a stop at the mudroom for work boots, and she was making her way past lawns and gardens to the stables.

In spite of the early hour, she was not the first there. Benjam, small and thin, cropped hair gone completely grey, his face permanently tanned from years of living out-of-doors, was already at work, mucking out the stalls of the half dozen riding horses she still kept.

Ignoring his protests, she took the shovel from him and shook his dry, cracked hand. "Thanks Benjam. Sorry I'm late. I'm back though."

She had to raise her voice to be heard above the chorused greetings coming toward her from the stable inhabitants.

The old man grinned proprietarily, his inspection of her indistinguishable from that with which he favored his four legged charges.

She grinned back, somewhat embarrassed by such enthusiasm. Though keenly aware of the bond between them, the natural reticence of the Pennsylvania Dutch to hang out their feelings in public, held her tongue. Besides, how could she put into words all she felt for the man who had been mother and father to Sam and her even before the untimely death of their parents. Had it not been Benjam's ability to see life with simple clarity, uninfluenced by the wealth and power surrounding them, the compass by which the twins had set their stars?

Still grinning widely, Benjam followed her into each box. While she shoveled, he reported, making no distinction between human boss and equine charges. Hopping to the side of each sleek animal in turn, he patted its shoulder, demanding of her, "Don't she look bee-yoo-ti-ful?" Then jumping to her side to give her shoulder the same sort of pat, he inquired of the horse, "Ain't you glad she's back?" Only when he got to the last stall did some of the smile fade. "Sam's worried about Nimbus," he muttered. "Thinks he's got a dicky knee."

"Oh? I thought my brother sounded cranky this morning."

Nimbus had been his mount for twelve years now. "What does Cousin Susan think?"

Benjam shrugged. "Ain't sure neither, I don't think. Wants to move 'im over to her place where she kin keep an eye on him."

"And Sam doesn't want that?"

"You know Sam. Sooner part with 'is right arm."

"I'll talk to him. He'll be gone for a while. This would be a good time for Susan to come and get him, give him a good work-up."

She finished the mucking out, then moved on to feed the stock, stopping to admire Handsum's newest piglets before collecting the day's eggs.

Death On Delivery
A Pennsylvania Dutch Mystery

In the mudroom, she removed her work boots, washed hands and face, and barefoot, took the eggs and a raging appetite inside.

* * * * *

In the kitchen, Mrs. Honeycutt was dusting powdered sugar on something. Sal groaned.

"Oh. So yer home naw vunce," the good lady grunted. "It's high time. Suppose now you want yer eats."

"Just a boiled egg and toast, Mrs. Honey. Be good to have some really good bread again. I've missed that. You have me spoiled. How you've been anyway? Where's Honeycutt?"

"In the spring house. Turning the sauerkraut vunce. Set yerself a piece. Yer brother's in already."

In the small dining room, Sam was dipping into compotes of eggs, sausages, and fried Yukons. He invited her to join him.

She shook her head. "Mine's coming. I've got three weeks of eating everything not nailed down to make up for." She gave him a one-armed hug, dropping a kiss on the chestnut hair so like her own, then took her usual place across from the larger version of herself.

Sam nodded, his mouth full. "Understandable. Can't check up on the restaurants without eating." He took another forkful. "Been on the scale yet?"

"No. Haven't had time."

"Uh hunh."

"Well, I haven't. Besides, aren't you always telling me to forget it?"

"Yeah. If you only would." He speared a sausage link. She tried not to look. He jabbed it at her. "You should try one of these. I changed the recipe a little."

"I'll think about it."

"Good! And here's something else for you to think about. Mrs. Honey's out there making a batch of sour cherry fritters for you. You can start thinking how you're going to refuse them without hurting her feelings."

Sal groaned. "Oh no! Not sour cherry fritters!" She eyed him bleakly. "I hope you've done something more than find new ways to torture me while I was gone. Have you seen anything of Walt?"

Sam said he'd taken some friends to lunch at Ringside Seat, Walt's newly opened sports bar, and that business was brisk. "Did a nice job taking care of us too. Growing up finally. He's using my barbecue sauce now. Says it goes over big. Frankly, I still can't believe he and Barney actually went ahead and started their own restaurant. It's not as though there's no place for them with Pleasant Company."

It was an old argument. She changed the subject. "I hear Nimbus is off his feed. This hot weather you think?"

The discussion turned to horses and the job Cousin Susan was doing running Thaxton stables. Asked, he admitted he'd finally relented. Susan would pick up Nimbus while he was away. Talk turned to their restaurants and the purpose of Sal's 'vacation.'

"You said there were reports of trouble with the *Geese*.* Vas gibt?"

What "gave," she said, was that several friends had said that women dining alone were getting short shrift.

---

* The responsibility for the twin's three top of the line restaurants: the Red Goose in Manhattan, the White Goose in Paris, and London's Grey Goose is Sal's. Famous for their Pennsylvania Dutch cuisine, including the indigenous seven sweets and seven sours. Sal visits each several times a year, monitoring the quality of everything from bus persons to decor, and that, of course, includes the food. She could no longer go incognito, there being little staff turnover, but she could, and did, go unannounced.

"And were they?"

"Just in the Paris store. You recall we'd promoted Charles to Maître d' last year? Seems he thinks women dining alone bring down the tone of the place. He thought to discourage this by making them wait in the bar for long periods, even declining to accept a reservation from them."

"You read him the riot act?"

"My version of it. He's worked well for us until now, trains the wait staff well, so I hate to lose him. I gave him a second chance. Oh, by the way, I stopped over at Uncle Peter's to see how Janus* is doing."

"Running the place yet?"

She laughed. "Not yet. She's training to be a jockey. They say she'll be really top notch if she can keep her weight down. She loves to eat."

"She will. She's a determined young lady."

"Isn't she, though? Speaking of determined people, Denver Kildare tracked me down over there. He still wants to buy the Geese."

Sam gave her a sharp look. "You getting bored with it?"

"Perhaps."

"Okay. We'll give it some thought. You did get away for a couple of days though, didn't you?"

She said she'd wrangled an invitation to work near Atlanta with the Habitat for Humanity crew. "For three glorious days! I loved it! There's something so... adventurous about the smell of rough lumber. Remember the remnants bin at Grandfather's lumber company...."

"...And the hours we spent looking for just the right piece...."

"...Begging nails from Adolph...."

"...Always insisting grandfather'd fire him if he knew."

---

* Character from 'Dead in Pleasant Company'

She smiled indulgently at him. "You did the hammering though. I seemed to hit my fingers more than the nails."

"I suppose it's a guy thing. Anyway, you're the one who came up with the ideas."

"Some of our happiest moments."

"Uh hunh." They remained in the past for a bit. "Anyway," she said then, "my previous experience didn't seem to impress the Habitat folks. After an embarrassingly brief assessment of my carpentry skills, the crew chief relegated me to the role of 'go-fer'. I spent three days carrying 2 by 4's, huge coils of wire and lengths of plastic pipe to the more coordinated workers."

Sam laughed. "That should have worked off a few pounds."

"Should have. Would have, but you're forgetting Atlanta's great restaurants. Naturally I had to check them out. Some of them anyhow."

"Naturally." He of the I-can-eat-anything-and-not-gain-an-ounce metabolism. "It's your job. Market research. Just protecting our investments. Nicht wahr? It's a dirty job but somebody has..."

"Ach! Sie ruhic!"

"Put it this way. My three weeks away did not auger well for guarding either flank or rear."

He laughed at that. "Well," he pushed his chair away," I've got to get going. So what are you going to do while I'm gone?"

"Go to work, of course."

"Of course, but you're a lieutenant now. Doesn't that mean you can delegate a lot?"

"Good heavens no! I've still got both Juvenile and Victims. Warmkessel said he wanted me to take Theft and Fraud as well."

"What you wanted, isn't it?"

"Theft and Fraud, yes. Anything but Violent Crimes. Speaking of which, anything new at this end about the deliverymen murders?

He shook his head. "Uncle Rueben says the DA is pulling strings among his council buddies to get the investigations brought under his umbrella."

"Really? That would be devastating for the Chief." She sipped her coffee. "You don't suppose Cousin Madeline has anything to do with that?"

"Everything, if she's anything like she was as a kid. She was always in the thick of anything contentious going on among the cousins."

"Not in the middle of them. On the sideline, egging everyone on. She played a great game of 'Let's you and him fight.'"

"Speaking of cousin Maddie, I hear she's lost her boyfriend."

"Oh? Warren Watland? I'm sorry to hear that. Her affair with him was beginning to make her almost human."

"Almost."

"I wish I liked her better. Losing your first love is never a picnic, and at her age... if she's lost him she could use a friend."

"Maybe, but not you. She's always hated your guts."

"I know. I wish I knew why."

"Forget it. Anyway, she can't be that upset. The family says she's spending a big hunk of her dough in backing his political career."

"Oh? For... "

"Lieutenant Governor I hear. Forget them. Let's talk about me."

"Okay. What about you?"

"I'm off as soon as the plane is ready."

Sal downed the last of her coffee. "Anything new with the *freundschaft?*"

"Not much. Wish you'd talk to Aunt Fiddena though. Lately she's giving everyone a hard time about going to church."

"Oh? Because of the heat?"

Sam nodded. "'Doc' says it's too hot to drive in that ancient Packard without air conditioning and she won't let anyone else take her. Maybe you could..."

"I'll try. Anything else new?"

"I assume you saw the new piglets? What do you think?"

"They look great. If they evaluate well, let's get more."

"Okay. I'll look for a good source while I'm over there."

The important topics covered, they chatted on a bit anyway. Three weeks was a long time to be separated and now they'd be apart again.

Finally he said he had to leave. "Want to get airborne before it gets too damned hot. Roselma is going along this time, remember."

"I know. We chatted by e-mail yesterday. She's been well?"

"Other than needing new reading glasses."

Sal grunted. "Yes well, there's a lot of that going around." She watched as he rose to go. He stopped to give her shoulder a squeeze. "Well, 'Bro.'"

"Yup. Try to keep out of trouble 'till I get back, eh?"

"I will if you will."

"See you in the funny papers."

* * * * *

Naturally, all three 'girls' were in attendance when Sal arrived for lunch. There was the usual fuss over Sal's new slimmer figure, now not quite so slim as three weeks ago, but still unnatural as far as the great-aunts were concerned. They made a point of telling her so.

"Never mind that, Aunt Fiddena. What's this I hear about you not listening to the doctor?"

"Oh fudge! I've riden in that Packard to church ever since I was three years old and I'm not going to change now. This is not the first time we've had hot and humid weather you know."

"No, but you aren't three years old any more. Look Aunt Fiddena. How about if I pick all three of you up and take you? I'd really like that. I don't see enough of you."

No one was surprised at Aunt Fiddena's meek submission to this proposal. Sal's knack for persuasion was part of the family lore. This time, however, the aunts seemed particularly smug. Only driving home after lunch did Sal realize they, too, had gotten what they wanted. It meant she would have to go herself, an experience she was all too often inclined to skip in favor of a Sunday morning drive in the countryside.

"Wiley old girls," she thought.

At two-thirty, Sal put away the last of the Thaxton Foundation grant proposals, sent e-mails to her offspring, reminded Mrs. Honey she would be on three to midnight for the next three weeks, so would not be requiring dinner, and headed for work.

CHAPTER 3 Jamie

Children and fools tell the truth.

Wednesday morning.
All his short life, Jamie Truman had been the smallest boy in his class. In death, he looked even smaller.

This morning he'd awakened from a fitful sleep to a leaden sky, amassed with black clouds heavy with rain. He had dressed slowly, putting on his best shirt--a long sleeved cotton with large navy blue and white checks--and the new jeans bought with his paper route money. Then he had sat on the edge of his bed, listening to the familiar sounds of mother and *him* getting ready for work, waiting for them to leave.

His mother called up the stairs to tell him it was time to get up. He could hear her voice falter toward the end, could hear *him* telling her to stop smothering the boy. "He can take care of himself," he heard *him* say.

Standing well back from his window, he watched their cars drive off. Mother backed her five-year-old Escort uncertainly on to the street, turned left and headed for school. *He,* of course, did not take his own red Porsche to work. The red Porsche was reserved for their "little trips." Rather he waited at the end of the driveway for his ride.

He had gone back to sit on his bed for a long time thinking. The phone rang once or twice but, although he knew Mrs. Stanhope was off for the day, he ignored it. It would be either somebody selling something or somebody from school.

School! The Corrigibles! His friends! The thought made him ache. Why the Corrigibles had made him a member of their tight-knit gang was a complete mystery to him. Other boys had never liked him. Mother was horrified by his inclusion in the group, had forbid him to have anything to do with the odd assortment of fellow travelers in his class. He had learned not to talk about them to her, yet they were the only good thing that had happened to him since his real father left.

In a strange way, the Corrigibles were a big part of the reason he had to do this. He had failed to live up to the gang's "no secret" code, and now his secret, his shameful secret, would be uncovered.

It was all his fault. He was too weak. He was a coward. He could not get up the nerve to tell the gang the truth. Main Duke was big on telling the truth. But what was the use? They wouldn't believe him. To them he was the luckiest boy alive. He had a father who liked to do things with him. Fishing weekends at their cabin, camping at the shore. And he got to do these things in a Porsche. A red Porsche.

No. They'd never believe him, and why should they? Even his own mother didn't believe him.

Now his shameful secret was going to come out anyway. Not only would his secret be exposed, but he had failed to protect his friends.

After weeks of trying to dissuade *him, he* had insisted on inviting Turt and Robey along this weekend. They would surely tell Main Duke and, well, there was no telling what Main Duke would do. Main Duke had a whole vocabulary of special words for men like *him.*

What would they think of him then? The thought made him sick again. He threw up in the bathroom, though there was little left to disgorge.

He returned to his room, once more vainly listening intently for any sound. Certain now he was alone, he went to the small roll top desk his real father had given him on his first day of school. They had plans. He, Jamie John Truman, Junior, would study hard and be an architect too, so the two could work together when he got big. Then one day they took his father to the hospital and he never came back.

Then *he* came.

He didn't have to think about what he was going to write. He had written it over and over in his head.

From his closet shelf, he took the baseball cap once worn by Roger Clemente and the box containing the new brown and blue hound's-tooth sweater. It was the latest Christmas gift from Aunt Dawn. Aunt Dawn's sweaters were always two sizes too big. Once or twice he had tried to mention this in his thank you note to her, but Mother always made him rewrite it. The sweaters were expensive, ordered by phone for a boy his age from the best store in town. He should be grateful. It wasn't her fault he was so small for his age.

This one was nice and soft, something called cashmere. Robey Robinson had gone crazy when he saw it. "It's a Bill Blass Original!" Robey seemed to live for clothes. He could have the sweater now.

The cap was for Fingers. He liked to pretend he played for the Phillies.

His black trunk yielded a set of calligraphy pens, his CD collection and the new portable disk player which had made him the envy of the school. These would go to Wheels. She was always either riding her bike or dancing around. As for the pens, Flirtie Gertie would go crazy over them. Gertie really *was* crazy according to Main Duke, who had overheard two counselors talking about her but, crazy or not, she sure could draw. She made a lot of signs and posters and stuff. For a moment Jamie longed to be around to see the signs she would make, and be, at least a small part, of the affairs they would announce. But no. Alive he would not be allowed to give the pens away. His mother would call her mother and get them back. It was all useless.

He took his bike keys out of his jeans pocket and put them on the desk. Turt, short for Turtle because of the way he walked, could have his bike. Maybe they would let him have his paper route too.

That left only Main Duke. Jamie liked Main Duke the best. He got his savings account book out of his secret hiding place and put it on the desk and wrote right in the front of it:

"I leave all the money in this account which was earned by me to my best friend Main Duke Theodore Reinhardt. Signed, Jamie John Truman." He thought a moment, then added the date.

He arranged his legacy around the note on the desk so they would all be seen together. That way nobody would have to hunt for anything. He did not want to be a nuisance.

His task complete, he went down the few steps separating living and sleeping quarters, through the large silent house with its conversation pit, its terrace room, its hot tub. In the large pantry, he selected a box of black plastic bags and removed three of them. He stopped and thought a bit, then went back for one more.

Back in his room, he began to pack his belongings. Clothing from the pine dresser went into one bag, those in the walk-in closet into another, toys and games into a third. Next he stripped his bed of the adulterated sheets with the racing design and the matching comforter, stuffing these into the last of the bags. He found space enough in one of them to accommodate the last thing that belonged to him--a bedside lamp, its base shaped like a racecar.

He looked around the empty room with a sense of peace he had not felt for a long time. Without the lamps, the room was almost as dark as night. He was glad he had thought to bundle his things away himself. No one would bother to unpack these neat parcels. His privacy, so violated in life, would not be trespassed on in death.

Packing complete, he went once more to look out the window, searching through his mind for one reason he should not do this, but the clouds, hanging even lower now in thick charcoal humps, seemed to call him, to lend him strength.

He had considered carefully the point of impact. It seemed most appropriate to punish the part of the body which was the source of his torment, but could a person die from such a wound?

The gun felt awkward in his small hand. He began to worry if he would use it properly. The real thing felt quite different than he expected.

* * * * *

He needn't have worried. Even a rank amateur can kill with the rifle's end pushed hard against the brain.

* * * * *

The blood from the gaping hole finally caked and dried. Now and then a breeze, from the partly open window, flipped the note, held down by the boy's disc player, back and forth.

CHAPTER 4 Batter up!

Well whetted is half mowed.

Plainfield Police Department. Wednesday. 3 PM.

Lieutenant Charlie O'Connell grabbed her the moment she left roll call. Though well aware she was not one for public embraces, he'd, none-the-less, thrown caution to the winds and exercising his right as mentor, enveloped her in a warm hug. After all, hadn't he recruited her? Hadn't she proved an exemplary police officer? And hadn't she, under his supervision, re-vamped the entire Juvenile program. And hadn't it covered them both with glory?

She had accepted his accolades as patiently as possible. Juvenile had been an interesting challenge to be sure. Now it was time to move on.

But she was finding any sort of movement difficult. Released from her friend's grip, her efforts to get from his office to her own were proving hairy. The whole place was in an uproar. News of this morning's murder, passing between the changing shifts, meant being stopped at every turn. She had yet to reach her own desk, and had already fallen well behind in her efforts to catch up after her hiatus.

Finally, extricating herself from the throng, she sprinted down the hall toward her office. Her phone beeped. She dug it from her pocket and puffed, "Hello."

The voice was unexpected and venomous.

"*Lootenant* McKnight!"

No mistaking that voice. Acting Captain Longnecker. Calling from the desk in the large command room from the sound of it.

"Vell yer Highness! Finally gettin' to vork! Didn't see ya at roll call. Guess yer too important these days to show up vunce."

"No sir. I was... " She stopped. No good playing it straight with him.

He finished it for her. "... busy. Ich weiss! Hop-nopping viss that *freundschaft* of your'n."

To say it was he who had come to roll call so late that most officers had already filed out, would only invite further vitriol.

"Good afternoon Captain. Sorry I missed you. How can I help?"

"Help me? This ain't about nothin' so lowly as me. No sirree, Chicky. Yer wanted in the commissioner's office *mach schnell*"

"The commissioner's office? Not the chief's?"

"You heard me. The commissioner's. Anyways, the chief's there too."

"He is? And they want me? What for?"

"How the hell do I know? Probably waitin' to kiss yer Thaxton fanny for showin' up. Ennyvays, they sett to hop to it. 'En venn yer done there, ya can hustle yerself dawn to my office fer a review of the department cases. Versteh?"

"Yessir."

If he'd hoped to rattle her, he was doomed to be disappointed. According to Charlie, the *Evening Call* had been making much of the new juvenile program. Naturally that would irritate Longnecker. As for the case review required of each officer of her rank and above, she'd already caught up with current cases with O'Connell.

But why this curt order to "hop to it?" Could it be the chief was going to turn over Fraud and White Collar Crimes to her as promised? She brightened, offering up a small prayer that would be it.

She resigned herself to further delay, waved off her waiting secretary with a brief, "Sorry, Dolores. I'll be right back," dropped her papers on her desk and headed for the sixth floor.

* * * * *

Earlier in Police Commissioner Frey's office.

But in Commissioner Frey's office, it was not fraud on the official mind, but murder. Multiple murders!

Now, mid-afternoon, the commissioner's office appeared to be the target of an alien invasion. If, in this case, the invaders carried press cards, microphones and notebooks, their noisy presence in the outer office where Lainie Summers held sway, was no less ominous.

Lainie Summers, immaculate and unflappable, silver, neatly waved mane topping her tall, big-boned frame, was presently holding them at bay. One large white earring lay on the desk, a silent testament to the perpetual phone calls. The other still adorned her pleasant bony face, keeping company with the crisply white bracelet and beads falling well down her chest. Taken together on this hot and humid day, her crisp ensemble, like blue-green ocean waves topped with a riff of white, suggested a cool and pleasant oasis.

Normally, Lainie, who had served three commissioners as secretary, aide-de-camp, factotum and general dogsbody, manipulated the press with ease. Today, however, she'd had to pull out all stops against the ever more creative enticements of the media, whose pockets, due to the newness of the fiscal year, were bulging. In addition to outsiders, she'd had to balance mounting pressure from the mayor, city council, and a deluge of both influential and uninfluential citizens.

Not that she wasn't used to it, of course. She was the commissioner's lightning rod, taking from her boss's critics their most strident and belligerent demands, and passing them on to her boss, reduced to manageable proportions. At the same time, it was she who translated his often vitriolic and actionable comments into language at once pointedly clear and well within the rights of citizens. There seemed always those who, having come to the commissioner's attention through their abuse of that document, insisted when cornered, on standing firmly on their Constitutional rights.

But today's uproar had hit a new high. All those grisly murders! Eleven hard working Plainfielders had gone unsuspecting to their deaths and the primarily intelligent, tolerant and impassive Pennsylvania Dutch had had enough. Like the rasping of crickets in mating season, the good citizens of Plainfield were speaking out. Fortunately, it was just six months to city and statewide primaries, and elected officials were vulnerable to suggestion.

At last count, nineteen requests for radio and television interviews lay in the center of the commissioner's normally spotless desk. Twice that many requests from print media formed a staggering pile to one side. A third pile, pink telephone message slips, lay to the right. An even higher stack of well filled personnel files, sent over from the chief's office, took up most of the upper half of the desk.

Yet the jumble on the desk was but a pale reflection of the state of the commissioner's mind. The man himself paced back and forth, as far from his desk as possible. The press onslaught had already strained tact and political savvy to the breaking point. And now, his own police chief, his life-long buddy, had let the side down as well.

He pushed the memos aside irritably and pulled the personnel files toward him. The uppermost of these bore the name, history and records of the chief's choice to head the new Special Investigative Team. It was not the commissioner's choice and he was not going to go along with it.

The commissioner blamed himself. He had gotten lazy. For years now, his next in command had needed no more help from him than an occasional pat on the back. As chief, Warmkessel had rid the Plainfield Police Department of the dishonest, the incompetent, the unfit, turning its one hundred and eighty-six men and women into what one reporter called a "keen, lean machine." But, he had gone into a tailspin after losing both wife and adored son a couple of years back. Since then, the police department pretty much ran itself.

Then these bizarre killings started, and Warmkessel had come back to take full charge. But was he the same chief? Had he lost his judgment, his fire? Was that why this killer had gone uncaught?

And, Frey added to himself, pushing aside the uppermost file, anyone can be unwittingly influenced by personal considerations. In this case, no doubt his judgment was clouded by this officer's work with Victims Of Crime, the chief's own project.

Nor was the commissioner alone in his misery. DA Watland, a frown crunching his symmetrical features, had marched into his office hours earlier, like the ex-Navy gunner he was. For nearly two hours now, he had provided the company said to be loved by this intolerable state.

Not that the D.A. and the commissioner were anything like bosom buddies. No, indeed. Only the extreme danger the situation posed for each of them, supplied the catalyst for this unholy alliance.

For Watland, too, had been hounded by the ubiquitous press. It was from them he learned of this latest murder. They had tracked him down at a meeting of the United Funds committee, of which he had just been named Chair.

He had replied a series of grim, "No comments," to those reporters too close to avoid, and hurriedly escaped.

Once gaining the security of his own office, Watland had sent for his top assistant DA. The killings were on Maddie Grimm's docket. Besides, she always knew what to do. He needed her cool head now more than ever.

But Maddie was not there. Someone said she had gone to view the scene of the latest murder and had not yet returned. How like her, he thought, to be Johnny-on-the-Spot. Thank God he could depend on someone.

Feeling lost, he'd left his office by the back door, walked up two flights of service stairs to the commissioner's office, knocked and entered through *his* back door. There he seated himself in the most comfortable chair--the commissioner's own, crossed his sharply trousered legs and laid his aching head against the back. Surely these late bridge evenings with Louise and her parents would come to an end once they were married. They were taking their toll, but he did not wish to offend his future in-laws. He wanted the Chalmers solidly behind him, the commissioner's chair not being, by far, the chair to which he aspired.

But there were many careful steps to take before he had the support he needed to challenge the incumbent. He was no fool. The publicity gained, when he prosecuted the deliverymen killer, could either give him an incredible boost, or drop him forever into the pit of lost gubernatorial hopefuls.

And thus it was that for the past few hours, commissioner and district attorney, protected from the public onslaught by Lainie, had huddled over the game plan.

The two men were in full agreement. Someone had to grab the ball and run with it, and that someone was Chief of Police Warmkessel. Frey's job was to use his 'bully pulpit' to get behind the cops. Watland's position, (taken firmly--his publicist having advised him his image needed firming up,) was that he had done his share for now. Hadn't he assigned his best assistant as liaison to the police? It was up to her to see that the police provided his office with proof they could take to trial. His personal contribution would come later, in court. All the chief had to do was produce a team leader that would get them out of this mess.

The two men had, of course, avoided mentioning their more personal stakes in the chief's choice. Rather, they piously reminded each other of the enormous responsibility and power the chosen person would have. They needed someone with wide experience, young enough to hold up to the long days and nights to come, old enough to have developed good judgment. Someone, they said firmly, who could inspire the troops.

Yet the name placed before them was the least experienced of all Plainfield's officers, with no experience at all with crimes of violence.

Frey complained. What could his old friend be thinking? Warmkessel's choice was too new, too untried, too, not to put too fine a point on it, female. They couldn't take a chance on having someone make an even bigger mess than they already had. The two men were prepared to dig in their heels.

At the moment, however, their heels were cooling. Chief of Police Warmkessel was already late. Where in hell, they demanded of each other, was he?

As if on cue, Warmkessel's voice floated in from the outer office. A peal of laughter stung the waiting men further. Outside somewhere, a mad killer was loose. Here they were suffering serious bouts of anxiety. And Warmkessel, their hope, their regrettably only hope, was telling Lainie jokes!

Lainie ushered him in still chuckling. She lingered in the doorway as the massive figure reached out and enveloped the commissioner's carefully manicured hand, and pumped it vigorously.

"Stow it, Tom!" Her boss was terse. "The cameras aren't rolling." Frey waved him to a seat. A round of musical chairs followed. Watland moved well out of the line of fire to a chair near the window. Warmkessel took the newly vacated commissioner's chair, the only one that could accommodate him. Frey settled across from his subordinate, prepared for battle.

Knowing the best defense is sometimes an attack, the chief wasted no time launching an offensive before Lainie even had the door closed.

"Did you look over her file? Shall I send for her? I can get her here in two shakes. Of course, I haven't spoken to her yet. She might refuse. She is very definitely her own person, but I..."

With the door now fully closed, Lainie Sommers was temporarily cut off from the discussion. Those last words hung in the air. *"Her* file?" *"She?"* Good Lord! In this stronghold of chauvinism? What could the chief be thinking? He must be out of his mind.

At her desk, she inserted a small object into her ear. Warmkessel's voice, serious now, came through perfectly. She listened for the anticipated explosion. Frey and Watland, co-captains of the chauvinist team, would never stand for it.

Nor were they. Throughout the ensuing battle, Lainie's money was on the chief, at his best when the odds were against him. And she suspected her boss, for all his bravado, believed it was his friend, still "in the field" as it were, who was doing the department's real work. It is a conviction familiar to many who have come up through the ranks--that fieldwork is greatly superior to deskwork, however exalted the desk. In today's fracas, however, to bet on the chief would take real guts.

The commissioner's voice was coming through sketchily.

"... sorry, Tom." "... just won't do." "... lieutenant less than a year," "... use her some other way," "... need someone at least... captain..."

Then the chief. "... exceptional officer in every..." "... best choice we have."

Frey again. His voice suddenly louder, more hopeful, like a raft bound sailor sighting land. "Wait a minute! Isn't she a troublemaker? Isn't she the one who stirred up that whole mare's nest...?"

"... About woman officers taking their share of night duty? Yeah. But that's all over and it's worked well. I tell you what, Earl," Warmkessel's voice dropped to that boys-in-the-back-room tone, "if McKnight was a man, I'd be thinking there would be a satisfactory replacement for me down the line. We need someone like her..."

But Frey cut him off. "... no experience with violent crime. I think that let's..."

The chief louder. "Not true. She did solve those murders up at Hawk County a couple of years back. Besides, she..."

For some minutes Lainie's ear was employed in taking phone calls. When she inserted the earpiece once more, Watland had the floor.

"Oh for God's sake! Be honest! You just want her because she gave you that damned Victims of Crime thing! Just because you, yourself..."

"Shut up Warren." Apparently Frey had had enough.

Lainie tapped her fingers together in silent applause.

The chief seemed to have taken command of the floor. "This... this madwoman... I tell you the truth, she has us hog tied seven ways from Sunday. If these killings could be solved by good police work, they would be, but they can't. And that's the long and short of it. And we *got* to stop her. And not only because everybody's rapping our behind, either. It is just bad for a community, even one as good as Plainfield, to get the idea that someone can literally get away with murder. We can't afford to let the police department become a laughing stock." The chief was in dead earnest now. "Earl, we gotta have the best our force has to offer, and right now that's Salome McKnight! We can't afford to play 'give-the-deserving-cop-a-break'. There'll be problems with her appointment, I'm sure, but..."

Low mumbles cut her off until her ears plucked the "P" word out of the rest.

"... want something for the press, don't we? I tell you they'll eat it up! The *Call's* been raggin' us 'cuz the PPD has never appointed a woman to head up a Special Investigative Team."

"Hell! If we start letting the press make our..."

"Wait a minute Commissioner." Apparently a thought had struck the district attorney. "The chief may have something there! It'll be one woman pitted against another. Almost poetic, don't you think? The press will eat it up!"

Oh you wily bastard, Lainie thought. A dull thumping now punctuated his words. "Think of it! If she comes up aces everybody's covered with glory, and if she bombs," a distinctive creak indicated a settling back in his chair.

"Which she won't!"

"Of course not! I don't *think* she will either, but I mean *if* she *does,* well, at least that will shut up those press gals for a long time."

The commissioner was incredulous. "God, Warren. You're a sneaky bastard! After all these years, you still surprise me!"

"Me, too," Lainie thought. Which was even more surprising, as there was not much she would put past the district attorney.

But Warmkessel hung on to the reins. "Whatd'ya say? Will you go along with my recommendation?"

"All right! All right!" The commissioner tried to sound more persuaded than defeated.

On the other hand, Watland was playing it cleverly. By keeping his comments to the barest minimum, he could wash his hands of this decision should this woman bomb, as he fully expected her to. That would open wide the door to bringing the investigation over to his office. On the off chance that she succeeded, of course, well... He *was* here, wasn't he?

The door swung open and Watland emerged, buffing the already perfect shine on his nails with the small brush he carried in his vest pocket.

But Commissioner Frey was not going to be in this alone. His voice followed the district attorney.

"Well?" The tone demanded a response.

Watland shrugged. "Well what? You have my thoughts on the matter. It's really a police decision, after all. Go with Tom's suggestion, if that's what you both think. It'll be on his head anyway. Besides, it never hurts to stay in with those Thaxtons." He returned the brush to its nesting place, threw a perfunctory nod at Lainie, and left, leaving the door between the two offices open.

"Okay. Okay, Tom. You win. Guess it's the best we can do."

Warmkessel gathered up the woman's file. "Fine. That's fine. And thanks, Earl. Can Lainie take care of the rest of these?"

Taking a 'yes' for granted, and again giving Earl's hand a bone-crunching shake, the chief was gone, leaving the office seem unusually large, empty and silent.

CHAPTER 5 The Call

Those who look into somebody else's well sometimes fall in.

The office of Chief of Police Warmkessel. About 5 PM.

They had not found her easy to convince. Plenty of others, she had pointed out, were more experienced officers, were better equipped for the job.

"Like who?" Warmkessel had replied with ungrammatical irritation. "Hell girl! We don't get this kind of thing here enough to give anybody much expertise! Once in a while somebody blows his temper, an occasional hit and run. Sure, we can do that, but this kind of subtle, psychotic stuff is really more in your line than anyone else here. Anyway, look how you handled that teacher's death up at Hawk County. If it weren't for you, some fourteen year old kid would be serving life down in state prison."

Sal had scoffed at that. "I must say I'm surprised you bring that up. That was far from a stellar piece of investigation on my part. Not only did I have plenty of help, we were lucky. And I knew the people involved. Besides, did you forget I almost succeeded in becoming the next victim myself?"

Warmkessel had interjected. "Maybe, but that's the closest we've ever come to having to find a nut-case like this. And then there was that weird Tunnelson thing a year or so back. You were the one who got that all straightened out too, weren't you?" He leaned closer. "Look Sal," he hurried before she could comment, "this killer is bright, too damned bright. I keep getting the feeling she's out there some place laughing at us. We need someone who is just as smart, someone with imagination, and, damn it, Sal, that's you!" He paused then, adding with a sudden grin. "Anyway, I asked your brother. He says you can do it."

"You asked Sam? How? When? He's..."

"Airborne. I know. Mrs. Sweeney got him for me."

"She did? I'll have to have a talk with her." Adding, "Even so. I simply don't think I'm the person..."

Her objections fell on deaf ears, but she had stuck to her guns until the chief ended it by telling her to consider the assignment an order.

So there was no getting around it. Certainly the job had to be done. Riding back down to the fourth floor, she made her first decision. She decided to stop praying. She had prayed she had been called in to be given a new assignment, hadn't she? This was, she told herself, just another example of life giving you what you asked for, and having a good laugh in the bargain.

* * * * *

She returned to her office just in time to pick up the ringing phone.

"Warmkessel here Sal. I forgot to tell you. Frey has scheduled a press conference tonight to announce your appointment."

"Tonight?"

"In about an hour."

* * * * *

Naturally, those representatives of the media already on hand--you recall the clutter on the police commissioner's desk--were first to get out the news. These journalists, most of them celebrities themselves, assured that the announcement got full play.

Still, they were not happy. Their customary behind-the-scenes machinations had thus far failed to produce any hint of the subject of the forthcoming press conference. It was maddening.

Forced to be amicable in this one-horse town, they passed the time over drinks in the Holiday Inn bar, devising ways to teach the local yokels the fun and profit to be had in leaking a few gems to the press.

But they were not idiots, and the Plainfielders had earned a grudging respect from them. They knew the last SIT leader had left Plainfield, and a new one would have to be appointed. They knew Chief Warmkessel. They also knew he was not one to let grass grow under his feet. The promised press conference could mean only one thing.

But who would it be?

As the hour for the press conference neared, it became apparent there was only one room large enough to accommodate them--the large community room of the beautiful, white, octagon-shaped, Thaxton built, Plainfield Community Center.

Consulted, Mayor Reuben Thaxton conceded the use was entirely proper. It was a groundbreaking decision. Until now, its most newsworthy use had been as a forum for the debate over whether the city should consider Ground Hog's Day a paid holiday for city workers.

When the appointed hour arrived, the room was jam packed with "pros" armed and loaded for bear. Back at the home studio, network researchers stood by to fill in with facts. Talking heads stood ready to tell the world where the Plainfield cops were getting it wrong.

Suddenly, those in the front rows reported seeing a woman in the wings. The possibility that the new leader might be a woman, raced through the crowd like trout disappearing from the Catasauqua River on the opening day of trout season.

Sensing the genesis of a hot news story, they switched to making charitable promises to be kind to the--well, 'poor slob' is the way one woman put it. A lamb to slaughter. After all, they were pros. They could afford to be noble. They knew what to expect. The chosen would arrive with a prepared statement, which they would then make it their business to disembowel. The chosen, (to avoid appearing unprepared,) would be forced to say more than planned, increasing the likelihood of saying something they could really get their teeth into. Sound bites all 'round!

What happened that evening though, can best be told through the eyes and ears of someone actually there.

Truth to tell, we were all caught off guard right from the get-go, one woman network broadcaster e-mailed her husband.

We didn't even see her at first. When this gal walked into the large conference room, she was pretty much hidden by local VIPs. We figured her for the press officer or someone's 'go-fer.' I recall telling Bob Houseman, in tones of purest snidery, she gave new meaning to the term 'little woman.'

That was before I got a good look at the suit she was wearing. So help me, it looked like the work of Harry's London tailor! I had an impulse to run home and burn the entire contents of my closet. Lucky you! I was too far away to do it!

I saw her shake her head at the Police Commissioner, who apparently thought he should introduce her. Without fanfare, (and better still from our point of view, without notes,) she merely stepped up to the podium and waited for us to settle down. She was so short (about 5'2" I'd say), the podium hid all but her face and the upper part of her chest.

Then she began to speak.

"Can we please get started?"

The tone so matter-of-fact, my reaction was to shut up mid-sentence, probably for the first time since I left Sister Margaret Marie's ruler. (I'll bet you like her already!) She has a great speaking voice, low and pleasantly authoritative. I just sat back and relaxed. It felt as though Nanny had come into the nursery to chase away the bad guys.

Apparently the effect was universal, because pretty quickly everyone else shut up too. During the seconds she waited for us, her eyes moved slowly about the room, seeming to take in each person present.

Bill Cosgrove remarked, afterwards, that if he ever wanted to commit a crime, he would certainly not do it here. "That woman's got eyes like an x-ray. She'd simply call the Bobbies and tell them where to find me."

"I am Lieutenant Salome McKnight of the Plainfield Police Department. I have been asked..." Well! You probably saw our reaction to that! You could have knocked us over with a feather! Not only a woman, but Sal Thaxton McKnight! The famous Thaxton twin!

We'd heard she'd lost a lot of weight. We'd even heard she had joined some police force or other, but we simply had not recognized her. You know how good she is at keeping away from the press.

She gave us a few seconds to quiet down before going calmly on. "I've been asked to put together a team of officers whose task it is to find the man or woman responsible for the death yesterday of Mr. Donald Thurston, and for the deaths of ten other men. I expect to have the names of the rest of the team available for you shortly. I will see that you get them immediately." Her eyes continued their earnest surveillance. "Now I know you all have different deadlines and work in different time zones, so I will name one officer as your contact, available to you, let's say from eight a.m. to eight p.m. Will those hours be adequate?"

Death On Delivery
A Pennsylvania Dutch Mystery

Nothing in her tone gave you the idea you could push her around, just that she really wished to give us what we needed. We were so taken off base by this reasonable approach, all we could do was chorus agreement.

"Good. You will understand that, at this time, I am unable to tell you anything more about the cases themselves," she went on smoothly. "I have been on leave, and only got back today. The press officer will serve you better." This delivered with such straightforward common sense, nobody but Art Jorgen rebelled, and you know him! That perennial adolescent is set automatically to object! One wonders how he gets these plush assignments! He could only work for a network that equates confrontation with news, facts aside. Rumor is his network pays him according to how obnoxious he is.

Anyway, I digress. To get back, she looked us all over again and continued. "Given the parameters I've just set, do you have any questions you reasonably think I might be able to answer at this time?"

A stroke of genius, not? Expecting we apply the standard of reason to our questions. Good, huh?

Thus encumbered, I don't need to tell you the conference was short. She took maybe half a dozen questions. Those that were pertinent were answered completely, fairly and to the point. Those relating to anything else, she simply and courteously ignored. Nor did she fall for our old, reliable trick of re-phrasing the few valid questions she'd already accepted. After one or two futile attempts to get her to go for that, she looked directly at us, said she felt sure she could count on our cooperation in getting to the bottom of these unspeakable crimes, thanked us for coming, and left the room.

Honestly, darling, I felt out of breath, and I hadn't moved from my seat!

There followed some very personal thoughts not germane to this story.

* * * * *

As the district attorney had predicted, the implications were not lost on even the most unimaginative of reporters. That evening, some variation of the *Plainfield Evening Call* front page banner, looming over Phyll Dayly's by-line, "Does It Take One To Catch One?" appeared throughout the international press.

Perhaps it was not too surprising that it was women journalists who were most vocal. In an unfortunate comparison to barnyard hens, they flocked that night into Plainfield's Media Club, where the appointment of Salome McKnight, and her handling of the press, were the only subjects of discussion.

In the wee hours of the morning, Phyll Dayly said it for all of them. "Wow! If she continues like that, I give her a week to either be stoned or have this murdering bitch caught."

* * * * *

But Sal's appointment did not go down well everywhere. One of Plainfield's senior police officers sat at his desk, paper and pen in hand, trying to write a letter. It was more than an hour since he had angrily clicked off the evening news, an hour in which the anger and disappointment had continued to build.

He was sick of it! Sick of disappointment, sick of being passed over. They could all go to hell! His wife was right. The thing to do was to get out. He could open that PI agency. Or maybe he would buy into one of those home businesses he was always reading about. After all, the duplex was paid for and he would have the rental from the other side to live off.

He went back to finding the right words for his letter--words that would make them feel like the unappreciative jerks they were.

* * * * *

The television was tuned to the newscast in at least one of the three spacious three story colonial homes occupying one side of the "U" called Elk Run Close. The woman watching the press interview, kept her eyes riveted on Sal McKnight's face, seen in close-up as the final credits rolled.

The watcher laughed shrilly, turning off the set with a sharp jab of the remote control.

"Those fools! That woman! Isn't it just marvelous darling? Look who they picked! Isn't that the greatest darling? Don't you just love it?"

Still laughing, the woman mounted the stairs of the empty house and went to bed.

* * * * *

At a small neighborhood Hawk County bar, high above and beyond the lights of the city, a middle-aged man watched the late night newscast with unblinking eyes. The news team uttered their final implausible pleasantry to each other and bid the viewers good night.

The bartender pointedly turned off the set. His lone customer continued to stare at the darkened box, then pushed his glass forward for another refill. The bartender assessed his customer. Not that he needed another tonic water. He simply seemed unable to move from the spot. Closing time or not, the bartender decided to let him have one more.

For a moment, he wondered what had caused his long time customer to quit drinking a couple of years back, but soon he was absorbed in counting the day's drawer. When he looked up again, the bar stool was empty.

* * * * *

Hong Kong. The Mandarin Hotel. Thursday.
The concierge had taken the call himself. A somewhat confusing message to be sure, as calls from America often are. This one was from a very young lady, claiming to be Mr. Sam Thaxton's niece.

The concierge shrugged at that. Who was he to say? He, himself, had a spare niece or two with whom he wiled away an occasional hour during the long night shifts.

He pushed a memo into the message box for the Mandarin Suite. Every hour or so he checked the box. The girl had sounded very excited. What was it? She discovered she was pregnant?

Thaxton didn't seem the type, but then, who did? Anyway, if she was a diversion for the man, it could be really interesting because this time the reservation form said *Mr.* and *Mrs. Sam Thaxton.* He wanted to hang around for the fireworks. But when the concierge went off duty several hours later, the message was still in its box.

CHAPTER 6 Friends

The more ve get araunt abaut, the more ve find be-jesus aut.

Hawk County Alternative Program for Youth At Risk. Wednesday 3 PM

Just as his former teacher was beginning her workday, that of the young Assistant Maintenance Person was drawing to an end. At three o'clock on the nose, "Duke" Reinhard grabbed his jacket and dashed out. It was not like him to run off on the dot like that, but the urgent note taped to his locker meant trouble. Had it been from Shari, he wouldn't have given it a second thought, but Kit "Wheels" Gaumer was no fool. So today, instead of heading for the parking lot, where his old Chevy waited, he bounded up the familiar stairs to his former classroom.

He no longer took the familiar steps three at a time as in his student days. That was because Mr. Shramsky's boys, straggling up from their basement classroom on their way to their waiting van, would surely do it too.

Usually, he stopped to chat with these young versions of his former self, boasting he'd been worse than they, the worst student in the history of the whole of Hawk County. To them, struggling to make it through a single day without incident, he was a god. He had been there! He had made it!

But not today. Today he turned a deaf ear to their pleas for attention, their protests following him up the stairs.

No one stopped him now. Now he had the run of the school. Now he was sought after by the same teachers who once did everything they could to get him thrown out. That was before Teech came along. Teech talked Ol' Pete into giving him the job as assistant to old Jeb Daniels, now deceased.

And it had all worked out well. Teachers no longer had to do their own "donkey work." For the first time they had someone to carry cartons of books and supplies up and down the four floors of the elevator-less building. As to finding something lost, he was a godsend, knowing, as he did, the five county buildings inside and out. Hadn't he been kicked out of all of them at one time or another?

No time to reflect on this serendipitous and surprising outcome today though. He'd have to really snap to it to get up the only stairs before students began coming down.

The thud of feet said he was too late. Now he'd have to stand aside and wait while students from the top floor, the first to be released, poured out and down.

Naturally they did not run. Running was not permitted. Ol' Pete was very firm about that. Rather, they confined their gait to the fastest permissible walk, a pace finely judged to come within a hair of being called "run" by whichever teacher was doing the defining.

It was a fine exercise in psychology, as each teacher had his own idea of just where that distinction lay. The group would surge past one teacher, slow for the next, surge and slow, surge and slow, the whole mass of students moving as one, down the three flights with no cue beyond a quick sidelong glance at teachers standing guard outside their respective doors.

It was, perhaps, five minutes before he could proceed.

Death On Delivery
A Pennsylvania Dutch Mystery

Outside room 8, he stopped in the open doorway, observing the class inside as they prepared to leave. The teacher was hollering at the top of his lungs at the class, engaged in all kinds of horseplay. His class, too, had been like this at first, each trying to out yell the other after a whole day of enforced quiet.

It had taken a while, he couldn't remember just how long, before they had accepted the necessity for talking in normal tones while they waited for their bus, always the last to be called. Nor could he remember how Teech had managed this transformation, but he was sure of two things. He had helped her do it and it hadn't been by hollering.

Duke listened to the teacher's high-pitched yell with disgust. He had tried to explain to him that you couldn't keep kids in line with threats. Things were a thousand times better when he and Teech were there.

He thought about Teech while he waited. He shook his head in benevolent puzzlement. She sure had been a funny lady. Called them "Mister" or "Miss", for one thing. Sounded funny. Welfare used their last names sometimes too, but only when they were in hot water. Mostly they were called "re-tard," even by their families and classmates. Except for Harry, who was called Dum-Dum because he couldn't talk, and Screwy-Louie because he was... well, screwy, no getting around it.

But you had to give her credit. Teech had taught him to read when everybody said he was too old and too dumb to learn, and to take care of the monthly miner's pension that came to him.

Yes, she *was* a pretty good teacher all right, but she wasn't very smart, or she wouldn't have gone to be a cop. Everybody knew people hated cops, which meant you either lied to them, or you sucked up to them. He didn't know which was more disgusting. On the other hand, everybody treated teachers like they were little tin gods, when most of them weren't worth the space they took up. Now his old class was stuck with this pansy Soroka character. Not that it was exactly the same class he'd been in with Teech, of course. Only four of his old classmates were still there.

He waited out of sight until he caught Tommy Mudra's eye. Tommy, called "Mechanic" by the gang and even a few of the teachers, was eighteen himself now, and hoped to graduate this year. Duke signaled him and went to his car to wait. He would follow the school bus until Mechanic and Wheels could hop off.

* * * * *

A half-mile down the road, the bus door opened and Mechanic popped out followed, not only by the expected Wheels, but by Flirtie-Gertie and Turt as well.

"Fer cripes sake," Duke exploded, "You didn't *all* hafta come!"

Mechanic slid behind the wheel and began adjusting the rear view mirror with hands, permanently oil stained.

"Well I did," Gertie snapped. "I'm his lab partner! And Wheels goes wherever I go an' that only leaves Turt."

"Oh yeah?" Main Duke sounded aggrieved. "I thought Wheels..."

"Well you thought wrong! I just asked her to write the note 'cuz I knew you'd listen to her!"

"Ennyways," Mechanic interceded, "What's the diff?" They took off in the opposite direction of the school.

"Okay. Okay." Duke conceded, facing the trio already settled in the back seat. "But you know I could get in trouble picking you kids up off the school bus."

"Bo-ooy" Gertie said, "since when did you care about getting in trouble?" Duke's concern for avoiding trouble was both recent and unsettling.

"Cuz," he growled, "I realize that everything I do the rest of you think you hafta do too."

They continued to spar. Duke now taking the position that skipping school was a natural exercise, certainly nothing to get all hot and bothered over, Gert holding ground, the others chipping in from time to time on whichever side said something with which they agreed.

But for Mechanic, literally in the driver's seat, it was a rare chance to take the four-laner all the way down to Plainfield. Still at it, they pulled into Jamie's driveway, some forty minutes later.

They "oohed and ahed" at the Truman house, which seemed like a palace to them. Main Duke pushed the bronze bell button. The sound of the melodious chimes brought another chorus of "oohs and ahs." There was no helping it. Each had to take a turn pressing the button. But, despite Main Duke's warnings that someone would surely call the cops at the racket they were making, no one came.

They gathered around the wide front door discussing what to do next. It began to drizzle.

Gertie peered through the long side glass panel. "Nobody's here. The whole house looks empty."

"Hold on!" Wheels had wandered around to the side of the house. "Hang on! Here's his new bike. He left it out. Jamie must be somewheres around. He always locks his bike in the garage when he goes away."

"Hey! Come here!" Mechanic pointed. "Look at that." He pointed to a partially open window. "I better go close that. It's raining." He was already half way up the maple tree next to the open window.

Gertie yelped. "That's Jamie's window, ain't it, Wheels?"

Wheels didn't answer. She was giving the bike a wide-eyed examination.

"Just like Jamie said! A mountain bike. Heck! I could ride it like nododdy's business!"

"Never mind that! Keep yer hands offa it! An' you come down here! That's none of yer business! You guys are gettin' outta hand lately!" Main Duke looked aggrieved.

But Mechanic had already reached the window. As he reached out to close it, his attention was caught by something just visible from his precarious perch. "Hey! Does anybody know if Jamie's moving? I seen a bunch a bags full of stuff in there."

"Never mind bags! What about Jamie? D'ya see him?" Duke began to climb too.

"Wait a sec. I'm going in."

Mechanic was over the sill and inside. He straightened up, turned and let out a yelp, quickly clapping both hands over his mouth. He remained motionless until Main Duke reached him, then made a dash for the bathroom.

Main Duke stared. "Jeez! He's dead! Jamie's killed hisself!"

Main Duke was as familiar with death as any young person raised on the streets, but never had he seen anything like this. He remained standing there for a minute, wondering who needed him most, his live friend or his dead one.

He took in a deep breath, then went and knelt at the slight body with a bloody hole where the head used to be. A gust of wind from the open window blew the dead boys hair back and forth.

From below, they could hear the others shouting as the rain began to pelt them. "We're coming up too!" Gertie's shout galvanized Duke to action.

"The girls mustn't see this!" He dashed to the window and yelled down. "Ferget it! Stay there! We'll be right down." Slamming the window shut, he dove into the bathroom to assess the condition of his friend, now recovered but white faced. "Come on! You gotta go back down and take the others home. I'll stay here with him until someone comes. His mom should be home soon."

But Tommy did not move. "I can't believe it! He's dead. Jamie's dead." Tears stood in his dark eyes like still pools. "I can't just take them home! I wanna stay too. *They'll* wanna stay. You gotta tell 'em!"

The older boy gave the younger an assessing look, then without another word, went back to the window, opened it, stuck his head out and called down. "All right! All right! Shut up! Go to the front. We'll let youse in." He gave Mechanic an awkward pat on the shoulder. "Go on. Go down and let 'em in."

Already drenched by the downpour, the three lodged noisy complaints. Gertie, torn between admiration for Duke's boldness in letting them in, and anger at his earlier neglect, erupted. "Bo-ooy. Aren't we gonna get in trouble getting into Jamie's house like this?"

"Shaddup a minute, will ya?"

They looked at him in surprise, then saw his haggard face. Turt peered up at him. "Where's Main Duke?"

"With Jamie."

They followed him upstairs. "What's wrong with Jamie?" Gert, demanding validation. "He's sick, isn't he? See? I *told* you something was wrong." I-told-you-so written in every movement. Her worry having proved correct, she adding righteously "Let me up. I can take care of him. After all, my mother's a nurse. I know what to do. Ain't that right Duke?"

Skinny legs propelled her past the others like a grasshopper to a new leaf.

Duke grabbed her arm. "Stay here! Sit down!" He pushed her down on the carpeted stair, holding her down with one arm, motioning to the other two with the other. "Youse guys, too. Siddown! Jamie don't need your help. He don't need nobody's help no more."

He took the spate of protests for a minute or so. Then just as suddenly relented. "Oh, heck! You might as well know."

His voice dropped. "Jamie's dead! He's killed hisself!" The silence was so palpable, even the rain seemed to be affected, falling now without a sound. "We're just gonna wait here until somebody comes home. His mother should be home soon."

They stared at him for a minute or two, then, without a word, Gertie got up and left the room. Turt and Kit followed to the upper level. Duke watched them for a minute, then shrugged his shoulders and followed.

In the dead boy's room they stood in a shocked, silent half circle around the body, the head now covered with a pillow case depicting racing cars that Main Duke had pulled out of one of the trash bags.

Gertie spoke first. "We hafta call the cops. You have to do that when people die like this."

"Cops? You want us to call the cops?" Turt was appalled. "They'll say *we* done it. They'll take us all in! We can't call the cops. Let's just get out of here." He grabbed Mechanic's arm and moved to the door.

"Hold it!" Duke's voice stopped them. I don't know if Gert here is right, but we ain't leaving Jamie. That's fer sure. Period."

"Well I *am* right. That's what we had to do when my aunt did it. That's what you have to do."

Turt struggled to absorb the duel shocks of his friend's violent death and their uninvited presence in this house. He ventured tentatively, "Can't we wait until his mother comes home and let her do it?"

"No! The one who finds the body has to do it! We better do it now! Gertie sounded positive. "Hold it! I know! We'll call Teech. She'll tell us what to do."

The very mention of their former teacher's name produced unanimous relief. Gertie looked up the number of the Plainfield Police Department and Duke dialed.

CHAPTER 7 Call for Help

The hurrieder I go, the behinder I get.

Plainfield Police Department. Tuesday 8 PM.

Too charged up to follow Warmkessel's order to go home early and get some rest, Sal repaired to her office to think.

She sank into her chair, feeling somewhat punch-drunk. The offices on either side were dark and quiet, allowing for reasonable concentration. The rise and fall of voices of duty officers, shuffling back and forth outside her door, served only to create a reassuring curtain of normalcy, of business as usual.

There was no point in rehashing her doubts about the assignment. Rather the only way to ease her anxiety was to see if she could get a handle on the unwanted task.

Until now, she had done her best to keep out of the deliveryman murders. Murder had become, in the past few years, an acquaintance both formidable and all too personal. Fortunately, family and business had provided endless avenues of escape.

She began to read the reports of the ten earlier murders. As she read, she let her mind drift back, recalling the official reports presented at daily roll call, as well as the infinite variety of hypothesis set forth by the exhaustive media coverage.

The official reports themselves were slim. Results from the crime scene units were alike in their fruitless search for forensic clues. She began to understand the PPD's reliance on various profilers and other outside experts. Nevertheless, her toes crunched away madly as she read.

She pulled the evidence bags toward her. Each contained a list of items found in the pockets of the victims, and in some cases, the items themselves. The Crime Scene Unit had thoroughly investigated the, mostly unremarkable, objects. They had made a diligent search for any hint of a connection, either among victims, or between victims and murderer. None had been found.

As she read on, two conflicting aspects of the deaths cried out: the exact duplication of the crime each time, and their sheer ingenuity. The first, she thought, pointed to a purposefulness, a rigidity, which could best be thought of as abnormally compulsive. The second pointed to a mind at once creative and intelligent.

She was not as bothered, as had been the experts, by the apparent lack of motive. Killing itself could be a motive, a way, possibly, of reducing intolerable stress. To focus on it seemed futile.

Then, too, it seemed the police had let themselves be waylaid by the fruitless search for forensic clues. The chief had said he felt as though the killer was out there somewhere laughing at them. Was she? Were those pristine crime scenes more than a need to leave everything obsessionally neat? Yes. That fit. She would not be the first serial killer to deliberately challenge the cops.

But whether purposeful or mere serendipity, it seemed obvious to her, as she sat studying the reports together like this, that the police had let the killer yank them about by the nose. Was she enjoying it? Perhaps that was what her toes were telling her.

Death On Delivery
A Pennsylvania Dutch Mystery

An hour later, she sat back to think. The way she saw it, it all boiled down to two main considerations: first, how, and second, who. Her predecessors were reasonably intelligent, all competent. With time a diminishing commodity, it would be to her advantage to use the work already done up to this point. How could she best maximize those efforts and on whom, among the PPD, could she rely on to help?

For the first, how the murders were committed without leaving a single usable clue, it seemed a more careful review of the eleven cases was called for. Tedious work, but a plan to determine that, in a fairly short time, presented itself almost immediately. She would leave that for the morning.

She felt better then. A coded message sent to Dolores' computer, gave her a "heads up" on their new assignment. Adding the *Urgent, Top Secret* code, and a red light began to blink on the secretary's system.

Finally, she sat back to consider the "who." The plan in mind meant foregoing working alone, or with the help of her sergeant only, always her preference. Eleven cases to be considered meant help. How much help would depend on the qualities of those chosen.

If Warmkessel was right and the solution to these murders took a different sort of police work, a different point of view, (and she accepted the logic of that,) then she must choose officers with those same qualities.

But what qualities? She thought a bit longer, then with a rather nebulous list of characteristics in mind, made her way to Personnel.

* * * * *

It had taken a key and special permission from the chief to enter Personnel. She had searched through the files, thinking about the men and women she knew, or knew about. Some seventeen files got a close look. All but six were returned.

Again Warmkessel had dispensed with strict rules and given her permission to take home those six.

"Anything," the chief had said morosely, in answer to her request. "Don't want to rush you, but you see how it is. The situation is urgent." If he could have some names by some time tomorrow, he would sure appreciate it.

She had told him she'd do her best, locked the files in her briefcase, returned the crime scene items to Properties, and gone home.

* * * * *

27 Longmeadow. In the dead of night.

The garage door closed behind her with a silent thud. A few isolated clumps of fat, steamy raindrops had dried within seconds of falling on scorched pavements. Now puffs of warm, moist air blew at her as she walked through the dark, starless, new night to the rear entrance of her home.

Invariably, she enjoyed this hundred-yard trek from the former stables to the back of the house. This, albeit short, walk through the wide range of weathers this corner of the world experienced, helped her feel in real contact with the earth. She thrived on the changes--her boredom threshold being virtually non-existent. Even in the midst of a heat wave, one knew there would follow in more or less predictable order, rain, hurricanes, tornadoes, cold waves, snow, blizzards, wet spells, dry spells, all interspersed with perfect days and nights. Save for the intense humidity, which now weighed remorselessly down on her, she loved them all.

Two foot thick fieldstone walls Great Grandfather Henry Harrison had pulled, piece by piece, from his own land, and filled in with mortar he made himself, kept the house cool in spite of the prolonged heat.

Death On Delivery
A Pennsylvania Dutch Mystery

The barn-cum-house was as cool and inviting as it had been two hundred years ago when it housed G.G.H.H.'s cows. There was no need for air conditioning. Ceiling fans kept the air moving, a central de-humidifier kept out the damp during unusually wet springs, or when the banks of the Catasauqua River flooded.

The quiet house welcomed her all right, but any attempt to sneak into the kitchen unseen came to naught. Mrs. Honey 'schussed' her upstairs, insisting on bringing up a tray, "so's youse can keep up yer strength vunce if yer gonna do that chop."

Midnight repast gone, e-mails to children sent, (they do not like to get news of their mother second hand,) a futile call placed to Sam, and she was ready for bed.

Propped up against several oversized pillows, she looked those six over again. Besides Masters, three other officers seemed to have one or more of the characteristics needed. She would call them in the morning before they left for duty.

The decision made, she locked the files back in her briefcase, and turned off the light. Still suffering from jet lag, she dropped off to sleep almost immediately

DAY ONE

CHAPTER 8 Rick Masters

Kissin' don't last, cookin' do.

Wednesday A.M.

Rick Masters patted the top of his classic Volkswagen, carefully inspecting it for dings or the first signs of rust. The paint job, his own design, neatly split the car in half: sparkling white on one side, a deep, brilliant black on the other, the two separated by a long "s," extending from the front rooftop, and curving gracefully downward to the rear wheel cover. It had cost him a bundle, including the special lacquer topcoat, but he expected it to keep the body of the car in as pristine shape as he was keeping the drive train.

Inspection passed, he headed for work. He was early, but he wanted to stop for breakfast and the Loot expected you to be on time.

Though barely six o'clock, the day was already hot, with no sign of relief in the cloudless sky. Waiting for his order at a PC Junior, he reflected that a year ago he would not have been in such a rush to get to work. A year ago friends had expected him to turn down the chance to work with McKnight, his views on the subject of women supervisors being well known.

Death On Delivery
A Pennsylvania Dutch Mystery

Not that he didn't like women. Fact is he liked them a lot. He tended to put them on a pedestal and they, naturally, tended to fall off. Disappointment and disillusion all around.

He accepted that the disillusion was mostly his own fault. He expected a lot. He wanted women to look good, sound good, smell good, and be trustworthy, intelligent, and reasonable, also fun loving, passionate and feminine. He didn't even care if a woman was more intelligent or talented than he, as long as she didn't use it as a weapon.

Looking forward to marriage when the time came, he had naturally given the matter considerable thought. If and when he took the plunge, he would want his wife to be a person in her own right, with ideas, with opinions, able to convince and be convinced by reasonable discussion. Having met two women like that so far,(his mother and his boss--the said lieutenant,) did much to keep the flame burning under this impossible dream. These two were out of range for him, but where there were two, there would be one more.

And when he did take the plunge, he would not refer to her, or even think of her, as "the wife", as was the custom here among the natives. Yes! A reciprocal relationship of earned trust and respect would underlie the love, the passion, that would form the basis of their marriage. Otherwise, he would remain single. Which, of course, is why he was.

When his breakfast came, he pulled up under a tree to eat, resisting the temptation to eat while he drove. Another influence of the Loot's. She had, she confessed, given up her love of eating while driving when she first put on her uniform. Eating while driving was the cause of many a fender-bender and worse. It was simply not in her to ask more from the public than she was willing to commit to herself. In the same way she had quit smoking, when the school at which she was teaching passed a no smoking policy for students.

A dishtowel protecting the seat, he dug into a fresh asparagus and cheese omelet--a PC Junior specialty. It was such delightful food choices, in fact, which kept him here in Plainfield. Ever since he discovered the Pennsylvania Dutch tradition of offering seven sweets and seven sours with their entrees, he'd been hooked.

Beyond the basic need of a non-cooking bachelor for good food at reasonable prices, Rick loved to eat. Corn fritters, corn on the cob, squash, pickled cabbage, apple sauce, stewed rhubarb, fried zucchini, fried eggplant, tomatoes, stewed or fried, and succotash, buttered or pickled red beets, corn relish, chow chow, macaroni salad, macaroni and cheese, cucumber salad, cucumbers in sour cream, lettuce with hot bacon dressing, beet salad, carrot and raisin salad, Waldorf salad, tomato salad, fresh fruit salad, Jell-O salad, and potatoes: mashed, fried, scalloped, even hot potato salad, to say nothing of the ubiquitous Dutch filling. And it didn't end there. Desserts were just as varied. How to choose among the home made pies and tarts: lemon meringue, strawberry, sour cherry, apricot crumb, blackberry, blueberry, raisin, pecan, rhubarb, coconut cream, lemon cream, apple tart, apple or peach dumplings. Don't care for pastry? How about homemade cake or pudding. Beyond all that, with nearly everybody here having a garden, you could expect homemade preserves for the freshly baked bread.

According to the Loot, who had been just about everywhere in the world, in no other place could you be as confident of getting good food. It was, she told him one day over lunch, the reason she and her brother had gone into the restaurant business. Accustomed to the abundance of choice in Pennsylvania Dutch restaurants, they were always appalled, as they traveled, to find little beyond the same half dozen entrees, one or two vegetables, and less than a handful of desserts available. For people like Rick, it was a gastronome's heaven.

The last of his breakfast gone, he shifted gears and headed eagerly for work.

The "Loot's" early morning call could not have pleased him more. Over this past year he'd become quite enthused about police work. The Loot was clearly the boss, yet she let him have his own wings. And she was a fine cop. He had seen her in situations that would challenge the toughest, and she had always landed on her feet.

Not that she was what you'd call easy to work with. A lot of cops complained about being assigned to her. She was damn particular for one thing, possessing some kind of radar, which tipped her off when you weren't doing your best. Several times she had sent him back to catch something he had missed. On the other hand, cops who worked with her had a tendency to win commendations and promotions, and Rick was ambitious. He had his eye on a Jaguar he could never afford on sergeant's pay.

During her three-week leave, he had done his utmost to maintain her standards, and he had been looking forward to seeing her usually serious face lit with that sun-come-out-from-the-clouds smile when she read his reports. Now, however, with this new job, all of that would get lost.

But that was OK too. The smartest thing the chief could have done was to throw this job in McKnight's lap. She could do it if anyone could, and he would be there to help. If nothing else, he had proved to himself, by his performance while she was gone, that he was as worthy as anyone of the chance.

* * * * *

The Loot was just picking up the phone to take an incoming call as he arrived. He grinned widely and nodded a greeting, getting an equally pleasurable smile in return.

The aroma of freshly brewed coffee and tea, evidence that the Loot had also arrived early, pulled him to the credenza holding sway against the single windowless wall. No styrofoam cups here, he took one of the hand thrown dark blue mugs from its hook, opting for tea. He made a pretty decent cup of coffee himself, but his tea tasted like bilge water. Mug in hand, he moved to the long windows, waiting for the phone call to come to an end.

The drapes, pushed aside as far as they could go, gave an unobstructed and startling view. No more than ten minutes ago, the whole of the horizon had been painted a clear, flat blue. Now large pillows of pure white loomed to the south, while the sky to the east was matted with thick clouds of varying shades of grey. It looked, for all the world, like the rumpled comforter on his bed. Not right at the horizon, but a bit higher up, the grey mass was pierced by a thin band of molten gold. The lone traffic light on Applebutter Road flashed red, green, yellow, each color as brilliant against the grey as lights on a Christmas tree.

He observed the ebb and flow of Plainfield's orderly early morning traffic with the critical eye of a cop. It seemed somewhat more harried than usual. Had it to do with the sudden appearance of clouds after months of heat wave? The approaching Labor Day weekend? Or were Plainfielders getting frantic over the discovery of yet one more dead deliveryman?

He found the last possibility encouraging. In his native Los Angeles, the news would have barely earned a second look.

Waiting, he congratulated himself on his decision to make his home here. Originally on loan from the L.A.P.D., a couple of years back, he'd been charmed by the natives with their distinctive accent and upside down word order. Not many of them still said "throw Papa down the steps his hat," but there were still plenty of engaging colloquialisms to be heard among the natives. Coming from a section of the country where "I" was held to be sacred, he had grown quite fond of these unassuming, incurious, bone-honest, hard-working Pennsylvania Dutch.

Second cup of tea gone and now fully ready for action, he turned to find the Loot still on the phone. He tried to guess who was on the other end--tough as the Loot was mostly saying "yes sir." Somebody senior? But who? Warmkessel? The commissioner himself? Impossible to tell. Almost anyone would get this same earnest respect from her.

When she caught his eye, she raised shoulders and eyebrows simultaneously with a helpless gesture, nodding wordlessly at the green case-folders covering her desk.

A dozen of them, ten of them thick, detailing the investigations of the earlier murders. The eleventh was slim. A single page outlined the initial findings for yesterday's killing. Clipped to it were two memos. The first, from Chief Warmkessel, turning the case over to McKnight, another from McKnight to Warmkessel, naming her team. This he read with particular interest.

The list brought his eyebrows to full mast. Corporal Adam Adamson he knew by reputation. A smart-ass. Thought his opinion was the only one that counted. A second corporal. Emily Haines. A knockout with gorgeous red hair. Plenty of guys tried to date her and been shot down. A curious choice. Done some good undercover work for Fraud with that charity scam, but hardly preparation for hunting down a vicious murder. How was the Loot planning to use her? That she had a plan in mind, he was sure.

The third name was an even bigger surprise. Sergeant Burger. Fourth-of-July Burger. What could his parents have been thinking? Imagine going through life with a name like that! No wonder he became a cop! In the PPD since God made apples, and only made it to sergeant. How good could he be? Wasn't he retired or about to? On the other hand, this Haines kid was damn young. Too young.

They seemed an ill-matched lot. He knew why she picked him. He had proved himself, but why these other three? Was this an example of the flights of fancy she was rumored to have? If so, this, when so much depended on her judgment, was a hell-u-va time to show up. Still, finding his name in the space designated to name her next in command, was somewhat reassuring.

The other officers began to drift in. He looked up to nod briefly at each. The woman was first and right on time, but the other two were late--the older sergeant by nearly eight minutes, Adamson by twelve. Lucky the lieutenant was on the phone!

"Sorry about this," the Loot nodded at him, briefly covering the mouthpiece. "It's the Governor. Will you introduce everyone? I think they all know who you are."

He did so, noting the reaction among them as he said names. This was never going to work! A team had to respect each other, trust each other to jell into a working unit.

Another glance at the Loot, who gestured with her free hand, indicating he should play host.

Again he complied, pointing out the urns of coffee and tea, the mugs, the china cups and saucers stacked below, pints of milk and orange juice in the built in refrigerator. However early she'd been, she taken time to fill the "larder," including, apparently, a stop at Pleasant Company, as a box of breakfast goodies waited beside the bowl of fruit.

Rick had grown accustomed to the varied reactions to the well-stocked credenza. Today he got them all: awe (from the girl,) envy (Adamson), and disgust (Burger.)

Adamson made himself right at home, helping himself to crullers and tea. The girl eyed the bowl of fruit, needing an extra nod before helping herself. Burger scowled at the set-up, giving it a thorough search before taking a pecan bun then demanding a "reklar" cup.

"If you mean styrofoam, there isn't any. These," he lifted his mug, "are as regular as it gets."

Burger shook his head, but grabbed a mug, filled it half way with coffee, topped it off with milk and three spoons of sugar. Repast in hand, he snubbed the blue leather chairs, moved as far away as possible from the others flopping into one of the plain, straight back chairs around the table.

Masters was amused. His own initial reaction had been much like Burger's. It had taken a while, but now he couldn't stand styrofoam at all anymore. True, the blue china cups were still a little far out for him, but they stirred a collage of memories. A tearful young prostitute, diverted for a restful moment from hours spent pouring over mug books for the face of her attacker, by a wide-eyed examination of the hand painted roses inside the cup. The stiff faced mother, fresh from identifying her son's drowned body, both hands clasped around the cup's warming bowl, sipping the hot, reviving brew as she struggled to accept her loss. The middle-aged secretary, caught embezzling from her long time employer, staring into the bottom of the cup, as if for some evidence that life could ever be good again.

The way the Loot treated them, both victims and victimizers were allowed a tiny gleam of light. He'd accused her of being too soft for police work, but she simply said that, though punishment had its rightful place, the end goal of a civilized government should be to restore its citizens to a productive life whenever possible, and the key to overcoming the past is hope. Besides, she'd added, every one has a right to simple courtesy.

He wondered if she would feel the same about this killer when they caught her. And catch her they would. He had no doubt about that.

As today's lot settled with their choices, he sat where he could look them over without seeming to do so.

Burger had all the signs of the inveterate cigar smoker; the perpetual droop of his uniform shirt pocket caused by the constant bulge of two or three cigars, the lips, slightly tilted to the side, a permanent small gap in the corner. What would the Loot do when the smelly stogey appeared? He himself, had quit smoking cold turkey a while back when the chief told him, over end-of-shift drinks, he had done so. If the chief could do it, he could do it.

In sharp contrast, Corporal Haines was, simply put, a knockout. Reddish blond hair hung long and straight over slim shoulders. It was hard to get past the girl's beauty. He stared at her until she turned, giving him the full impact of two deep green pools, shaded by silky blond lashes. The contrast between her very feminine beauty and the business-like uniform was jarring. She had given him a small, polite smile before moving to take up a conversation with Adamson, whom she seemed to know slightly. As for that young man--the only one not in uniform this morning-- Masters decided there was no competition for the girl there, unless she was one of those who saw herself a cure for that particular propensity.

Unobtrusively, Masters watched the three. The girl settled to read the files on her lap. Adamson, perfectly brushed straight black hair, faultlessly pressed white shirt open at the neck, neatly tucked into tight grey pants, a pale blue sweater on his shoulders, was exploring Sal's office like a man planning to redecorate. Burger had given the briefest of glances in Adamson's direction before shaking his head and returning his attention to the case files. Then he, too, settled down to read.

CHAPTER 9 Emily

What you ain't got in yur head, you better have in yur feet.

Emily Haines clamped down hard on the handle of her cup. The clink of cup against saucer had already drawn sharp glances from several of the group.

Her hand had been shaking since Lieutenant McKnight's early morning call woke her with the invitation to join the new Special Investigating Team. It was the last thing she expected.

At first she thought perhaps it was a dream. She wanted to push the *re-call* button, ask if she'd heard correctly. But how would that look?

She'd had to remind herself she was not an imaginative person. Besides, the call had included some very un-daydream-like instructions. But Emily Haines, a mere corporal? On a SIT? Probably it was some minor thing she was wanted for. Never mind. She would be cool. She would show up as ordered, prepared for anything.

Her hand shook all the while as she got her small son dressed and breakfasted, making that task more daunting than usual. She'd heaved a sigh of relief when she dropped him off at day care.

Emily knew the lieutenant of course. The woman was a Thaxton, and everybody knew the Thaxtons. But that Lieutenant McKnight was even aware of *her* existence? That was quite different! True, she'd been one of McKnight's students at the police academy a couple of years ago.

Emily had found the older woman a rarity in her life--a woman worthy of admiration. She remembered the classes well. Not only had McKnight made the work seem interesting and important, but she knew how to keep the class in line. There were always one or two male students who seemed bent on seeing just how quickly they could get the women teachers rattled--something they rarely did with male instructors. McKnight had handled the troublemakers without threats or shouts.

Emily had watched her carefully, trying to see how she did it, but up 'till now she hadn't a clue. All she knew was the guys in class soon vied to fetch her film projector, or run to the cafeteria to fetch her coffee at the mid-class break. Most impressive though, was that after the first few classes, the male officers spontaneously stood when she entered. Her first thought, after hanging up the phone this morning, was that, with a little luck, she would get another chance to observe the woman up close. Emily Haines wanted to be a sergeant some day, but to do that she would have to learn how to handle the smart-asses.

The trembling fingers finally quiet, she stole a look at the woman from under the screen of her lashes. The lieutenant, she saw now, looked much the same as she had two years ago. No beauty, the young woman thought with the unconscious arrogance of one who has never known anything else. Even seated, you could see the older woman was short, too short to ever rate high for looks. Silver beginning to show here and there in the chestnut hair. Ordinary sort of face. Nice wide-set grey eyes. Well shaped brows. Judging the other woman's appearance by her own, Emily felt well ahead in every aspect but those eyes.

Taking advantage of the lieutenant's averted gaze, her eyes dropped to the woman's desk for a closer look. Pretty top, she thought. Burled something, someone had called it. Whatever that meant. She made a note to look it up. Big. At least four feet by six feet, with lots of nice swirls! She wondered how they made those swirls. Maybe with onions. Dad used to make plain white pine look like expensive knotty pine by pressing a cut onion into the raw wood. She'd have to look around the garage sales for an old desk and try it. That big surface would be great in the basement for cutting out patterns.

She looked up to find the lieutenant's eyes resting on her. Embarrassed, Emily turned away, but not before she caught a smile on the older woman's face. Gosh! What a difference!

She felt better then, and with a quick glance at the lieutenant and a murmured, "I missed breakfast," helped herself to an apricot.

Judging the wide arms of the mission oak chair adequate to accommodate her snack, she sat down somewhat gingerly, and moved her survey on to the rest of the team.

Two of them she dismissed immediately as possible romantic candidates. Not that she was looking, of course. It was, she told herself, just a girl thing.

The sour looking old guy she would avoid as much as possible. These old geezers were always a pain. The nice ones wanted to father you, filling you full of advice you didn't want. The others, resenting women on the force, entertained themselves by making the same old cracks, most of them dirty, all of them insulting. All of them made passes at you, when they thought they could get away with it.

That was not a problem she would have with Adamson. Nevertheless she liked him. You could be friends with him. He made a good escort, courteous and considerate, and you didn't have to keep your guard up. She'd had a date or two with him. At one party, she met a couple of guys who worked at the best shops and boutiques, and offered to let her know in advance of the best sales--real sales where better things were marked down, not the kind where they brought in a lot of cheaper stuff to be sold as regular stock.

Munching her fruit thoughtfully, her appraising gaze came finally to the man in the blue leather chair. He appeared to be absorbed in the contents of the green file-folders on his lap. Tom Sellick type with thick brown curly hair, broad shoulders, big hands and feet. That was supposed to mean they had other things that were big too. Her face flushed at the unbidden thought. Quickly, she turned her eyes away.

For a few moments, Corporal Emily Haines felt her hard won self-possession slipping. She forced herself to remember that at thirty-one, she was already a corporal with two commendations on her record, and that Lieutenant McKnight had, for whatever reason, selected her for this team. Police work suited her fine, and she was good at it. As she sat back in her chair to eat her snack, Adamson caught her eye and winked.

* * * * *

Adam Adamson nodded approval at his counterpart. Not in his category as a cop, of course, but he liked her. Still, he was surprised to see her here. Whatever could they have in mind for her?

But she was not the woman who held his interest at the moment. Adamson's reaction to Lieutenant McKnight's early morning call was to generate a review of what he knew about the caller. Dissatisfied, he'd decided to forego his early morning health regimen this once. He seldom missed this daily workout. Not only was he vain about his figure, but he was still looking for that 'certain someone' and the gym was prime hunting ground. But this time professional aspirations took precedence. He had, after all, a future to think of. A stop at the library was called for.

He dressed carefully, deciding on 'civvies' rather than the anonymity of a uniform. Like Masters, Adamson had his sights set high and a well-dressed police detective could find himself in a position to meet the right sort of people. Now, fate had given him his chance.

The small sacrifice paid off. Listed in all versions of Who's Who, the most recent gave him facts. His imagination filled in the rest.

McKnight, Salome Thaxton: b. 19--. Thaxtonville. Along with twin brother, the only children of Walter and Salome Thaxton. Walter was the youngest of Henry Harrison's eight children. Parents died in crash of their airplane when the twins were five. Married Gunther McKnight (deceased). Three children: Joseph, Walter Jr., Lucienne.

Ah. A single parent. Perhaps she was looking for someone to lean on as she raised her family.

Education: Earned Ph.D. after volunteer work with disturbed adolescents piqued her interest. Took a job in public educational setting before joining Plainfield Police Department where she reached the rank of lieutenant in three and a half years.

Business: With brother, opened first Pleasant Company restaurant in Plainfield at nineteen. Developed to include 500 restaurants, three up-scale restaurants and nearly two thousand PC Juniors.

Awards: Numerous business awards. Congressional Medal for help in capturing the internet terrorist at turn of the century.

Charities: Thaxton Foundation, Angels of the Air

Related References: See Henry Harrison Thaxton, Thaxton Foundation, Business Women of the Year, Congressional Medal of Honor Winners, Organic Farming, Employee-owned businesses.

Adamson stared at the book. Sounds lonely, he thought. His imagination conjured up images. He saw himself in a fantastically tailored tux, (for which she, of course, would have insisted on paying,) escorting her to Country Club affairs.

He would be charmingly indifferent to the difference in their ages. And kids were no problem. He really liked kids, and was not likely to have his own. Further delightful images presented themselves. His 5'11" figure, faultlessly turned out, squiring her to the kid's ball games, their graduations. The whole family in their private box at the theater, (he had already begun to think of it as *their* box,) where she would naturally want to introduce him around. He entertained these tantalizing visions a few seconds before returning to earth.

Skimming over the library's many references at a quiet desk, he realized now he had already met the twin brother, when Thaxton Industries suffered a series of break-ins a year or two back. Adamson, then newly elevated to corporal, had been sent to make the initial inquiries. The big man himself happened to be there when he arrived. Adamson had tried to make an impression on the man, not really expecting anything specific, but hoping he could, at least, impress his name on the man's memory. But the old guy just shook his hand, thanked him politely, and beat it.

As for Salome Thaxton McKnight, his new boss, the more he read, the more she began to pique his curiosity.

Eagerly, he pulled up the computerized newspaper files. The Thaxtons were noticeably absent from the Society pages.

He turned to the Business pages. Surely these would be more help. However, though there were frequent references to one or more of the Thaxton businesses, whether publishing house, real estate, restaurant or harness racing stables, every story ended with the same caveat. The family's wealth could only be estimated as their varied companies were all privately held.

Mention of the stables directed him to the Sports sections. Here the stories were more numerous with reports of harness races won, and the sale or purchase of high priced equine stock. Sam Thaxton's Olympic trials received quite a big play. He tucked that information away for later study. Of immediate interest, was the Thaxton Stable colors. He could, he thought, do a lot with indigo blue and silver.

Still, his search was not a total loss. Over the years, the Plainfield Evening Call had devoted full pages to Thaxton gifts: the Plainfield Library, the Thaxton Preserve, the County Hospital's enormous children's wing, the University's new physical education facility, now considered the nation's best Olympic training site, to say nothing of the huge, white, octagon-shaped Plainfield Community Building.

No wonder she was chosen to head this team!

Mention of the Community Building jabbed at him. It was time to get there and to work!

The fifteen minute drive to the station provided ample time to consider how best to handle her in the light of this new knowledge. Not that he anticipated any problems with her. He genuinely liked and understood women, and thought, correctly, he worked well with them, especially when they were a bit older.

Then they were either looking for someone to take care of, someone to take care of them, or tough cookies who thought they didn't need anybody. In Adamson's hands they were all malleable. Age, beauty, intellect aside, he treated them gallantly: called attention to their sensitivity, their uniqueness; phoned them when they were ill; remembered their birthdays. His technique had seldom failed him, and was no less effective because it was both unconscious and superficial, perhaps because at heart, he was really a rather nice person.

He'd been a bit put off to find her so absorbed with the phone that his arrival earned the merest nod from the woman at the desk. Nevertheless, he'd submitted gracefully to introductions. As soon as he could do so unnoticed, he'd seated himself on one of the indigo leather chairs where he could study the woman inconspicuously.

She had, like him, chosen to wear "civvies" rather than the uniform chosen by the others. He liked that. It spoke of kindred minds. Moreover, her suit earned his approval. Obviously expensive, it did very nice things to the wide-set grey eyes which he had already proclaimed her best feature. He would enjoy helping her select the right clothes. Imperfect figures were such a delightful challenge!

He gave some thought to what he might call her. Women liked special nicknames. "Sal?" Probably everyone called her that. "Sally?" Too girlish. Her full name then. "Salome." Yes. It fit her. Kind of old world and biblical. He would have to find out how she pronounced it, Sal-ome, like the dancer or Sal-o-may, like the biblical temptress.

He had seen no signal, but the other three officers were making their way toward the far end of the room. Regretfully, he picked up his cup and saucer and went to join them.

* * * * *

The four newly designated officers sat in an erratic circle, making sporadic self-conscious remarks to each other in muted tones. Empty cups and mugs pushed aside, they waited as the lieutenant took call after call. At last, with a final "Thank you sir, I will sir," the calls came to an end.

"Forgive me," she said, coming quickly around the desk to firmly shake hands and give each officer that quick penetrating glance which had so impressed the journalists.

She gestured toward their empty cups, nodding approval. "It looks like you have all been well taken care of. Thank you for playing host, Sergeant. You and I," Masters got a smile and a nod, "have three weeks of catching up when we get a chance. For now, thanks for your excellent work while I was gone. I've read your reports. Good work! We'll talk later." She turned to the others. "Will you bring your drinks and the case-files over here?" She indicated a large round worktable along one wall, a sense of urgency accompanying her words. "I am eager to get started."

Leaving the others to carry the case-files, Adamson moved quickly to garner the chair next to the team leader. From this vantage point, he could continue his appraisal of this astonishing room, while the others occupied themselves with the usual mundane preliminaries.

The cherry credenza, the china cups, the crystal fruit bowl, had already been granted silent approval. Now for a careful study of the burled cherry desk. He had seen it some... oh, yes!

It had been featured in an article on the state's history, appearing a while back in Architectural Digest. Fantastic!

His eyes moved on. One wall, floor to ceiling windows, drapes pulled back to expose a view of Hamilton Circle, the wall behind their table completely bare, and a third consisting mostly of glass windows and doors looking out on the main squad room.

Only the wall above the credenza was not bare. It held two paintings: a large ink and watercolor hanging a few inches above the credenza, and a small oil a little to the left. He was sure the smaller was a Kadinsky, but could not place the artist in the larger. Above the Kadinsky hung three small round cherry frames containing pencil sketches of children, presumably her own.

He applauded this tasteful but modest salute to family. Obviously, the woman had good taste. In fact, everything about the woman spoke of it. The scenario this realization produced was so intoxicating, only the sound of his own name in a room falling suddenly silent brought him to earth.

CHAPTER 10 Adamson

A person wrapped up in hisself makes a mighty small package.

"Planning an auction, Corporal Adamson?"

For a moment, Adamson appeared hand-in-the-cookie-jar embarrassed, but only for a moment. After all, what had he been doing but paying the team leader the compliment of admiring her taste. Surely she could not object to that?

He produced a self-deprecatory smile.

"S-s-sorry Lieutenant." He gave her the approving nod of a fellow traveler. Then, looking directly at her, permitted a captivating smile to reach his eyes. "It's just... your office, Lieutenant! I just *love* it!" The smile broadened. "The Kadinsky is wonderful of course, but who did the watercolor?" He tipped his head towards her own.

"Thank you, Corporal," she said mildly, "Glad you like it. However, given the circumstances perhaps you could find a more appropriate time to browse?"

She turned away, fighting irritation. But at whom? Adamson? Herself? She recognized well that roving attention, knew it was more than a simple interest in his surroundings. In his place, she too, might have employed this all too familiar defense against boredom.

Worse yet, the appraisal itself was not altogether displeasing. It was pleasant to find someone else who thought the Kadinsky print exciting, rather than vaguely 'pretty,' or worse, 'cute.' As for the watercolor, she had to admit it was gratifying to hear someone say something other than that it was 'nice,' then 'very nice,' on those rare occasions when she admitted it was one of her own efforts. Yet Adamson had given it the same approving study he had given the Kadinsky, and she was vain enough to be tickled.

She pushed vanity aside. They would all be better off if she let him know that, in this group at least, he was not going to be an island on to himself.

But was he? Four officers, new to each other, suddenly called together to work under a fifth, also new, on a case which had already been the focus of the most public harangue ever to hit Plainfield? It was not, she thought, a circumstance for ebullience.

But neither was it a time for the faint of heart. Again she considered how to proceed. Burger, too, had remained apart from the group as she talked. Eyes down, his face bore the expression she'd seen often in adolescent students, young people who, though capable and bright, were sullen and rebellious. It came, she thought, from being ignored, from having their own ideas too often rejected. It began in their earliest years when adults, given the task of bringing the young mind to fruition, chose instead to foster their own egos by keeping ascendance over their charges. Parents, coaches, youth leaders, even ministers did it, but teachers were among the most guilty.

The result was the young developed an attitude of tough disinterest. Like perfect fruit left ignored too long, they got sour, sometimes rotten. Was Burger a case in point? Had she made a mistake in choosing him?

Yet his records had shown him to be an exceptionally good cop, despite his being passed over for promotion when men like Longnecker kept moving up. What had held him back?

Death On Delivery
A Pennsylvania Dutch Mystery

Attitude, she guessed. Unresolved anger. Resentment. One of the generation which had never fully bought the idea of women as police. Would it affect his working for her? He would have her gender, as well as her enviably quick rise in rank to hold against her.

Her hope lay in his presence. She'd half expected him to turn down her offer to join her team. Yet here he was. How now to draw the best out of him?

"As a starting point, I want to know what you think about these murders. We've all been following the case, at least to some degree. It's impossible to avoid it. We've had, not only the ever-present press reports, but those from the various SIT teams at roll call, as well as a cursory look at the case files here this morning. Does anything jump out at you?"

She had not expected an immediate response and got none. Casting a speculative look over them, she decided on a mild offensive. "How about it, Sergeant Burger? You were on one of the earlier SITs. You have valuable experience. Will you give us a start? What is your assessment of the investigations so far?"

A risky approach--to put the most irascible officer on the spot first. If he dug in his heels, retreating into a whirlpool of past injustices, she would have to eliminate him. It would mean a bad start, a circumstance to be avoided. But she had to know.

Keeping her demeanor formal and official, again she let the silence in the room lengthen. Burger was accustomed to taking orders. As long as he viewed her, however reluctantly, as Officer In Charge, he would respond.

The tactic worked. She was right to start with him.

Burger shrugged and took a deep breath. It was evident he had given the cases some thought.

"I sink naw," he began testily, "the same thing I sought from the beginnin' naw vunce."

"And that is?"

She waited, giving him time to dig around in his memory for specific examples. It took a bit of hemming and hawing, but, once started, a virtual torrent shot forth.

Surprisingly, Burger's opinion tallied pretty much with her own. He complained they had let "everpuddy en' his brudder yank 'em about by the nose," and that, aware of their lack of experience in "this here kinda thing." they had "follawed dawn every possible blind alley, like a sow to the call of his mate." The cigar came out for a firm roll,

"You refer to the profilers?"

"Fer one, yeah. Not only though. Remember when the chief appealed to the press for help? That brought ever' kinda loony outta the woodwork!" He hitched around in his chair self-consciously.

He reminded her that in the beginning, they thought the death was a suicide. It did not occur to them that Plainfield had produced a 'nut-case killer.' "Partikular one that'd strike again! I mean," he said, vexation thickening the Pennsylvania Dutch accent. "Plainfield, for Chrissake! Hell! I still don't believe it!" The cigar reappeared as if by magic.

"It don't wonder me how come ve didn't get nowheres. Ve cum to depend on that there DNA and that there stuff to solwe our cases," he complained. "Like ve lost the use of our eyes and ears! I ain't sayin' this new fangled stuff ain't no good, I'm chust sayin' that's not the only way to do it. Vat I mean iss..." He looked about distractedly, patted his shirt pocket. "Oh hell!" He shook his head again. "Nevah mind. I don't know vat I mean." He thrust the cigar back in his pocket.

Sal moved to her desk, opened a drawer and returned with an ashtray. "I offer you this as temporary first aid, Sergeant. Smoke if it helps. I want you all as relaxed as possible this morning." She acknowledged the looks she was getting from the others. "The air cleaning system here is quite good, and we will accept the minor inconvenience of whatever smell remains as a trade-off for the moment. We won't be spending too much time together inside once we get underway," she added. "I can't help hoping, though," she smiled at him ruefully. "That you don't smoke one of those really... *strong* smelling ones."

The unexpected offer took him off guard, breaking the developing tension. "Oh jeez! Ya didn't hafta... Awful nice a ya though. Danke!" He looked at the cigar again. "Maybe later. I kin manache a while without it. Anyways, vat I was chust tryin' ta say iss, there hasta be some reason why one inwestigation after another comes up viss the same empty bak. I mean, ten times! Eleven naw! A bit of a stretch, ain't?"

"Yes, that bothers me also." Sal got up and went for the coffeepot. "Why do you think that is?" She re-filled empty cups.

"You von't like it."

"I don't have to like it."

"Vell then," he glared at the un-lit cigar, "fer vun thing, venn I vorked on'em, ve had a helluva time gettin' anything done. Hell! Ever' body and his brother second guessing you: the captain, the DA, the noospapars, your locker buddy, your *wife* fer God's sake." He paused for breath.

Masters nodded agreement. "I know what you mean. I got the impression the damned media was running the investigation. They'd interview some expert or other and suddenly that's what the PPD seemed to concentrate on."

"And," the lieutenant said musingly, "I suppose once they'd adopted a position, they'd feel obliged to stick with it. I wish now I'd followed the news more closely. I'm afraid I gave it up a while back." Yes, she chided herself. You did pretty much behave like an ostrich, didn't you? You let your past experience with murder traumatize you, adopted a 'see no evil' posture. Childish of you. Just what did you think you could avoid?

"An'," Burger was going on, "the only thing the pressure from the press did was bust up the teams."

"Yes. I wanted to ask the chief about that. What do you know about it? It's most unusual to change a SIT before the case is closed, but we're the fourth."

"Ya vell. Ya better ask him. There's plenty a reason though."

The group fell silent. Adamson took it as long as he could. "It took them forever to give up that ridiculous suicide theory. Whose brilliant idea was that?"

"Who d'ya sink?" Burger's voice dripped with disgust. "That lame brain Longnecker! Bad enuf it was a ridlicus idea in the first place, but then he evens stuck to it, even after the second and third. Shows he don't know nothin' about workin' men. As if a guy like that would try ta bump himself off in one of them high-class apartments. And with champagne yet! That man's an idiot!" For the first time, he looked directly at the lieutenant. "Guess I ain't supposed to say that, am I? Him being a captain an' all! I suppose ya'll want me to shuddup now, or leave, or somethin'."

Nevertheless he went doggedly on before she had time to respond. "Ennyways, it's not only him. That ther lady DA got the brilliant idea our killer was the same as the one in Florida! Nacherly, that got the FBI in. We wasted a bunch a money and time on that. Hell! I think the DA still believes it, evens though ve proved it couldna bin that lady. Hell! The Florida dame was locked up at the time of a' least one of 'em!"

"I see."

"That damned DA is just itching to prosecute a big case. Get 'er boss's face on the telly," he muttered. "Gonna run fer President or somethin' I hear."

Another silence.

"I've been wondering, Lieutenant," Emily Haines put the question tentatively, "and this may sound dumb, but could we be making a mistake in assuming it's a woman? After all, the perpetrator was almost certainly wearing a disguise, so why not a man?"

"You may have a point there, Corporal Haines," Sal said. "In any case, it is good to question assumptions. We'll keep this one in mind. Keep it up." She scanned their faces. "What else?"

They looked at each other then down at their legal pads like students on the first day of school. Adamson began to doodle.

Impatience seeped through. "Corporal Adamson? Sergeant Masters?"

But it was Burger again. "An' here's another thing." The cigar reappeared, got a firmer roll. "It seemed like there was allus a lotta confusion around the inwestigations." He hesitated, waited for a comment, got none, plunged on. "It seems like ve vas allus in a hurry. Naw I'm chust wonderin' how thorough the grount was covered." He limped to an end.

"Confusion? What do you mean?"

He frowned. "Can't say I 'member ezzackly. Chust somethin' in my memry that hit me a coupla times as I was readin'."

Sal studied him, decided he had given them as much as he could for now. "What do the rest of you think about Sergeant Burger's comments? Corporal Haines?"

But she was wrong. Burger had apparently gotten his second wind. "Vat I meant vas this. Thirty years on the force an' I sink you can always do a better chob, especially after it's all over, but at the time, it's different. Especially viss these here murders. Truth is," Burger admitted, "ve're spoilt. The kinda murder ve get arount here iss nearly always open and shut. I mean, usually your 'perp' is the closest one handy at the time. It's chust a matter of haulin' 'em in and takin' down the confession vunce. So we don't have to really..." he took some time to select the right words, "...really dik wery deep. Versteh?" He turned up his palms and looked at Masters. "Denkst du nicht?" He took another breath. "Naw maybe if we had our old chief back."

That earned him a look from the team. The beloved chief's decline was not discussed openly.

It was Adamson, skimming through the files as he listened, who replied. "As you said, maybe we have come to rely so much on Forensics to prove our cases that now, with so few physical clues available, we're lost. But, I must say Sergeant Burger, according to the official record here, it was you who came up with the idea of lifting footprints electrostatically, wasn't it? Gave us a description of the woman, the only real clue we have to date."

"If," Burger said grudgingly, "ya consider that a description."

"Wears a nine and a half shoe. Probably 5'8 or 9. About 115 pounds. It's something."

"Mebbe. She coulda been wearin' over-size shoes to throw us off."

"It's still something," Adamson said. "Whatever made you think of it?"

Burger shrugged. "I'm a detectiv, ain't I? It's chust bad luck that these killings always seem to happen at times when we were already short handed. I ain't sayin' the inwestigations got short shrift, I'm chust saying that the wheel that squeaks the most gets the most grease, and ya gotta make decisions about what's urgent and what's important."

Sal was so focused on a possible, and appalling, inference of what had just been said, she almost overlooked this last bit of wisdom.

Death On Delivery
A Pennsylvania Dutch Mystery

"Ach vell!" The older man was saying conclusively in the absence of any other response. "She asked what we sink and that's what I sink. I shoulda kept my mouth shut."

"Not at all, Sergeant. You've given us a lot to think about. Certainly what you said deserves a closer look." She took in the group. "I want all of you to feel free to say what is on your minds without fear of criticism. Remember, we are just brainstorming now. How about it? Does anyone have anything to add?"

Somewhat mollified, Burger resumed his seat. Adamson raised a hand. "What I find troubling is our total inability to figure why she kills delivery men. Usually serial killers go for well, hookers say, or some lot that lets them feel morally superior, but delivery men?"

Masters grunted agreement. "Yeah. That's the big one, isn't it? These guys are good, hardworking guys. What in the hell do you suppose she could have against delivery men?"

"Or perhaps just *one* deliveryman," Sal said. "Yes, indeed! That's the question. However, I think to focus on that now would just distract us. What I *do* want to focus on is this. *Someone*", she said with some heat, "right here in Plainfield, has found a way to plan and commit cold-blooded murder right under our noses! And," she kept their eyes, "I don't believe we can blame it on some stranger. Whoever is doing this *knows* Plainfield. And you and I are going to find out who and how. It could be the toughest job you've ever had, because, in this case, *we cannot fail!* Despite the odds against us, we will be expected to pull a rabbit out of a well-worn hat. And quickly."

"Well," she paused to check her notes. "I think this discussion has been quite helpful, don't you? It has been for me anyway. I begin to see more clearly where our challenges lie."

She checked her watch. "All right. Before we go any further, I want to set some procedural ground rules, then

I will ask each of you whether or not you are willing to commit to them.

"To begin with, plan to work around the clock with no leave breaks until we get the job done. We'll start each day together, meeting here each morning at six o'clock sharp." Four heads stared back at her. "I realize that is a bit early," she confessed sweetly, "but that hour before the shift changes, is the quietest here. That will be helpful in keeping interruptions both from the media and others, to a minimum. Feel free to either bring along a breakfast or help yourself to whatever the larder here has to offer."

"As for today," she kept their eyes, "we will start off by looking at the earlier investigations. Also, I am trying to arrange a meeting this afternoon with Dr. West, the county psychiatrist assigned as consultant on the case. You'll be looking over his reports this morning as well. You may have some questions for him."

She looked at her watch again. "Look, it's 10:00. I'd like to give some thought to your observations here this morning. I hope to have a method for collecting what facts we have and thus, what facts we will need. I believe those facts, however unpalatable, will not mislead us and we will have our killer. Suppose you take a break now and reassemble here for a brown bag lunch. Say eleven-thirty? Any questions?"

If her intent was to draw them together, to inspire the troops, she'd failed. She had gone too far. Their faces said it. Once again she had erred in estimating just how much they were with her. It was not the first time she had overwhelmed her audience. She wanted to kick herself.

She looked to her sergeant for help. Masters jerked to attention. "Right. Right. Of course Lieutenant. Sounds ambitious, but we all understand the importance of moving right ahead. And I think we know that none of us would be here if you didn't think we were up to it." He looked around the table with a grin, then at her.

Her sergeant's response chided her. His grin reminded her to lighten up.

She managed a grin back. "I see by Sergeant Masters' face he thinks I've gone too far. Sorry. I do expect a lot. Sergeant Masters can testify to that. However, each of you has been chosen because of your capacity for good work. Nevertheless, yours is the deciding vote. You have a right to know what you are getting into. So if you feel you are not ready to commit to this team, you have every right to ask to be replaced. I have to say I hope you won't. I selected each of you carefully and I believe I've chosen well. As for me, I do not consider this a one-way street. I'll do my best to earn your good opinion, but I do not ask for it as a gift, nor do I demand it. The only thing I *do* demand of you is your best effort. What do you say? Anyone want to be replaced?"

She gave them time to respond. No one did. "All right. That's it for right now," she said with finality. "Please be back on time. I warn you though, this may be your last free time. You should expect to be on call around the clock until we have the job done, so please use this time to make any arrangements you need." She stood then, nodded a brisk dismissal. "In an hour and a half then."

* * * * *

Adamson caught up to Rick Masters, already halfway out of the door. "I've heard about her powers to persuade. I see she operates on the 'you get more flies with honey' principle."

Masters laughed. "You ain't seen nothing yet! Wait 'till you've been 'McKnighted!' See you back here in an hour and a half, buddy. Gotta run now."

Rick dashed down the hall just in time to catch up to the new computer operator, a lithesome blonde said to be the niece of Chief Warmkessel. Adamson stood and watched Rick operate for a few minutes, then shrugged his shoulders and walked off to the squad room where he had left his belongings. "To each his own," he thought.

* * * * *

Emily Haines and Sergeant Burger left at a more leisurely pace, heading in opposite directions, each absorbed in thought. Emily was forming a resolve to learn just how to be so clearly in charge without sounding bossy. It would come in handy if she decided to marry again.

* * * * *

The older man admitted to himself this meeting hadn't been as bad as he'd expected. Not that that meant anything. Nope! He still didn't expect a whole lot outta this "team." One thing he knew, he wasn't gonna ass-kiss like those other two guys. She'd hafta take him like he was or lump it. Same thing he told his wife.

But he was thirsty. He hurried off to do something about that.

CHAPTER 11 A Plan

The safest bank iss vot you keep in your heart.

As the fledgling team scattered for a final fling with their diverse interests, Sal closed herself into her private office to work on last night's idea. Her plan was a bit more structured than that to which these officers were accustomed, and she anticipated some resistance. Nevertheless, it was the quickest way she could think of to maximize the work already done.

Unanswerable questions continued to plague her. Why *had* the department failed to get a handle on the brutal and mysterious murders? It seemed their very uniqueness, coupled with their nearly exact duplication, should have netted more. Why hadn't it? If she had any chance of succeeding where others had not, it seemed critical to learn where they had gone astray.

The three previous teams had amassed mountains of information. She felt certain, such was her confidence in the PPD, that much of it was potentially useful, however it was impossible to tell at this point. The case files were a confusion of steps taken and not taken, of facts recorded and not recorded. Like it or not, that, along with her choice of divergent thinkers, made some sort of structure necessary.

She managed to remain on task despite the intrusion of several phone calls. Chief Warmkessel waxed enthusiasm when she reported the team was off and running, waned nervously when the names of the eccentric four were revealed. Another, from Assistant District Attorney Madeline Grimm, put through by an apologetic Dolores, was, she felt certain, fully intended to jar her. After an icily perfunctory inquiry about Sal's health, Cousin Madeline followed with a completely un-Thaxton like jumble of small talk, going on for some minutes, scattering about frequent mentions of "Warren" and the district attorney as though they were two different people. Sal hung on. Sooner or later her cousin would come to the point.

It came so suddenly, Sal almost missed it.

"... let you know I would *appreciate* being included on the team." She had, she confessed with the most cousinly of confidences, experienced quite a lot of resistance from those *other* officers, but she was *sure* closer collaboration between the DA's office and the police would produce better results.

Sal did not have to ask "better for whom?" Maddie would certainly want Warren Watland to be there, at the right time and place, should anything develop.

Still, the phone call achieved its purpose and all her early reservations returned. Had she remembered Madeline had been the DA's point man on the murders from the beginning, she would have found some way to keep out of them, a broken leg, a case of mumps, nothing would have been too much bother.

The distrust between the two cousins had always been an enigma to the Thaxton freundschaft. The family chided Sal endlessly for this. It was up to Sal to keep the cousinly fences mended. Sal sighed. It would be another time the courthouse dining room, where the law firm of Thaxton uncles and cousins regularly lunched, would be the depository of countless reports of her performance, advantageously edited by her cousin.

Death On Delivery
A Pennsylvania Dutch Mystery

She shrugged philosophically. Perhaps Madeline had changed. People do. They were both older now. Yet all the while Madeline was talking, Sal's toes were kneading vigorously.

She went back to her task. For some while she worked steadfastly, so oblivious to sounds around her that when the phone rang suddenly for a third time, she jumped.

She looked at her watch. Eleven o'clock and nearly ready. Just enough time to proofread what she had and print out the necessary five copies. She reached back and pushed the button on the speaker, so she could talk without stopping her work.

"I'm so sorry Lieutenant. I know you said you didn't want to be disturbed." Dolores' voice shrank to an apologetic whisper, "but I don't know what else to do. I've got two hysterical callers on the line. They're for Juvenile. What do you want me to do with them?"

"Sergeant Eisenhard is taking that for now."

"Yes, ma'am. But he's off until tonight and, anyway, they're insisting on talking to you personally. They seem to know you."

"Oh? Who is it?"

"I don't know exactly, but line one is from that place in Hawk County where you used to work." Sal stopped breathing. Pete. What in the... "The caller on line two says he is the Main Dude. They both sound really excited."

"Main *Duke*," she corrected automatically. She could not help grinning. "*And* Hawk County?"

That meant Pete Hammond. Or something about Pete Hammond. Had something happened to him? She pulled in a deep breath.

"I'd better take them. Line one first, but get back to 'Main Duke,' otherwise known as Theodore Reinhard." His face, bossy, rebellious, proud, demanding, was immediately before her. The room took on a sudden brightness. "Ask Mr.

Reinhard if he can hold on. If he can't, get a number at which I can reach him." She punched the second button

"Good morning. This is Salome McKnight."

"Oh. Good morning, Dr. McKnight."

Not only was this not Pete, but the high-pitched, nasal whine on the other end was as far from Pete's deep, measured voice as possible. Yet this voice, too, produced a flood of memories. Violette Fister, the school secretary, sounded frazzled, not an unusual state for her. "I hate to bother you at work, Dr. McKnight. I know how you hated getting personal phone calls at work when you were teaching here, but Mrs. Treadwell insisted."

"That's all right, Mrs. Fister." She found herself adopting the same conciliatory tone which, for all the years at the boot camp, had constituted the whole of her verbal exchanges with this woman. How she raised two boys, and successfully by all accounts, was a puzzle.

"Don't worry about it. I hope you and your boys are well."

"Oh, yes, we're all fine, thanks. My oldest has just won a football scholarship to Villanova." Briefly the whine left the voice. "He'll start this fall."

"How I envy you! None of my children show the slightest interest in college. You've done well with those boys." The few words seemed to cheer the woman. "Can you put Mrs. Treadwell through now?"

"Yes, Dr. McKnight. I've got her on the line. It was so good to talk to you again. We really miss you here. Here's Mrs. Treadwell."

The slight emphasis on the "we" was not lost on Sal. True, in some corners she had been missed, at one time at least, but for others her departure from Hawk County had been a cause for rejoicing.

"Ellen Treadwell, Dr. McKnight. You probably don't remember me. Social worker from Hawk County?"

Good Lord! Forgotten her? It was 'a consummation,' she thought, 'devoutly to be wished!' "Yes, Mrs. Treadwell. I remember you." All too well.

"It's about your boys," The crackle in her voice had earned her the sobriquet 'the wicked witch of the east.' "They're in trouble again."

It was an accusation all too familiar.

"My boys?" Sal deliberately misunderstood. "You've had reason to make contact with Walt and Joe?"

"Walt and Joe?" The question threw her as gratifyingly as Sal could have wished. She felt better.

Stymied, the social worker struggled to regain her perch, but she had been sidetracked. "Who are Walt and Joe?" Her voice reflected a faint hope. Perhaps there was another student problem she could lay at the feet of the woman who had been her nemesis.

"My boys. You said you were calling about my boys," Sal said reasonably. "Although they are really young men now. And I can't say I ever really thought of them as *my* property just because they are my sons."

The dawn came. "Oh," she said faintly. She recovered. "Oh, no not those boys." Treadwell dismissed her children airily. "No, I mean your *class*. You know. Theodore Reinhard, Leonard Wilson. That whole group. *You* know."

The Main Duke on one line, social worker on another. What next? County superintendent?

"I haven't taught that class for several years now, Mrs. Treadwell. I believe Mr. Soroka is their teacher now, isn't he? You need to make contact with him." Several years it might be, but it was no effort to think back. What *had* they been up to? Had they gone back to hanging substitutes out the window by their toes? And why Reinhard? He'd been out of school and working since she left, but she had followed his career. A lot hung on how well he did in his experimental position. If he had blown it, she would have his hide.

She reminded herself she no longer had any kind of hold over him, so what could she do anyway? Not, she said to herself, "that I ever had much of a hold over him." To her caller she said, "I thought Mr. Reinhard and Mr. Wilson had graduated. And if it has to do with the younger boys, you'll have to..."

"Oh, Mr. Soroka can't handle the class at all. Especially in this situation." Treadwell's contempt for the young teacher nearly matched that of the students themselves, unfortunately turned off by his polite, almost effeminate manner, and his insistence they behave 'like little gentlemen.' "I can't imagine why they keep him on."

The answer to that was simple. Gary Soroka was the seventh teacher the class had had since she left.

"Yes. The two older boys have graduated, but Theodore *works* at the school, you know..." This another accusation. "...so he's always *there*. And Leonard hangs around the school all the time, too, and they're always causing *some* kind of trouble. And now they've really outdone themselves! We don't know what to do with them and...." Sal started to interrupt her when she said the magic words, "...Colonel Hammond told me to call you." Sal wondered if the thud of her heart could be heard on the other end. "He says you're the only one who can handle them." This was admitted with the greatest regret. The social worker's tone said it. Surely there had to be some unsavory reason for this woman's lasting influence on this class. And on Pete Hammond, come to that.

Sal decided firmness was called for. "What is it you or Colonel Hammond want from me? "

"Commander Hammond would appreciate if you could come up here and talk to the boys. They have agreed to talk to you. If you are willing, he will arrange a meeting at your convenience. He suggests his office might be the best place, if it's not too far out of your way. He knows you are busy, but this is really serious."

"What is the problem? What have they done that is so awful?"

"Colonel Hammond said he'd rather tell you himself. He says if something isn't done immediately, they'll all just land down there at the police station anyway. He thinks you might prevent that." Again, the implied compliment was grudgingly wrung out.

"Oh. All right then. Hold on." She pulled up her appointment schedule. "Will you check and see if a little past four o'clock is suitable? That's all I have open today, and I'll be unavailable after that."

"Oh, I'm sure that will do fine. One of the small buses will have to wait to take the boys home, but Commander Hammond said to agree to any time you could come." Treadwell's assurance came grudgingly.

"Fine. Tell him I'll be there as soon as I can after four. And don't worry about Mr. Reinhard. I have him on the other line. Goodbye, Mrs. Treadwell."

Pushing the second button, she could not keep the smile from coming back. "Hello, Mr. Reinhard?"

"Yeah, yeah. Is this really you, Teech?" Her heart lurched at that. The voice rushed on. "No. No. I know, you're not 'Teech.' You're Miz McKnight. I'm sorry I forgot."

"Unless," Sal grinned, making the familiar rejoinder. "You want me to forget and call you 'boy?'" She couldn't resist teasing him. It *was* so good to hear this voice again. "How are you?" She was surprised to find how much she really wanted to know.

"Oh, hell, I'm allus fine. Sorry for the hell, Miz McKnight. Anyways, it ain't me that's in trouble. You heard about Jamie?"

"Jamie? No. What about him?" For a few seconds there was no response while an argument ensued with insistent voices on the other end. "Oh, all right, all right. Have it your way," one of the faint voices said. "If yer sure she's coming." Then Main Duke's voice. "Are you coming to this here meeting with Colonel Hammond?"

"Yes. I just told Mrs. Treadwell. I'll be there at a little past four.

"Oh, *her*." He dismissed the woman. "So you are coming. Is that today, I hope?"

"Yes, today. Will you be there?"

"Sure. You bet! This one's a lulu, Miz McKnight. Maybe it'll be too hard even for you. All right, all right." Again to someone on the other end. "I ain't tellin' her nothin'! Jeez! You can't even talk around this place!" Back to her. "This place sure ain't the same without you here, Tee--I mean Miz McKnight. This place has gone to the dogs since you left."

"All right, Mr. Reinhard. I'll look forward to seeing you later. Until then."

* * * * *

The connection severed. She had deliberately kept away from the once familiar world. Was she making a mistake in going now? But no. Pete Hammond had asked her to come, and he wouldn't do that lightly. She had seen him only once since entering the police academy, but she could see his face, his eyes intent on hers, as clearly as if he were in the room. Oh dear, she thought helplessly, I thought that was all history.

The light on the intercom brought her out of her reverie. She picked up the receiver. "Yes?"

"Just checking to see if you want anything before I go for lunch."

"No, but you'll have to add a meeting at four to my calendar. I'll leave right after our 2:30 meeting with Dr. West. I'll be at the Hawk County Boot Camp. You have the number. If I'm not in the commander's office, his secretary will know where I am. Go ahead and get some lunch now. The team will be back in a few minutes and we'll work through lunch. Forward my calls to the main switchboard. Have them take messages until you return."

She returned to her work, finding concentration difficult. She suddenly realized her personal radar was at work. Inside her shoes her toes curled tight, a sure sign that something notable was in the offing. Did they warn of pleasure or pain? Did it wait for her here, working on the case, or up at Hawk County?

She stared at her feet. "I've told you this before. If you are going to continue to harass me like this," she said out loud, "you're going to have to learn to talk!"

CHAPTER 12 Fourth of July Burger

There iss not a pot so crooked you can't find a lid to fit.

All eyes were glued to the fat, red grapes spilling cross the table in all directions, looking like so many children released from school. They had escaped, (the grapes that is,) from a hole in Burger's much used lunch bag. The crusty, senior sergeant made no attempt to rescue them, leaving that to his new teammates. In an unwitting, but hopefully prophetic forecast of the team's future accord, they had done so, returning them, one by one, to be scooped up and popped into the older man's mouth. As a beginning, it was, Sal thought, far from auspicious.

"Yeah, *I* haf," Burger was saying in reply to Sal's request for thoughts they might have had during the short break. "I bin tryin'," in went a grape, "ta put myself in the 'perps' place." Two more followed the first. The over-loud voice, the slightly disheveled hair, were unambiguous indicators of the manner in which the veteran had passed the time.

The four officers had arrived promptly at eleven- thirty to find Sal already seated at the round table, lunch and coffee to hand.

She had wasted no time, asking for new ideas even as they'd hurried to settle around her.

* * * * *

Death On Delivery
A Pennsylvania Dutch Mystery

Rick Masters *had* had several ideas. None, however, germane to the case. Suffice it to say, he had finally gotten Angela Hawkins to agree to dinner, assuming he was free to go. Working with McKnight, you never knew.

Adamson hadn't been so lucky. The green-eyed rookie he was sure was gay, wasn't. Or at least he wasn't admitting it. So Adamson had gone to his club, followed his weight lifting regimen, then back to his apartment to change.

Emily had called her fiancé who had agreed to meet her for coffee. There followed a repeat of last night's argument. She loved him more than she thought possible, but she was not ready for another marriage. At least not the kind Bert had in mind. Happy with police work, and being chosen for this team, was a real feather in her cap. She determined to do nothing that would make Lieutenant McKnight think she'd made a mistake. Besides, she wasn't sure she wanted to have more children, yet that was all he wanted.

They had quarreled and parted. Again. It was getting to be a way of life.

Of the four, only Forth-of-July Burger had given the puzzling murders any thought. What else was there to do between drinks at Louie's?

Not that he'd spent the entire time thinking about them. In fact, murderous thoughts, or violent ones anyway, would most likely have surfaced that morning, even if his initial outlook on entering the place had been more sanguine.

That was because the bar's only other customer, a middle-aged woman, had gotten there first and was already crying the blues to Louie. Her presence brought to the surface Burger's life-long grudge against the fairer sex, especially as it applied to here-to-fore male bastions. And here he was, fixin' to go to work for one!

Maybe he'd just go back and quit. Yeah! That felt good. That's what he'd do. A fresh beer encouraged further musing.

Hell! What right did a broad have in grabbing the first real murder case Plainfield had ever had? Another time a guy missed his chance in order to favor one minority or another. It should have gone to someone who knew what he was doing, like one of the other officers. Longnecker, for instance, although come to think of it, his specialty was the type cases where he could ham-fist his way to information, to a confession. Not him then. Webber then. Shankweiler. Miller. Hell, even O'Connell. He wondered if it was true what they said about black guys. He didn't seem any....

Gloomily, he stared into his beer, reviewing his own sexual adventures, limited to a once a month token tryst with his wife of thirty-two years. Done a lot of extra-marital looking, but somehow never got beyond that. Just didn't seem to be worth all the bother.

Come to think of it though, that was probably how this woman got herself picked team leader, even if she wasn't much to look at. "You know what they say," he told Louie with a glance at the other customer. "In the dark they are all the same."

Louie looked from him to the woman, and raised his eyes. "Not that much, they ain't," he told himself.

Oblivious to the bartenders speculation, Burger threw money on the bar and left.

He thought about quitting all the way back. Of course, if he quit he'd have to go back to checking the phony gun licenses some artistic genius had been floating all over the county. Hell. At least this case was innerestin'. Maybe he'd stick it out a little longer. Help her out. Show her the ropes. He would let her know, let them all know, that he knew his job.

The drinks had freed him up enough to talk.

* * * * *

"If I want to ice delivery men," he said around bites, "it seems to me the timing is gonna be partitelar important. So maybe it ought to be important to us too, *denkst du*?" His sandwich was so thickly stuffed, his jaw made a clicking sound with each bite. "I mean," they had to guess at what he said, "these guys ain't gonna hang around yakkin' away to no female. They're on tight schedules, so what ever happens, hasta happen quick. *Verstehen sie*?" He made short work of the first half and started on the other. They tried not to watch.

"I think I do," Sal said. "You refer to the way these men are murdered. You think that these men, accustomed to a tight delivery schedule, and on unfamiliar ground, would not want to hang around and chat. Therefore, whatever the woman does or says to them, it has to be well planned and quick. *Nicht wahr*?"

Burger stopped chewing to consider what she said before nodding vigorously. "*Ya. Ya gawiss.*"

"Looking at the murders from the criminal's point of view." She nodded encouragement at him. "Good idea. I can see how that helped you build the excellent arrest record you have," she added, reflecting a little honey wouldn't hurt. "Thank you Sergeant. Has anyone anything else?" The question hung in the air, a wallflower waiting hopelessly for an invitation to dance.

They continued to look at each other awkwardly, lunches unopened before them. It was as if Burger's repast had made them reluctant to begin their own.

She waved at their meals. "I'll talk while you eat, and have mine later, when you are working."

Emily's peach flavored yogurt, diet Coke, and cellophane wrapped peanut butter and cheese crackers, looked meager between Burger's and the feast in front of Masters: two turkey barbecues from PC Junior, a bag of carrot chips, a sour cherry pie, milk from the office refrigerator. The aroma, released as he unwrapped the familiar packaging from the first of his sandwiches, elicited an envious growl from Sal's stomach. He grinned at her, offering to share the bag of carrot chips. She shook her head.

Adamson's neat white bag, imprinted with his full name, yielded a square plastic dish of salad, and a small package of carefully wrapped rye crackers, obviously homemade. He had helped himself to tea.

"All right then," she said briskly, "I want to start with the press and how we'll handle security first, then I'll describe our next steps."

* * * * *

For half an hour they listened intently as she explained the plan. Emily Haines frowned. "What about this section marked *Profile*? I don't see quite how..."

"I think you will when you get to it. You'll look at the facts in your category, then sit back and think. What we want is a careful analysis of the facts. If we base our conclusions on those facts, however unpalatable, we will be a lot further on. She's made choices, a lot of them. If we examine those choices, they may reveal a sort of footprint which could lead us to her."

Adamson's slightly raised hand asked attention. Sal gave him a nod.

"So-oo, let me see if I've got this right. You want us each to choose one of these four forms, each covering a particular aspect of the murders." He studied the four forms in front of him, tapping each in turn with a forefinger. Poisons, Victims, Date and Time of the murders, or the Crime Scenes.

We begin by gathering the appropriate information for that category from the eleven case-files here." He tapped the green file-folders. "Right?"

Sal nodded. "It would be easy to let ourselves be intimidated by the large number of cases. I want to turn that liability to an asset. The murders *seem* to be nearly exact duplicates of each other in many ways, but let's see. Whether they are or not, each of these represents a deliberate *choice* by our perpetrator. Let's see if we can get a handle on how she thinks."

"Right." Adamson went on. "Then we look for the common factors among them, and answer the questions you've posed at the bottom of each form here," tap, "adding any questions or conclusions of our own."

"Right." Sal nodded him on.

Burger mumbled, "Goot! So he proved he can read!"

Sal ignored him. "Excellent synthesis, Corporal. That is one of your strengths. Very noticeable in your written reports. Thank you." Adamson's face reddened.

"As to the rest..." But Adamson, unaccustomed to such candid praise, could not let it go. Turning up his smile until it reached his eyes, he sought clarification.

"You've referred to reasons you chose us," he said archly. "I confess to my share of curiosity about that. We seem an unusual, dare I say a-typical, group." He uncrossed and recrossed his legs.

She had tried to shake the query away, but Masters spoke then, seeming to speak naturally for the group. "Yes Loot. I'm a wee bit curious myself. Besides, it might help us to work better for you if we knew what you see in us."

Not too unusual a request, you might think, when you've dealt yourself four wild cards.

She gave in then, replying without further preamble. She had chosen them, she said with the same cool frankness, because, as a group, they were intelligent, inquisitive, trustworthy, able to think beyond the obvious, and willing to take a calculated risk. "As to your individual strengths," she aimed her eyes first at Burger, "your experience is invaluable, as is your integrity, which has been tested and remained intact." The nod and look moved to Emily Haines.

"You are highly objective and analytical." On to Adamson. "As for you Corporal, you are intuitive, a creative thinker, and are widely informed. As for you Sergeant Masters, you know how to generate ideas and take leadership." She turned both palms upward in a gesture, inviting comment. "Will that do?"

The matter-of-fact statement of her attributes, offered without guile or intent to flatter, seemed to rattle, rather than re-assure the young woman. "But how do you come by this information?"

That, too, Sal thought, was a fair question. "Well, that, I suppose, is *my* strength. Besides a review of your files and a chat with those with whom you have worked, I've my own first hand observations of each of you. Two of you I have had in class at the academy," she nodded at the younger two. "Sergeant Burger I've observed at work on several cases-- the Protikin case and the Williamson Brothers matter, for example. Of course Sergeant Masters and I have worked together for a while now."

She sat back, hands in pockets, giving them time.

"Hmph," the grunt came from Burger, "It chust wonders me how anyone would want me on a *team!* Their allus complainin' I ain't a team player."

"Yes," Sal said frankly, "I'm aware of that. It is a charge leveled at most of us here at one time or another, including me. But let's face it, good cops, in the traditional sense, have had the case for nearly two years and come up empty. Time to give the divergent thinkers a chance, don't you think? Do any of you doubt you fit into that category?"

Adamson knew *he* did. Even among his friends he was often accused of being *too* different. Emily Haines, too, remembered her former husband's chief complaint. "You are always on some goddamn path of your own. Why can't you be like all the other wives?" But she couldn't. It had nothing to do with wishing or trying, just everything she did turned out differently--her home, her garden, her clothes, her cooking, her career. Could it be that it wasn't so awful after all?

Even the grizzled Burger experienced a thud in the pit of his stomach, as though an important part of him, lost long ago and valued only in secret, had been drawn out and openly admired.

Sal studied their faces. "Team playing has its place--and an important one--but it's not always conducive to breaking new ground, which is what we have to do to solve this case."

They seemed to be satisfied with that. She turned away, ready to continue, but Haines spoke, her eyes still clouded with doubt. "You said making such decisions is your strength. Are you ever wrong?"

"Sometimes, yes," Sal replied frankly. Again she prepared to start. The strained look on the other woman's face, forestalled her. "But I think not this time."

There had been a brief flurry while technicians brought in telephones and laptops. "Take note of the calendar I've put on your computers. We have Dr. West at two-thirty. I'd like to see what we've come up with before West gets here. After that I'll be leaving for an outside appointment. That will be a good time for you all to visit the most recent crime scene. Perhaps we can meet back here again later, say at seven? By then, I hope to have additional assignments for you. Please keep security uppermost in your mind as you work both in and out of the office. You can work on these lists until two o'clock or thereabouts. Directly on the computer if you wish."

Burger grunted. "Vell, lad--Lieutenant. It's the strangest way of doing lek vork I ever heard of, but I suppose that's the future waving at me. Nicht vahr?"

"I'm afraid so, Sergeant. Let's give it our best shot and see what we come up with. Mach's gut?"

"So geht's alle vile," he said philosophically.

They spread out around the large table, Burger grudgingly bringing up the rear. "At least we're gettin' to work instead of yakking. Be a lot easier on the feet," he conceded.

Sergeant Burger's feet seemed to be much on his mind lately.

* * * * *

At the comparative quiet of her own desk, Sal sat back to think through an idea which had presented itself earlier this morning as tentatively as a boy pinning a corsage on his first date. However, it was not long before the steady tattoo of clicking keyboards, mumbled comments, grunts of surprise, and the unending ring of phones, broke through her efforts to concentrate.

Alert for the first signs of heightened interest and the hoped-for group cohesion, she accepted the interruptions philosophically. The interest was there all right, yet even amid the hub-bub, the team still seemed somewhat ill at ease with one another: Adamson the most voluble, Haines tacking polite 'thank you's' to each request, Burger remaining somewhat apart from the rest. Only Masters, fielding questions in an assured voice, seemed to have adjusted to the new alliance.

Naturally, Adamson had wasted no time choosing the form marked *Poison*s, settling quickly to work. The first column took him only a few minutes, then, without a word, he got up and left the room.

Emily Haines watched his departure with raised eyebrows. *Crime Scenes* had seemed to be, by far, the most interesting of the choices, but she was finding a review of the earlier investigating officers, with the results of leads followed and abandoned, necessary but tedious reading. She also made a careful study of crime scene photos and coroner's reports. Some while later, she moved to a quiet corner of the room to think.

Mumbling something about "bein' back in school," Burger gravitated to the form covering *Victims*. He recorded the data asked for, mumbling to himself all the while, Then, list in hand, he grabbed a phone and began jabbing numbers with the end of his pencil. A brief verbal exchange with someone on the other end and he would scribble, flip through the next file, jab at the phone, and repeat the process. Soon the detective in him was absorbed.

For Masters, left with the *Dates and Times* of the murders to investigate, the case files were scant help. The Internet provided some of what he needed, however. A few quick notes, then he, too, left the office.

* * * * *

Community Building. Rooftop restaurant.

Chief Warmkessel and Mayor Rueben Thaxton settled down to lunch. They began, as was their habit, by congratulating themselves for having the forethought to include the eatery in the plans for the building. Not that they had ever imagined Plainfield would become a major media interest, but, as things were, they could escape the hub-bub of their offices for a bit.

Warmkessel was in hopes of getting his back patted by someone whose approval of his choice of team leader would be unconditional. Naturally, the mayor had obliged.

"I'm a bit afraid we'll never find the woman who's doing this," the mayor admitted frankly, "but if anyone can do it, Sal can."

Warmkessel took a poke at his salad. "At least the damned press has left town. The major networks anyway. Just the local stations left now. They'll feed things back to New York if anything breaks."

"And you're leaving it to Sal to handle that?"

Warmkessel nodded. "She pretty well set it up at the press conference. She knows how to handle them."

"Ought to. Been at it since she was five." The mayor gestured for more coffee. "You got everybody on board with that?"

"Yeah."

"You sound doubtful."

"It's the DA's office. They *say* they're with us, but..."

The mayor nodded understanding. "I'll have a quiet word with them. Maddie is family after all. She'll cooperate. And Sal will get us out of this. She knows what she's doing. You haven't seen my roses for quite a while. I've got a beauty, a clear blue, I'm trying to..."

CHAPTER 13 Sam

If you poke a snake's nest don't be surprised if you get bit.

Hong Kong. Mandarin Hotel. Thursday 3 PM

To his surprise, the message was still in the box when he came back on duty the next afternoon. Puzzled by this unusual turn of events, he sought out the registrar.

"Not yet," he said, shaking his head. "Someone called to say the party had been delayed. Didn't say why."

"Say where they were? Wife's with him this time."

"No, he didn't," the registrar said irritably. "That's his business. He pays for the suite. That's all that matters to me."

"Sure, that's fine for you. But I rely on his tips and he can't tip if he ain't here."

"Too bad for you." The registrar gave him a sympathetic look. "Anyway, they'll be here soon, I'm sure. After all, they didn't cancel. And if his wife is along this time, you're bound to make up for the lost tips."

"I guess."

He went off to take the first of the evening's calls, resolving to keep an eye on the mail slot behind the desk.

* * * * *

As the morning wore on, the sound level continued to rise. More notable now was the scrape of chairs being pushed back, the opening and closing of doors. Masters left the room several times, each time returning more disconcerted. Adamson was gone nearly an hour and came back, his expressive face a curious blend of triumph and dismay, like a small boy who had just hit the game winning homer into a policeman's window.

Nevertheless, by the time the agreed upon hour arrived, they were all back in the office, clustered around the large table comparing notes. The look on Masters' face brought Sal to her feet.

She motioned them to come together. Adamson came readily. Haines seemed loath to leave her work, and Burger, still somewhat estranged from the group, dawdled about as well. She decided it was time to bring the outfield in.

"I take it you've found something? Who wants to start? Sergeant Burger. Why don't we stick with you?"

Abrupt as always, Burger dug in. "I'm vorking on this here list of wictims, naw vunce. Here's vat I got so far." He hitched himself to his feet. "Looks like the inwestigating officers did a purty goot chob checking victims--backgrounds, associations, families, that kinda thing. Akshally, I know most of them officers. They are good men for this kind of vork. I don't think they would miss anything important, but there are a few points I wanna double check. Also there is some lek-vork I can follow up on." Apology entered, he went on. "But from vot ve got in the files here, we get this pitcher of the wictims. I got it on the computer if ya wanna look. She helped me get it on the form."

"She?" The teacher's correction came involuntarily, entered before the policewoman could stop it.

Burger made a face. "Yeah. She. Dolores. There's plenty she couldn't get on though 'cuz a connection among them was the favorite theory of several detectives. Here it is. Youse can all look at it but here's what I got for a profile of the wictims."

Death On Delivery
A Pennsylvania Dutch Mystery

VICTIM PROFILES

Murder #	Personal Data	Employment Data	Church Affiliation	Miscellaneous
1	Charles White – 34 w. Two kids, separated Plainfield Native	Flora Time 8 years	None	Teamsters
2	Wil Shumberer – 45 w. Six kids, married Plainfield Native	Dan Stroud's for 22 Yrs. Home Furnishings		Teamsters
3	Sammy Gangewere - 38 Married, Plainfield Native	Ace Electronics 10 years	Presbyterian	Non-Union Boss's Son/Elk's
4	Jack Haines - 36	Short's Bakery 6 years	Lutheran Not Plainfield	Teamster Bowls w. Midtown
5	Ephraim Ackerman - 24 2 kids, Coaltown Native	Morton's Produce 23 years	St. John's Methodist Choir	Non-Union
6	Chou Li Moon – 31, 3 kids Married, Vietnamese	Simpson's for 1 year. Home Furnishings		Teamster & part-time Student at Plainfield U.

7	Joe Cockran - 25 Divorced - no kids Lives w. girlfriend	Mid-Town Lumber 2 years	New Baptist	Teamster
8	Dave Grover - 33 Single, Plainfield Native	Ralston Sporting Goods 3 years		Non-Union, Bowls w Century & Woman Chaser
9	Alfred Keller – 41, no kids Divorced, Plainfield Native	Wilson's Delivery Service 3 years		Teamsters Barbershop Quartet
10	Doug Stoner - 26 Single, Plainfield Native	Office Products 2 years		
11	Don Thurston - 38 Lives w. girlfriend Plainfield Native	Wagner's Interiors 14 years		

COMMON FACTORS OF VICTIMS: Over 21. Worked long time at business. Mostly Caucasion.
QUESTIONS: How were the deliveries ordered? Why were these men chosen?

"Aches ranged from twenty-one--that's usually the minimum ache for drivers--those guys usually need to be bonded--to fifty-eight. Most were long time employees with the company, anywhere from three to twenty-two years. As I sett, they did a thora chob checking for a connection. They checked chust about everything you could think of for both the wictims themselves and their spouses: hoppies, habits and the like. Also churches, club memberships, insurance carriers, political groups, favorite recreation, bank accounts, schools they went to--the works. Evens checked the businesses they vorked for and their insurance carriers." He peered at them from under shaggy eyebrows. "There had been that rash of arson cases upstate where someone was burning up places so's to ruin an insurance carrier, remember? So I don't really see that they missed anything. Do you?" He looked in the lieutenant's general direction.

Sal considered it. "No. Go on, please."

"They did have one thing in common. Nine of the eleven favored beer over the hard stuff or wine. So go figger." He paused, giving them time to go and figger.

"We'll keep that in mind, although I can't see how it fits in. At least I don't..." She looked at Emily.

"No. No. It doesn't appear to be. Champagne, and a rather good brand of it according to the autopsy reports."

Sal frowned. "Hmm. It could be that the victim's unfamiliarity with the champagne has some relevance. Certainly something to think about. All right, Sergeant, go on please."

Burger brightened. "The favorite theory of several OIC's is that one of these guys was the real target and the others were chust iced to cover it up. They spent a lot of time checking that awt too, but I ain't buyin' it. But I remembered vat you sett about empty baks, so I fikkered all that nosing meant somesing, and here's vat I think. See what you think."

He shot the lieutenant another look. "I say fergit lookin' for common factors in the wictims 'cuz *the wictims themselves ain't important!* Not to this here lady. Outside of their being delivery men, that is." Not getting a response, he continued persuasively. "It don't matter a bit to this nut *who* the *guy* is, see?"

He sounded aggrieved, as if taking it personally. "In other vords, this nut-case doesn't actually choose the wictims herself. *Somebuddy else does!*"

He looked at his teammates then at Sal. "That way," he said with emphasis, "this here killer can... can..." He flipped his hands around in opposite circles, as if the resulting movement of air would clear away the obscuring fog and reveal the word he wanted.

"... Abrogate the responsibility for the choice of victim," Sal suggested.

"Yeah, that's it. Ap-re-gate the responsibility. We all know how these 'perps' try to blame somebuddy else fer their trouble." Feeling the sale slip away, he added hastily. "Somebody *else* actually sent them see? Then when they get iced it's *their* fault, not hers." He stopped. "What d'ya think? Anything?"

Rather astute is what Sal thought. He would have snorted with contempt had she made that observation out loud. She said it was certainly worth bringing up. "Will you raise that question with Dr. West? I think this is helpful. Is there anything else?"

"Chust the union thing."

"Union thing?"

"Yeah. It was in all the news."

Masters nodded, remembering. "Some said there was a fight to take over control of the local teamsters by some out-of-town group. Never found any kind of proof though, did they?"

"No, an' they ain't gonna either. Hell, I know the locals. They run a whisky clean outfit an' they ain't about to turn over their local to a bunch a out-of-town crooks. Tried to tell 'em as much at the time, but the DA's office was hot and heavy over the idea so's they kept on it. Free press for the DA. Made 'im look like a big time crime-buster. Personally, I wish he woot get elected Guvenor. He ain't doin' shit aroun' here. That Grimm dame does all the work. Not that I *like* that bit... her, but she at least does the work."

Assaulted by efforts to concentrate on the task while doing battle with a view of her cousin, so unfortunately close to her own, and the meaning of 'whisky clean,' Sal sought for a safer subject. Her finger went rapidly down the list of companies. "What about these businesses? I seem to remember they looked for a connection there."

He shook his head. "Nossing that I could see."

"Really? How is it she knows which ones to call? She'd want to be sure her order would be delivered by a man. A lot of businesses employ women drivers as well."

"By *one* man," Adamson corrected. "Was there ever a partner waiting in the truck?"

"Jeez, I don't think so. A'least I didn't see nothin'..." He looked at Sal. "I'll check though." He made a labored note.

"Which means," Adamson said, "she would have to order things to be delivered that could be handled by one man."

Haines was pouring over Burger's worksheet. "Maybe we should know how many Plainfield companies normally send one person out on a delivery."

"But," Masters objected, "that would mean..." he dropped to his chair, his face losing color.

"That she knows the area businesses well. Yes. Yes. That feels right."

They looked uncomfortably at each other, Masters particularly out of it. Sal looked at him. "You all right Sergeant?"

"What? Oh. Yes. Yes. I'm fine."

She nodded. "What do we know about the deliveries themselves, Sergeant Burger? Exactly how did she pull this off time after time? What kind of things were delivered, how were they ordered, when and the like. In fact..."

"Naw chust vait vunce! I got that too. I *sett* we couldn' get it all on the sheet." A look at Sal. "It's a bit detailed an' youse may not wanna take the time... 'Sup to you. Wanna know how far I got?"

"Yes, indeed. Please."

"Wuz gonna have'er type this all up but if we can jes..." He turned back to his much-scribbled notes. "Okay. First one, this here Flora-time. A lady ordered a weddin' arranchement over the phone. Expensive. Sett she'd pay extra to get it deliwered between eight 'en eight-thirty in the mornin'. Sett she'd pay cash at the door. Manaher's pissed they never did collect fer the flaurs. Been billin' the city fer 'em." A grisly smile crossed his lips. "Naw this here Stroud's outfit was sapposta deliwer a set a them whatcha-call nesting tables. Customer needed 'em in a hurry fer some kinda breakfast thing she wuz havin'. Then Ace here," he stabbed the form, "got a call from a real old lady. Woice shook so much they had a hart time unnerstanning her. She wanted one a them there DVD players ta saprise 'er grandson. Kept sayin' she didn't unnerstan what it was. Nice ol' lady, but helpless like, they sett. Asked fer it to be deliwered the next day so's she could surprise 'er grandson who jus grachated from high school with honors. He wuz leavin' to go campin' at ha'past eight so it had be there by then. Okay, let's see. At Short's a young girl callt an' ordered a wedding cake. Hold on! I can't make awt my onw writ... oh, yeah. Manacher sett she was real fussy about the color of the decorations. Had to be

Death On Delivery
A Pennsylvania Dutch Mystery

a partik'lar shade of peach." He smirked at this evidence of female foolishness. "Girl dropped off a sample of the color and a don payment the day before. Sett she wooden pay fer it if the color wuzn't ezack. Deliwery hat to be before eight-thirty 'cause the mother of the brite wuz to pay fer it and she had to leave at that time fer the church.

Asked if they would take a local check for the balance. At Mortons..."

"Wait a minute! Are you saying someone actually saw the killer? This is the first time I've heard..."

He shook his head firmly. "Naw. Venn they came in at seven next morning they found the sample and the dough in the mail slot. Nobody seen her. Okay. At Morton's, lessee..." he scrambled among loose sheets of legal pad, "oh, yeah. That's right. Morton's said somebuddy, they thought it was a man but later said it coulda bin a woman, ordered a case of oranches, needed first thing as she would be away the rest of the day. At Midtown Lumber..."

If Burger was aware of the flurry this compact recital was causing among his teammates, he gave no sign, merely trudging stolidly on. "... Young voman ordered a small microwave to be deliwered early the next day. Said it was on orders from 'er sick Ma's doctor. Said she'd pay extra if deliwered batween eight an' nine." Here his voice took on a different tone. "Now up to this time, the dapartment vas keepin' the details of the deliweries under wraps, but right about in here the dapartment made a big effort to warn stores about deliwerin' to women they didn' know and to report any suspiscious orders. Well, the bottom dropped outta that when customers got mad about bein' queschioned. Youse all know them Pennsylvania Dutch. They don't like no one minding their bizness. See, what happened was these here orders are always from a high class soudin' dame--some said she sounded like one of them Brits, but they all say she sounded like she had lotsa dough, en them's people no bizness owner in his right mind wants to offend. So when Simpson's got a call from a lady callin' 'erself Mrs. Morton Chacops they chumped at it."

Sal's mouth dropped. "Mrs. Morton..."

"Yup. One of yers, ain't she? Well it wun't her, a'cours, so ya don't need ta worry. Fack, she wuz off in England somewheres at the time. Anyways, this here lady vhat called fer a bedside taple for a weddin' present and described their top model exackly, even gave 'em the model number an' all. Well, this Mrs. Chacops is a Thaxton ain't she? Sister-in-law of the mayor? So nacherly, they went ahead an' deliwered it.

"My God!" Adamson fluttered. "This is incredible! The woman is brilliant!" He sounded envious.

The lieutenant seemed to be lost in thought.

"Vant me to go on? It's reely chust more've the same."

"Yes. Yes. We may as well hear it all."

"Okay, let's see vunce. Next was Ralston's. Somebuddy orderet a basketball backboard. Sed it wus fer her hubby's birthday and she wanted ta saprise 'im before he left for vork." He paused for comment. Getting none, he continued. "Next, Wilson's Deliwery Service. Told to pick up a box weighing near to twenty-five pounds. Sett it would be too bulky for a voman. That call came in, lessee, May 17th, one day bafore the killing.

Haines said, "That delivery service employs women drivers too. I know because I applied for a job there. I wonder what she would have done if a woman driver showed up."

"Cancelled, probably," Sal said. "After all, there could have been who knows how many unsuccessful attempts-- times when everything didn't mesh. She'd just have to call it off, wouldn't she? And as superbly as these scenarios are put together, that's just what I think she'd do." For a moment she grappled with the thought. Then asked, How many more, Sergeant?"

"Two more." He wet the end of his pencil with the air of a CPA. "Okay naw. Lady called Office Products fer a small desk for 'er granddaughter. Called jes the day before. Went on and on about the little girl's birthday and her wantin' this here desk an' haw 'er Gran wanted to have it there before the little girl came. Naw, this here's the last one. Wagner's Interiors. Like the others. Orderet a chair. About last Satidday. Sett she needed it ezzackly on this date. A surprise for 'er husband. Well, I guess that's it."

The recital electrified his listeners. Haines, in particular, had grown increasingly incredulous, but it was Masters who spoke for the group.

"I'm beginning to see why she's not been caught. She knows just what buttons to push."

"Yes. It *is* frightening, isn't it?" Sal sat deep in thought for a moment. Finally she looked up. "Well! That was quite a report Sergeant Burger. Well done! You have outdone yourself. Thank you so much."

The praise flustered him. He shrugged philosophically.

"My chop, ain't? Like allus."

If indeed it was like always, Sal reflected, he had certainly been short changed in terms of promotion. Was there something about him she was missing?

CHAPTER 14 The Team

He who puts his foot in his mouth bites his own toe.

Haines had gone next. Aware of the lieutenant's increasing concern over time, she'd offered the abridged version. "It's all on my form here. You can follow along if you want more detail."

According to Haines' report, there was nothing haphazard about the killer's choice of settings for her crimes. Not only were they high-end rentals, but all were at least partly furnished. She had left the places spot-less, leaving nothing such as a hair for our CSU. "Unless," she said with a touch of irony, "you consider the body of the dead man a clue. It, the body I mean, was always found seated at the head of the dining room table. Estimates of the time of death put it between seven-thirty and ten AM. Times are uncertain because of the delay in our being called in. In one case, where an apartment was sub-let, we didn't get called in until a neighbor came in to check on the plants several days later."

"As to the cause of death, we know more about that. Some sort of poison. I believe Corporal Adamson has more on that. Suffice to say, the ME believes the poison was ingested voluntarily--that is..." She raised her head to look at the group, wide green eyes almost black now with her back against the sun. "...As opposed to being forced down I mean.

Death On Delivery
A Pennsylvania Dutch Mystery

It was always ingested in a liquid, something alcoholic. The exact combination varies from time to time, but consistent elements are champagne, tonic water and fruit juice. Some kind of punch apparently." She looked up at Sal. Sal nodded her on.

"When the police arrive--they are usually called by the victim's employer, who gets calls from irate customers--the rooms are empty except for the items furnished by the management, whatever the man delivered, and the body. Just a minute...." She flipped through a sheaf of penciled notes. "Oh. Yes. I knew I had a note on that somewhere. The body does not appear to be touched in any way. That is, there are no marks of any kind. The ME looks for bruises or signs of a struggle, including needle marks, but only one man had any and he was an insulin taking diabetic. Also, there is no sign of any kind of weapon that would indicate he'd been knocked out or anything like that. Pockets appear to be intact." She stopped and picked up her cup with trembling fingers. She went on briskly. "Okay. Let's look at access to the murder scene. I don't have all the information I want about that, but at this point, we do know in each case she had a key. How she gets a key is another incredible story."

Adamson nodded. "Used different disguises, didn't she? The exact information was kept under cover, wasn't it?"

"Yes. Gag order, courtesy of the DA's office.

Looking at it all together like this, we can begin to see why. It's incredible enough on its own, but tied in with Sergeant Burger's report.... Well here. Look at the last column and you'll see what I mean.

"In the interest of time, can you give us some sort of summary?"

"I'll try, Lieutenant, although.... Well, anyway, in each case she rented the unit using some kind of ruse. These seem to have gotten more daring as she went along. In the early murders, she simply called or wrote ahead for an appointment to view using a variety of names. She arrives for the appointment early, dressed as a woman of varying ages, but always in the best of taste. One way or another, at some point in that initial interview she usually produces a large wad of cash, which, they now admit, they find distracting. Well, some of them do, anyway. She pays the deposits, which are hefty," envy glowed briefly in those eyes, "usually from the bankroll. Only one or two bothered checking her credentials. When asked about it, they are quick to say they consider themselves good judges of character, and they could tell she was the genuine article. A real lady. Some of them refuse to believe what she did at their facility even when presented with a dead body later."

"Wow!" Adamson's finger moved quickly down the last column. "What incredible ingenuity! She certainly prepared well! What attention to detail!"

"Yes, indeed. After the fifth murder the PPD tried to get apartment owners to screen their prospective renters better, check references more carefully, but then she simply switched and took the house-sitting job. A brilliant idea and perfect for what she had in mind. The only problem is it wouldn't work more than once. In a town the size of Plainfield, the word would go around like wild fire. Still once was enough, because when there was another murder in spite of the extra precautions, rental agents just returned to their former ways."

"Why not? I can see that!" Masters spread his hands. "Neither their employees nor their tenants were hurt, so what did they have to lose really?"

"I suppose that's right. Anyway, the last few times she appeared in guises that were just incredibly clever. Just look! Once she showed up as a mother of a small child in day care, next with a letter from Morgan Chalmers, another time she..."

"Chalmers? President of Union Trust? Forged, I presume."

"I don't.... Give me a..." She flipped quickly through the green files, selected one, flipped through the contents. "Here it is. It seems the letter was handwritten on Mr. Chalmer's personal letterhead. The apartment manager, a Mr. Joshua Werner, said the request referred to 'personal reasons' for the request, so he assumed that meant, well, something personal. Obviously he was not about to question Chalmers personally."

"That," Sal said, "took real nerve."

"And that wasn't the only one that did. Look! She posed as an Aide to the Governor. Had a letter from him too. This time the letter requested a short-term lease for his aide covering the three months preceding the primary. Again, the request was reasonable, the three months rental paid ahead, so it was accepted as genuine."

"Incredible!"

"Yes. Remember when the papers announced a new director of the county Red Cross chapter? That time she merely used that woman's name. They didn't bother to check her credentials at all that time.

Well! One thing for sure. She reads the newspapers."

"Wait!" Sal stopped her again. "How is it these apartment managers so blithely accept a cash deposit?"

"Well, she doesn't always. In most of the earlier murders she had a traveler's check or something similar. But when she does, she gives them some sort of story. On one occasion for instance, she said she hadn't had time to find a bank. Even asked the manager to recommend one!" She looked at the group and nodded. "This last time she posed as a nurse. The manager said if you couldn't trust a nurse who could you trust."

CRIME SCENE PROFILES

Murder #	Body Location	Est. Time Of Death	Notification	Site Access
1	Livingston Place	8:30-10 AM	Neighbor	With key. Cash deposit and references
2	Park Terrace Apts.	8-10 AM	Apartment Mgr. 1:00 PM	Letter references, pd. deposit. Asked key be left for her.
3	Grover Villages	7:30-9:30 AM	Manager 12:15 PM	Had small child. Pd. cash because ex-spouse would plunder checking acc.
4	Cleveland St. Manor	8-10 AM	Apt. Mgr. Call Log 11:30 AM/2 days later	Mgr. received call from traveling tenant - leave key for decorator
5	Manchester Heights	Indefinite	2 weeks/Apt. smelled Neighbor complained	Broke in with credit card. 10 professors on European sabbatical
6	3960 Hamilton Sq.	7:30-9:30 AM	Weekly Cleaner 12 Noon	Used governor's letter to pose as his aid. Short Term Lease during primary

Death On Delivery
A Pennsylvania Dutch Mystery

7	Pine Wood	8-10 AM	Maintenance Man 12:30 PM	Posed as new local Red Cross Director using Director's real name, so references all checked. Checking Account in same name
8	Maple Tree Village	8:30-10 AM	Maintenance Man 1:30 PM	Posed as Honorary Chair of Plainfield U. using letter from University President
9	Quail Crossing	7:30-9:30 AM	Neighbor/6 PM	Broke in again
10	Thornfield Estates	8-9:30 AM	Court Manager 10:30 AM	Not Available
11	West Side Towers	8:30-10 AM	Phone Repairman 12:45 PM	Posed as Nurse transferred from out of state with letter on hospital letterhead

COMMON FACTORS OF CRIME SCENES: Time of death between 7:30 and 10 AM. With one exception, victims were seated at the dining room table. Bodies discovered by landlord's employees.
MOST IMPORTANT INFORMATION: How access was gained.

"Dear heaven!" Sal shook her head. "The more I learn about the case, the more frightening it is. What kind of a person does she have to be to pull this off?"

"Brilliant I'd say, for one," Adamson said. "Creative, imaginative!"

"Persistent," Masters added. "Determined!"

"To say nothing of efficient. Organized." Haines said. "A planner."

Burger brushed it all aside. "Like I sett in the beginnin', a nut-case! Period."

They stared silently, first at each other, then, as one, at Sal. She shook her head. "I admit I am overwhelmed at how quickly, looking just at the available data, this is jelling into a picture. I can almost begin to see her, can't you? I wish... look, unfortunately we've got to move on. We've only a few minutes before we meet with Dr. West. Commendably thorough, Corporal Haines." She turned to the others. "Gentlemen. Is it possible to get the last two reports in? Then we can face West with as much information as possible." She looked at the remaining two. "Sergeant Masters? You've been looking as if you are sitting on a hot poker. What's up?"

But Masters, uncharacteristically hesitant, shook his head. "Why don't we hear from Adamson next?" He motioned the younger man to go ahead.

Adamson flicked at a non-existent crumb on his spotless shirt, and began dramatically. "We-el!" He made it two syllables, the second falling off down the scale, "you are not going to like this but here is the poison profile so far." Something seemed to be interfering with his usual pleasure in being the focus of attention. He could not stop his dramatic gestures and manner of speech, but he certainly was not enjoying it.

"Part of this is common knowledge. My poison profile sheet's on the computer for you if you like. As you can see, there have been four different poisons used: atropine, digitoxin, strychnine and cyanide. I went over and spoke to Joe Christman. As you know he's been working in Substance Abuse for years. I asked about the characteristics of each, where they might be obtained and by whom." He paused. "Christman said they are all fairly easy to get hold of in one form or another. They are all water soluble, quick acting, and in varying doses, fatal." He stopped. Whatever was exciting him was still there, vibrating in the wings. He went on, all eyes on him. "We-ell, I was *just* leaving a copy of the list with Sergeant Christman when he called me back. He was still studying the list. He said I might want to stop by the drug storeroom and talk to Bob Weinsheimer there." He paused. "We-ell." Again he said it in that naggingly familiar way. Sal could cheerfully have wrung his neck! Was he still trying to play "class clown?" But a closer look showed nothing but excitement there, so she held her tongue.

"I just trotted right down there. Weinsheimer looked the list over too, and repeated pretty much the same thing Christman had said. I asked him if he could describe how they actually *looked*! I'm not quite sure *why* but I did." He nodded self-approval. "Sergeant Weinsheimer said better than that, he could *show* them to me." He paused to let the implications hit home. "It seems each of them were among those confiscated by the police, or turned in during the drive we sponsored a couple years ago! In other words," he added making it perfectly clear, "they are all available right here!"

CHAPTER 15 Shadow of a Murderer

If you go barefoot, don't plant thorns.

Masters said, "My God!" And sat.

Adamson seemed to be having some difficulty believing his own report. "I'm not saying," he continued apologetically, "we should necessarily read anything into that. I mean, it could be a coincidence. None of those poisons are what you could call rare or anything." He turned to look at Sal.

"Just what are you saying?" Sal looked from Adamson to his list. "*All* of them," she asked faintly?

"Yes ma'am. But like I said, it doesn't necessarily mean... anything."

"No. No, I suppose not. On the other hand..." She studied the poison worksheet more closely. "As you pointed out, these are all quite common. Digitoxin for example. Anyone with heart trouble could have a supply on hand."

"As would any hospital, emergency team.... Even some first aid kits carry a supply." She continued to study the form. "Atropine. Commonly used in eye drops. I'm sure a lot of people... Arsenic. Strychnine. Both are readily available in various home and garden.... Anyone can get hold of them."

"Yes. As I said, it could be no more than a coincidence. We'll have to look at it in..." He eyed Sal warily. "You *said* to look at facts, no matter where they took..."

"Of course! Of course! Tell me this. How get-at-able are they down there? I mean, I know there's a guard there, and you have to log in. And there's a security camera, but how securely are they kept?"

"Well, anybody who works for the city or county can request a permit to get in."

"But they have to sign in?"

"Oh yes. In and out."

"So, there's a record of anyone making such a request. They're kept pretty well secured in there, aren't they? I know some are kept refrigerated, some not, but either way..."

"Well, you can't just go in and help yourself. Even if you sign."

Burger showed sudden interest. "Hell! Everybody en his brother goes in there. Hell! It's part of the tour! And nobody in his right mind is going to go in where they know there's a security camera going, especially if they plan to use it to bump somebody off."

"Not our lady anyway," Adamson agreed. "She's not that stupid."

"No. I suppose not. Unless.... Look Corporal Adamson. Have a good close look around there. Find out how vulnerable those cameras are. Could they be tampered with, for instance? You know what I mean."

"Yes ma'am. Will do."

Sal added to her notes, then checked her watch. Eight minutes to go. She did not feel ready to go on, but the pressure she felt earlier was not only building, but appeared to be spreading. "Well. Thank you Corporal. Fine work." She looked up at Masters. Surely she could rely on her sergeant to calm the waters. But for the first time since she'd known him, he seemed unable to look at her. "Sergeant Masters? Judging from your expression you have something. What is it?"

"More that you won't like I'm afraid. I'm checking times and dates. I've run off copies for each of us," he said, shaking his head. "I hope you can take all this in better than I seem to be doing. Frankly, I'm beginning to feel spooked!" He gave her an odd look. "I've done a lot of running around," he began, "and there are still a few holes, but you will see a pretty awesome picture beginning to emerge. I began by looking for any connection between ordinary things: day of the week, time of the month, like that, but found nothing. Then I remembered what Burger here said and that got me to thinking," he nodded approval at the other sergeant. "Remember he said something about the cops being short-handed at times during these investigations? I thought I'd check that out. I dug into the archives for the daily logs kept by each shift captain. I had to get security clearance from the chief before the records clerk would let me in. That was a little touchy, as I didn't want to tip my hand."

* * * * *

He had found Warmkessel in his office, looking hot, rumpled and miserable. Waving Masters into a chair, he had listened to his officer's request. "Certainly, certainly boy. Anything. I told Salome. Anything. Can you tell me what you are looking for?"

Masters had played it down. "We're just clearing away the underbrush right now, trying to get a better picture of... well, of what's been covered and what hasn't. I just wanted to check what else was going on at the time of the murders, see if anything ties in."

Warmkessel had sat up abruptly, spilling his coffee, the implications immediately clear. "Oh my God! What are you trying to tell me?"

Masters had tried to calm him. "Nothing. Nothing at all. It's just one of a number of things we're looking at. Nothing to worry about." He'd gone on to say he was sure Lieutenant

McKnight would be in touch with him as soon as they had anything to report. Yes, anything, he assured the chief again. He had stood, thanked the chief and left feeling sorry for the old man. Hell, he'd had enough trouble.

* * * * *

"Nevertheless," Masters continued, "if you look at the right hand column..."

TIME LINE PROFILES

Murder #	Date of Murder	Time Between Murders	Activities Involving Plainfield Police
1	June 12, 2001		Horse Auction, incl. a Derby Winner
2	December 31, 2001	6 months & 19 days	Holiday celebration & help provided to Lantzville during their police strike
3	June 1, 2002	5 months & 1 day	Seven States High School Baseball Playoffs
4	October 30, 2002	4 months & 29 days	NA
5	February 12, 2003	3 months & 13 days	Groundhog Celebration

6	May 28, 2003	3 months & 16 days	Provided assistance during plant fire in Dunston
7	September 2, 2003	3 months & 5 days	County Fair causing heavy traffic, police escorts for stars, more petty crimes
8	February 28, 2004	5 months & 26 days	Region wide Elks Convention 10,000+ people
9	May 18, 2004	2 months & 20 days	Flood in Edgewood and support for flooded towns to north
10	July 26, 2004	2 months & 8 days	State University Conference Threats on U.S. Education Secretary - keynote speaker
11	August 29, 2004	1 month & 3 days	NA

NOTES: Police coverage stretched for both planned and unexpected events.

"You can see for yourself, Loot," he said, giving her a hard look, "It looks like Sergeant Burger hit it right on the button. At the time of the murders, there was something big going on stretching the PPD to its limits--in some cases more than one thing. First there was the Horse Auction. You all know what a headache that always is. Plainfield is the major auction site at any time. People come from all over, including overseas to buy and sell horses, and that particular time we had the Derby winner here. About sixty thousand folks here with their horses and trailers and all. Quite a headache for the PPD. The second murder came New Year's Eve-- again a time when the department is normally stretched to its limits, and that was the year the Elk Run cops were on strike and we were asked to help out. The third murder came in the middle of the National Little League playoffs. Kids and their families here from all over the country. The fourth murder happened just when we were dealing with that flu epidemic. At one point there we were operating at half-staff. Remember? Then there was the oil fire at the processing plant in Dunstan. Went on for six weeks. Can't have forgotten that!" He slapped his paper angrily. "I don't know why I'm reading 'em to you. You can see for yourself." He had not taken his eyes off her. "Tell me I shouldn't be thinking what I'm thinking."

She shook her head slowly. "I can't. You have every right to..." She stopped.

"I just don't see how we can possibly put this down to coincidence, do you? Especially after what Adamson found. Are we wrong to jump to conclusions?"

Sal struggled to remain calm. "Someone here? Someone local? Perhaps someone in the department you think?"

"I quit thinking. And that's not all. Lieutenant, you said you thought the murders were happening with increasing frequency? Well, I had a look at that too. I admit I'm getting spooked! Just look!" Masters jabbed at his form. "Six months between the first and second, five between the second and third. Then, let' see, it's four months between the fourth and fifth and then... it looks like three months between them for the next several.

But he had lost Sal, who seemed to have sunk into some labyrinth of her own. He told himself she was not buying it. But why not? He prodded. "Lieutenant?"

"Oh. Sorry. I was trying to think.... These dates. There is something familiar about... Sorry," she said again.

"Only two months separate the ninth and tenth. You can see the time between murders seems to be escalating at an alarming rate!"

"Yes. I see what you.... And one between the last two. Yes. I wonder what...." Something clicked. Did this account for the sense of urgency she'd felt since she'd taken her first quick look at the case reports? If so, chalk up one for women's intuition.

Haines came alive. "Just a minute! Are you saying she is timing these deaths to fit into the PPD's schedule? That's ludicrous!"

"Not a bad idea, if she is," Adamson said. "If we have our hands full, she has a better chance of getting away with it."

They stared at each other. The message light on Sal's desk began to blink.

"That will be Dr. West. He'll have to wait."

"He won't like it," Masters reminded her.

"He'll have to. Look, it also might mean that the killer is confident she won't be caught or," she considered it before continuing, "or she doesn't care. Maybe *wants* to be caught. We'll see what Dr. West thinks about that."

The flickering red button blinked peripatically. "Dear heaven! I hate to leave this at this point, but we'll just have to. Look, is there anything that can't wait until tonight?"

"Yeah. There is. Something else the chief told me in confidence. I'd made a remark about how surprised I am that the PPD has gotten nowhere with these cases. Well! Listen to this. As you know, the usual practice in the PPD is for the original Officer In Charge to see the case through until it's closed, one way or another, but the chief had some real problems trying to keep the same OICs involved. The first one, Lieutenant Gorgoli, seemed to be making progress, then he quit. Warmkessel says to keep it quiet, but Gorgoli resented what he called interference from the DA's office. Personality clash, he said."

Perhaps not, Sal thought. The family had always spoken of Cousin Madeline's habit of sticking her nose in everywhere as being 'helpful,' but to strangers she could be a lot to take.

"Then too," Master's voice took on a conciliatory tone, as if apologizing for the department, "we gotta remember the first two were generally thought to be suicides. I think I can understand that too. There was some evidence that the first 'vic' had been having a lot of trouble both at home and at work--that's all in the first case-file. When the second came along, one of the second vic's friends said he'd talked a lot about the first guy. And, the DA's office said that showed he was jealous of the publicity the other guy got. His family and friends--friend actually, they could only find one, said he would do anything for attention." Masters face showed how much he thought of publicity seekers. "And, the main thing is, it simply never occurred to anybody, I mean *anybody*, that we had a serial killer until the third one. I mean, *Plainfield!*" Master's sense of universal order seemed to be under attack. "Hell, this is absolutely the last place you would expect to find a multiple murderer. Jeez! We don't run to violent death of any kind. One of the reasons I moved here! These people are *good*," he said, recognizing the rarity of that virtue. "They're gut honest. They don't even cheat on their wives! Why," his deep voice grew louder and higher echoing the outrage on his face, "most of 'em don't even *swear.*" He stopped, sputtering, then delivered the final ignominy. "They're *Pennsylvania Dutch,* for God's sake!"

Oh yes, Sal thought. It would not be the first time virtue had provided an environment for perfidy. But such cold-blooded murder? And she, too, had let her confidence in the people she'd known all her life blur her thinking.

"Nobody," Masters continued, "I should say but Lieutenant Gorgoli. Gorgoli was convinced from the first it was not suicide, but the DA would not buy it. Gorgoli even predicted there would be more.

"Really? That's the first I heard that."

"Me too. I got it from Gorgoli himself. He's still hopping mad about it. Shankweiler was named the second OIC. He stuck it out through the next few. But when the press descended on Plainfield like seven-year locusts, Shankweiler couldn't take having a microphone shoved in his face all the time, so he gave it up in favor of early retirement."

Masters went on, quietly now. "The chief said he had tried to get a special team appointed once or twice before, but the DA's office wouldn't support the idea, so the commissioner and the council didn't go along. It was dropped until Mayor Jacobs got involved. Apparently *he* reads the newspapers."

Yes, Sal thought. Sam had mentioned it among other bits of news from home when he telephoned her in England. According to her brother, the *Call* had run a series of editorials criticizing everybody for the failure to find the 'Lady Killer.'

"The chief blames himself, feels he really missed the boat but we know what a bad patch he was going through at the time. You know," Masters looked at Sal, "this whole thing can have a devastating effect on him if we don't pull this out. The entire police force is becoming a joke."

"All the more reason for us to not fail," Emily and Adamson said simultaneously.

"Yeah. I got a couple questions," Masters said. "Question one. How the hell does "X" come by all this information?" He tapped the table angrily. "That's for us to find out. And then there's question two. One for the shrink I think. What does it mean that the time between the deaths is getting shorter? I mean, we are talking really *alarming* here!"

"Yes. Yes indeed!" Sal thought the group seemed to feel it too. Finally, she sighed and spoke. "Oh my! But haven't we come far in this little while! And we do seem to have a clearer picture of the reason these murders have gone unsolved, wouldn't you say? If we *are* dealing with someone who has access to inside information, we certainly have added a new and pivotal aspect to the case. Yes, Sergeant, I certainly agree that it is alarming!"

She cast a quick look at her team. Was it her own apprehension they were sensing? Respect for this menace would keep them sharp, but she thought she saw the beginning of fear there now. She went on in a business-like tone. "All right. Let's see what we can do to bring it all forward. All right then. After we meet with West, you can go ahead with your individual areas as we discussed this morning. Let's see if we can find a way to predict when or where she might strike again. In addition, I want you to go and have a first hand look at the latest crime scene. I've asked them to keep it secured for you. Then, can we meet back here this evening, say at seven? At that time we will decide whether or not we are on the right track. Is there anything else that cannot wait until we meet again? If not, I believe our guest is here."

CHAPTER 16 Dr. West

What is coarser than dirt goes away of itself.

The traffic light at the intersection of Hamilton Circle and Applebutter Road seemed stuck on red. She looked at her watch again. Three thirty. She punched the familiar number in the car-phone, told the girl in the school office to tell Colonel Hammond she would be late.

The meeting with West had confirmed many of their guesses, but beyond breaking up the tension that had begun to develop among her team, had he been any real help? With little time available before leaving for her appointment, she had chosen to put off a discussion of the team's impression of the meeting until they had time to digest it all. West was sometimes a lot to take.

The county psychiatrist had virtually barged in among them, towing Dolores in his wake. He'd stretched one eager hand out to her, the other pushing thick, black rimmed glasses further up on his nose. The familiar gesture reminded her of the days when, as co-workers, they had been as friendly as possible when one is a fence-sitter and the other a jumper-in-with-both-feet.

Today, with her stomach tight and wanting only to get on with it, she had given his honest queries after her family short shrift.

West had seemed unaware of the tension in the room, smiling broadly at her with the combination of admiration and relief the indecisive sometimes feel in the presence of their opposite.

Salome introduced her team, all but Burger rising to shake hands. Burger came only to half-mast, put off from the start by West's limp response.

They laid out their findings before their guest. He listened carefully, leaning back in his chair, fingers spread and pressed together before him in thoughtful tents.

It was Burger's theory he addressed first. "Yes. Yes, I do see your point. Very profound question, Sergeant... Burger is it? The *way* she chooses her victims allows for classic anonymity. It is, perhaps, as significant as the victims themselves. It speaks to the *depth* of the psychosis, you see. As to what it means to her? I think it fits in very well there too. A significant factor in psychosis is the externalization of blame. A neurotic will internalize it--what most of us do--but not someone functioning under the burden of a psychosis."

Burger, who believed in calling a spade a spade, was only slightly mollified. "So she is a nut-case then?"

"Oh yes. Most certainly the woman is psychotic."

Burger grimaced at the subtle correction. Emily Haines cleared her throat. "Is it logical to suppose then, that we can expect her to stick to the same MO if... if she goes again?"

"Ye-es, I would think so." West frowned, examining the interior of the tent. "Although, I should warn you, you should not think of her acting logically--at least not the way you and I think of as 'logical.'" Crooked fingers put quotation marks around the word. "Her actions may *seem* logical to her, a faulty logic born of early trauma and the faulty perceptions formed during that time. Actually," he continued after a silence, "these murders have been very much on my mind. They seem to be inhumanly brutal and callous, so much so

I can't help thinking they have much in common with cult sacrifice."

The team had looked from the psychiatrist to Sal in varying shades of disbelief. Adamson leapt. "Sacrifice? You don't mean...?"

"Oh no. Not really. I just meant that the two are similar in that, in both, the individual must be able to separate himself from the 'purpose' of the ritual and the actual deed. In cults, the disjunct is helped along through the use of drugs. In psychosis, that disjunct is already present, built into the unconscious as it were. Then too," he added after a thoughtful pause, "the exact duplication of each death strikes me as being ... well, almost ritualistic."

Sal had hurried to keep her team from following down this blind alley. "If you are referring to the *flavor* of these deaths, I agree. To a point, anyway. There may be a similar detachment from the act of killing itself. That is," she added eying Burger's face, "the perpetrator may not have a real sense of taking a life. That correlates with the impersonal aspects of the deaths we have noted, including the lack of personal connection between the killer and the victim. So, yes, ritualistic in that sense, but not really a cult of any sort, would you agree?"

West back-pedaled. "Oh yes. Yes indeed. I was only making an observation. No, I don't really see them as cult murders. Cultists don't kill delivery men."

Adamson's next question also threatened to take them into unnecessary waters, but she had let it ride hoping it might be just the thing to "hook" Adamson's brain. "Can we explore some of the reasons a person develops this kind of psychosis?"

Hands once again tented. West had said musingly, "I wouldn't want you to hold me to this, even experts who spend a lifetime studying serial killers can't agree, but I think, after studying these cases carefully, what we are seeing here is an extreme manifestation of abandonment. Ye-es," he'd muttered thoughtfully to himself, his eyes tentward, "I would expect to find the root there. Yes, that would be my guess."

Burger snorted. Emily Haines looked puzzled. "Abandonment?"

"Yes, yes, indeed. I do believe so. Put very simply, someone who has, in effect, loved and lost."

"Great! Great!" Burger threw up his hands in surrender. "That should narrow the field."

Sal sought to divert the cognitive turn the discussion seemed to be taking. West got there first.

"Perhaps," he had said, "I have put it *too* simply." He cast a hooded smile on the skeptic. "Like any psychosis, this does not derive from a single, clear message, even of hate. A child can survive being consistently told anything, even that he is not wanted, or ugly, or any such one-pronged message. He can even survive if he gets mixed messages as long as they come from different people. One finds him acceptable, another doesn't. In both scenarios he may be insecure, unfilled, even neurotic, but not psychotic. That happens when the message is garbled, when the child gets one clear message one moment and another diametrically opposed the next--from the same primary caregiver.

"In this case," he continued to press his case, "this woman probably experienced a very close and satisfying, although not necessarily healthy you understand, relationship initially. This relationship probably existed for a time, perhaps for years. Most likely it was a parent-child relationship. If I were to guess, I'd say a daughter-father relationship. The child is led to believe she is the be-all and end-all of daddy's world and grows up with her identity, and that of her father, irrevocably entwined. They are one and the same. Then something happens and the relationship is abruptly severed. Father leaves to make a life with another woman for instance.

Or dies. In either case, the child is devastated; She takes the blame onto herself. She convinces herself she could have prevented it had she been more... oh, more perfect in some way. This gives birth to all sorts of compulsive behaviors in the effort to become that perfect person in the hope of winning the coveted approval. When the approval is not forthcoming, the child thinks she must be punished. With no authoritative person around to do so, she takes on the job of punishing herself."

They stared at him. "Look," he said persuasively, "It all fits. You said," a nod to Masters, "the time between episodes is getting shorter. It could mean that her control is diminishing."

"Do you think it will continue?"

"Oh yes. I think so."

Sal had shivered at that. "Yes, that is what we thought."

Adamson persisted. "So the motive lies in someone's past?"

"Let me differentiate between what you, as police officers, think of as motive and the *cause* of the psychosis. The psychosis is most certainly rooted in the past, but there is probably a more recent precipitating event. Some occurrence about the time of the first death I would think."

Burger didn't like it. "So you're saying she can't help herself?"

"I'm saying the psychotic's actions are beyond his or her control. The psychotic reacts to his psychosis as automatically as we respond to hunger or the need to empty our bladders. That's why mental illness is an accepted defense in our criminal system."

Silence followed this. Then Sal had spoken up. "Then what provokes subsequent episodes? Is each murder preceded by another event, or is it more likely the early trauma resurfaces from time to time in the hope of being resolved?

Or," she had considered it, "has "X" become addicted to killing?"

"Yes and yes. Any and all of the above could be operating in this case. Well put Dr. McKnight. Very well put."

"Thank you Dr. West," she'd said dryly. She was reminded of an old record she and Sam had found in the attic. 'Positively, Mr. Gallagher? Absolutely, Mr. Sheen!'

Case. Eleven men senselessly dead, eleven families ripped apart and here they sat in safety and comfort and called it all a "case." Surely, she thought, it called for some designation more ardent, less clinical. But West was off now in a world of his own.

"Studies do show, for instance, that once one crosses that particular boundary, subsequent killings get easier. Then too, when one has taken a life without discovery, one is left with an incredible feeling of omnipotence. After all, one really *does* hold the power of life and death in one's hands." He'd leaned back in his chair, nodding his head. "And that," he'd said musingly, "in turn would tend to pull the mind more and more out of balance."

She'd tried to put her finger on something he said that struck her as important, but the sense that they were running out of time overwhelmed her.

Adamson was talking. "Looking at the shrinking periods between deaths more out than in, wouldn't you say? "

"I'd think so. Probably by now your killer no longer sees anything out of the ordinary in what she is doing."

"But surely," Emily Haines protested, "such a person cannot pass unnoticed. Somewhere she has to be causing some attention."

"No, not at all. An experienced therapist might, should spot her, but by now people around her would be used to the way she acts and accept it."

Aghast, Emily pursued it. "Are you saying that all this... turmoil goes on inside without showing on her face?"

"Ah! You find that hard to believe? It's true though. Actually it is those faces which show the least emotion that conceal the most inner turmoil."

Again the blurred picture flickered in and out.

When West left, asked for a summary of their meeting, Adamson, his own hands unconsciously tented in imitation of the psychiatrist, made a credible job of summing up. But whatever was in the back of Sal's mind continued to elude her. She had sent her team on their way and left for her appointment at Hawk County. Perhaps the change of venue would shake it out.

* * * * *

Within ten minutes she had left Plainfield behind and the disturbing results of the morning's meetings with it. At the last Plainfield exit, she turned north onto the pristine highway meandering up Hawk mountain. She wondered if her erstwhile fellow faculty still referred to it as "the four-laner" in the same artfully studied mix of awe and derision. The scorn had been for the congressman who sought to assure both immortality and his chances of re-election by seeing to it that the pork in this particular barrel bore his name. Unfortunately, he had not bothered to ask how the natives felt about the proposed super highway. The result was that, not only had they stayed away from the polls in droves, they also stayed off the new highway, preferring the familiar small streets to "the city" on those few occasions when the city had anything of interest to offer. No one used it save the odd traveler, the even odder person in a hurry to get from Coaltown to Plainfield, and Salome, who had had to travel it every day for five years. In fact, she herself, had been viewed by some of the staff in much the same way as they had the highway: useful in an emergency, but not something they had asked for and, for the most part, did not want.

Unnecessary it might be, but there was no question the highway was an admirable piece of work. Carved between mountainous deposits of red carbon, alternating with flat layers of dark grey slate on one side, and the shallow blue-green river winding round deep working mines of white powdered lime, it was a Wright-like testimony to man and nature at their most harmonious. At one point, a cantilevered ledge of snow white concrete, wide and graceful, swooped over half the road, protecting it from constantly crumbling rock. All along the mountainous side, small trees and undergrowth pushed through sheer, red rock in search of precarious berths. It had provided living lessons for students for whom there was no learning without relevance.

She watched for her favorite spot where a mountain spring trickled, not over, but right through the rock walls. She found herself taking in deep lungsful of mountain air, its hint of rain a welcome after the hot humidity of town. The river was low now, too low now even for the wonderful trout and bass which lay in the spring-fed bottom much of the year, but it would recover. The hint of rain in the air promised it.

As it would have to. What else would CoalTowners do with their leisure hours? It was not Christmas, but the two-day school holidays granted at the opening of deer and trout season, CoalTowners awaited most eagerly. Rain or shine, on opening day, Hawk High was hit by a rare, but recurrent, form of spring flu, attacking males from seven to one hundred and seven. At one point, the joint county school board, under the momentary influence of an imported school superintendent, voted to put an end to this insidious outbreak. They declared anyone missing that day--teacher and student alike--would have to produce a doctor's excuse to return to class. The net result was a blizzard of crumpled sheets torn from the pads of doctors who had thoughtfully packed prescription pads along with their fishing tackle. She had not been able to decide whether to admire this assertion of personal right, or protest this blatant snub to the rule of law.

Climbing steadily upward on the four-laner, the past seemed to come to meet her. As clearly as if it had been yesterday, she recalled the ominous note struck by her first glimpse of the dark red Gothic-like structure, towered and gabled, clinging precariously to the edge of the mountain which served as the 'school' for Hawk County's boot-camp.

For five wonderful years it claimed much of her time and every bit of her interest and energy--just the thing to help restructure her time after her husband's death.

Her "boys." She smiled at the social worker's spiteful alias. She had not seen them since Liz Pealing replaced her on the joint committee more than two years ago, but now their faces appeared, like holograms, before her as she drove. Images floated toward her, faces grinning boldly, shyly, confidently, as fit each personality.

That first day they had straggled in one by one, casting a covert, suspicious glance in her direction, then collecting in the farthest corner of the room, like water rushing toward a corner drain.

'Fingers.' 'Turt.' 'Robey.' 'Mechanic.'

Yes. 'Mechanic.' A sudden grin broke out. Oil stained hands, jeans and shirt wrinkled beyond recognition from sleeping in the corner of his foster parent's garage, a trouble light plugged into a long series of extension cords, supplying both light and heat. Like an ugly duckling sequestered in a clump of protecting weeds, Mechanic had sought this refuge from the nine other more aggressive foster children in the household.

Two girls filled out the group. Shari must be nearly eighteen now. A woman really. She and Kit Gaumer, for whom the use of her given name, Catherine, earned such dark looks no one did it more than once, had been the only girls.

It was almost impossible to think of them except as a single entity. Long before they all came together in her class, mutual rejection and destitution had formed them into a tight cohesive group. Their grim histories had found their way into the core of her belief system, providing motivation in her present work, altering her approach to the work done by the Thaxton Foundation, slanting her political views.

A powerful influence, those five bittersweet years were, yet she was still troubled by unanswered questions. Was it possible to undo the damage done to these children in their early years as she had hoped? Or was Maude Greengage right? Did providing students with at least one place where they could expect reason and justice, do nothing more than make it impossible for them to "fit in" with their own world?

Was today going to be proof that Maude was right? The thought struck her with such force her foot eased up on the gas. Would Maude and the rest of the old guard faculty be there to say, "I told you so?" Come to think of it, wasn't that the message in Treadwell's tone?

No. Someone would have warned her. Liz Pealing for one. Their friendship dated from Sal's last year when, together with Pete and Sam, they had unmasked a murderer. Or Pete. Colonel Peter Hammond. His depth of understanding, his quickness to grasp the root of a problem, his willingness to find new solutions, had been established from that first day.

When the sign bearing the legend, *Hawk County Alternative School and Sports Camp for Youth At Risk,* appeared suddenly, she felt an ache almost beyond bearing. Better off she might be now, safer, more settled, but she had left joy behind here in this strange setting.

CHAPTER 17 Pete

The wheel that squeaks the most, gets the most grease.

The team stood together in the dining room of unit 64D. At the moment they were staring at each other. Masters was in charge.

"Anything?"

"No." Adamson answered, apparently for all. "The place is spotless."

"What d'you think, Corporal Haines? This crime scene fit your profile?"

"Yes, sir. As far as I can tell anyway."

"Where's the truck the victim came in?"

"Wagner's Interiors. Company got permission to take it away. It's been processed."

"I assume they didn't find anything."

"No sir."

"Have you had time to work out a possible scenario?"

"Sort of. It looks to me like the killer, by some ruse or other," she shot a brief glance at the group, "gets the victim to sit in a chair at the head of the dining room table and...."

"What makes you think that?"

"Common sense. Some of these men are pretty big and they would be hard to force to do something they didn't want to do or, I imagine," she added thoughtfully, "moved once they were dead, especially if the person we are looking for is a woman."

"The bodies are always seated at the table? I thought..."

She nodded. "All but the first time when the body was found on the dining room floor."

"You think she learned from that to be sure her victim was in place before hand?"

She nodded. "Yes. As I said, he would be too..."

"Heavy to move. Right. Go on."

A deep breath and she continued. "Once seated, he apparently drinks a glass or cup of whatever it is, from which he dies almost instantly." She stopped. "That's all I have right now. I would like to think about it some more."

Masters nodded. "You said you had a chat with the manager here? Anything special in getting access to the place?"

"Not really. Like each of the others, the killer had a song and dance ready for the manager. In this case, she asked if she could have the key so her mother could have a quick look at the apartment before they signed the lease--which they were going to do later in the day. The key was left here on the table."

"Really? How neat! Who else had...?"

"Keys? Maintenance has one; the manager has the other three, as the place was not officially rented. They change the locks for each new tenant, make five keys altogether. One remains in the manager's office, one goes to maintenance, one to security and two to the tenant. Tenants sign an agreement not to make any additional keys. If they lose a key, the manager provides them with a replacement--part of the security here. In this case, only maintenance and the lady were given keys. Security would not get their's until the place was rented."

"Master keys?"

She shook her head. "They do not use master keys. Maintenance and security use their own when they have to get in. The manager says he rarely uses his. Not with the kind of people they get here."

"Okay. We know how she got in. Anything else you can tell us about the rest of the scene?"

"Well, from the chalk markings here, this body was found exactly like the last nine."

Masters studied the report of the scene-of-crime officers. "Haven't been a helluva lot of help, have they? What about this Williams character? Anybody talk to him?"

"The manager says not. Says he disappeared yesterday before he could be interviewed, and according to the manager he hasn't shown up today. I have his address."

"Good job, Haines. Thanks. Here, Sergeant, you better check this guy out. Take Adamson. See why he disappeared. Maybe he knows something."

* * * * *

Sal parked and entered the quiet building. From the floor above, a deep male voice, engaged in urgent conversation with a softer one, saturated the quiet building. For a moment she could not breathe.

Suddenly, the years slipped away, and she felt as awkward as an adolescent. She was not ready to see him. She would take advantage of his busyness to get hold of herself.

Quietly, she moved through the main hall to the other end of the building where her old room lay. It was empty now, cold without the familiar faces and voices. She moved across the large room with its huge windows, past the cloakroom where Turt begged to sit so he could work away from the eyes of other students, across the room toward the huge storage closet where she had found the body of a hated teacher.

The condition of the room shocked her. Where were all the books and supplies she had spent entire summers selecting? The closet was empty too, save for a few boxes of graded reading materials much the worse for wear.

She sat a moment at 'her' desk, shaking her head at other changes in the room. Nearly everything was broken or scattered, including some musty looking jars on the science lab table, the very table for which she had fought so hard. With its independent gas jet and small working sink, they had performed a full range of experiments in biology, chemistry and physical science. Now the jet hung crookedly from its mounting, black holes showed where the faucets had been removed.

For five years she'd held her ground to provide her "special" students the same quality learning environment as other students, a place of which her troubled students could be proud. Why, she had demanded of administrators, should nothing be required of them but that they sit quietly and do what they were told? Why not use the classroom to let them discover true ways to get "high," put them in touch with their brains, show them they could solve their own problems, acquaint them with the thrill of accomplishment, introduce them to the excitement and beauty of nature? If they had too little family at home, let them be family to each other. Introduce them to dialogue, to negotiation, to standing one's ground without violence. How else could cycles of ignorance, neglect, abuse and poverty be broken? Why should they not expect to live in a world that is, at least occasionally, reasonable and fair? Four out of five students in the entire school did not live with either parent. Where would they learn how to be parents themselves if not by caring for each other in the place where they spent the bulk of their day? Had it worked? Did they still watch out for each other? Once again she wondered if today's emergency would prove her philosophy had failed?

She was sorry she had stopped in. How could you possibly teach in a room like this? How had Pete allowed it? Was this what 'her boys' were up in arms about?

The sound of a chair being pushed back, somewhere over her head, reminded her it was time to be on her way. She could not put off the reunion any longer.

She retraced her steps, returning to the stairs leading to Pete's office. What, she demanded of herself, are you worried about? Pete will have changed, forgotten what had grown between them. Or worse, will have remembered and would be a little embarrassed by the hundred and one ways he had expressed the warmth of his feeling for her. Perhaps, too, she would look at him and wonder what she had ever seen in him.

His door stood slightly a-jar, as if waiting for her. She tapped lightly on the glass panel.

"Pete?" His name felt wonderful on her lips. A chair creaked loudly, and a split second later he was pulling the door wide open with one hand, reaching for her hand with the other.

"S.J.!" His pallor was startling, and she thought him thinner, but the encompassing grasp was the same--warm, firm and familiar. The look in the dark eyes, as they took her in, brought a sudden flush to her cheeks and she could not look directly at him.

His voice husky, he said her name again. "Well, Salome Jane McKnight. So you're here. I wondered if you had forgotten us."

Forgotten indeed, she thought. Ha! "Yes, I'm here. Didn't Mrs. Treadwell tell you I would come?"

"Oh yes, but from her tone of voice I rather gathered there was some doubt." He had lost none of his native accent. "I guess I forgot there never was anything doubtful about you."

"Just Ellen's way, I suppose. She doesn't change."

"No. She seems to remain quite steadily in one place. Actually, I imagine you'll find everything much the same. "They smiled, their eyes met briefly for the first time. She looked away. "Except for your old class," he amended. "Haven't done very well replacing you. Even Maude Greengage complains that no one can handle that class like you could." He smiled ruefully. "Rather amusing that." He did not look amused.

The combined scents of after-shave and cigarettes assailed her. She felt a need to sit. She pulled her eyes from his, and gently disengaged the hand still locked in his.

"Oh! Sorry." His face reddened and she felt her own cheeks flush. "Afraid you'd disappear, I guess. Sit down. Sit down."

"*I'm* not going to disappear, but you look as if *you* might," she said, trying to sound casual. "Have you been ill?"

"Oh, no. No, I'm fine." He brushed the question aside. It was a palpable move to change the subject, but she did not dare question it. "It was so good of you to come, S.J.. I know how busy you are. I've been hearing about your new assignment. You must be as good at police work as you were at teaching--as I knew you would be. I hope they appreciate what they've got."

Pete fumbled for his cigarettes, holding the battered pack out to her. She shook her head. "Right. You quit. I remember." He lit one with a lighter taken from beside an ashtray already full of butts. "I tried to quit a couple of times, but I always go back."

"I know. It's tough. I stopped when my daughter threatened to start if I didn't--one of the hazards of raising autonomous, reasonable children I guess. I do sneak one or two at home, now that they're all out on their own. Anyway, with me it's food." She smiled foolishly at him.

It took a moment to realize he was asking about her job. "Oh yes. In some ways I find police work more satisfactory.

It's easier to see results, for one thing. Still, my work here was great basic training for what I do now. Prevention is so much more..." The roar of a souped up engine, followed by the screech of brakes, floated up through the open window.

"That'll be your boys." He reached for his telephone.

"My boys." She smiled again, shaking her head hopelessly.

"That is the way everyone still seems to think of them, I'm afraid--how they appear to think of themselves actually. You have certainly left your mark on a lot of lives here. It is not true, you know, just as I told you when you left five years ago, that we are all expendable."

Into the telephone he said, "Mrs. Fister, you keep those boys down there until I ring for them, even if you have to hog-tie them." He covered the mouthpiece with his hand. "She could do it, too. She and Frank have bought a herd of cattle and she works right along with him." Back to the mouthpiece. "I haven't had time to fill in Dr. McKnight."

"Tell her I asked about her. She wasn't in the office as I came through."

He nodded, listening to the secretary. "She looks wonderful." The brown eyes swept over her. He interrupted the flow of chatter on the phone. "Yes. Yes, I'll tell her. She asks about you too." He cradled the phone. "Mrs. Fister says 'hi and we all miss you.'" His smile faded and his mouth opened then closed.

Before he could say more, she pointed to the multi-buttoned instrument. "New phones?" Inane, but the only thing she could think of to avoid the abyss threatening to open under her feet.

"Yes." He accepted the redirection. A man accustomed to not getting what he wants, she thought, pain stabbing her heart. Why didn't he fight? "Now I get instant contact with every blessed Tom, Dick and Harry in two counties.

It certainly didn't help any this time." It took her a few moments to realize he was talking about the new phone.

His voice lowered, then dropped away as if lost forever. He cleared his throat. "Salome, I've got to tell you about this thing before those boys break down the door. We're really at a loss to know where to turn."

"Good heavens Pete. What is it?"

He sighed. "Do you remember Jamie Truman? He came to us after you left, but we staffed him when you were still on the Joint Committee a year or two ago."

The question surprised her. Jamie had not been one of 'her boys,' so why...? "Yes, I remember. Quiet, shy boy. Small for his age. Placed in Anne Buford's class while we tried to find out what was wrong with him. A bright boy. Referred by counselors in his private school. Said he was a paranoid schizophrenic, didn't they? I had a problem with the diagnosis as I recall. He was supposed to be re-evaluated. What was the result?"

He shook his head. "Never happened. Parents put up such a fuss about having him tested again so soon, we were forced to go along with it. I did everything I could to have West test him, but I was out-voted. You know how they are. He fit the pattern. The general consensus was that his parents knew best. After all, his mother is a teacher and his stepfather a scientist. God, what a travesty! He fell right through the holes! Dammit, Salome, there are just too many of them we miss."

"I take it Jamie Truman was one of those? What's it all about?"

"Salome," he reached for her hand again, but whether to protect her, or reassure himself, was not clear. "The boy's dead. By his own hand."

She stared at him. "When?"

"Sometime yesterday. I'm not sure just when." She waited, knowing that was not all of it. Suicide was not entirely unknown to Hawk High. "He left a note. One of your boys found it or I doubt we would ever have seen it." He seemed to be stalling. "Damn it," his fist hit the desk. The dark eyes glittered. "His note accuses the step-father of abusing him terribly, so much that he would rather die. And we thought he was one of the luckier ones because he had parents!"

"Sexual abuse?"

"God, Sal! His parents are educated, intelligent people-- father one of the country's top electrical engineers, mother's trained to see the signs. She must have known. How did our people miss such a thing? How could I?" He got up to stare, unseeing out his window. "Why didn't the boy come to me?"

Sal knew too well the pain when your best efforts go to naught. She reached for the phone and punched a number. "This is Sal McKnight. Give me Juvenile. No, I *can't* hold. Cut in on the line then," she snapped. "This is an emergency." In another brief moment. "Carl, this is Sal. Look at the day book from," she looked at Pete, "Tuesday?" Pete nodded. "Tuesday or Wednesday. A juvenile suicide. The name is Jamie Truman." She waited. "Reported when? *This* morning?" She listened again, relayed the information to Pete. "The report was just sent over to my office an hour ago. I must have just missed it." To the phone she said, "Yes, you did the right thing, but I still want to see the log. Who has it?" Again she listened. "What action is being taken?" This time she listened a little longer, then, "Right. Okay. Tell Eisenhard to expect a call from me. I'll want to see him. No, tonight. He should leave a number where he can be reached. I'll get it from the desk later." She hung up and sat back opposite Pete. "How did you find out?"

"From Soroka."

"Soroka? How did he..."

"He came running up to my office after somebody in the class said this would be his last day on earth. I hauled them up here. It seems that some of the boys have gotten the whole class riled up, and they have signed some sort of pledge to avenge Jamie's death. They found him, did I say that?"

"But why do they think Mr. Soroka..."

"Can't get a straight answer about that. They insist I know. Worse, the Reinhard boy's in on it too. You know Duke once he gets his mind made up."

"How did they come to find him?"

"Shari got up in arms yesterday when Jamie did not show up at school. Apparently they had a joint report of some sort due. They were quite a pair, you know. Wrote an entire little musical together, and it wasn't bad either. Jamie seemed able to see right past her psy..." He dropped to his chair. "Anyway, she kept trying to call him throughout the day and got no answer, so they didn't think he was sick. The housekeeper would have been there if he was, so they all went down there."

He tried not to think about the many school rules broken, tried not to think about six of his students piled into Reinhard's car. "When they got there, Lenny Wilson saw Jamie's window was open and went to shut it because it had started to rain. They found him."

He stopped to sip the unwanted coffee, now cold. The voices floating up from the secretary's office a half flight down grew louder.

"Have you seen the note? Do we know exactly what it says?"

The 'we' caught him off guard. He turned to look at her. "No. Duke again. He took it because Mrs. Truman tried to tear it up after she read it. The police have it now. I understand Mrs. Truman objected strenuously."

"Did they tell you what it said?"

He nodded. "A sort of will. He seems to have left everything he owns to his friends."

"The Corrigibles? I see. Where are Jamie's parents now?"

"His mother is at home under doctor's care. Says she thinks the gang is responsible for the note, although she does admit it is Jamie's handwriting. She says Jamie has been telling a lot of lies lately." Pete sat back down. "The father is away on business, she says. Claims she doesn't know where."

The not too distant voices from below got louder, but neither seemed ready to move on.

"Pete, I don't see yet why you think you need my help. You can handle Duke and the rest of the gang. What are you leaving out?"

"Hell, Salome, they've threatened to *kill* Soroka!"

"Soroka? Why?" She stopped. "Oh! They think he's gay, don't they? And they equate that with..."

"Pedophilia. Yes. God knows we've tried to explain..."

She shook her head. "There must be more to it than that. The Corrigibles never went in for violence."

"Well, they have now. Make no mistake about it. They say no one will ever know which one of them did it, and even if they do get caught, most of them are still juveniles."

"By 'they' you mean..."

"Duke Reinhard is doing most of the talking, but it is clear they are all firmly united in this. The worst of it is a lot of people here believe that they would get away with it too. They believe they've got you to protect them. And I have the awful feeling that the gang believes it too."

She felt herself getting angry. "And you?" She looked at him.

"Good God, Salome! I don't believe it. Not for a minute! And so I told them all too." He, too, was angry. "I know you too well. I also think the gang doesn't really believe it. I think they know you would not be a party to any such thing, but they go about *acting* as though they believe it. And, as you well know, the new "zero tolerance" regs leave me no choice. I must act on it."

They could no longer ignore the all too imminent voices

"Okay Pete. We'll think of something. Let's let the tough guys up here before they break down the door."

"Yes. Yes. I guess we'd better. Salome, I hate to saddle you with this."

"Don't worry about it. I supervise all juvenile cases, so it would have come to me anyway, so stop worrying."

Pete pushed a button. "Send those boys up here Vi, but you tell them if they don't come up quietly they won't be let in."

He dropped the phone, moving quickly to stand in front of the closed door, arms across his chest, feet firmly planted.

As the footsteps approached, he roared at the oncoming herd. "I *hope* you are all prepared to be *gentlemen*. And *ladies*." This apparently to the last stragglers. "Are you?"

There were some mumbles to this question. Through the frosted glass Sal saw someone moving toward the door.

"Hold it!" The roar was stupendous. "I'm waiting for an answer!"

"Yeah, yeah."

"Is she in there?"

"Is she really here?"

"Teech's here! I told ya. Teech's..."

The roar came again. "If you are referring to Dr. McKnight, yes, she is here. You will get to see her *when* you answer my question and not before. Are you prepared to be ladies and gentlemen?"

A chorus of "yeah, sures" and one bold, "ain't we alwus," echoed loudly in the large hall.

"All right then." Pete's roar diminished too. "Ladies first. And the rest of you chaps, one at a time."

CHAPTER 18 The Corrigibles

The deeper ya dik, the yellower the gold.

They found him, at last, in a corner booth of the TipTop Diner behind an enormous plate of spareribs and sauerkraut. Adamson slid in beside him. Burger squeezed in across from them, and mopped the sweat from his face.

Adamson began. "Mr. Williams. You're a hard man to track down."

"Yeah? So what? You can just tell that bitch I ain't paying no more alimony 'cuz I ain't working." He sopped up the sauerkraut juice with a hunk of rye bread. Burger motioned to the waitress to bring him the same.

"Really? We understood you were working at Greentree Village."

"Yeah, well you understood wrong. I quit."

"Really. Pretty sudden, wasn't it?" A forkful of sauerkraut muffled the answer. "Working there yesterday, weren't you? Now you say you quit. May we ask why?"

"It ain't none of yer business, but you guys got cop written all over ya, so's I'll tell ya anyway just to show you what a square shooter I am." He sopped and chewed. "I quit 'cuz I ain't workin' no place where that she-devil murderer is hanging around! That dame eats workin' men like me alive!" He chewed on another meaty rib. "Nope. Not for me!"

"That's strange. We heard you were helping her out. You were right there with her, weren't you?"

"What the hell you talkin' about?" He put his fork down and glared at them. "Say, who the hell are you guys anyway?"

"Plainfield PD. Special Investigators. Corporal Adamson. This is Sergeant Burger."

The witress placed a heaping platter in front of Burger. Adamson raised an eyebrow. "Hungry," Burger said.

The man stared from one to the other. "What the hell dywa want with me? Hell, I coulda bin the next victim. You should be protectin' me!"

"What we're trying to do, Mr. Williams. Can't do it very well, though, without the help of public-spirited citizens like you. So, how about it? Tell us about that morning."

"Tell ya what? There ain't nothin' to tell. I went ta work, did my job and went home."

"That's not the way your boss has it. According to him, you made up for coming late by leaving early. That puts you there just about the time the body was discovered."

"Meaning what?"

"Meaning we want to know what you were doing every minute you were there. For instance, you left early. That right?"

"Yeah, that's right. I was sick." The waitress took away the plates and brought a piece of raisin pie topped with ice cream.

"You ought to be sick. How can you eat like that? You'll get as fat as a house."

"Not me. Work it off. Anyways, you have your answer, now beat it."

"No rush. You and I might as well chat while my... partner here has his lunch. So, let's see." He checked his notes. "According to your own log, you finished 64D at eight thirty. That right?"

"If that's what I wrote, that's what... hey wait a minute. When was this guy bumped off?"

"Right around eight-thirty, give or take. Help the killer out, did you? Carry her bags?"

"Jeezuz! Wait a minute! Just between you and me and the lamppost, I didn't evens go in 64D that day! Honest! I was late, and a little hung over--you know how it is--an' I was tryin' to catch up. I knew it was clean, so I skipped it!"

"So that's your story now, is it?"

"It ain't no story! It's the truth. I had a party the night before, and I couldn't get the bastards to go home, and I only had a coupla hours sleep, and I was still bombed!" He hung his head. "God! I musta been right there when she was doin' it 'cuz I was right outside 64D when I looked at my watch and it said ha-past. Oh God! Now, I'm really sick!"

Burger poked a fork at him. "Where did you go then, after you checked your watch?"

"Just downstairs to the next job. That lying bastard Jonesy said the job should take five minutes, but it took near half an hour."

"Yes," Adamson agreed, "I imagine in your condition it would."

"Then what," Burger persisted.

"Then? Then I went over to C building. After that..."

"You drive over there?"

"A'course. Need my truck, don't I?"

"Park your truck in the lower service level?"

"Yeah, sure."

"See anybody down there when you were loading up?"

"Nope. Nobody. Place was like a tomb."

"Seen a nurse down there?"

"A nurse? No, I told ya. Nobody."

"How 'bout as you drove away. See anybody then?"

"No. I tol' ya!"

"Nobody? Repair men? Utility trucks? A delivery truck?"

"Wait a minute! That's right. There was a van there. I wuz afraid he'd be blocking me in."

"Where was it from? The delivery van, I mean."

"I don' know. Just a truck. Parked right next to an old jalopy."

"Old jalopy? What old jalopy?"

"The cleaning lady's."

"Cleaning lady? What cleaning lady? Someone you know?"

"No, a'course not. I don't hob-nob with cleaning ladies."

"Then how did you know she was a cleaning lady?"

"How d'ya think? She *looked* like a cleaning lady." They looked at him. "She was packing her cleaning stuff in her trunk while I was putting my stuff in my van."

Burger put his fork down and looked at Adamson.

"What sort of cleaning stuff?"

"The usual. Bucket. Mops. Bags of garbage. Like that."

"Garbage? The apartments have their own dumpsters at each unit. Why would she take garbage with her?"

"How the hell do I know? Ask her. Maybe it wasn't garbage. All I know is she put two plastic garbage bags in her trunk along with a bucketful of rags."

"What did she look like?"

"Look like? She looked like a cleaning lady. I tol' ya."

"Tall? Short? Fat? Thin? Dark? Light?"

"I don't know. Medium I guess. She was bending over to put her stuff in her trunk."

"Fat? Thin?"

He shrugged again. "I don't know. Not fat though. Normal I guess. Maybe a little on the skinny side. Depends what you mean by skinny, don't it?"

"Hair?"

He shrugged. "I don't know. Covered with one of them there Dutch caps."

"Dutch caps?"

"Je-sus! Do I hafta draw a pitcher? I tol' ya she was a cleanin' lady!"

Adamson turned. "Hold it! Are you saying she was one of those girls from the company that sends people out to clean in Dutch outfits?"

"Yeah. That's what I said. A cleaning lady."

* * * * *

The two girls came in first, accepting the 'ladies first' order graciously, as if used to it. They came in together just as on that first day long ago, only now both obviously taller, older and, in Kit's case at least, prettier.

Smiling broadly, Sal offered her hand to each girl in turn. Long painted nails on one, small rough hand on the other, mute testimony to the difference between the two.

"Miss McCutcheon. Miss Gaumer. Still good friends I see. How nice."

Still bone-thin, still scrawnily blond, face still pockmarked, Shari seemed not to have changed in the intervening years. Kit, however, was barely recognizable. Now curling brown lashes half raised over golden eyes, sunlight plucked strands of gold from the brown mass, falling freely well below her shoulders, framing her small face. That it hung loose, rather than pulled unceremoniously back, secured by a rubber band or bit of string and shoved under a painter's cap, spoke more to Kit's estimate of the importance of the occasion, than to the fact that she was a young woman now. Seventeen, but Beauty still slept, not in a tree-enclosed bower, but in a garage under one or another engine.

All three seemed suddenly shy. But, just as on that first day, Shari's uninhibited tongue bridged the gap.

"Oh, Mrs. McKnight! Are we only glad to see you! These boys are really *wacko!* Gosh, you look *beautiful!* Oh, Mrs. McKnight! Do we ever miss you!"

An influx of grinning males cut short any further gushing.

"Hi, Teech--I mean Miz. McKnight."

"Hiyah Teech!"

"Are you coming back to stay?"

"Now we'll get some action!"

Again Sal extended a hand to each. "Mr. Wilson. Something new has been added, I see." Smiling, she took his hand, lightly touching a thin line of blonde hair on his upper lip. "Mr. Mudra. I hear you are going to graduate this year! That's great news! You too, Mr. Dietrich. I saw your parents the other day. They are quite proud of you."

She waited for a mumbled "yup" before turning to the one she knew she would have to deal with, if she were to help. "Mr. Reinhard. You are looking very well. I have heard glowing reports of your work here. I congratulate you. You have set such a good example for the younger students. Well done!"

She gestured them to sit down, indicating the large chair directly across from her for their leader. She could not help smiling. "It is very good to see you. You are all certainly looking well."

And so they were. The boys sported clean shirts, although certainly Reinhard was clearly more man than boy. Shoulders filled out, thickened neck, his muscular upper arms spoke of strenuous physical activity.

"I just heard about Jamie. My sergeant said you called and asked for me yesterday. I'm very sorry I was not there to take your call. The report is on my desk waiting for me, but I understand you have all behaved very commendably in calling the police, and in making certain we saw Jamie's note. You have been good friends to Jamie."

Give them a chance to think of themselves as young people who do the right thing under trying circumstances. Yes, Pete thought, that is just what she would do. Recognize how difficult it could be to stay within the law. Maintain their sense of self-worth. Draw herself into their circle. Make them allies. And all with a few words.

She was speaking quietly. "Colonel Hammond said Jamie's memorial is tomorrow. You'll all be going I assume?" She looked at Pete.

He nodded. "Yes, anyone wishing to attend the services will be excused from school for the half day. We will be providing transportation for students as needed," Pete said, slipping, as he nearly always did in the presence of others, into the safety of administrative jargon.

"Have they been talking with a counselor?"

Before Pete could answer, Reinhard spoke angrily, "We don't need no counselors. What good are they? They don't know nothing important. They didn't know enough to help Jamie. How d'ya espect them to know enough to help us?"

Shari burst into tears. "Yeah. If they were any good Jamie would still be here, instead of being dead."

Lenny Wilson put an arm around the girl, sending an aggrieved look at his former teacher. "We don't need nobody no more! We needed you once and you went off and joined the cops!" He spat. "We know who done this to him and we're going to take care of it ourselves! Don't worry about it!"

Sal nodded sympathetically. "Yes. I understand. It is like you to want to take care of Jamie. Do you have a plan to do it?"

They had expected, were primed for, an authoritative demand to keep out of it. Her tone of acceptance stymied them. She went on before they could re-group, handing them an acceptable alternative. "I imagine that, at this point, your main wish is to see Jamie off with as much care and respect as possible. As you have rightly pointed out, we have failed to take care of him until now. Not you. You have been his faithful friends. How do you think he would like us to say goodbye? As you heard, Colonel Hammond has arranged for transportation for any student wanting to go. Is there something else we can do?"

Though her words had included the group, it was their leader on whom she focused her attention. For a brief moment, he was the boy who had been unceremoniously escorted to school by a persevering truant officer. A hunted lion at bay, defenses up, ready for any challenge. Five years of negotiated truce, each allowing the other dominion over his own territory, stood at risk.

She knew better than to try an appeal based on authority. Even to rely on a claim on their feeling towards her would be tossed on the same heap as any other effort to deny them their rights. It was precisely their joint battle to defeat such challenges that provided the glue holding the group together all these years.

"No, but thur's plenty *we* can do." Duke Reinhard's gesture excluded her. "We're gonna make sure it don't happen no more either. We ain't gonna let some other poor sunnava...." Duke looked at Pete and reined in.

The strength of their anger appalled her. She had assumed their affection for her, their trust in her, had remained intact, in spite of her own efforts to forget them. Now, clearly the bond between them was broken. For a moment she considered drawing on her authority to bring them to heel.

She studied each pair of eyes, assessing the strength of their determination, seeking a key to open the door again. She could persuade either of the girls to tell her what she needed to know, but if they could not be trusted with the group's secrets, the gang would hold it against, not only them, but against women in general for the rest of their natural lives.

She drew a card. "I was hoping you would permit me to help in some small way." She looked at the young man who had been in the center of the crisis a few years ago. "Tommy, you've been Jamie's 'big brother' in class, haven't you? Can you tell us what we can do to help?" Knowing they would not speak without their leader's consent, she added, "that's if Mr. Reinhard thinks that's all right. What do you think Mr. Reinhard?"

His trust in her stretched gossamer thin, she put her money on his own strong sense of justice and fair play. She held his eyes and waited with a relaxed confidence she did not feel.

Finally, he shook his head with disgust. "Never mind. I'll tell you myself. We're gonna get that fag Soroka--that's what. When we're done with him, there'll be one less queer around to mess with little kids!"

She waited for a moment before speaking quietly. "Do I understand you hold someone responsible for Jamie's decision to take his life? It is very upsetting and painful, I know, but wasn't that his choice?"

"Choice? You call that a choice! You're not a man, Ms. McKnight! You don't know what it's like! I mean you're a good lady and all that--but you don't know about the kind of people some people are."

Sal refrained from pointing out that police officers had a fair acquaintance with how many people are. As in the old days, she tried for a dialogue. "Yes, I suppose there are some kinds of people I don't know much about. What kind of people do you mean?"

Shari began to answer, but Duke threw her a look that would stop a train.

"Pacifically," Sal kept back the smile at the memories the mispronunciation called forth, "I'm talking about fags, queers and weirdoes. Guys you don't know nothin' about."

"If you mean homosexuals, I know enough to know that they run the full gamut--the same range of good and bad as you," she gestured to the group, "or me or any other group of people." She continued reasonably, her eyes directly on Duke's. "What does this have to do with Jamie?"

"If you think that they're the same as us, then you don't know nothin' about it. Jeez, Tee--Miz MucKnight! You'd think that being a cop you'd..."

"I just meant the same in that..." She felt she was losing ground. She switched tactics. "Can you tell me what all of this has to do with Jamie?"

"It has everthin' to do with Jamie." Duke's face took on the stubborn look she knew so well. "We'll take care of it. Don't worry."

She looked at the others, their eyes fixed on their leader. "Well, okay," she said gently, "but it seems to me the last time you said that, you wound up in court. Isn't that right?"

Silence.

At the door, Pete made a move, but Sal signaled him to let things ride. After a few more seconds, she said matter-of-factly, "You did call me and ask me to come here. I'm sure you had something in mind when you called. Can you tell me what it is? Or was?"

Shari stood up. "Duke, I want to say something and I don't want you to stop me. After all, we're all in this--not just you."

"You all agreed you'd leave it to me," Duke retorted.

"We agreed we'd leave it to you to call Mrs. McKnight and tell her about it--ask her what the police could do first--then if they couldn't do anything we'd take care of it ourselves."

The rest of the group chimed agreement.

"If you want to know what the police are doing about Jamie's suicide, I can't tell you. The report just came up to my desk while I was on my way here. A Juvenile officer is checking out the report at this moment. I will certainly look into that delay for one thing. I understand you were all together when he was found," her eyes moved slowly from face to face, resting for a moment on each, "and that you," she indicated Duke, "called the police and the ambulance. That was the right thing to do. Thank you. As the people who found the body, you are important to the police investigation. I understand he left a note. I have not yet seen it, but if it is as I've heard, as Jamie's friends, you are the best, possibly the only, persons who can help the police. We will need you to give statements."

They rustled importantly in their chairs, and the tense air abated slightly. She continued. "An officer will be at school to talk to students. Perhaps you could start by telling them who knew Jamie best, besides you." The rustling stopped and they became very still again at the thought that some other students might help the police if they didn't. She pressed her advantage. "Perhaps you would prefer I send a car for you. Will you all be able to come down to headquarters tomorrow and make statements? Perhaps following Jamie's memorial service?" Time would give them an opportunity to consider the long-range effects of their actions.

"Black and white or unmarked?" Naturally the question was from Mechanic.

It took her a second to shift with him. "Which do you prefer?"

A spirited debate ensued. She let it continue for a bit, then looked at Duke. She decided it was safe to return the reins to him. "It's up to you."

"Okay. Okay. We'll take a vote. Who wants black and white?"

Lenny and Tommy's hands flew up.

"Okay, now who wants unmarked?" The two girls raised more sedate hands. He counted each group carefully and declared. "It's a tie."

For the thousandth time, Sal wondered at this compulsion to state the obvious. A result of a dulled intellect, or the habit of a lifetime of explaining a complicated society to a drug and alcohol addicted mother? Another question she had left unanswered.

He was digging into trousers beyond baggy, so loose they had to be held on by a black leather belt wrapped once and again around his waist. A relic, perhaps, of one of his many 'dads.' "We'll flip a coin."

"No. *You* decide." Shari insisted petulantly. "You're the boss. Shouldn't he? Don't you think he should?" She appealed to the rest of the group.

"Nix on that stuff." Duke's firm reply settled the matter. "I'd have half of you mad at me no matter what I said--and for no good reason," he said, showing he had not lost his sometimes surprising wisdom. "Kit, you call it." He held the quarter ready on the tips of practiced fingers.

"Heads is unmarked." Kit answered without hesitation.

"You got it." The coin flipped, was caught expertly, and immediately displayed on open fingers. "Heads it is. Okay, Miz McKnight. We won't do nothin' till after the fun'ral anyways. We'll all be waitin' tamarra. You'll be there a'course?"

Their pleading, cajoling, insistence filled the small room. Sal glanced up at Pete, still on guard duty. How could she possibly reschedule her already packed calendar? Then she thought about the chilly reception she was likely to get from the other faculty there.

"Yes. I'll be there," she heard herself saying.

Pete's voice boomed again, directing them out. "And I'll expect you all to be on your best behavior tomorrow! Come on! Come on! You'll see her tomorrow."

He closed the door on the noisy exodus, returned to sink back into his chair. Only then did he notice she had already begun to gather her things. His face drained of expression. "You have to go right away? We have so much to catch up on."

She rose quickly. "Yes, Pete I must. Sorry, but I've got to get back. You'll be there tomorrow?" He nodded. "Good. I'll see you then." At the door she turned to look back at him, "Are you satisfied with this meeting? Is that what you wanted?"

"Oh, yes! Couldn't have gone better, could it? I see you haven't lost your touch. It's just," he sought for courage to say at least part of what he had planned to say, "I thought perhaps we might talk about it over dinner. Surely they let you eat down there." He followed her to the door. "I remember you always said how much you liked Dominoes- -veal rosemary, wasn't it?"

"Yes. Yes, it was. I'm surprised you... That is, I don't remember ever going there with you. I mean..."

"You didn't. But I go there fairly often and I thought if you could spare the time, we might..." He shook his head. "No, never mind. I know they've heaped this other thing on your plate. Another time perhaps."

He sounded so desolate; it was all she could do to refrain from making some assurance, agree to another time. But they had tried before to contain their feelings within the boundaries of friendship. They had not been successful then and she did not want to find out if it would be any different now.

"Sorry, Pete. Thanks for understanding. I'll see you tomorrow."

"All right, S.J. Till tomorrow then."

She could feel his eyes follow her from the open doorway as she descended the stairs. She stopped at the secretary's office.

Violette Fister was just closing things up. A bit awkwardly as country women do, she came round and hugged Salome.

"Everything go all right? He," her eyes moved upward and returned, "was in a real tizzy. I told him you'd take care of it."

"Well, I'm not sure it's taken care of yet, but we've bought enough time to let them cool down a bit. How's... everything?"

"Don't ask! Actually, it's not the same place since you left. I'm thinking of quitting. Would have already if it weren't for him." Again the eyes moved.

"Oh? How is he? Is it my imagination or does he look ill?"

"It's not your imagination. He was a lot worse before the divorce became final last year. Put a little back..."

"Divorce?"

"Yes. Real messy too. Must have been the year or so after you left. He took the boys to visit his family for the summer. His wife was livid. Called the cops and everything. Caused a scene at the airport. But the boys wanted to go with him so there was nothing she could do. While he was gone, she filed, asking sole custody. Didn't get it, thank God! The divorce was final, oh, a little less than a year ago, but the custody battle still goes on. Silly, really. The oldest one is nineteen now, so it's only the seventeen year old. Colonel H's trying to hang on until the boy's birthday this summer."

"And then?"

"Oh, the boys want to stay with him."

Sal sat silently, remembering a conversation between Pete and her over dish washing one day.

"I had no idea. I must go now, but I'll try to... to keep... I'm glad you stayed with him. He needs you."

The secretary shook her head. "It's not me he needs, Dr. McKnight."

*****

He lit another cigarette, listening for the sound of the outside door clanging shut, echoing through the empty building. When it came, he rose from his desk and went to his window. He watched for her car to appear at the bottom of the driveway, stop at the sign there, move cautiously forward before pulling forward onto the highway.

The metamorphosis from rage to control, this rag-tag gang's return from destruction to dignity, had taken, what... ten minutes according to his watch. Again he thought how untrue it is that we are all expendable.

He remained so, watching the highway as the homebound traffic thinned to a trickle, long after the white car was out of sight. A knock at the door brought him back.

"I'm leaving Colonel Hammond. Want me to lock up?"

"Yes, Mr. Watkins, go ahead. I'm leaving too."

"Yup. Okay." The janitor shuffled along, letting the younger man precede him, down and out to the parking lot. "Goin' to stop at Rosie's?"

"No. No I think not tonight. Got some work to do at home." He was not in the mood for even the undemanding camaraderie of his regular bar mates.

Why did he feel so desolate? All that he had hoped for had happened. She had come. She had calmed the students. She would see them again, and doubtless talk them out of getting into trouble. What else did he expect?

It was not what he expected, but what he wanted that clung to him as he drove home. When he reached his own door, he resolved to ask her again. And again. And again.

*****

"Mr. Wilson. You've been quite a piece of work! Burger threw a couple of bills on the table. "Does your boss know you're on drugs?"

"Drugs? What dya mean? I ain't..."

"We'll keep an eye out for you, Mr. Williams." They headed for the door. "Oh, and Mr. Williams?"

"Now what?"

"Don't leave town, will you? We'll be in touch."

CHAPTER 19 Seventh Inning Stretch

If a sorrel iss not tricky, its owner is.

The sound of tires rumbling over the wood plank floor of the covered bridge a quarter mile from her own home brought Sal to earth. She had no idea how she had gotten home. The red and charcoal mountain had passed unseen, the spring fed rock, the sky, crowded with photo opportunity clouds, all unnoticed. She was due at the office at seven. When had she decided to go home first?

He was free! The barrier between them gone. She reminded herself to act her age, but her heart continued to leap adolescently about. Perhaps, she thought, her subconscious knew what it was doing. Home was as good a place as any to come down out of those particular clouds. She would use a change of uniform as the excuse for stopping at home.

Naturally, she could not get by Mrs. Honey without being fed. She agreed to a sandwich and settled in the corner of the breakfast room for a quick meal.

"May I put the game on for you? It's the first game of a double header. The Phillies are ahead four to one in the eighth?"

"Oh?" The ordinary question seemed from a different world. "No. No thank you Honeycutt. I'd better not. I've got some work to do."

But work eluded her. Instead, her thoughts rattled erratically around one fact. Pete was free!

Safe now to take him up on his dinner invitation.

No, she had better stay as far away from him as possible. She did not want to be needed.

Seeing him today had made her want him more than ever. She should not have gone.

If only she could talk to him. Alone. She would call him back tonight.

No. She would see him tomorrow. She would wear the navy suit and silver blouse he liked so much.

Another thought jolted her. What had been the final break in his marriage? She had encouraged him to take back his rights to be a father to his sons. Had that proved the irrevocable break for them? Had she known that to encourage him would result in divorce? Had she done it on purpose?

Finally, she gave up, pushed her half eaten meal away.

Her cell phone drew her guiltily back. She did not answer immediately. Perhaps it would be Pete. She had warned her team they would need to put aside their private lives for the duration of their task, and here she was ready to....

It was Lucienne, reluctant to accept her mother's assurance she was not in jeopardy. But with the break, her mind returned fully to work.

Almost fully.

* * * * *

Wednesday. 7:15 PM. Sal's office.

From the outer office, she could see the team, bustling about in her office. Two other officers waited in the outer office. Dolores beat them by a hair. "Sergeant Eisenhard has been waiting for you, Lieutenant."

Sal motioned him to wait. "I'll take Corporal Trenton's report first."

The press officer described the situation with the media as much improved. "It seems to help that I'm always on tap to answer questions, although I must admit I can't quite get used to seeing myself on the tube. I try always to have something for them, however trivial, and that helps too. I guess you've heard that a number of them have their own experts on the prime time newscasts. They pretty much agree nothing is likely to happen this soon. Do you have anything new? No?"

"Not for release at the moment." She looked at Eisenhard. "But we may have something later from Sergeant Eisenhard. He will let you know. Good job, Corporal."

"Well, anyway, with Labor Day coming up, a lot of them are going home. You know where I'll be if you want me," she said, hurrying off.

Sal turned to the waiting Sergeant. "I'm glad you're here Sergeant. Is that the Truman file? Good. I have more for you. I just came from the school. We'll need a strategy. Let's take it in order though, starting with your report."

"That would be the letter the boy left, I think, Lieutenant."

The note, written in tight, sometimes illegible script, was long and rambling, as though the writer was reluctant to say goodbye. There were frequent references to what *HE* was making him do, references so ripe with shame, guilt and fear there could be little doubt as to the meaning. Jamie had told *her*, but she had not believed him, had always sided with *HIM*. The boy expressed the hope someone would see that his belongings got handed out according to the "will" he had left. A list and a savings account bankbook were attached.

Eisenhard opened the savings book. "One hundred and eighty-two dollars and eighty-six cents. Money from his newspaper route."

"When did you get on this? The desk report just came in this morning."

"The official report from the mother, yes. But a call came in from the victim's friends yesterday. About 3:45. They demanded to see you, but finally gave it to the desk. He handed it to me. I checked it out. I arrived at the Truman house about half-past four and found the boy's friends waiting outside in the rain for me. They had been asked to leave the house. One of them, a young man they called," he checked his notes, "Main Duke, had the note. He said Mrs. Truman wanted to rip it up so he grabbed it and kept it. Inside I found the housekeeper hysterical, the woman asleep, the father gone and the dead boy still in his room. I called the coroner. He took the boy. I took the note and the stuff the boy left in his room. It's kind of eerie. The kid had packed all his belongings, even the sheets and stuff off his bed, into large plastic trash bags. I just took everything away with me, including his bike, since it is mentioned in his note."

"You talked to his friends?"

He nodded. "I would have had to even if I didn't want to. They were furious, partly with themselves for not doing something about the boy's stepfather, the *HIM* of the note, according to them. Said Jamie never said anything to them, but the bastard had invited two of the younger ones to spend a weekend with Jamie and him. Promised to take them to a ball game in his Porsche."

"But that..."

He shook his head. "Apparently he had already tried something with those same two at Jamie's birthday party last year. Got them up in Jamie's bedroom to show them the present he gave Jamie." He sorted through his file and pulled out a photograph. "This is it. It's a lamp. The base is a replica of his red Porsche. You can see what the boy did with it before he killed himself." The lamp lay smashed to pieces in the bathtub. "I take that for an indictment."

"Dear heaven!"

Seeing her face, Eisenhard held up a moment.

"Yes. He told someone, as kids nowadays are taught. He told his mother." Sal felt sick. "You said she was asleep when you were there?"

"Husband gave her something to knock her out, according to the housekeeper. Then he left. Didn't say where he was going. I gave the housekeeper my card and told her to make sure Mrs. Truman called me as soon as she woke."

"And did she?"

"Yes. About ten last night. Apparently the pills she had taken had worn off, and the housekeeper told her what I'd done. She was furious! Wanted everything back. I told her they were being held as evidence of a crime, and if she wanted them back she would have to come in and file a claim, but first she would be wise to file a formal report of the boy's suicide. She finally did that this morning."

"You have a preliminary PM?"

He nodded. "Death due to self inflicted gunshot wound to head."

Sal paled. "What about his charges. Does the PM support them?"

Again he nodded. "Clear evidence of frequent and forced anal intercourse. Recent too. That region of his body is pretty full of scar tissue."

Sal swallowed. "Where is this prize specimen?"

"Nobody knows. Both his secretary and his wife have promised to call as soon as they hear from him. I talked to each of them about an hour ago. Neither has seen or heard from him. Or so they say."

"His car?"

"With him as far as we know. It's not in the garage."

She took a few precious moments to think. "Look, let's get out an APB on him. Get a picture of both him, and his car, if possible, from Mrs. Truman. If not, get a picture of that model from a car agency. Let's get it on the tube. No public accusations at this point. Just say we think he can help us. Also, put someone on to watch both his home and work. Don't expect either of these women to report him. I've met him. He is handsome, highly intelligent and a manipulator, especially with women. They won't want him caught at work either. He is their fair-haired boy. And let's not wait for Mrs. Truman to come in. I want to see her too. Can you get her here in..." she looked from her watch to the busy team inside her office, "in an hour?"

"I think so," he said grimly.

"Good. Come for me when she gets here."

* * * * *

"Good even..." Sal's voice trailed off in astonishment. The familiar room was barely recognizable now. Blue leather chairs pushed back to accommodate a large table stacked with papers. The rose shaded lamp and crystal vase had been shoved into a corner. A huge, detailed, city map, on which Emily Haines and Masters were drawing red and green circles, covered the long office wall.

"Looks like you have been busy." Sal joined them at the table. "What do we have here, Sergeant Masters?"

"Right. Think we have a coupla things. Came up in finishing our profiles. Remember it looked as though each of the murders was committed when the PPD was unusually busy. I wanted to follow up on that. See if it was coincidence or something else. I tried to figure how far in advance the extra assignments are put out. Well, that's a bit of a bug-tussle because sometimes they are assigned well ahead of time and other times as the crisis arrives. I took a look at Emily's profile and learned the delivery order was usually placed within a couple of days of the murder. So I asked Emily to run the daily logs through the computer, going back four days prior to the crime. Then I thought about Adamson's findings. So I asked her to do the same thing with the entry logs from Drugs, this time going back no more than two days prior. I figured if someone was helping themselves to our own stock, they wouldn't want to have it around longer than necessary."

Sal nodded. Masters went on. "Emily set up the search program and gave it to Dolores to run. She's doing that now. Then we went to the crime scene. Only thing we found out there was a *missing witness* statement. Apparently maintenance man there, named Williams. I asked Burger and Adamson to track him down. We've kinda gotten used to starting with Sergeant Burger. Okay Sarge? Want to bring the Loot up to date?"

Burger was busy at the map. "Maybe Adamson kin do it. He's a better talker."

Adamson nodded agreeably. "Sure thing, Sarge. If you're sure? Okay then. Well, according to this Williams guy's log, he must have been right there about the time of the murder. Warmkessel's men had not been able to find him at the time. They'd left instructions for the manager to call them when he came to work this morning, but he never showed. We got his home address and went there. No soap. We asked around and one of his neighbors suggested we check around at nearby restaurants because, as he put it, 'he would be dead hungry by this time.' Found him at the TipTop diner. You know the one on University Avenue? Well, he was there all right. Looked pretty well hung over. His story was so convoluted we could not believe a word he said. At first he claimed he had finished checking the place out for the new tenants at eight-thirty, as his work-sheet said, but Burger here got the truth out of him."

She did not ask how. "Which was?"

"He was in the hall right about eight-thirty, but he never went into 64D. He had gotten to work late, and then found he had the wrong key, so he just skipped it. He's pretty heavily into 'coke,' and he'd had a party the night before. Anyway, at first he told us he hadn't seen a soul anywhere in the halls or the grounds, but the good sergeant here, who could write a book on squeezing information out of a reluctant suspect, stayed on him and came up with something. It turns out he saw one of those 'Dutch Girls' packing cleaning stuff in an old car in the service garage just as he was leaving."

"Dutch Girls?"

"Yes ma'am. That cleaning service. Advertises on the tube. *'Nobody cleans like a Dutch Girl.'*" Wear those blue and white uniforms and the little white Dutch caps. Said he hadn't mentioned it before because he really didn't think about it."

"And he saw her... where?"

"In the service garage as he was leaving. That would have been around nine."

"What was she doing? Did he see?"

Adamson nodded. Burger looked smug. "Putting a couple of large plastic bags in her trunk, along with a bucket with rags in it. She was carrying a pair of those yellow rubber cleaning gloves."

"I see. Did you..."

Burger got even smugger.

"Of course! According to their main office. Dutch Girls had no one assigned anywhere in GreenTree Village anywhere near that time."

"I see." She gave the two men a sharp look. "Did you..."

"We did. We split up the list of crime scenes and checked. Out of the eleven murders, so far we have found people who now say they saw a Dutch Girl after four of them."

"But how is it none of this is on record?"

Adamson shook his head. "They all say the same thing. Nobody ever asked! It seems these Dutch Girls are a familiar sight in those up-scale rentals, so nobody really notices them."

"Yes, of course! Merciful heavens! That's an excellent piece of work, gentlemen. That should help."

"They'll follow through with it, of course," Masters said. "Right now we're trying to get a better handle on future attempts, figuring to prevent any more deaths. We figured to take advantage of one of the few things we know about her, she's consistent."

"Reasonable," Sal said.

"So first we marked each of the murder sites on this map, marking each with a red circle. The number inside the circle represents its place in the chronology of the murders. Next, we decided to expand the crime scene profile to include the types of apartments and neighborhoods where the crimes occurred, then to look for other possible sites in the area, which had those same features. Corporal Haines and I spent the afternoon going around, getting a feel for the kind of place she likes. As it turns out, they have a lot in common. We added these possibles to the map, marking them with green circles.

"Notice the sites are not in geographical order. That is, the killer didn't go from one point to another, but all locations are within city limits. Which I, that is we, think worth noting. I--we--think it qualifies as the sort of thing you wanted us to pay attention to."

"Yes. What conclusions have you drawn?"

"We believe it's possible we have identified the next possible site."

"I see. How many..."

"Twenty two. We figure a four-man team at each site, two to watch the apartment, two for the delivery van, should do it. That's the down side."

"Four men, at twenty-two sites, for twenty four hours? Is there an up side? Can we narrow it down somewhat?"

"We've been working on that. Emily thinks we can. Emily?"

"I may have two things that could help. From the crime scene data, we see the time of the murders--always between seven thirty and ten o'clock. I've tried to work out the reason

Death On Delivery
A Pennsylvania Dutch Mystery

for this, and I think the early end of the time period may be that she has to wait for the stores to open. This is assuming that deliverymen are her target, which I think we must accept. Why they are, I have yet to understand. The delivery is always..."

"What about the other end of the time period?"

"I can think of only one reason that holds water. That is, that she has to be somewhere else by nine-thirty or ten."

"A working girl you think?"

"Or a mother with a child in kindergarten. There are a lot of possibilities. Could be a University student."

Sal looked at Adamson.

"Got it," he said and went to a phone.

"All right. Go on."

"The request is always that the delivery be made as early as possible, so it is usually scheduled first--that's usually eight o'clock or shortly thereafter. Some of the places, the bakery, the flower shop, and the drug store for instance, open at seven, but do not begin delivery before eight. The lumber company is the only exception. They quit delivering at four each afternoon so they can load up the truck ready to pull out again right when they open the next day. They usually deliver to building sites, so the early hour is no problem as they just drop their loads off and leave. I believe we can cut down our observation by confining it to those hours? Maybe four or five for each site instead of twenty-four."

Sal nodded. "That should work. I'll have to take this to the chief, of course, but he says he'll give us anything we want. Look, I want this set up as soon as possible. There's no telling how soon... wait. The weekend's coming up. Has she ever struck on a week-end before?"

They looked at Masters. He checked his list. "No. Never. But this is a big weekend. The extra work assignments are out already."

"I can't believe she would strike so soon again. That would be a departure for her. That's all to the good. We can make good use of the time. It will take a while for us to set it up."

Dolores tapped and entered, holding a printout. She looked stricken. She looked from Masters to Sal and back again.

"The Labor Day is upon us and we'll already be short handed. Also," Sal continued, "she probably scouts out the scene first, don't you think?"

"Meaning we should have started yesterday."

"Yes," Sal said. "In any case, it will be good practice for us. Good job group. Let me put in a call to Chief Warmkessel."

Masters, looking at the secretary's face, went over and took the paper she was still holding out in front of her, as if contaminated.

Masters stared at the paper. He looked at Dolores. "You sure?"

Her face answered for her.

"Oh. That the computer check?" Sal approached. "Any good?"

Masters cleared his throat. The paper in his hand was shaking now. Dolores was in tears.

"All right, Sergeant. What have you got?"

He looked at her, then out the darkened window. He rose, like an old man, and went to lay the paper in front of her.

"Sorry, Loot."

There was not much on the paper. Just one name, in fact. Nevertheless, it took a moment for it to register.

The paper read:

Madeline M. Grimm

CHAPTER 20 Jamie's Mom

Little children step on your lap: tall ones step on your heart.

They stood together, staring down at the paper. The office went deadly quiet, the silence setting her apart. Sal dragged her eyes away from the ominous paper to look at Masters.

"Madd..." She shook her head slowly. "Just the one name? This can't be the whole.... That's not possible! There must be an explanation. I mean, she's the ADA assigned to the case. She has a legitimate right..." She looked at Dolores briefly, then again at Masters. "Oh no, Sergeant. We've missed something. Or misinterpreted something. Have you included all the possibilities in your searches?"

"I believe so, Lieutenant. We were pretty careful."

"Who designed the search?"

"I did," Emily Haines replied. She took the paper from Sal's hand. "No! That can't be!" She, too, seemed to have difficulty taking it in. "I must have made a mistake."

Sal grabbed at the possibility. "Do you think so? Can you review your setup?"

Masters intervened. "She set it up right. I checked the program before we ran it."

Sal looked at Dolores. Though she knew the answer, she asked it anyway. "Are you sure you ran it right? Oh, sorry

Dolores," she said to the woman now in tears. "Of course you did." She had to accept it. Dolores would have checked her results, checked and double-checked.

Sal shrank into a chair. "There has to be some explanation."

They did not answer. Her own words echoed back at her from their faces. *"If we first collect all the pertinent facts of the case, then base our conclusions on those facts, they will not mislead us and, however unpalatable, we will have our answer."* She had insisted facts would not lie, had asked for cold, hard facts. They had collected and compared cold, hard facts.

Masters regarded her steadily. "Sorry, Loot," he said again. "You okay?"

Emily Haines filed a protest for her. "Maybe she has been supplying someone with..." She watched Sal's changing expression. "I don't believe it! That beautiful woman? She has everything she could possibly want! Looks! A great job! All the money she could ever want! I don't believe..." She faltered.

Disbelief. Again Sal's words hung in the air. Criminals relied on it. Murderers counted on it.

"Explains a lot though, don't it?" Burger seemed to find it more palatable than the others. "I mean, viss her in charch at the DA's office, and bein' in on all the inwestigations and all..."

Sal could see it too. It was barely even a challenge for one who had the District Attorney in her pocket, who could manipulate the grieving Chief as effortlessly as a child.

They were all looking at her, waiting for her to say something. She rose and began to pace. "I need to think."

She shut everything else out, studying the forms, considering them separately and together.

Adamson approached. "Does she fit West's psychological paradigm at all? I mean, I suppose you know her pretty well."

"This morning I would have said so," she said faintly. But was her cousin this master of subterfuge? Was she so manipulative?

"Wait! This is not fair!" Haines turned to Sal. "Lieutenant. This is monstrous that you should be forced to carry on with the case now. We should get hold of the Chief and...."

"No." Sal faced them. "Let me think. If my cousin really is involved somehow, it is better that I should bring... handle it. Unless you think I will not be fair?"

They did not think that.

"Good. Thank you. Corporal Adamson's question is valid and should be answered. Let me..."

Almost instantly, a flood of memories inundated her. Times when a gathering of cousins had suddenly turned into something nasty, unpleasant. And, all too often, Madeline had always seemed to be at the core of it somehow.

She recalled, too, West's description of an unhealthy close relationship between parent and child, one subsequently abandoned. It had struck her at the time as being nebulously familiar. Did that fit? Her heart sank. She recalled now how the young Madeline was constantly at her father's side. More often than not, he had even gone so far as to take her along to work. But had it changed? The answer was yes. A second daughter had come along, supplanting the older Madeline in their father's eyes.

The awful thing about the memory was how the cousins had mimicked the petted and spoiled Madeline, rejoicing that she had had her come-uppance.

She became aware of the silence. They were waiting for her to say something. "God help me, but I don't think we can rule her out."

"Hang on," Masters said. "Let's look at it together. See if we can find a hole. She would have, did have as we now see, access to the drugs. We have to assume she is smart enough to know how to use them. She certainly knows when the department is busy, although we know that is not the only reason she picks the dates she does. Maybe if we knew what else governs the dates, it could help, one way or the other, don't you think?"

"Look for a connection between the dates you mean?"

"It could help. Point one way or another."

"What about all those different scenarios? Could she make them up?" Emily had moved to sit beside Sal. "Is that like her?"

"You mean the stories concocted to obtain the rentals? Oh yes. Madeline could have been an actress had her father permitted it." The very thought made her toes curl up tight and stay that way.

Her heart ached. She had to talk to Sam. She wanted to escape, to be alone somewhere where she could take it in, but she was trembling too much to trust her legs. Besides, her team was waiting.

She closed her eyes for a minute, then opened them. "I'm sorry. We have no choice but to act on it, just as we would if it were anyone else." She took a deep breath, looked each of her officers in the eye, and gave instructions.

* * * * *

Wednesday 8:30 PM. Sal's office.

Sergeant Eisenhard appeared on the heels of the departing team. He paused just inside the doorway.

"I have Mrs. Truman here, Lieutenant. Do you want to see her now? Her attorney is with her."

Sal struggled to clear her head. Had she really thought any of this important? She would just turn this case over to Eisenhard. It was, after all, his baby. She looked up at him, opened her mouth and shut it again. The look on Eisenhard's face was enough.

This case was no less urgent. Weren't many other young boys at equal risk? "Yes," she said faintly. "I'll come. Is everything set in place as I requested?"

"Yes, Lieutenant. I got the pictures and descriptions out, and the surveillance people were in place about ten minutes ago."

"Better get somebody to his office as well. Question everyone. Find out when he was seen last. Have them look for signs of his being there today--wastebaskets, appointment books, messages--you know the drill. You'll need a warrant."

"Right. I'll get right on it."

"Go ahead and lay that all on first, then bring Mrs. Truman in. I want you here when I question her. Use my phone."

While the officer arranged for the augmented instructions, Sal forced her mind to consider the boy's case. She re-read the notes the boy had left. When Eisenhard ushered in the woman and her attorney, she pushed a button under her desk. Almost inaudibly the video camera, set high into a corner of the ceiling, began its work. People charged as child molesters often brought retaliatory charges against the arresting officer. Spouses, too, were often in denial. Typically, Jamie's mother had, so far, shown no inclination to help. Could the woman herself be involved? It was not inconceivable. At the very least, she had failed to provide a safe environment for her child, a crime of the first order in Sal's eyes, and one for which there could be little defense. Was her involvement even more heinous? Or was the woman as much a victim as her son?

Sergeant Eisenhard named names, indicating chairs for the guests. Then, as instructed, took one himself between the couple and the door, affording him a clear view of all three.

Sal perched on the edge of her desk, leafing through the dead boy's file, observing the woman and her attorney under lowered eyes. Faces and voices often told more than words. Her silence seemed to irritate the attorney.

Perhaps it was the behavior of his client, Sal thought. The woman was highly agitated, her spindly frame moving jerkily in her chair, hands opening and closing the brass fastening on her handbag. The indeterminate blue eyes were clouded with apprehension and whatever barbiturate she was taking. A beige dress, stylishly soft, hung on her with an air of despondency, as if regretting the chance to be on a younger, a more joyful body.

The woman's appearance contrasted sharply with that of her attorney. His attire--a herringbone tweed jacket and cap, spoke of membership in an old, established firm.

When she finally looked up, he approached, hand outstretched, a broad smile on his face. Whatever he had expected, it was neither this crisp handshake nor the cool anger in her eyes. It put him slightly off his game. His eyes took in the office, resting for a few moments on her desk. He retrieved his hand and used it to lightly rub the burled cherry surface.

He turned to take a long look at the sergeant, paging through his pocket notebook. He considered raising an objection. Wasn't this Eisenhard's case? Why were they dragged here to the lieutenant's office? Case officers usually did their own interviewing. But after a shrewd assessment, the attorney settled back in his chair, shifted his expression to ingratiating, flashed a smile at the lieutenant, returned the queen to his hand, and led with his ace.

"Nice office!" He nodded approval, studying her face as if trying to place her. "I don't believe we've met. Name's Jason."

Sal ignored him, her attention on his client. He continued to look her over. With the ace already played to nothing but chicken feed, he was forced to play dirty. He asked, his tone thinly disguising the conviction that he already knew the answer. "How in the world have you managed to hang on to an office like this?"

Sal ignored that as well. He was neither the first, nor last, to imply she had either bought or slept her way up in rank.

He waited for the anticipated protest, ready to become charmingly apologetic. But it did not come. He rose, slid a card from an alligator skin card case, and handed it to her. Trump!

"Name's Harold Jason. With Thaxton, Stephens, Jacobs, Weinsheimer and Butz. I don't need to tell you who we are."

She took the familiar indigo blue and pewter grey card and dropped it on the desk.

"Nice desk, too, may I ask where you got it?"

"Yes," she said, eyes still on the boy's mother. It was her to whom she spoke. "I'm Lieutenant McKnight, Mrs. Truman. Thank you for coming in."

Jason put his hand on the woman's chair, thrusting himself between his client and Sal. "My client is here of her own volition, Lieutenant. For the record, she did not have to come."

Sal gave him a brief look. "Oh? And is there any reason why you would not want your client to help us get to the bottom of this? She is the boy's mother. The boy's champion. Not being a mother, you may not understand how painful it is when your child, especially your only child, dies. Surely Mrs. Truman wants to help us." She altered her tone slightly. "Unless there is some reason..."

The woman erupted tearfully. "No, of course not! But what the boy said is simply not *true*! You don't know my husband. He is the kindest, most generous man imaginable.

And he adored Jamie! Why he even adopted the boy legally so he would bear his name! Why he gave Jamie everything he wanted."

Disbelief. Child molesters relied heavily on it too. Again Sal considered turning the whole thing back to Eisenhard. As if reading her thoughts, Jason turned again toward the other man.

"I thought the good Sergeant here was in charge of the case."

Yes, Sal thought. That way it would be so much easier for you to champion the missing husband, to tap the curious bond which seemed to spring, unaided, among males of any age.

She had no problems with the bond, envied it, if anything, but it sometimes developed a glitch when it came to charges of domestic abuse, preventing charges from being brought at all, if possible. If not, minimize the crime as something, if not actually socially acceptable, at least understandable. They could even claim the boy liked it, that he had been a willing participant. She'd heard it all before.

But would Eisenhard see through this scenario? He was good, but he was also new, young, a nice person, unfamiliar with this kind of rape, as Sal wished she were also. Disbelief. It worked best on good people like Sergeant Eisenhard.

And like you, a voice said. You see it in this case because of your experience, because the boy's note had the ring of truth, and confirmed by the boy's disposal of the bed sheet. You see it here because it is not your family.

Family. Yes, that could account for the woman's refusal to accept the truth... except no. Those tears were not for her son, for his torment, for his loss. Nor were they for the missing husband. Right now the woman's tears were strictly for herself, for the fear of losing 'her man.' She had bought the dogma that a man was a requisite part of a woman's life, that any man was better than none. Had she given even a moment's thought to her son? The pitiful condition in which she had allowed herself to be presented, telegraphed Jason's 'poor little woman' hand for the defense. What else had he in mind?

If she could build a bridge between herself and the woman, perhaps Mrs. Truman could begin to accept the truth, a first step to being able to stand on her own feet.

Sal waited for the tears to stop before asking softly, "Where is your husband, Mrs. Truman?"

"I don't know," she whined. "I've said it over and over. I just don't know! I really don't! He travels a lot. I often don't know where he is."

Sal smothered her irritation. Had the woman forsaken mind, body and soul, to the whims of the man in her life?

Sal replied mildly, as though the woman had said she never put carrots in stew. "Doesn't he usually tell you where he is going?"

"Only in a general way," she wailed. "He'll say he's going to New York or Washington or whatever, but that's all."

"What do you do if you have to reach him?"

She wailed. "I *ask* him that all the time! He just says to call his secretary. I have her home telephone number in case I need it evenings or weekends. But he is usually home for weekends. He loves spending time with the boys."

On this last her voice faded to a whisper. She began again to cry.

Jason patted her arm. "Lieutenant, really, I must protest! Surely you cannot question the integrity of Mr. and Mrs. Truman. The Trumans are well known for their community work, especially Kyle. You are talking about some kind of monster. Kyle Truman is an upstanding citizen. Plainfield would benefit if we had more like him."

"If statistics are to be relied upon sir," Sal rejoined, "this community, any community, already has too many like him."

"You can't be serious! You can't believe the lad's note! He wasn't quite right, you know. Been in special classes for the last few years." Ignoring his client's ineffectual efforts to protest, he continued. "The school says he's emotionally disturbed--I don't really know the technical term for his problem, but..."

"Childhood Schizophrenia with a tendency toward paranoia, is the--" she stressed the word, "*technical* term for it, Mr...." she picked up the card, looked at it, dropped it back on her desk, "Jason. It's a term used to describe young people who have a crippling fear of their world. Jamie had, I understand, a deep fear that the world is not a safe place. He believed," she said evenly, "that the people around him were out to hurt him, that there was no one he could trust. Pretty crazy, wasn't he?"

"Oh come *on,* Lieutenant! You know how these adolescents are. There's been a flurry of these cases in the newspaper. The kid probably read about them and decided it was a good way to get some attention. Kids'll do anything to get attention."

"Yes, won't they?" Even Eisenhard knew the man had hit a nerve. Sal spoke evenly. "For the right kind of attention they will do anything: take drugs, eat too little, eat too much. Get pregnant. Steal. Lie. Even kill themselves. All for a little attention. Yes, I do know. So unreasonable of them too, don't you think?" She looked directly at the attorney for the first time. "I doubt, however, that he is sticking things up his own anus. Have you seen the ME's report?"

He stared at her.

"Do you have children, Mr. Jason?"

He took the question as an olive branch. After all, this woman was clearly off base. "No, not yet, but I..."

Sal interrupted him. "Good. Don't." She went back to eying the woman. "Perhaps we can be spared one more deaf, dumb and blind parent. What do you think, Mrs. Truman, shall we encourage Mr. Jason here to have sons?"

The woman shrank back into her chair. Again the lawyer put a restraining hand on her arm. "Let me handle her," he said under his breath.

"Yes, do." Sal leveled eyes at him. "I'm waiting."

"Lieu-*t*en-ant! Really! I must protest on behalf of my client. She has done *nothing*. You have no right to treat her as though she had."

"Oh, on that I entirely agree with you," she nodded. "She has done nothing. When Jamie tried to talk to her--she did nothing." To her own ears, her voice sounded unforgivably venomous. She fixed her eyes on the other woman. "When she saw or heard evidence of her husband's predilection for young boys, she did nothing. And now that it is too late for Jamie and we are trying to ensure he does not continue to violate the bodies and trust of other young boys, she still does nothing! Right you are, Mr. Jason. She has done, and still does nothing! Perhaps you are not aware, Mr. Jason," she said coldly, "of the countless tragedies of one kind or another that are the result of 'doing nothing?' That is especially true when you have chosen to bring a child into the world."

Jason's jaw dropped. He moved to protest, but she finally had the woman's attention.

"Saw and heard--what are you talking about? Saw and--I never saw or heard *anything*! I don't know what you are talking about."

Sal controlled her temper. "Oh? Tell me, Mrs. Truman, you are a classroom teacher?"

The woman nodded reluctantly.

"The Plainfield Police Department holds regular workshops in child abuse and neglect specifically for teachers. Have you never attended them?"

She said nothing.

"I'm sure you have. They have been required for quite a number of years now. Can you remember anything you learned there? Anything at all? I'm sure you expect your students to remember in a similar situation, don't you?"

She waited.

It was the attorney who answered. "*Really,* Lieutenant, I must protest! You cannot expect Mrs. Truman to be an expert on child abuse--always supposing this is such a case--which I don't for a minute say it is, just because she is a teacher."

"And what of you, Mr. Jason? What of the legal responsibility all professionals have to know the signs, to know that more often than not the molester is a trusted family member..."

Her voice faltered. And not only in child abuse cases, sometimes in murder too. "...Or close family friend, to recognize signs of bribery or coercion, to know the molester's high need for secrecy," she paused, forcing her mind on this case. "For instance, Mrs. Truman, tell me about these weekends your husband 'liked to spend with the boys.' How were they spent?"

"I don't know." The woman whined. "I wasn't there, was I?"

"You weren't there? Where were you?"

"Oh I don't know. Kyle wanted that time so he and Jamie could get closer.... Oh my God! This can't be happening! Not to me. We are the most popular couple at the Club and that's because of Kyle. People don't really like me, you know, they just put up..."

"Mrs. Truman, we have more than Jamie's letter. Two of Jamie's friends have described advances your husband made to them. They could be lying, of course, but I don't think so. I know them well, and I am prepared to give credence to their allegations." Oh yes, she thought, you knew *them* well. But how well did you know your own cousin?

The woman covered her face with her hands.

Sal went relentlessly on. "They blame themselves you know. Children who have been molested. That's why Jamie took this way out, why they think they can't tell anyone. They are ashamed."

"Please! I've heard enough! You're trying to make me feel guilty! Oh, God! This just can't be happening to me!"

"No one ever thinks these things can happen to them." No, not even you, she told herself. "But the point is, we must find your husband. He will be given every chance to clear himself, I promise you. The point is to find him quickly before the newspapers get hold of this--which they are certain to do."

"Oh my God, yes. The newspapers. The television. Everybody will know. Yes, yes, but what can I do?"

"You can think about where your husband might be. Has he taken any money out of the bank since you called him yesterday with the news about Jamie?"

"I don't know where he might be, and I don't know about the money."

"Do we have your permission to make inquiries at your bank?"

The woman hesitated, looking at her attorney for help.

Sal continued. "Look, Mrs. Truman. Let's try to arrange our priorities. You are in for a very difficult time in the next days and weeks. Your whole life will be different. I want you to be able to look back at this some day, knowing that, at least from this moment on, you did everything you could for Jamie. After all, he did say that your husband sexually molested him frequently, and threatened him to keep him silent. Can you imagine how frightened, how sick with pain the boy must have been to want to die rather than continue living with your husband?"

But the woman seemed unable to think of anything but the immediate problem. "He'll kill me when he finds out. He hates people to know his business."

"Yes, he has used anger to keep you from asking questions, from thinking." The way women use tears, she thought. The battle of the sexes. "Mrs. Truman, I think we have gone beyond worrying about whether your husband gets angry or not. Now you need to give the information to Sergeant Eisenhard. We can do it all with a court order, but I think you will like yourself better if you help. We will need you to speak to your bank when we get through to them."

Eisenhard took the proffered checkbook and glanced at Sal. She nodded, and he disappeared with it.

"All right now, Mrs. Truman. We'll be finished soon. If your husband wants to 'get away,' where does he go? Do you have a summer home?

"Yes, of course." Not to have at least two homes was apparently even more unthinkable than a child-molesting husband.

"There's our place in the country, of course. Kyle's parents are there now. I don't think--," she hesitated. "I don't really know if he would go there with his parents there. He's never really gotten along with them. He hates his father." She hesitated again. "I suppose it's possible he's gone..." She stopped.

"Yes?"

"Well, he talked me into buying a small place at the lake. I've only seen it once. I'm not even sure I know how to get there. Kyle said it was a man's place, reserved for Jamie and him."

"What was the occasion the one time you went there?"

"Well, I had to sign the papers. Actually, he wanted me to sign without seeing the property, but we were buying it with my money, and I insisted on seeing it. I'm not altogether a fool," she said defensively.

Fine. She could forego the innocent act to protect her money, but not her child. Sal was sick of the woman.

"Can you give us addresses for these houses?"

Again the woman gave a helpless shrug. Finally the attorney was allowed to rescue his client. "I can get them for you if my client agrees. May I use your phone?" Obviously he wasn't going to leave his client alone.

Sal went on. "Have you complied with Jamie's final wishes yet? I would like to be able to assure his friends..."

"I'm not going to give his things to those boys." It was the most energy she'd shown so far. "Mr. Jason says I don't have to. We gave him most of those things. When Kyle comes back he will tell me what to do."

"When your husband gets back he will have his hands full."

In the silence the attorney's phone conversation could be heard. "Lieutenant McKnight," he told the phone. He listened, then, "Oh, yes sir. Yes sir, I'll do that. Thank you, sir."

He hung up the phone and returned to his client's side, handing Sal her note pad with two addresses. Sal motioned to Sergeant Eisenhard, who had returned and resumed his chair in the rear.

"Anything yet?"

"No Lieutenant, but they're working on it."

She returned to her task. "Mr. Jason, I understand you advised your client that she did not have to honor the last will of her son." She withdrew the note from the boy's file. "What did you find wrong with it? It looks all right to me. Holograph. Dated. Signed." She waited. "Not witnessed, of course, but then it's not a monumental estate."

"Ah... no, Lieutenant. That is I didn't know... that is, I didn't realize... ah.... Your Uncle Reuben sends his congratulations and to tell him if he can help in any way."

"Thank you." For the first time she thought about the effect of one Thaxton female accusing another of being the first female serial killer in history. Will they be so willing to help when they find out? And how would the 'prestigious' law firm of Thaxton sons, cousins, and in-laws, be affected? What of the rest of the Thaxton aunts, uncles and cousins? Would generations of honest, capable work stand them in good stead or would the long fingers of crime entangle them too?

"In any case," Jason had decided groveling was called for, "I think I need to speak to my client." He brought out his fourteen-carat smile. "Look, Sal, maybe we can start over. I didn't realize you were going to be taking the case yourself. Have to admit you threw me a little."

She interrupted him again. Interrupting twice in less than an hour! "It's Lieutenant, Mr. Jason and I liked you better when you were more concerned with protecting your client's interests than with making peace with me."

An officer appeared at the door and spoke to Sergeant Eisenhard. He brought her a phone. "Excuse me, Lieutenant. We have Mrs. Truman's bank on the line."

"Thank you. Sergeant. Mrs. Truman? All we want to know is if your husband, or someone, withdrew a sum of money since--oh, let's say, since noon yesterday. Check all accounts--savings, money market, line of credit... everything."

The boy's mother took the phone, spoke, listened. Her thanks was the merest of sounds. She put the phone back on its cradle as carefully as if it were fine crystal. She didn't speak until she had returned to her chair. Then her voice was low. "He withdrew eight thousand dollars from our joint checking account and twenty five thousand from each of our money market accounts. He also went to the vault for the safe deposit box. They don't know what he did there."

There was silence again.

"Well it's your business. We will find him. But if it were my money, I would instruct my attorney to close all accounts immediately. And we will need a list of the contents of the safe deposit box."

Mrs. Truman began to explain. Sal shook her head. "Don't tell me. You don't know what is in the box." Was there no limit to her abdication? "Look, let us have the list of what was in it before your marriage. Is that possible?" Even she looked to the attorney for an answer.

He nodded. "Yes, of course. We will cooperate fully in any way we can. I'll get it to you within the hour."

"Thank you, counselor. Give it to Sergeant Eisenhard. Now can we return to the issue at hand? May I assume we have settled the question of the boy's will? His friends are a very loyal and close-knit group. They are to each other the family none of them has had."

That last was unfortunate. The woman hit the ceiling. "Jamie had a family! A real family! I never liked his going around with that gang. That's why I let him have a paper route. That, and Doctor Swain thought it would be good for him."

Yes, no doubt he thought the more time he spent away from his home the better. "I'm sorry to hear you object to that group. They are a nice bunch of kids. Your son couldn't have had better friends. But, getting back to the boy's last wi--"

"All right, all right. I don't care! My boy is gone! My husband is gone! What do I care what happens to a few toys?"

"Good. Thank you. That will help. Now about the other things, I understand he packed all his belongings in plastic bags.

"Yes, yes. Take them. Take them all away," she wailed. "I don't care, I tell you." She covered her face again with her hands. "I can't believe this is all happening to me."

"I think that is wise of you. I'll have an officer take care of the bags. That will be one less problem for you. We will let you know as soon as we find your husband. If you hear from him, we expect the same from you. He is now a fugitive. Charges have been filed against him on behalf of the other two boys. We will keep it as quiet as we can. Once again, thank you for coming down. And Mrs. Truman?"

The woman, leaning on her attorney, turned.

"Your son's friends will be at the service tomorrow as will others from school. Try to be gracious to them. They too, loved your son."

"Oh. Then you do believe I loved my son," she asked, faint hope rising.

"Of course. I never questioned your love for the boy."

The boy's mother stood up, looking down, found the answer in the Aubosson rug. "I guess it's what they mean when they say sometimes love is not enough. I never understood that."

And this sad woman was not alone in that. Sal thought of the countless people she'd faced just in four years in quiet, civilized Plainfield. How many men, women, even children claimed love as the motive for their acts. Love of money, position, spouse, child, even God, and the trail of destruction, of heartbreak, of death, they left behind.

"No," she agreed. "It hardly ever is."

* * * * *

She had one more thing to do for Jamie. She phoned the Victims Of Crime people to call on Mrs. Truman without delay. The woman had some tough truths to face, and she did not want another death on her hands.

DAY TWO

CHAPTER 21 Goodbye Jamie

Rain before seven, sun after eleven.

Jamie's friends had come to say goodbye. Their lowered voices, their shining faces, their hair kept rigorously in place with Shari's hair spray, helped to mitigate their idea of funerary attire.

Turt had plumbed the family's only closet to borrow the jacket of his father's blue suit. Once the rage of the fashion world, the style called 'leisure suit' had been an appellation less accurately predictive of the wearer's lifestyle, than of the clothing manufacturers. The garment recalled a golden age for men's haberdashery, a time when a single style united CEO and salesman, professor and refuse collector, in a common bond--an enviable feat. By the millions, men had been persuaded to discard single and double-breasted suits in favor of the pseudo casual look. Naturally, a few years later, a return to the traditional suit pushed the "new look" to the back of the closet--providing, as I say, a leisurely retirement for many a clothier.

As for today's version, discovered in the farthest recesses of his foster parent's closet, the young man now sported with all the hauteur of the fashion innocent, a denim blue jacket with little buckles suspended from collar and cuffs, zippers at a slant, two at the breast pockets, two at the side pockets, and a fifth at the small 'ticket' pocket. From one of these, his house key hung, causing a pleasant tinkling sound every time the boy moved--which being Turt, was almost always.

Robey sported a white jacket with vertical orange and green stripes. It very nearly fit him. He had turned up the bottom of the sleeves, securing them inside with masking tape. A straw hat, (a skimmer), would have set it off nicely. Lacking this, he wore the striped blazer over neatly pressed jeans.

His half-brother, Tommy, refusing any jacket as 'wimpy,' wore a plaid weskit made for one of his foster brothers by that young man's current girlfriend. He had dressed it up a bit with a black bow tie, pre-tied of course, boasting a handy strip of elastic to keep it firmly in place.

Lenny was so skinny that none of his dead grandfather's clothing was suitable. He settled for a button down-the-front sweater he had been given as a gift. He hated it. This would be its first and last appearance. With it he wore a wide, striped tie, secured, somewhat creatively, by his grandmother.

Only the Main Duke wore both suit coat and pants. He had purchased them at the Salvation Army store for six dollars, in preparation for his first job interview two years ago.

The girl's outfits were, in comparison, somewhat more traditional. Shari's dress, a pert pink and white number with roses across the front where the hoped for breasts would someday bloom, had been short when it was bought new for last year's Spring Concert. Shari had a solo part. She had grown four inches since then. It was touch and go as to whether she could actually sit down in it, without attracting apprehensive stares from the other mourners. In sharp contrast Kit's skirt hung halfway between knees and ankles. No sissy roses for her. The skirt, a plain bright red, was enough concession to a regrettably approaching womanhood. It was topped by her most prized possession, a grey sweatshirt bearing the legend:

Best Overall Athlete

Special Olympics

Hawk County

They all wore sneakers. Some of them did, to be sure, have other footwear, but they would, to a person, rather themselves be dead than be seen in them.

Two persons represented Jamie's school. Barry Soroka, his unfairly maligned teacher, and Colonel Pete Hammond. Ellen Treadwell, having come down with a severe cold, heroically forsook her responsibility in order to prevent the spread of germs.

But for his stepfather, Jamie's family was there in full force. Several aunts and uncles, and a handful of cousins sat in the second row, behind the boy's mother. She was protected from the curious and faintly condescending glances of the dozen or so mourners by several tranquilizers and her sister on one side, and a volunteer from Victims of Crime on the other.

Just as the minister rose to begin a pallid address--after all, he hardly knew the boy--Sal, in full uniform, entered quietly and took a seat midway between the boy's family in the first two rows, and his friends, who had been seated three-fourths back by a no nonsense looking usher.

The service was mercifully short, mercifully as the 'gang,' agog over seeing their former teacher in uniform, had, in order to get a better look at her, begun bobbing up and down in their seats, like a coffee pot beginning to perk.

As soon as the service finished, a man, identifying himself as Mrs. Truman's brother, stood up and asked that no one, except close family members, follow the group to the cemetery. This, taken as the rebuff it was, further agitated the group. A belligerent discussion of this latest blow, conducted in sibilant whispers, promptly ensued.

Sal drew the Main Duke aside, introduced him to the Juvenile officers, leaving it to them to get the gang into the promised official cars and transported to headquarters. She directed Sergeant Eisenhart to bring them to her office, after taking their statements. A few brief words with the two educators, and she was gone.

For the two Juvenile officers, the forty-five minute drive was one to remember. Excited almost beyond speech by the official mode of transport, the young people adopted a proprietary air regarding the woman now the officers' superior. They had, after all, known her first. A casual question of what the Lieutenant was like as a teacher produced an excited array of anecdotes.

They seemed pleased to report how their perennial struggle against learning anything had met its match. Pressed for specifics, they recounted some of the ways she had devised to coax, trick, bribe and cajole them to reconsider this attitude. They now seemed to find their teacher's ability to outwit them at every turn, hilarious. In later years, as the legend of Sal McKnight grew, these stories, edited once more by these second hand tellers, would become part of the heritage.

But that would happen later. Suffice to say that today, by the time the seven arrived at headquarters, the Corrigibles and the officers were on a first name basis.

* * * * *

With the Corrigibles safely in the hands of the police officers, Sal hurried to her own car with unseemly haste.

Her thoughts raced as she drove back to Plainfield and her, now nearly incomprehensible, task.

The long drive provided plenty of time to think, to review the team's findings and the steps they had taken since then. Had she done the right thing? There had been no time for sleep, and now the much needed clarity of thought eluded her.

She forced her mind back to the events of last evening, looking for something left undone. After the boy's mother had been escorted out by a somewhat chastened lawyer, Sal had sought out Chief Warmkessel.

As she began her report, the chief was something like his usual self, cheered by the progress made in so short a time. But that was short-lived. When Sal told him the name of their quarry, he had objected loudly and firmly. A Thaxton? A name associated with untouchable judges, honest attorneys? A psychotic killer? Impossible! Surely, he had insisted, Sal, the perceptive Sal, would have seen something, would have known.

But the thoroughness of the team's work was convincing. He reviewed it all himself, followed it every step of the way. In fact, it was in trying to convince him, she had succeeded in more firmly convincing herself. In the end they agreed. At the very least, they had enough to consider Madeline Grimm a suspect, and act on it.

Once persuaded, it had taken the chief but a minute to see the implications. The sudden rise in antagonism between the two departments, the spurious effort to place homicide under the DA's umbrella, the provocatory behavior towards the three earlier Officers in Charge of the case.

Sal had given short shrift to the offer to find a replacement for her. It was her family, her job, and that's all there was to it.

Citing the escalating times between murders, she had insisted they act without delay. They would have to do everything possible to prevent any further deaths. Together they had reviewed the sites chosen by the team as possible future rentals. Warmkessel had suggested one or two changes, then they went to work manning them.

After the initial shock of finding the long sought killer in their midst, a request for extra duty for one-fourth of the force seemed insignificant. With the complete PPD roster before them, they had selected forty-four men and women to begin surveillance of those twenty-two sites. The chief proved he had not lost touch with his men, giving her quick, illuminating sketches of each as they went through the roster.

They spent twenty minutes pairing them, and another twenty getting them on the phone, each taking half the names. They had to go back to the roster for replacements for the five who were beyond reach.

It was midnight by the time they finished. At the chief's insistence, they had taken the elevator to the rooftop restaurant, ordering sandwiches and coffee. For the first time in her life, Sal could not eat. Instead, she tried again to reach Sam, while Warmkessel woke a judge for permission to place a tracking device on the suspect's cars.

By 2 AM, the thirty-eight men and six women, pried by the emergency call from bedroom and bowling alley, housework and homework, restaurants and garage workshops, arrived at headquarters, dressed comfortably as instructed.

Together, they had paired the officers off, given them a limited brief, which did not include the identity of their suspect. On arriving at the assigned site, they were to monitor all entrances, the tenant parking area, and the garbage loading areas, keeping them under close surveillance. If problems arose, they were to call for instructions.

The chief stressed the importance of reporting *all* activity, but in particular, to look for a woman alone, probably carrying a case or bag of some sort. They were particularly interested in a Dutch Girl, should one put in an appearance. Finally, they were warned to report *everyone*, even if someone showed whom they knew or recognized.

If anyone of interest showed, one officer should follow, while the other remained on site, keeping an eye out for an early morning delivery.

They were to stay on their particular site until nine thirty. The chief ordered cell-phones be issued each officer. They were to call in every half hour, reaching either Warmkessel or Sal in their respective cars. Then the surveillance pairs were dispatched in order to locate and reconnoiter their assigned site, probing for any problems.

For the next few hours, Warmkessel and Sal had been kept busy, answering questions as they were called in, going to the site when requested. Sal kept one cell phone line open for her own team. To them she had assigned the job of following the suspect, leaving to them the specifics of that task.

Just before dawn, Sal went home, showered, ignoring the temptation of the wide expanse of her bed, and changed into her uniform. The new day, projected to continue hot and humid, with thunderous threats of rain, promised to be even more difficult than the one just past. Sal had some vague idea the uniform might help.

By 7 AM Masters reported the team's decisions. They, too, had paired up, Masters and Adamson, Burger with Haines, to tail the suspect around the clock. They had decided to pick her up at her home. Masters and Adamson would take the first shift. They would arrive before dawn, early enough to attach a computer chip to her car, as there was no way to conceal ground surveillance equipment. Still, the chip would do fine and she could be followed at a safe enough distance.

The teams would switch tasks. The pair not on the suspect vehicle would remain at headquarters with the monitoring equipment. A third cell phone, with a specially designated number, would ensure all were on call at a moment's notice.

The first report came in shortly after eight, just as Sal was pacing up and down in her office. Everything had gone as planned. Masters and Adamson had reported in. The suspect had driven her Mercedes to the office about eight o'clock, as expected. Nothing doing. They would be relieved by Burger and Haines at nine.

At nine-thirty, the established cut-off time, the twenty-two surveillance teams were sent home, and told to be ready to repeat until further notice.

Fifteen minutes later, Sal had corralled Sergeant Eisenhard and another officer from Juvenile and, again in separate cars, headed for the boy's funeral.

* * * * *

But whatever satisfaction derived from this review was negligible, and even that did not last. The boy's funeral had swelled the level of her own distress to intolerable proportions. The battle to mitigate those aspects of human nature which permitted today's tragedy was, she decided, a losing one. Inadequate and destructive parenting, the unwillingness of family, friends and school to believe the evidence of their eyes and ears was depressing. As was the question raised by these events.

Did the same tragic faults lie at the bottom of this young boy's death and the almost unthinkable murders conceived and committed by her own cousin?

A larger, more immediate problem assailed her. Where did her responsibility lie? Family or work?

Not for the first time, she would have to choose between loyalty and duty. Loyalty to family?

She had put off thinking about her responsibility to the family. Thaxton *freundschaft* tradition called for a gathering of resources to support, protect and defend the family member in trouble--regardless of source. Outsiders might be welcomed as a spouse or partner, but should a choice be necessary, the Thaxtons all lined up along bloodlines.

That's all very well and good, Sal thought, but we have never before produced--at least as far as she knew--a multiple murderer. True, Grandfather Stephens might have come to the attention of the police, had his father not been an ambassador and his uncle a judge. Grandfather Stephens' maiden efforts to finance his many inventions were reputed to have sailed a bit close to the wind. His subsequent success, however, had polished his reputation in family annals, and by now his methods had been mercifully forgotten. But he was an exception. The Thaxtons were, after all, Pennsylvania Dutch.

Her job as a police officer? One or two treasured friendships lay shattered because of her stubborn refusal to make the popular choice.

In the end, she knew she would have to do what was right. She just wished she were more certain she knew what that was. She had to talk to Sam.

* * * * *

In desperate need of time to herself, Sal parked her car and hurried through the busy government building to the haven of her office. That there was a chance her office *would be* a haven and not the hive it had been, lay in her instructions to the officers to take the Corrigibles to a PC Junior and feed them. She would have perhaps a half hour's respite. It was not nearly enough, but better than nothing.

The phone rang, splitting the silence. She cursed herself for forgetting to turn it off.

It was Sam. Her earlier call to him had caught him in the bosom of Chung Li's family, knee deep in the finer points of souse production. After assuring himself she was all right, he'd cut short her apologies for bothering him.

"Something's happened. You're worried about doing the right thing. So give."

She gave, sticking to the short version of the team's findings. He interrupted the allocution only once, to give quick orders to get the plane ready. When she finished, he said she was doing the only thing she could.

"You haven't told the family?"

"No. I'm just..."

"Or your kids either?"

"No. Secrecy is so important..."

"Right. Absolutely right. Leave it to me."

"Really? But won't you..."

"Never mind. I'm coming home."

So the family would be told and quickly, and Sam would do it for her. Yet, in spite of the lifting of this enormous burden, things were moving too fast. She needed time to think.

The office was dark and quiet. She poured a cup of coffee, grateful someone had made a fresh pot. Perhaps it would help her revive. She was hungry. She forced herself to sit back in her chair and breathe deeply, the residue of one of the countless diet regimens tried. It didn't help much. Normal people, she told herself, lost their appetites when tired or upset. Why couldn't she survive happily as fictional detectives appear to do without lunch, a boiled egg for breakfast, a salad for dinner. None of their sandwich halves for me, she thought grumpily. "More like a steak smothered with pork chops," she told herself with a sigh. She sat back again and tried to think.

It was useless. The conditions for thought simply were not there and if she closed her eyes another second she would fall asleep.

Plan B, she thought. Talk it over with someone she could trust. Sam, for instance. Who else? What about Pete? He was sensible, trustworthy, and no doubt he would drop everything and come if she called. And he was free now. Why not? She reached for the phone.

CHAPTER 22 Madeline

Frogs croak. Birds chirp. Storm coming.

The phone began to ring on the other end, but before it could be answered, Dolores tapped and entered, moving as close to a run as she could manage on the tips of her toes. She shut the door firmly behind her.

"I'm so sorry, Lieutenant," she whispered frantically, glancing over her shoulder. "Miss Grim is here. Sergeant Burger and Corporal Haines are with her." Surprised at the first bit of news, to Sal, the second was astonishing. "She insists on seeing you immediately!..."

There was no time to react. Madeline burst through the door and stalked into the room, the two officers following sheepishly at her heels. Sal had a sudden horrifying urge to laugh. Sam had often imitated their cousin in an effort to get his twin's attention. The expression on Madeline's face today, bore ghoulish witness to the accuracy of Sam's youthful mimicry.

She managed to keep a straight face, but during the whole interview, which followed, the impression that this was Sam remained. She had to remind herself sharply, that this was the real thing.

"Salome Jane Thaxton!" The voice was exactly the way Sam would do it: peremptory, arrogant, only this time overlaid with ungovernable fury. "Just what *are* these officers doing following me? Don't bother to deny it!"

Sal looked from the deeply flushed face of the tall, elegant woman, to the beet-red faces of her officers. Before she could open her mouth to reply, the woman rushed on.

"I'm no *fool*, you know. I'm not one of your precious students! I know a 'tail'," she raised her head on that proud neck even higher, "...to use the slang to which you are doubtlessly accustomed by now, when I see one. She looked at Sal as if the other woman was a pail of particularly unpleasant garbage. I have ordered enough of them myself!" She jabbed a slim smartly painted forefinger at Sal. "If this is your way of nosing into Warren's and my private affairs, let me take this opportunity to inform you that I do not *appreciate* it, nor will I tolerate it! I shudder to think what Warren will say when I tell him!" Her chin took a sharper tilt upward. "You have no doubt heard he is planning to announce for *governor* shortly. Everyone knows that, and I am giving him my support. And that includes my share of the Thaxton money! And *you* are *not* going to butt in and spoil it, like you always do! No indeed Salome Thaxton," she continued without pausing to breathe, looking down at Sal. "You and your *brother* have gotten away with this sort of thing all your lives, but your precious uncle can't protect you any more! I know too much about you, you can depend on that!" Here she paused to suck in a breath.

Dolores wavered halfway between the intruder and the door, her face reflecting her dilemma. Should she stay and protect Sal, or go for help? With Burger looking ready to plug her, and Haines eying the distance between them, Sal knew she had to say something. But lungs filled a-fresh, Madeline had leapt once more into the breach.

"You have never liked me," she said, now haughtily majestic, "either you or your brother. You think I don't know why you took this job, but I do. You took it just to harass me, to show me up!" She spat viciously.

"You...think...you...know...so...much!" Each word got its share of vitriol. "Who cares if you have a doctorate anyway? They don't mean anything. You can buy them anywhere. I don't suppose that's how you got *yours*, is it? No," she answered herself, "of course not! You were always such a prig! Tell me," she twisted around so her body was still facing Sal, but the audience had her face, "are you still such a tattle-tale? Oh wouldn't your *friends* like to hear how you used to run to your precious auntie with stories about me?" She turned back. "Don't think I don't know how you used to tell tales about me when I came to visit you. Let me tell you, I didn't appreciate it then and I don't appreciate it now! So," she paused for another quick breath, "either you get your men off me, or I will tell fath-- Warren. I'm sure the family would love that, wouldn't they? *Thank* you very much, *Cousin* Salome! That's all I have to say!" She turned on her heel and whirled toward the door. "And you...."She pointed a bony finger at the two stunned officers as she passed, "stay here!"

The group was stunned. They stared at Sal, open-mouthed, unable to speak. It was up to Sal to do something, but what? What to address first? The officers' failure to keep the woman under surveillance? The total misunderstanding of the officers' surveillance? Accusations of childhood treachery?

She forced herself to consider the scene as a police detective. From amid the officer's apologetic efforts to explain, and her cousin's elocution, Sal selected the most salient fact.

"She knows we were tailing her, but she has no idea we consider her a suspect! She thinks it is a personal attempt to spy on her and Warren Watland." She shook her head

Death On Delivery
A Pennsylvania Dutch Mystery

helplessly. "It's so awful I don't know whether to laugh or cry."

"My vote's fer cryin'," Burger said gloomily. "Ennyways, it don't make no neveah mind. Fact is, she' on to us."

Haines wailed. "We've failed! Our first task and we've failed miserably. What are we going to do now?"

"I don't know. How did she spot you?"

It was their turn to claim ignorance. Burger was disgusted with himself. "Ve followed procechures. First time I evah got caught." He gave his partner a look.

"Oh, I know it's my fault! I was so afraid we were going to lose her, I probably got too close. I'm so sorry, Lieutenant. I've ruined the whole thing. Now she'll be on her guard and we'll never catch her."

Sal pushed that aside briskly. "Forget it, Corporal, I had forgotten how..." She started to say paranoid, suddenly realizing how accurate the label no doubt was in this case, "... suspicious she is. And she is, after all, familiar with police procedures. I should have thought about that."

"What's going on?" Masters had appeared out of nowhere. "Those kids in the outer office are acting like all hell's broken loose. That skinny girl with the pimples grabbed me. Keeps asking if you're all right. Adamson's trying to quiet them down. Fat chance! Seems you have a real fan club out there, Sal." He tossed a grin at her. "We got something new here? Cop groupies?" For the first time he saw Burger and Haines. "Hey! What the hell are you doing here? Did you lose her? Damn, I'd better..."

Succinctly, Sal related the scene with their suspect. When she finished, he looked at their faces: Burger's clouded with shame and disgust, Emily's pinkly embarrassed. He spoke laconically, "Gosh, I miss all the fun! If I'd known we were trying out for Jerry Springer..." He left it hang. He strode to his favorite chair, sat back and crossed his legs. "Let's see now. You got one commotion in here, and another one imminent in the outer office. What else did I miss?"

As if in answer, Sal's phone rang loudly. Dolores' voice came. It's "District Attorney Watland, Lieutenant. And Sergeant Eisenhard wants to see you. I think they've found Mr. Truman!"

* * * * *

A commotion ensued just on the other side of the outer door.

"Who do you..." That was as far as she got. The rest was smothered in a jumble of youthful voices and limbs. She nodded to Masters to herd the noisy group back to the outer office. To the phone she said, "Mr. Watland?" She aimed for normalcy. "How are you?"

He wasn't buying it. "What in the hell is going on over there?"

"I'm afraid we have a situation developing here. We had better..."

"Listen McKnight! Can the baloney! What are you trying to do? Ruin me?"

"Ruin...? Certainly not! Don't be ridiculous!" For the third time in as many minutes, she realized she had said the wrong thing. Nothing so riles the ridiculous as being so accused. "Look Mr. Watland. This is not the best way to discuss this matter. Could we meet for a few minutes? I could come there, or perhaps you would prefer to come here?" She checked her watch, "say after lunch?"

Strike two! This was not protocol. The District Attorney did not call on a Police Lieutenant. Nevertheless, to her surprise, instead of exploding again, he appeared to be considering it--perhaps, she thought, from the standpoint of a future statesman.

He mumbled something about a lunch, adding something to the effect it was probably better to have this out away from his staff. "As long as," he finished, managing to make this clear without actually saying so, such was his discursive talent, "it won't become a habit." He agreed to drop by her office at half past one.

Sergeant Eisenhard entered. Mr. Truman had, indeed, been picked up and was being held for questioning on the basis of the stepson's note. Eisenhard was worried by the accused man's outrage. He was, after all, important. His boss, the head of Plainfield Steel, was on the phone, threatening to sue. Would the boys stick to their stories? What about the foster parents? Would they support the kids?

At least something was going as expected! The news provided a welcome diversion, however temporary. She grasped at the chance to deal with a world more normal-- normal for her, anyway. Yes, she assured Eisenhard, the two boys would stick to their stories. As for the parents, they had an extra edge there, as both boys were wards of the state.

"What about the rest of them? They're more than Dolores can handle."

"I'll have a word with them."

She paused on the way to speak to her team. "While I talk to my young friends out there, will you set your heads around what we are going to do about our suspect? She is alert now, even if for the wrong reason, and she is very, very sharp. It won't be easy to fool her. If we are right, and I am increasingly certain we are, I don't think we can wait. All right, Sergeant Eisenhard. Let's talk to your guests."

CHAPTER 23 To the Rescue

Goot children bring goot luck.

The Corrigibles were being themselves. Robey and Kit were at the computer, he watching wide-eyed as one after another printed page was scanned into the main frame, without any visible assistance. She, crunched down on thin haunches, traced with her eyes and one tentative forefinger, the mechanical operation. Turt stared at the large electronic county map with the many colored lights depicting the location of streets, bridges, traffic signals and underground service lines.

Adamson was being buttonholed on one side by Tommy arguing the superiority of Chevys over Fords, while Shari gazed at him adoringly as she fingered his lapel. Lenny was, where else, at the snack machine, whether buying or figuring how to get at the coin box, was not clear.

Main Duke, very much at home sitting on the edge of the secretary's desk, seemed to be telling Dolores how to "get around the Loot." When said Loot appeared, he slid upright and gave a sharp whistle.

Dolores and Adamson heaved a sigh of relief to see how quickly they all stopped whatever they were doing and gathered around Sal.

The young people took the news of their friend's father's incarceration coolly, nodding with satisfaction. Turt and Tommy were taken to separate rooms where a court stenographer took statements.

Sal addressed the others. "The officers who drove you down will take you back when the boys are finished. In about an hour I should think. You can wait here unless you have something else to do?"

Apparently they hadn't.

"I will need Corporal Adamson," thus reprieving him, "and Mrs. Columbo has quite a lot to do, so I'm afraid you need to sit quietly here in the outer office for a bit. Can you manage that?" She looked at Main Duke.

"'Course. Piece a cake. We know how to behave. You learned us, remember?"

"Yes. *I* remember. I wasn't sure that you had." She glanced at his perch on the secretary's desk.

Only minimally abashed, he said trucently, "Oh yeah. Yeah, I guess we wuz a little out of hand there for a bit, but we wuz perty excited, I guess. We'll settle down now, like we wuz in church. Don't worry, Loot."

* * * * *

"Will they stay there," Adamson kept his voice low as they left the outer office.

"I think so. A few years ago I would have been more certain, but now? They're pretty upset over Jamie." She sighed. "I need time to think. I've never before been at a loss regarding what to do with them. I can't decide if I'm overwhelmed or merely out of practice. They need time to get used to their loss. With the three day Labor Day weekend upon us, they will be at loose ends, any kind of school activity is out. Is there something they can get involved in for a few days, something they could tell their friends about? Can you think of some group that needs a few willing hands?"

He shook his head. "Most of those organizations will be pretty much closed for the holiday weekend. Maybe the others can come up with something."

But the rest of the team, grouped disconsolately around her desk, showed no sign of inspiration.

"You going to bind and gag those kids to keep them out of trouble," Masters asked sourly.

"No," she said casually. "No. I thought you could teach them about police work. Perhaps," she added with an attempt at humor, "you could teach *them* how to tail our suspect."

From the cracked door, several of the Corrigibles heard that. Lenny leapt and rushed into Sal's office. "Hey! Now yer talkin'! Yeah! We could do that!"

"You mean tail that lady that just come screaming out of here?" Main Duke sounded derisive. "We couldn't help hearing that lady, could we now? They probably heard her in Timbuktu." Main Duke pulled a chair up to Sal's desk, bending over her earnestly. "Listen, we could tail her, no sweat." They rushed to surround her, just as they had in the past. "That," their leader went on, "would give us something to do. I bin tryin' to think a somethin' that'd keep these guys busy anyway, and this'd be perfick! You know how we are! You know us a long time, ya know." He hitched himself closer. "Look. We seen all these 'tective movies. We seen how it's done. But," he said, knowing a thing or two about making concessions, "these here officers could go along and stay back some place where they can't be seen. In case," he said sagely, "you wuz worried."

"An' we could report to them every fifteen minutes. I got a watch, and so does Shari." Robey spoke with the serene confidence of one who has not encountered much he couldn't handle.

The gang was exultant. Their leader had A PLAN. Just like Hannibal Smith. "And you're always telling us how smart we are," Shari added.

Main Duke rushed on. "Look! You guys have walkie-talkies don't you? We got a car, a motorcycle and a bike. We can follow her no matter where she goes. What's she done? Nicked the family silver? Well, never mind. It don't matter what she done. All we need to do is follow her, right? Come on, Loot! Look, you know us real good, right? You know how smart we are--you told us that lots of times. And, heck, I'm old enough to go in the service, but I got all these people to take care of so I don't. And following a lady ain't no harder than being a soldier, is it?"

"And you always said we should think about someday doing something for someone else because we all got so much help from welfare and that stuff, and now here's our chance." Shari's contribution contained more than a trace of unction.

"Stop! Stop! You're turning all my words back on me!" She smiled in spite of herself.

Main Duke turned to his loyal followers with a nod which said, "I guess that's how to do it."

Sal looked at her team for support in refuting this preposterous suggestion, but they were all more or less grinning.

"Personally," Adamson said, "I think it's a great idea."

"Yes. It just might be." Masters considered it. "I do, too. As the young lady, Kit is it? said, we can be there, but out of the suspect's sight."

"Matter of fact, it sounds ideal to me. They wouldn't really have to stay concealed, just take turns hanging around like kids do," Haines interjected.

"Yeah! Yeah! If we had, say three groups of us, always with one set of wheels..." Shari started.

"We could keep her in sight, no matter where she goes," Kit finished.

"And we can mix up our groups every once in a while," the suggestion from Robey was made more to the other Corrigibles than to her.

"So we'd never really look the same." The discussion was among them, something about it as valid as any business meeting.

"Sure! Nobody ever pays attention to kids anyway," Shari said with sad certainty.

"I think she has a point there. I doubt if our suspect would see *them* if they were right under her feet!" Emily Haines, still burning from being made to look a fool, said hotly. "*She'd* pay them no more attention than she would a stray dog."

"And you *did* say we'd need an innovative solution, and if this isn't innovative enough..." Adamson was beginning to enjoy himself.

"And we can wire them, so they are always in touch with us. That way we'd be doubly sure not to lose the suspect. And the kids, excuse me, the Corrigibles, won't be in danger," suggested Haines.

"And we can follow along in our own private cars. That way we could take over if something breaks," Masters added.

"And I think you'll agree it *is* urgent!" Haines again.

They stopped then, exchanging pleased glances before settling on Sal.

Sal sought for words. The Corrigibles engaged in official police work? Impossible! The whole lot of them had lost their minds. Hadn't they?

"Look, Lieutenant," Masters said, "I know this sounds like a rather bizarre idea. Maybe it's even illegal, for all I know. But you were picked to run this show because you come up unusual solutions, not so? And you decided on us for the same reason. Is the idea of letting the kids help any

Death On Delivery
A Pennsylvania Dutch Mystery

more strange than the four of us? Suppose we all just take a minute and think about it. For instance, is it illegal?"

"I... I don't..."

"I think the main thing is, if they" he nodded to the young people, "will stick to the plan, and not get out of hand. You know them. What do you think?"

"No," she said hesitantly. "They wouldn't get out of hand. It's just..."

"Honest to God, then. I say try it anyway. We can always back off."

They were all silent again. Even the gang demonstrated their occasional good sense by remaining quiet.

"What about the rest of you. Sergeant Burger? Tell them why it won't work."

"I think it's the dumbest damfool idea I evah hurt of," he said with disgust. "It's so damn stupid it might just vork! I'm tellin' ya! Ve didn't do *nothing* wrong tailin' her this mornin'. She must be some kind of a witch to have spotted us! Besides, I agree with Haines here. That there lady wouldn't give these kids a first glance, much less a second. I say try it."

Sal was struck by their arguments. If the two groups were willing to work closely together, as seemed obvious, it could do for tonight, giving her time to come up with something else. And, it would be a perfect way for the gang to work off their animus over their friend's death.

Albeit reluctantly, she agreed, making it clear the arrangement was temporary, and would be abandoned the first time any one didn't follow the plan.

Sal's watch spoke. In half an hour District Attorney Watland would be here. There was no time to waste.

After a brief conference, it was decided Sergeant Burger would show them the necessary techniques of surveillance. Adamson would teach them how to operate the walkie-talkies, a newer and more sophisticated version of their own.

Corporal Haines would go to the electronics lab and get the required 'bugs,' leaving Masters to map out and supervise the overall plan.

Masters nodded. "If everybody's clear on what their role is, let's get on with it!"

The agenda settled, Main Duke faced his followers. "Okay now. Listen up! It's about this here lady." He pushed his thumb over his shoulder in Sal's general direction. "We gotta stop calling her 'Teech.'"

Sal was completely taken aback. The effort to teach them the advantages of addressing adults properly, had met with only marginal success. Their habit of addressing her as 'Teech' first, before quickly changing to her name, she had always felt was a game they played. In so doing they could have their cake and eat it too.

Main Duke's pronouncement pleased her enormously. And why not? The spontaneous application of acquired knowledge is any educator's dream. They were actually going to begin to call her by name! Maybe they had learned more than she thought.

She reminded Masters to make sure the gang's legal, physical and moral rights were protected. "Several of them are not eighteen. They will need special consideration." They agreed to reassemble in her office at three o'clock.

She decided to grab a quick lunch. Her thoughts already centered on the meeting with Watland, she gathered pad and pen, hoping to make a few quick notes while she ate.

As she closed the door, the voices of the expanded team, chatting excitedly away, followed her encouragingly. Then Main Duke's voice above the rest.

"Go get 'em, Loot!"

CHAPTER 24 The District Attorney

Closed eyes hide the truth.

Pacing up and down in the broad space behind his desk, Commissioner Frey was telling her, for the third time in as many minutes, she had better be damn sure she was right. Sal, outwardly composed, sat on the other side of the desk, Chief Warmkessel, reassuring as a St. Bernard, in the chair next to her.

Arms flailing, the commissioner's rumble increased as he paced. He turned away from his lesser beings and began to address the floor. He knew what the trouble was. It was all his own fault. He had pushed too hard for action. He had been too optimistic in promising the press results. Worst of all, he had agreed to let a woman head up the team that was supposed to save them. Now she comes up with this crazy accusation. My God! She might as well accuse the Governor, the President for Pete's sake. Had his mind been working, he might have, given certain recent holders of those offices, thought of examples more apt.

Even his dependable chief of police was letting him down, coming to him with this flight of fancy. The commissioner faced his old friend, and erupted.

"Damn it Tom Warmkessel! How can you go along with this? It's criminal! This is nothing more than a personal problem between these two gals. Warren says Miss Grimm warned him when Sal was appointed there'd be trouble. She didn't want to criticize your lieutenant here, after all, they *are,* cousins, a fact which seems to escape your lieutenant, but she told Warren it has been going on for years. And now that Maddie is an ADA, well, it is easy enough to see why they don't get along. But to go this far! You know Maddie Grimm as well as I do. It's utterly inconceivable! Why that woman has been doing everything she could to assist these investigations from the get-go. She is brilliant. One of the best on our staff. Why she virtually runs the department when Warren is away! You must be wrong. Why I knew her grandfather, for God's sake! She's had a rough enough time since her father died. Have you ever looked at her workload? Her string of convictions?" He slowed down as speech failed him, came back to his desk and sank into his chair. From there he stared at them before continuing.

"Look, I know you know your jobs--but what you've told me so far is all circumstantial. Hypothetical. It could never hold up in court, assuming we would ever agree to take it that far. Even if it weren't her, Warren wouldn't take it to trial, not with this little to go on, no DA would."

"We agree. Nor would we ask him to with what we have." The chief's voice was calm, reasonable. "As you say, this woman is a very smart cookie. She knows what it takes to make a case. It is because of that we need, actually Lieutenant McKnight needs, to put some questions to Warren. If he were willing to talk to us, we could save a lot of trouble." Every ounce of the big man projected earnestness.

"Where is Mr. Watland?" Sal asked, not pushing. "We had a meeting fixed for two o'clock but he never came. Am I to take it that it's off?"

"Look! He called me, and I sent for Tom here. Told him I'd handle it. With his wedding just a couple of days away, he's got his hands full. So do I for that matter. I should be up at the lake! I've got a wagon load of company up there for the holiday weekend." He looked at them again, not liking what he saw. With a savage thrust, he threw his pen at his desk. "Oh hell. Might as well get it over with. But I want the meet right here. All of us."

He rolled his chair to his desk and reached for the phone. "This whole thing could blow up in our faces," he moaned between gritted teeth, "if you're wrong. It could mean all our careers!" He frowned at them from across the desk. When his glare did not appear to move them, his own eyes dropped and he went grimly on. "But I guess I don't have a whole lot of choice, do I?"

No, Sal thought. Even when rules were applied differently to society's favored, there were limits.

Frey pushed the button on his phone. "Lainie. Get Warren for me, will you? Tell him it's urgent." Waiting, he said, "Look, we gotta keep this questioning as casual as possible, and if, as I suspect, you're wrong, you'll just have to eat it. Find some way to make it up to him."

His phone buzzed. "Warren!" He spoke with false bon hommie. "Glad we caught you. Is it possible for you to drop into my office for a few minutes? It's important. Yeah, I know. Yes, we'll be there. Wife wouldn't miss it. She serves on the VOC board with Louisa's mother. Yes. She's here now. The chief too. I've talked to them both, and I think you'd better... When can you make it? Right away would be fine. See ya in a bit."

He dropped the phone in its cradle. "The fat's in the fire now." He roared for Lainie.

Lainie appeared at the door. "You rang sir?" She asked, mildly mocking.

"Coffee. Get some coffee, will you?"

Observing his mood, she omitted the salaam with which she might have greeted such imperial orders. It was not beyond her to ignore his demanding requests completely, but never when he had company, his public image as important to her as to him.

In less than a minute she returned with a tray. She asked primly, "Anything else sir?"

"No. No, that'll be it. Sorry about yelling like that." He threw her a quick entreaty.

He motioned them to help themselves. Sal didn't really want coffee, but took some anyway, thinking this small social gesture would help to tone things down. For a few minutes they sat and sipped, absorbed in their own thoughts until Lainie tapped and announced, "Mr. Watland, sir."

It had been some time since Sal had seen District Attorney Watland. She had forgotten how handsome he was. Blue eyes, blonde hair brushed straight back set off by a suit of charcoal grey wool and a spanking white shirt. He was not as tall as either Frey or Warmkessel, but neatly proportioned with broad shoulders and a trim waist.

His eyes swept the room with one quick, assessing glance. "Hi Earl! Tom!" He granted each a two handed handshake. "Got your invitations I hope? Will I see you Sunday?" Without waiting for an answer, he moved on quickly and took Sal's hand in both of his. "Sal! Sorry I missed you earlier today, but I'm sure "Mad" took good care of you. Expect we'll be seeing the Thaxton twins at the wedding Sunday." Still smiling, he pushed aside the coffee tray, and after checking to see that it was clean, sat on the corner of the desk. "Okey-dokey. What's up? Getting anywhere with this case?"

Mention of his imminent wedding served only to add to the discomfort of the two men, but Sal was thrown completely. Wedding? What wedding? True the commissioner had mentioned the wedding as the reason for his intercession on Watland's behalf, but she had just assumed it was some sort of family thing.

Sal was not the only one jarred by the man's flippant manner. Frey, too, seemed at a loss for words, replying uncertainly. "Uh... well... yes, at least we think so. But... uh... we need your help. Got a few questions we need to ask. I'll let the chief explain. It's his baby. Chief?" Exercising the universal prerogative to leave the dirty work to the help, he nodded at Warmkessel.

"Okay. Okay. And I just want to start by saying thanks" he faced the district attorney, "for coming at the last minute like this." He hesitated, looked at Sal's steady gaze, and dove ahead. "Look, sir. We think we've got a line on the serial killer--but," he hastened ahead as he saw Warren's expression brighten, "you're not gonna like this, sir."

Warren laughed. "What's not to like? Get enough on her to make a strong case and I can get it on the docket before the primaries. And what is this 'sir' business, Tommy?" The chief twisted in his seat uncomfortably. "Come on, old buddy. What is it? You got a poor case? Who is it anyway?"

Warmkessel, too, reached for senior officer privilege. "I think it would be better if Lieutenant McKnight explained. Sal?"

"Yes sir. Well sir..." A crisp tone hid her nervousness. How much should she tell him? But she knew that if she expected him to believe her, after all, preposterous assertions, he would need all of it. Even then... "Well sir..."

To say it had not gone well was to put it mildly. Already assuaged by her own guilt and pain, her explanation of how and why they had come to this pass seemed woefully inadequate, even to her. A thought plagued her. Were they wrong? Had they jumped to conclusions? Had she wanted to believe her cousin a madwoman? At any rate, her exposition produced no more than a tolerant half-attention from the district attorney. Until...

"What? An inside job?" Watland nodded. "Hmmm. That's hard to believe but it would explain why we haven't gotten.... Good thinking, Sal! Makes good sense. I just don't know why Maddie didn't.... Who did you say was on your team?"

Sal forbore to say she hadn't said. Up to now he hadn't asked. "Sergeants Masters and Burger and Corporals Adamson and Haines."

"Really? I always thought that Adamson was a bit of a flake. And Burger? You mean Fourth-of-July Burger? That old Pennsylvania Dutchman?"

Sal nodded. "The very one. He's been enormously helpful."

"And Haines? Who's she?"

"Emily Haines. Bright young woman. In her third year."

"Oh yes. Redhead. A real beauty. I told Vice to use her. A real femme fatale that one."

"Also an intelligent, dedicated, hard working detective," Sal said.

"Well! Well! All circumstantial of course, but if you can tie it all together.... What can you give me in terms of motive? In a case like this where the 'perp' is clearly a nut case, you'll need to connect it all up. I take it you've pretty much narrowed it down, is that it? That why you need me? Who is it?"

A look at Sal's face and Warmkessel took it up. "Well sir, we have good reasons to believe," the chief's eyes flicked from Sal's face to Warren's and stuck, "that it is someone in your department."

"*MY* department?" He shook his head. "Impossible! Maddie would have spotted her. Who could it be? One of the secretarial pool?" The faces around him said no. "One of my investigators? Who? No, it just can't be! No one could get by Madeline Grimm. Why she's been on the case from the beginning. Worked her butt off on it, too. Nobody could get by her!" Watland looked from the chief to Sal. Whatever he saw on Sal's face pulled him up short.

"Wait...a... minute," he said, pulling himself upright. "*Maddie!* You're serious! You think its *Maddie?*" He snorted disbelief, looking from one to the other waiting for a denial. "Madeline Grimm! Christ! That's almost funny! You must be crazy! Maddie and I have been the best of friends for years. Hell! We started in the department at the same time. I'm the one got her to go to law school, for God's sake! Damn it! I damn near married her! What in the hell are you talking about?" The fair face suddenly flushed dark red. He whirled, took one long step to stand over Sal and glower. "I suppose this is your doing?"

The commissioner interceded. "Now calm down Warren. Lieutenant McKnight very properly brought her findings to Chief Warmkessel and then to me. We've seen the work her team has done, and we believe it's... at least possible. We have all agreed that you could help clear it up immeasurably if you would answer a few questions."

"Help! Help what? Make a person I care about take the rap so you can garner a lot of press?" Watland was shouting now. "God! I can't believe this is happening. I thought you were my friends!" He glared at the two men.

Frey spoke quietly. "We *are* your friends. You know that. And nobody feels worse about this than I do. I only want what's best for all of us. I think you know that too." He tried to put his arm around Warren's shoulder. Warren shook it away.

Warmkessel started to speak, but the commissioner got there first. "Look Warren. You know how this stands. Eleven men dead and, according to the shrink who worked with the team, the," he, too, paused to choose the right word, "deaths seem to be escalating. They think that may be because she is getting away scot-free. Now maybe we are crazy, I'm inclined to think so myself, but Lieutenant McKnight and her team have done a lot of work on this in a very short time. But it *is* credible, and we can't ignore it. We can't stick at helping them if we can do so by answering a few questions. We just can't afford to leave any stone unturned."

"You expect me to stand by quietly while you railroad Maddie? Is that the kind of respect a public official can expect around here?"

Warmkessel hurried to assure him. "Nobody's going to railroad anybody. We don't work like that here as you well know."

This time the commissioner's hand remained on Watland's shoulder. "Look," he drew the word out, "if we are wrong, we will be overjoyed to admit it. But only you can help get at the truth. It is no more than we ask of any member of the public we are, after all, all sworn to serve. If you will just answer a few questions for us, we can put paid to it."

The mention of public office seemed to grab Watland's attention at last. He stalked to the window, turning his back to them. "All right," he said in a low voice. "I'll answer your damned questions, but, take it from me, you are dead wrong. Maddie is a little strange at times, it's true, but who wouldn't be after the life she's led. But she is certainly *not* a multiple killer! I know her better than anybody. She couldn't kill anyone!" His face flushed. He seemed to think the second statement a natural consequence of the first. He threw himself into the commissioner's chair, swaying back and forth. "Go ahead with your questions. I may or may not answer them." He threw her a black look from lowered eyes and spat. "Traitor!"

The single word struck her like a blow. It was no more than she had already told herself, told Sam. Her brother had scoffed. "You know better. If she's in it, it's because she put herself in it. She could have no fairer person than you to look into this. You would do the same if it was your own child."

He was right, of course, but that certainty brought little comfort. The problem of how to begin remained.

* * * * *

"Thank you." Frey nodded to Warmkessel who looked at Sal.

Sal felt far from ready. This was nothing like the meeting she had hoped for. She would have preferred to go slowly, asking general questions about their office routine. Now not only was he on guard, but his dander was up. It would be like pulling teeth to learn anything useful. She tried to produce a reason to turn the interview back to Frey or Warmkessel, but could think of none. The task was hers. She wished she felt up to it.

She began with a crispness she did not feel, thanking him again. "I wish there was another way to do this, sir."

The interview went from bad to worse.

"Think back to the beginning of the week. "Were you especially busy? Especially un-busy?"

"As a matter of fact, the entire past week was pretty wild, what with my wedding and this... this... thing," he delicately referred to the last murder. "The place was a madhouse." He confessed he'd been staying out as much as possible. He and Louisa had been shopping for the house.

Sal had tried to sound sympathetic over these domestic challenges.

Watland insisted they could always find him if needed. Yes, of course, Maddie ran things, knowing the procedures better than anybody.

She asked, "What about this past Tuesday? Anything special about it? Can you recall that day?"

"Not that I remember." But he hesitated over that.

"Could you check your calendar?"

He was irritated again. "My secretary knows who I want to see and who I don't. If she's not sure, she asks Maddie. We have to keep it pretty accurate. I'm on all kinds of boards, and now as chair..." He pulled a cell phone from his pocket and consulted it. "Oh yes. That's right. I had the Charity Tea that day." He flushed a bit at the memory, "Anyway, there's proof it *can't* be Madeline! That was the day of the last murder, wasn't it? Well, as it happens, I had lunch with her that day." A tiny frown came and went.

Lunch with Madeline? Sal felt a stab of relief. Could that mean they were wrong? Could she have calmly gone from murder to lunch?

He had been checking his calendar. "Actually," he said, volunteering something for the first time, "I had a lunch meeting scheduled with some of the staff, but it was canceled."

"Canceled?"

"Yes. I believe Maddie said several of the staff couldn't make it."

A coincidence? She asked if that happened frequently. "I mean, I imagine scheduling those meetings must be difficult. I suppose something often comes up at the last minute?"

"Of course not! For one thing, I seldom call meetings and when I do, they are announced pretty well ahead of time. You know how it is to get a bunch of ADA's together. That's why we meet over the lunch hour."

"So, what did you do?"

"Actually, I was pretty pissed," he said, grimacing as if tasting something bad. "I remember now. I had wanted to get them all together to straighten out a few problems we've been having before I went off on my honeymoon. I shot off a pretty harsh memo to them." He nodded approval at himself.

"So, you and Miss Grimm had lunch together?"

"Well, yes." He shifted uncomfortably in his chair.

"But there's nothing really unusual about that, though, is there?"

Death On Delivery
A Pennsylvania Dutch Mystery

"Lunch with Maddie? Well, not so much lately. With the meeting canceled like that, we were both free, so naturally..." He frowned again.

It had not sounded natural. Something was worrying him about that lunch, but what?

"Where did you go?"

"I don't know. Tony's I think. You can check my charge card."

"Tony's? Over on West Madison? Isn't that a bit far to go for lunch?" Expensive, too. Not really approved for reimbursement, Sal thought.

"Yeah, I guess so, but it is a favorite of Maddie's. We used to go there a lot."

Sal had fished about for a way to ask him how Maddie was taking his wedding. "I imagine you had a lot to talk over if Maddie's going to be running the office while you're on your honeymoon. Perhaps Maddie thought you needed to talk over things that might come up while you were away. Do you think that's what she wanted?" His frown deepened. "Or perhaps Louisa joined you?"

"No-o-o. Actually Lou and Maddie really don't seem to care for each other much."

"Oh. They've met then?"

"Once. I brought Louisa in to the office a while back. Maddie said later she thought it was not good for staff morale, so I didn't do it again."

Sal was tired of hinting around. She'd just have to ask. "Maddie taking your impending marriage all right?"

"Yes." He scowled though. "It's a little surprising actually. I had really expected to have some trouble with her. I never really proposed, but I know she expected that we would marry some day. We'd even begun to look at houses. But she never said a word to me. Went on, almost as if nothing was changed." He was thinking about it now, apparently for the first time. "In some ways it's a bit embarrassing. For one thing, she still calls me 'Darling' when we're alone, but that's just habit I guess. She's sort of well, proper in an old-fashioned way, and Plainfield is not the kind of place where everybody calls everybody 'Darling.' I guess it's just habit, but I must remember to talk to her about that."

Chances were, Sal thought, there would be a lot more important things to talk to her about. She continued. "You have a nice lunch?"

"Oh yes. Although Maddie did seem a little wired. I thought she might have something special she wanted to tell me--that's why I thought she wanted to go to Tony's. It was always our, sort of special occasion place."

"But she didn't?" Why his frowning discomfort when he talked about that lunch? If Madeline was the one they were looking for, she would have committed murder just hours before that lunch. Again she searched for the right question. "Anything unusual happen at lunch? Out of the way?"

"Oh no. She was her usual bubbly, affectionate self. Called me 'Darling' a lot as I said, held on to my arm--that kind of thing. I believe she's planning to move."

"Move? From Elk Run Close?" Not likely, Sal thought. Not from Thaxton Square. Not from one of the four huge family-owned Colonials which faced each other majestically across a wide expanse of garden.

"What made you think so?"

"I don't know. All through lunch she kept asking me about what I thought of living in different places. I wanted to tell her about the house Lou and I bought, but it didn't seem to be the right time for some reason. She just chattered on." His eyes widened a bit.

"Remembered something else?"

"No. Not really."

But he *had* noticed, remembered something else. He was cooperating, but his heart wasn't in it. She searched for another string. "How did she look?"

Bingo!

"Well, I admit that's the thing that struck me as odd. But it's nothing, really." She waited. He looked at her, then responded peevishly. "It's nothing. Just that she was wearing a blue cocktail dress I bought her years ago. She looked great in it--I complimented her on it, though frankly it seemed a little loose. The only thing is, it was not a dress to wear to the office. Or even to Tony's for lunch. Anywhere for lunch for that matter. That's what I thought was a little strange. Maddie has great taste. A lot different than when I first met her, of course. She used to dress like a rag-a-muffin," he smiled at the memory.

"Can we go back to your conversation? You said something about houses?"

"Yes. She wanted to know what I thought about different houses--well I guess apartments, really. She was saying she thought that it would be wiser to live in an apartment at first. She wanted to know what I thought about that."

"And you answered?"

"I said I thought it was fine if she was looking for an investment. She said yes, she thought that would be the best thing all around. She's got enough money to do whatever she likes."

Something he said a minute ago was significant, but she couldn't place it. She asked instead if she had asked about any place specifically by name?

She held her breath. Was it possible she had asked about one of the places they had identified as a possible future murder site?

"Ye--es. She did name a couple." To Sal's inquiring look he said defensively, "Look, my mind was on other things.

Lou's family has invited five hundred people to this thing, including people from all over the world, and she wants me in on every little detail. She's a helpless little thing, you know. Nothing like Maddie."

No, Sal thought, nothing like Maddie. Nobody had taught Maddie that men like Warren might prefer women bright and efficient, might want them as lover, friend, companion or partner, but they still married the other kind. Helpless women, whether feigned or genuine, made a man feel strong. If the helplessness was genuine, the man soon tired of it--helplessness can be so exhausting. If it wasn't genuine, once the knot was tied, the poor guy would find himself pretty much led around by the nose. Either way, it wouldn't be too long before the competent secretary began to regain her appeal.

Most men, that is, Sal thought. A face popped unbidden to mind and was thrust back again. Sal knew Louisa Chalmers from school. She would be helpless only as long as it took to get the paper signed.

He went on. "I had a hard time paying attention to her that day." He stopped and looked at them quizzically, some of his bristle returning. He had remembered something again.

She fished around for a way to pull it out. Perhaps a change of focus would let it float back. "Where did you meet Miss Chalmers?"

"Well, let's see. We were introduced at the Club's Christmas Party. I saw her just casually a couple of times. Then I took her to the Spring Fling--two years ago that would be..."

"They are held in March, aren't they?"

"Yes. The last Saturday in the month, I believe."

Two weeks before the first death, Sal calculated.

"Was this the first time you had attended the Fling?"

"Oh, no. I've gone every year since I came on staff ten years ago. Old Mayor Butz expected it of us then, just as I do now. Makes for good relations with the community."

Yes, Sal thought. Especially if one has dreams of glory. "What about other years. Did you go alone before you met Miss Chalmers?"

"No. I don't remember who I took that first year, but Maddie and I went together for a number of years. She knows everybody--or her family does."

"With whom did Miss Grimm go when you took Miss Chalmers?"

"I don't know. I think she was sick or something that year. Maybe she was there. I just don't know," he said, impatient again.

"I'm sorry sir, I'm almost done. Just one or two more questions." He stared coldly at her without speaking. Excusing herself, she went to the outer office, returning almost immediately flipping through a telephone directory. She placed the open book before him.

"Sir, could you look over those pages and tell me if you recognize any of these apartment names as one Madeline mentioned?"

He gave her a look of utter disgust, pulling the book closer. The yellow pages were treated to the briefest of glances before being pushed away.

"This is just plain stupid," he said hotly. "It's a damn good thing you are not on *my* staff." He looked directly at her for the first time. "I don't know what the hell you're trying to pin on Maddie, but I'll fight you every foot of the way." He stopped suddenly, a thought striking him. He turned and stared at her again. "And Maddie's cousin, too! I guess it's true what they say. With a friend like you, who needs enemies?" He looked, first at the commissioner then at Chief Warmkessel. "Do you really mean to tell me you two are going along with this crap?"

Warmkessel said quickly, "It's not a question of 'going along' with anything. There's nothing to go along with at this point. It's only that Miss Grim does appear to have had the opport..."

"Opportunity! Jee-suz! What the hell is going on around here? God. I must be having a goddam nightmare!"

Warmkessel's deep voice rumbled soothingly. "Now listen Warren. You've known me a long time. Have I ever done anything to hurt you?" Watland slumped down in the chair and stared morosely at Warmkessel. "The answer is 'no' and you know that if Madeline has nothing to do with this whole thing, you are the one most likely to help us prove it. Now," he said calmly reassuring, "Lieutenant McKnight said she is almost finished. Let's get it over with, and we can all get back to our work. Okay?"

Watland uttered a sound and grabbed the book to him once more. He looked over the pages Sal had indicated. The room was silent for a few minutes, except for the sound of the pages being turned savagely. Finally he spoke, his voice hoarse and low. "I don't know. They all sound so much alike." He turned the page. "Here's one, I think. *Kettle Creek Estates*. I'm pretty sure she mentioned that. There was another one I seem to remember she mentioned twice. Some country sounding... *Timberlake*? No. No, but something like that. Sorry, that's the best I can do."

"Thank you. That could help. That's all I have unless...." She looked at the chief and the commissioner, both of whom shook their heads. She rose and offered the district attorney her hand. "Thank you again, sir. Once again, I apologize for worrying you."

"Just a minute!" He jumped to his feet, leaving her hand dangling. "What about all this now. Have I given you anything that can clear her?"

"You have given us a number of points that can either corroborate or refute what we already have. Should you remember the names of any other apartments at any time, we would be enormously grateful if you would let us know."

He turned to go, the starch seemed to go out of him. "Just one more thing, sir. It goes without saying that all of this has been in the utmost confidence. Please do not discuss it or mention it to anyone."

He said, this time justifiably peevish. "Why is it when people say something goes without saying they always say it? Anyway, I don't intend to say anything! I intend to forget the whole thing as soon as I leave here." He began to leave the room, then stopped and turned, his hand on the doorknob. "Whether you are right or wrong," he said, his voice shaking, "I'd just as soon not see any of you next Sunday!"

And the door closed firmly behind the departing district attorney.

* * * * *

The meeting, however unsettling, was not totally useless. From her car, Sal made two phone calls. The second was to Masters.

"I've had an idea. Get on to Phyll Dayly. I think she could be a real help. What we want is to find out if the deaths are connected with Warren Watland. Nearly everything he does is considered newsworthy so there should be something. Don't forget the society pages. Start with the murder dates and go back a bit. Talked with Phyll and she agreed to help. She'll hold everything until we give her the go ahead. It is a faint hope but better than no hope at all."

CHAPTER 25 Ernie

Pure hearts do good deeds.

Ernie Maddox cleaned away the debris from underneath his father-in-law's lawn mower. He ran his hand carefully along the blade, checking for nicks or rough spots. Finding none, he oiled the blade carefully, removed the spark plug, cleaned it, replaced it, and pushed the mower next to his truck, ready to return. He'd had to borrow the bigger machine, his own not able to handle the long neglected lawn of his, their, new home.

It had taken three days of his first week's vacation to clear all the junk out of the detached white frame garage. For the next three days, he had scraped and torched off layers of paint--he counted nine--from the one and a half car garage. Painted it the same pale putty color he had already painted the house. Joni had selected a color several shades deeper for the shutters and trim, and the old house, formerly so uncared for and drab, now looked, even to his eyes, beautiful and somehow elegant.

He wondered briefly if it was okay to describe such a modest house as elegant. Next week, his second vacation week, he would bring home his precious wife and son. Ernie Junior was only five days old, but he had already put up a tough fight against jaundice when Joni's milk, laden with medication, had not been satisfactory for him. Quite a scrapper my kid is, he thought, he'll do well in this world, with his sweet mama and a dad who could teach him a lot of important things.

Thirty-four years of drifting around had provided Ernie opportunities to learn a lot, both good and bad, but especially bad. That was all behind him now. He had met Joni at a neighborhood street dance two years ago. They both knew from the start they had something really special together and, since Joni wouldn't have it any other way, they were married six months later. In church.

He lifted the heavy mower as if it were a toy, and put it in the back of his six-year-old pickup. He'd lost count of the number of trips this truck had made to the city dump, clearing away all the junk the former owners left behind. Not a compulsive saver himself, Ernie could not understand the need people seemed to have for saving everything.

Before he met Joni, his own bachelor apartment, one very large room with a tiny kitchen on one end, a dining area in the middle and the living room bedroom on the other, had been scrupulously neat. Now this, their first house, would be the same. Joni liked things neat too, and their house sang with light and color.

Ernie knew he was acting like a damn fool, but he kept imagining what the next years would be like. Him and Joni and the kid and maybe one or two more, all together in their "nest," his Mom called it. His chest thumped so hard he thought he would burst.

He didn't know why his luck had changed so much. He had always been a second stringer--until he met Joni that is. Since then, everything kept coming up sevens.

Ernie had turned over a new leaf. No more pot, no more cigarettes, no more than an occasional drink, certainly no more all night drinking parties. He'd given them up gladly. A kid needed a good example to follow.

Tomorrow was Friday, the day the doctor said he could take his family home. He thought he'd stop by the church, not to go to Mass or anything--he wasn't really a churchgoer--but maybe he'd light a candle for the baby. Maybe one for Joni, too. Just to be sure.

Joni was just about the best wife a man could have. She actually seemed to like spending her days planning and cooking meals just to please him. But, when he nodded with satisfaction after his first taste or said, "It's pretty good," her face would break out into a smile that would knock your socks off.

All for him. Jeez.

They had noticed the changes in him down at the shop too, and just before his vacation the boss had told him that when he came back he would have a new job. Day Supervisor! He would be in charge of scheduling deliveries and assigning the men to their trucks.

As he closed and locked the garage door, he could hear the phone ringing in the house. He sprinted for the back door, but by the time he got there, it had stopped. He called the hospital to check that everything was all right with Joni and the baby, then climbed the stairs to take a shower.

He was pretty sure he heard the phone ring again while the shower was running. He wasn't worried about the caller. It was probably another one of those damn sales calls. Several times this week, he had dashed into the house at the insistence of the ringing phone, heart thumping with concern for his wife and new baby. It would be somebody selling windows or rug cleaning or insurance or some damn thing. A couple of the calls hadn't even been real live people, just a computer on the other end. Jeez! What was this world coming to? How did women who stayed at home stand it?

Maybe it was his boss. Maybe they had changed their minds about his promotion. Jeez! He hoped not. Joni had been so proud, going out and buying a bottle of champagne to celebrate.

He called the plant. Sure enough. The boss had called. Well, his boss' secretary actually. She was stumped. The boss had already left for the long Labor Day weekend to go fishing at his cabin in the Pocono's. In the boss's absence, Willy Kern had accepted a request for an early delivery on Friday morning, momentarily forgetting he had to appear in traffic court at that time. Since Ernie was the dispatcher now, she'd tried him. When she couldn't reach him, she had called Harry Stone. He had agreed to do it.

The call was from the sister of an old and favored customer. She wanted their best portable color television as a gift for her son. She'd asked if she could possibly get it as soon after eight o'clock as they could. The young man would be out running between eight and nine, and she wanted to surprise him. But Harry, one of their older drivers, hadn't been feeling well lately, so he told the girl to tell Harry he'd do it himself.

Besides, Joni would not be ready to leave the hospital until noon. The delivery would give him something to do until it was time to fetch his son.

Son! What a great word! He hoped the boy would take to baseball. The other sports were okay too, but baseball was his passion. It was a game of strategy, skill, strength, and... something more than that. Brains, that was it.

Wouldn't it be something if the kid was good enough to play for the Phillies!

He thought about that a bit.

Jeez!

CHAPTER 26 Huddle

Busy hands save trouble.

Friday. 3 PM.

Despite a seeming inability to remain still for more than a few seconds at a time, the Corrigibles had been introduced to the basic tenets of surveillance by a needlessly skeptical sergeant. Of all people, Burger should have known that any kid, who has spent his life keeping out of sight of well-meaning officials from welfare, school and police, has developed that skill to a fine art.

Emily Haines too, had found that several of the boys already had a good basic knowledge of electronics--they had not spent hours watching television for nothing. She was uncertain whether they would be able to wear the bugs with the nonchalant concern they seemed to evince. She needn't have worried. Nonchalance, especially while in possession of some prohibited property, was also part and parcel of those young lives.

As to the cell-phones, they were not that different from those owned by Main Duke and Fingers, who carried his grandmother's. (She takes her role of guardian seriously.)

True, the PPD versions were more powerful and had some additional features, but after a few minutes of practice, they had it.

The ground surveillance equipment was another matter. The police had finally succeeded in impressing them. Shari and Kit were quickest to master its use.

Hearing satisfied reports from the team, Sal suggested the kids be taken up to the rooftop restaurant and fed. It had, after all, been several hours since they'd eaten.

As they filed noisily out, Masters threw a searching glance at Sal, asking wordlessly, if she was all right. She knew, having stopped at the lavatory, she looked beat, but she gave him a determined nod. "Come back when they're settled. I want to talk to you about my meeting with Watland."

So the team was told of the difficult interview with the district attorney. She made it deliberately sketchy. There was no point in describing the man's craven behavior.

"So we can't expect any help from him?"

"I don't think so Rick. I imagine that at this moment he's busy finding a way to remove himself from any kind of involvement. I hope you've had better luck."

He nodded. "You had a great idea there. I asked Phyll for any news stories involving Warren Watland and Louise Chalmers. In little more than an hour, we had what we wanted. Phyll agreed to sit on the story, in exchange for first crack at it when it breaks."

He drew out a strip of paper and put it next to the Time Line Profile. "I haven't had time to put it on the computer, but here's how it fits in."

The new information looked official and somehow less personal there, as though this was nothing more than a classroom exercise.

"As you will see," he pointed to the entries on the strip of paper with the sharp point of a pencil, "except for the first one, each murder followed within a few days of a report in the Call's Society page about Watland and Chalmers. The first was the announcement that the two had been appointed co-chairs of the country club's Spring Fling. That appeared May 5. The first murder was on June 12, a little more than a month later. The second story, involving the two, appeared on December 20. They printed a photo of the couple dancing together at the club's Christmas Cotillion. The second body was discovered December 31."

"Then there was nothing until the next Spring Fling. A photo of the pair appears May 19. Another body is found June 1."

"October 8. The Call shot a bunch of pictures of the two at that charity auction they have each Fall. Story appears October 17. Body appears October 30. Then there's nothing until this year's Spring Fling May 18. Body found May 20."

Sal wriggled in her chair, but Masters went grimly on. "On August 18 there is a photo of the pair as partners in the club's sailboat race. Body is found September 2. The couple announce their engagement February 15. Body is found five days later. On May 8, the couple announces a wedding set for Labor Day weekend. Body is found May 18."

"July 20 the couple is shown in front of their new home. Body found July 26. Last photo appeared August 22. Body found August 29, one week later.

Their eyes seemed glued to the pieces of paper. They sat for a few moments, unable to speak. Sal felt them waiting for her. She apologized, "I must say, I am having almost as hard a time accepting this as Warren did, yet there it is in black and white."

Her own words came back, mocking her. *"If we gather the information carefully then base our conclusions on those facts, they will not mislead us and, however unpalatable, we will have our answer."*

She seemed completely unaware that the rest of the team had returned to quietly follow the story told by Master's pencil. When she finally spoke, it was more to herself than to them.

"It's all circumstantial true, but there can be no other reasonable explanation. No way we can put this down to coincidence."

"Not when you take into consideration how it all fits in with the department's busy periods. Emily is checking to see if Miss Grimm signed into the Poisons Lab close to each time."

Sal said nothing.

"There's this too," Masters said grimly. "If, as you said, Grimm had formed a serious attachment to Watland--her first, I think you said, and he suddenly broke it off...."

"Fits into West's abandonment theory, doesn't it?" Adamson tried not to sound as if he was relishing it.

"And," Emily was clearly not enjoying it, "if Watland's wedding is this week-end, doesn't that mean, an additional 'episode' is imminent?"

Burger snorted. "And the department is already overbooked for the holiday week-end."

Again they were silent.

"Okay then," Masters said calmly. "When?"

"Soon," Sal said.

"Day after tomorra, I'd say," Burger said. "That should narrow things down. What can she get delivered on a Sunday?"

"Sunday morning if she sticks to that part of it," Emily ventured.

"But she won't need to, will she," Sal asked. "She doesn't have to go to work on Sunday."

"Oh? You think she sticks to the early morning so she can get to work on time?'

"Well, yes. I suppose I do," Sal said. "Actually, I said that without thinking but, yes. I think getting to work on time is the most important thing to her."

Again the room was quiet while they thought.

"So. Let's see. What can she get delivered on a Sunday morning?"

"Flowers."

"A prescription from a drug store."

"They deliver Sundays?"

"Seitz does. In an emergency."

Quiet again.

"Doesn't leave much."

They agreed it didn't leave much.

"Monday then. That's a holiday. Is that better?"

"Well, it's a major furniture sale day. She could order something ahead of time and arrange to have it delivered Monday."

Sal thought that possible. "Get on the phones. Notify the stores on our list to refuse any delivery this weekend and report any request for such a delivery."

Emily shook her head. "You really think she'll continue now that she knows we're watching her."

"I'm afraid I do. I think she feels she must stop this wedding, that she is forced to go ahead. She's gone too far to back down now. Besides, I am sure she believes we are not clever enough to catch her." She sighed, tears gathering. I almost wish we weren't, she thought. She heard the Corrigibles returning to the outer office. She drew a breath. "So. Where are we?"

"Ready to go," Masters said. "But look, don't you think you ought to step out of this? I'm sure everyone would not only understand, but expect you to."

"And leave someone else to wash the Thaxton family linen?"

"No, not at all, but..."

"Thank you Sergeant. I appreciate your concern, I really do. Chief Warmkessel and the commissioner suggested the same thing. And I'm quite sure that you could do this without me. But it is my responsibility now, not only to the job I do, but also to my family. If it must be done, it is better that I have a hand in doing it. Let's just get on with it." She stood and straightened her skirt, replacing the jacket she had put on a lifetime ago. "If our new associates are pizza'd out, I'd like to hear what you have arranged."

* * * * *

The entire group now assembled, Rick Masters reviewed their strategy.

The plan was for them to pick up Madeline at her own home after she arrived home tonight. The Corrigibles would work in shifts, in groups of two and three, each group assigned a car, each accompanied by one of the police team.

If she followed her usual MO, there would be nothing doing until the early morning hours, but to make certain, surveillance would commence from the time she arrived home from her day's work.

Team #1, Duke and Shari, accompanied by Officer Haines, would arrive at the Grimm home well before the suspect. They would "case the joint," identifying possible exits, places where the watcher's car could be concealed yet still allow visibility. By 5 PM, an hour before the suspect would arrive home, they would split up, out of sight, watching the various entrances. Did the lieutenant know the place? How many doors were there? Three, she thought, a main entrance, a back entrance and an entrance to the basement. It was a traditional colonial house--the oldest one in the Thaxton *freundschaft,* but she had not been there in years and only a few times as a child. Even then, Sal recalled, they had been expected to play in one of the girl's bedrooms, never allowed the run of the place as in the homes of the other cousins.

This team would be in place until 7 PM. Then they would go home and get some sleep so they would be ready for their next shift. They would set their alarms for 2 AM and be back in position at 3.

Meanwhile, Burger would drive Kit and Robey back to their homes where they would pick up bicycle and motor bike respectively, and bring them back to the station where they could be quickly commandeered in the morning. Then, using Burger's private car, they would take the second shift from 7 to 11 PM. They would then be driven home by Burger, leaving their bikes at the station. They would get some sleep and be ready for Burger to pick them up at 5 AM at which hour they would again relieve Duke and his group.

At 11 PM Lenny, Turt and Mechanic, picked up from Lenny's where they would all stay as they frequently did, would take over the watch until 3 AM. After their watch they would take a nap in Adamson's car, whose car this team would be using and be ready to be deployed again in the morning as the need dictated.

It was decided that Sal and Sergeant Masters would act as decoys, Masters making himself visible at the DA's office, purporting to look for clues to the "real" killer, but actually verifying Madeline's presence there. He would try to observe any signs he could of preparations--calls to delivery companies, messages that she would be out of the office the next day or two, etc. He would also check on the whereabouts of the DA himself. Meanwhile, Sal was to make herself visible and busy at her office or go home, the point being to behave as though Madeline's visit had stumped her and she was giving up. Going home, acting as though it were business as usual, would lend verisimilitude to the plan. Perhaps, they suggested, she could get some sleep.

Actually however, she would be in instantaneous touch with each of them and they with each other through walkie-talkies. The use of walkie-talkies, they thought, would confuse the suspect, who would doubtlessly keep her radio tuned to the police band. To circumvent this, they had developed code names and code words to use on the police radio, should that be necessary. The Corrigibles and the officers had spent some time memorizing these codes while they waited for Sal. Perhaps, they suggested, she would familiarize herself with the codes while they got things rolling. Sal would stay in her office as usual until about six.

"When do you plan to start," Sal addressed the group.

"Today. It is Saturday and she has never hit on a Sunday, but that's all the better. It will give us a chance to work out the bugs."

Sal nodded, thought the proposed plan over carefully and had only one suggestion to make, that they show the Corrigibles the places marked on the map, which they had identified as the next likely spots, always keeping in mind that they could be wrong.

That agreed to, they began to look around at each other. Sergeant Masters stood up, looking over the confident faces of the expanded team to Sal, sitting, arms folded, on the edge of her desk. "Well, Lieutenant. It's your call." He waited.

Sal looked them over, then gestured helplessly. "Okay. Let's do it."

A cheer went up. They broke into their respective teams like the home team taking the field. And, with the ease of a practice that was already old hat, they took off.

DAY THREE

CHAPTER 27 Jockeys up!

Look for trouble at home first.

Main Duke and Shari, with Emily Haines in jeans and tee shirt, telltale hair tucked under her son's baseball cap making a plausible third, took first watch. They arrived at the suspect's home shortly after 2 o'clock.

With the suspect herself still under Masters' watchful eye back at her office, their assignment was to arrive well before the suspect was expected home. They were to reconnoiter, get the lay of the land and give the novice teams time to knit.

They took their time.

The suspect's home was one of four block-long Colonial homes facing each other across a park. Built by Henry Harrison Thaxton for his four youngest offspring, only two were currently being used as residences. One of these, originally built for their father Walter and belonging to Sam and Sal, was occupied by Cousin Peggy since they preferred to live in the country. Uncle Peter's residence on the north side of the square had been turned into a library. Uncle Theodore's stood empty until his daughter Susan could be persuaded to live anywhere but the Thaxton stables.

Madeline, the only living child of Nora, had been brought up and still lived in the south residence.

Private roads separated the four homes from the park, now a rose garden open to the public.

The residences were similar in that the entrances, a *porte cochere* providing protection from the elements for guests and family alike, were on the short side of the residence. The garages were on the opposite side.

It was well they were early. Even with the sketch of the layout of the property their lieutenant had provided, the initial trip around the outside of the Grimm home took nearly half an hour. Finding a place to park Main Duke's car took another.

Save for the caretaker who oversaw all four homes, they did not expect to find anyone around at this hour, and they saw none. The suspect did not keep any regular household help, relying on a cleaning service. The five-car garage presented a brief challenge as all the windows had been blacked out. The Main Duke attempted to persuade Haines to let him attend to the lock in his own way, but there was nothing doing. Then Shari managed to squeeze her pole-like body in between the tall hedges guarding the building, where one window had been left clear. She reported it was empty save for one old car. Described by cell-phone to the lieutenant at headquarters, Sal said the ten-year-old station wagon had been used primarily for errands by the Grimm's housekeeper, now departed. A detailed description of this car was forwarded to all of the teams, as the team reasoned this was the car most likely for the suspect to use, rather than her distinctive Mercedes.

In this they proved to be wrong.

As all entries to the house were necessarily approached by a driveway, which circled it, the three watchers decided they could wait together, parked just inside the front hedge between it and a stand of evergreens. This position afforded them a clear view of the entire driveway, while they themselves were well hidden both from street and house.

At 6:20 the suspect arrived home. They watched as she parked the gold Mercedes in the garage, watched the automatic door close with a thud. To their surprise, once inside the house there was no sign of her presence.

When the second team arrived promptly at seven, the house was still quiet. The switch went smoothly. Main Duke simply left his car there and he, Shari and Haines left in Burger's old car, with Main Duke at the wheel. Burger, Kit and Robey took over the watch in Main Duke's Chevy. At 2:30 AM, Adamson, Fingers, Turt, and Mechanic approached. The third team had not slept much, they were far too excited. But with four on the team, one could doze off while the others remained awake.

But no one did. They talked quietly in the dark, exchanging stories of childhood and school, experiences which differed as widely as if they had come from different planets. Certainly nothing in Adamson's parochial school background prepared him for the stories he heard, sitting quietly in Main Duke's old car.

Adamson prodded them to talk about "Teech." He would, he thought enviously, have given much to be spoken of in those tones of mingled proprietorship and respect by this odd bunch of kids. He was not that far removed from his own adolescence to remember the universal disdain the young hold for adults. Adamson thought that, in many ways, they were older than he. So he whiled away the hours satisfying his curiosity about his superior.

It was her choice of learning materials which provided the most salacious listening. "Teech" had brought in the state *Driver's Manual* and *Chilton's Auto Repair* to entice Mechanic to struggle through the detested lessons. Shari had fashion and teen magazines, Wheels news stories of the Indianapolis and the like. Fingers recounted, with ghoulish glee, the time Turt was caught with a copy of *Playboy* in his desk. They were all taken aback when the expected bomb never went off. This particular offense had always been good for a three-day expulsion, a free vacation as far as the gang was concerned.

But "Teech" hadn't turned a hair. After all, hadn't she said students were allowed to bring their own reading material? She merely inquired which part of the magazine he wished to read. Turt had had to stick to his choice until he had struggled through just one page. At the end of the day he had been reprieved. "Turned him right off 'girlie' mags to this day," Fingers tittered.

But she had made it clear that while she might use unorthodox methods or materials, she dropped her standards for no one, although they had seemed unreasonably high to them for much of that first year.

She had chided them for letting their teachers get away with not teaching them to read, do their math. She reminded them teachers were paid with tax dollars, a telling point for Main Duke, already paying taxes. They ought to *demand* their money's worth.

Thus encouraged, their outlook took a sharp change. It became *their* homework, *their* books, and finally *their* standards, *their* education. For Adamson, that explained the attitude of equality the kids and their former teacher had toward each other. By the time Main Duke, Kit and Emily Haines returned for their second shift, Adamson had been completely won over by his companions.

The second round of shifts started quietly enough, but about 5:30, Main Duke stirred the other two, dozing lightly. He thought he saw a dim light appear briefly in one of the upstairs windows. The suspect was awake and moving about.

* * * * *

Warren Watland stirred uneasily in his sleep. Was that the phone? Yes. It rang again. He swore angrily. Damn all anyway! The damned Plainfielders expected him to come running at all hours of the day and night! When he was in the state house, he'd have a number that was really private!

It rang again. He would pretend he wasn't home and let the message center take it.

* * * * *

Haines wasted no time calling the other teams, but held off calling headquarters until there was something more concrete to report.

They did not have long to wait. At 6:00 the suspect appeared, dressed in a crisp, white linen suit, carrying a briefcase and handbag.

The watchers looked at each other in silent surprise. What could she be doing up so early, and dressed like that? Not planning to go to work surely. In addition to the early hour, all city offices were closed for the holiday weekend. They reported this departure from expectations to the lieutenant, already waiting in her office.

In fact, she had scarcely left it. She had returned briefly to her home after the meeting broke up yesterday, partly to mislead Madeline, as directed, and partly to touch base with her daughter, home for the holiday weekend. As the two chatted a bit, her phone rang. When Sal answered, the line went dead. Madeline calling to verify her whereabouts? Sal was certain of it. Having shown herself to be home, she returned to her office, leaving instructions with the Honeycutts and Lucienne to say she had gone early to bed should she receive another call that evening.

As she had the night before, she had again napped briefly on the blue leather sofa. In the wee hours, she and Masters had taken turns manning the phones, retreating to their respective locker rooms for a quick shower and change of uniform. Now, already surrounded by a litter of half filled cups of cold coffee, they were taking turns pacing, reviewing their evidence, anticipating the myriad ramifications of the decisions they'd made. When the phone rang a little after six they were relieved. Masters punched the button on his unit.

"Okay Haines. What's up?" He listened, told her to hold on, and repeated the information to Sal.

"Looks like she's going to the office," Sal said.

"Today? This early?"

Sal nodded. "Oh yes. It's entirely like her. The fact that it's a holiday only means the office will be quiet and she can get some work..." She stopped.

"Work done?" He grimaced. "Like what?"

Sal said she didn't know. She wished now they had had time to put surveillance equipment in the DA's office. She said as much.

"At least we could have 'bugged' her office phone."

"Not without the proper warrants," she said.

"I suppose this means we're wrong. Do you think so, Rick?" Maybe it isn't even..."

"If we are, we'll just have to take one helluva lot of ridicule," he said grimly. "Better we should be wrong than right and let another death happen on our watch. So what do you want the teams to do? I say go on as planned. Like we said, it'll be damned good practice."

* * * * *

With orders to stick, the teams held a hurried strategy meeting. All three cars and Robey's motorbike would take off in pursuit, changing the lead vehicle every two blocks. They would keep the suspect in sight of at least two vehicles at all times, one directly behind her and another two hundred yards or so back.

They almost missed her.

They continued to follow her through the relentless humidity and a sun-less dawn. She drove so slowly they were beginning to wonder if she had spotted them and was merely accommodating them. Only Haines did not believe that. "She's just pre-occupied. See how she stares straight ahead, never changing her pace? My husband used to drive like that."

"Look at that! She just ran that light!"

"Ran right through it!"

"Never even seen it, if ya ask me."

A few blocks later they watched her come to a full stop at an intersection where the light was green.

"Look! What she doin' now?"

"What the hell's she up to?"

Several cars between them began to blow their horns loudly at her, then pass impatiently around her. They too dropped off, fearing they would be seen. Worse, their forward car had gone on ahead without them.

Burger grabbed the walkie-talkie. "Car Two! Pull off! Pull off! Ya lost yer quarry!"

"What the hell..." Car Two heard and obeyed. "Where is she?"

"A block behind you. Waitin' fer a green light."

But just then her car moved on at the same moderate pace.

Burger called for Kit. "You have the motorbike. Get out there," he ordered. "It's up to you. You seen her car. The traffic's light. Catch up to her and keep her in sight 'till we can regroup."

Just as Kit got her quarry in sight, Madeline ran another red light.

Kit shouted into the wind. "What's the matter with her anyway? She color blind or somthin'?"

"I don't think so," Emily shouted back. "She's just spaced out. Look at her! Her eyes never move!"

Death On Delivery
A Pennsylvania Dutch Mystery

The morning traffic, already light, began to thin out even more as they proceeded westward. Then again she stopped at a green light. This time there was no one directly behind her and Adamson, now the following vehicle, had to pull off into a gas station.

But this time they were more alert, and the procession quickly regained its planned procedure.

She did not stop until she reached Thurber's, a large twenty-four hour grocery store, boasting an in-house restaurant, as well as bakery, flower and gourmet shops. It was five minutes to seven.

They tried to guess what she could be wanting here. A discussion ensued regarding how to keep the target covered without being seen themselves. The parking lot was huge and at this hour only a handful of vehicles was in sight. One side, the one nearest the doors to the store's restaurant, did contain perhaps twenty vehicles. It was there Burger instructed The Main Duke to park.

Adamson drove his team around to the employee parking lot in the rear, where several tractor-trailers were backed up to a large loading dock. He found a spot where they could watch the rear delivery door and settled down to wait.

Burger took a position next to an abandoned car. There his team could get out and pretend to tinker with their car while keeping well in sight of the parking lot exits. Burger himself, astride Kit's bike, circled the store slowly to ensure they had not missed anything.

Satisfied now that the store was secured, Burger cycled to a nearby PC Junior and brought back breakfast.

They wiled away the time, continuing to get acquainted. An early shopping nun triggered a discussion of what it was like to attend Catholic school. When Adamson recounted the seemingly endless rules they had to follow, the uniforms they wore, the Corrigibles all had the same reaction. If everyone had to wear the same clothes, well--they might as well be in jail. When he told them how they had to kneel, sit and stand at a signal from Mother Superior's "cricket," they broke into muffled, but nonetheless hysterical, laughter. Even jail wasn't that bad.

Back in the office, Sal and Rick paced nervously until they could stand it no longer. Nearly an hour had passed since the teams and their quarry had arrived at Thurber's. What was she doing there? Having breakfast? Certainly a white linen suit was not appropriate for grocery shopping. She could stand it no longer. Sal demanded, "What's going on out there?"

"Not a thing. Her car is still here and she has not come out."

"Send one of the Corrigibles in the store to look for her. Better yet, send two of them. That will look more natural. I'm on my way!"

Main Duke and Kit were out of their cars before the rest could move. They ran to the door, then moved casually inside. Five minutes later, they came running out with the news. The suspect was nowhere in sight!

* * * * *

It took the team a few minutes to grasp the meaning of the announcement and shoot panicky questions at them.

Yes, of course they were sure. No, they hadn't missed anything. Yes, they had even looked in the ladies' room. The suspect had simply disappeared!

While Haines reported this to Sal, Burger went inside and questioned the employees. They had, indeed, seen the lady in the white suit, but they had not seen her leave. Perhaps she had gone out the employees' door at the back.

Burger raced through the store and checked the employee parking lot. Save for one fewer tractor-trailer it looked the same. The cars, which had been there when they arrived this morning, were still there.

He returned to the now assembled group, arguing about what to do next. As he approached them, Sal's fast moving car pulled into the lot and headed straight for them.

CHAPTER 28 Madeline Again

Foolish people leave long shadows.

In the ancient, well preserved hotel, the elevator door swished shut behind its only passenger. Without waiting a further signal, it immediately began its ascent, accompanied by the slightest rattle of its brass gates. The passenger, a nun of indeterminate age, pressed the button marked 16, releasing it only long enough to set a heavy grocery bag on the floor. As she bent over, her black cowl bumped the elevator door, knocking it slightly askew. She righted it quickly. Anyone watching would smile at her distress, as if she were expecting the Archbishop to enter at any moment. But, of course there were no watchers. She was nobody's fool.

Quickly she returned her gloved hand to the panel, her finger remaining steadily on the lighted button. As she rose, she studied the gloved finger, frowning slightly. These gloves were, perhaps, a mistake. Should she ever leave one behind, they would be readily traceable. Only one store carried the fine silk lined lambskin, imported from Ireland each year for their best customers, of which she was one.

She stifled the rising worry, recalling this particular pair would prove untraceable in any case. She had slipped them into her handbag while the sales clerk was off searching drawers for a certain fawn shade another customer requested.

More to the point, it would be most unlike her to lose one. Father had taught her very early on not to lose things.

The truth was that gloves were necessary and she could simply not bear to have those vinyl or fabric types next to her skin.

Still, she reminded herself to remain cautious. Her success was due to her first hand view of the ill-conceived and arrogant misconceptions of others, leading them to make foolish mistakes. Special days, such as this, tended to excite her and excitement could lead to errors, if she weren't careful. Understanding one's own weaknesses, anticipating every eventuality, these, too, contributed greatly to her success.

The fine old-fashioned elevator lurched upward. The red and gold flocked walls hung with octagon shaped mirrors, the brass handrails, the carpeted floor, the crystal chandelier with matching twin sidelights shaped like gas lamps, the folding brass gates, its very elegance seemed to surround her protectively.

Her finger on the button prevented it from responding to any other call. Many of the new elevators didn't have this override feature, an unfortunate concession to the hustle of today. She always took advantage of it whenever possible. It was annoying to interrupt her own trip every floor or so to take on or let out passengers.

The idea of using this particular apartment had been truly inspired. She couldn't decide which gave her most pleasure, her cousin's shame when they all saw proof of which of the two was smarter, the family's embarrassment when they realized their mistake in favoring *that* one over her, the expression on Warren's face when he saw all she had done for him.

She faced forward, waiting as patiently as she could. The elevator seemed much slower today than before. She hummed softly to herself, to "keep her mind busy." In third grade, Miss Mull had adjured them: "busy mind happy heart."

The nun's habit hid her extreme thinness. Still, she believed that she was not yet thin enough. She would never be pudgy like her cousin. Her plain cousin.

Her plans called for her to be in the apartment just at 7:10. At that time she was unlikely to meet anyone else. The night cleaning crew always left the building at six-thirty on the dot. From her office across Hamilton Circle, she often watched them pour out of the building together, quickly spreading out in different directions, some to toss the filled garbage bags into the dumpster, others to place large vacuums, waxing machines, buckets, mops and brooms into a white van, all the while calling cheerily to each other in the manner of people who have worked together for a long time. From her high perch they looked, in their dark uniforms, like a small colony of the beetles they so assiduously kept from invading the big old-fashioned kitchens.

For a moment she envied their casual camaraderie. But Warren had taught her to see that nobler ethics of society were merely avenues for the more practical to use on the way to their destiny. The only rules that counted were the ones you made yourself. It had been Father's philosophy too.

But if social meetings were a trial, those involving her work were a different matter. Her best source of information was those interminable meetings with the police. Her keen interest in the ways and means detailing the commission of crimes, her analysis of those mistakes, big and little which caught the unwary, and the devious ways in which the stupid had been caught, had served her unexpectedly well. Not only had they impressed her boss with her dedication to her job, but, tucked away in her memory as an encyclopedia of what not to do, they had proved enormously useful. In each case she had used her intelligence and wit to create a scenario of how the crime *should* have been handled. She had gotten very good at it.

So good, that she knew, without a doubt, that they would not catch her. Ever. Not that she was a criminal. She wasn't. She was an--an equalizer, like the man on television--an avenger. She was an Avenging Angel--that's what she was. They should give her a medal.

One lesson learned was to balance flexibility with constancy. She had a perfect plan and, for the main, she stuck to it. For instance, she didn't always rent apartments. Once or twice she had rented houses. Once she had answered an ad to housesit. Still another time she sublet one of the new and expensive mobile homes. Or was that twice? Yes. Yes it was. She was pretty sure. But one thing was clear. Wherever she celebrated, the surroundings were always in good taste. A girl has a right to be fussy when she gets married and Warren, too, had become accustomed to fine things.

Dark eyes shining, she watched the numbers over the paneled steel doors blink on and off. Eleven... twelve... fourteen.... As soon as the light blinked off for the fifteenth floor, she removed her finger from the 16 button and once again picked up her heavy grocery bag. The elevator oozed quietly to a stop, the doors hissed open and she slipped quickly down the broad, carpeted hall.

There was no possibility that the key wouldn't fit this time. Not like the time in Hacton when the new key had been so poorly cut it would not turn the lock at all. Such shoddy work was simply inexcusable. She'd had to cancel the wedding that time. To ask for a second key would be calling attention to herself--a risk she never took. But the frustration had only made her more determined than ever to continue. As always, she had put the experience to good use. The unscheduled interruption in her plans made her consider that perhaps she had been confining herself unnecessarily to using leave time. Actually, it wasn't even necessary to stick to vacation time. Today, for instance, she had simply told her secretary she would be meeting with a possible informant in the morning and might not be in until noon. That would give her plenty of time. She would be back in the office before anyone missed her.

She dug into her deep pocket for the hotel key. It worked easily, and why not? She had pocketed it some time ago from the table in the foyer of this very apartment. She'd had no particular use for it at the time, but it pleased her to have her own key when the rest of the family had to get one from the concierge.

CHAPTER 29 A Spanner in the Works

Best to look for somethin' where you know it isn't.

"What happened?"

"We don't know! She was here and now she is just gone!"

"But her car's still here!"

"How sure are you that you haven't missed her?"

That earned a united chorus of insistent no's and one plaintive complaint. "Y'know Tee... I mean Loot," Main Duke said aggrieved. "That lady is nuts! She stops fer the green lights an' goes right through the red! It's a wonder we ain't all dead!"

Sal did not seem to hear. She looked at Burger. "How sure are you she didn't see you?"

"I'm sure," he said firmly. "Hunnert percent."

"Then she must be in the store somewhere. We must check it again. There are so many nooks and crannies, it would be easy to miss her. I think you will do to reconnoiter," this to Emily Haines. "Your disguise is simple but effective. So it's up to you and the Corrigibles, Corporal Haines. Split up though. Let the two girls take the rest room. Divide up the rest between yourself and Main Duke. Make sure every inch of the place is checked thoroughly."

"Yes ma'am." They turned to go.

"Just a minute! Not like that! Not like a herd! You know better. Spread out. Go in one at a time or in small groups. Have you any money?" She waited while pockets were checked. "Make sure everybody has at least a few dollars or you will attract unwanted attention from the clerks. Be especially careful of the restaurant and the gourmet shop."

More slowly now, they moved to the doors springing open automatically as a sprinkling of early shoppers came and went.

Meanwhile, the four officers paired up to circle the huge parking lot, a task made easier as the number of shoppers increased. They assembled at the side of the lot where three large dumpsters held sway.

They looked at Sal. "Okay. What next?"

Sal was stumped. "I was so sure she was going to work today, especially when they told me how she was dressed, but she must be up to something, otherwise why disappear?" She looked at them. "Think! Knowing what we know about her now, where is she?"

Burger scowled. "Must've gotten past us somehow, ain't?"

"With all of you watching, Sergeant Burger? Surely someone would have recognized her."

"Mebbe she did somethin' to herself so's she looked different."

Sal stared at him. "A disguise? But why? You are all sure she didn't spot you so...."

"Unless it's a regular part of her routine," Haines said, returning with the straggling Corrigibles.

"Part of her... You think she might be going to...." Sal tried to mask the shock she felt.

"I don't know. I'm just saying we should consider it. Is it possible?"

"Possible? Of course it's possible. If Sergeant Burger is right, she could have easily changed inside the store. There is quite a nice restroom in there. I could kick myself for not having thought of it sooner. So who *has* left the store since you came?"

"Hey!" Fingers darted into their midst, eagerly insistent. "We seen that nice old couple, 'member? They that returned all those bottles and cans."

Adamson shook his head, "Yes, but I don't see... Besides, her car's still here."

"Who else?"

"There *were* two women," Shari put in.

Emily nodded. "Yes, but I did look them over carefully. They were both too young to be our suspect. Anyway, they were together so I doubt..."

"There was that tall guy. A construction worker of some sort. Definitely a man though."

"Right. I seen him, too." 'Turt' agreed, pleased to contribute.

"Who else? Anybody see anyone else?"

They concentrated on remembering. They shook their heads.

"No, just..." Adamson looked up puzzled.

Shari looked at him, a frown finding its way around her pimples. "The nun!"

"A nun?" Sal repeated softly, then louder. "A nun! Just one?" A consensus built around the nun. "How did she leave?"

Shari shrugged. "Just got in her car and drove away."

"Back in the same car in which she came?"

"Sure."

"You saw her come then? So she came in after you did?"

Another spirited debate regarding the time of the nun's arrival. "Hold it! Did anyone actually see her arrive?"

Another round of shaken heads. "Must have been here before us," Turt spoke the obvious.

"Wait! You saw her come out of the store, get into her car and leave. Where was she parked?"

"Over there. By all them other cars." Mechanic indicated the rows nearest the restaurant. "The car she drove away in was anyway. I seen it when we drove up."

Sal did not bother asking if he was sure. If it had anything to do with a car, he would be. "And you saw no one else leave?" She looked at each. "It's very important."

They were sure.

She stood still and thought. "You followed Madeline here and saw her go into the store. Right?"

Full court agreement.

"But you are certain she did not come out. Right?"

Again agreement.

"And she is not inside now. You're sure?"

Solemn nods.

"Let me think." She thought. "Can anyone suggest any other answer? Corporal Adamson?"

He shook his head. "I'm for Burger's disguise idea. We know she's used disguises before, so what's to..."

"Are you saying you think she's on her way to another..."

"Yeah. I suppose I am."

Sal again said she had to think.

"What about the man you said was a construction worker Corporal Haines? You said he was tall. Madeline is tall. Could he have...?"

But Haines shook her head firmly. "He passed right by me. It was definitely a man."

"All right. That leaves only one possibility." She spoke quickly. "It is simple as well as fool proof, awe inspiring. She must have parked that second car here earlier, possibly as early as yesterday, possibly right after she left my office. Yes, that fits. That must be what the yelling was all about. She knew that if she could distract us from tailing her long enough to get that car in place, she could lose us, even if we put a tail back on her. Cars often stand on these lots for days at a time. She could leave it here as long as she wanted to." She paused. "Was your Nun carrying anything?"

A conference produced consensus. She had carried a large paper grocery bag and a smaller plastic one.

"Probably has her clothes and briefcase in one," Sal said, her mind racing through the possibilities. She turned to face the group. "We'd better shift gears and do it quickly. Looks like we're facing the worst-case scenario and she's looking for victim number twelve. Rick, let's have a look at our map. We need to re-think this. If this is actually going down today, this morning, it could mean it's a rush job. Which," she said, surveying the site map now up on the patrol car computer, "could mean her choice of site is limited."

"One of the larger sites catering to temporary residents, where a single woman would be less conspicuous?"

"That's logical. Wait. I've a yellow page directory on the floor behind the passenger seat of my car."

She thumbed through it quickly. "Here," she circled several ads with a pen. "WoodRidge. Campbell Station. GreenTree. They all fit. Any others?"

"No. None specifically advertising for singles or short term rentals."

"All right then. Let's assume she picked this branch of Thurber's because it is on the way to her destination. And look. WoodRidge and GreenTree are each within a ten-minute drive. We'll focus on those two, but we won't forget the others. Corporal Haines. Get on the phone now and make sure our other surveillance units are in place."

"Shall I tell the units assigned to these two sites she is on the way?"

"Yes." She nodded Haines on her way.

Masters pulled up to the group and stopped. Sal nodded and went on. "We'll break up into two groups. Half with

Sergeant Masters and half with me. We will reunite as soon as one has something definite. But we need to know what to look for. What kind of a car did the 'nun' get into? Mr. Mudra?"

"'94 Coup de Ville. Grey. Four door hardtop. Standard trans. Good condition with a long scratch in the hardtop."

"Good. Great in fact. Thank God you were along. Give that to Corporal Haines and ask her to get that out to the others. Also put out a general APB for it. Wait! Also put out an APB for a nun traveling alone. Tell them to report to you. Sergeant Masters, you and Adamson take your team to GreenTree. We'll take WoodRidge. Keep in touch."

* * * * *

The teams divided quickly. Masters and Adamson took Kit and her bike. Fingers, Mechanic and Turt would follow in Main Duke's car. At WoodRidge, there would also be two vehicles and a "mobile" unit. By twenty minutes to eight, both teams had arrived, conferred with the police teams already there, and positioned themselves strategically.

Kit at one site, Burger at the other, were astride bikes, assigned to keep the nooks and crannies under observation, and keeping an unobtrusive eye out for the suspect should she arrive on foot.

At WoodRidge, Sal checked the reports of yesterday's surveillance team. Only three of the twelve buildings had vacant or newly rented units. A plot plan indicated those which had been rented within the last week. A note at the bottom of the plot plan gave the home and office telephone numbers of the manager.

Sal called the manager's home. A very sleepy, hoarse voice of indistinguishable gender answered.

Sal identified herself, apologized for waking the voice, said she could not wait for the office to open at ten o'clock, and asked for the information needed. The manager grumpily informed her that both the recently rented units had been rented to young newlyweds. Yes. He had met the couples. Yes. Both of them. The others were still vacant, but none of these were furnished units anyway. There was a waiting list for those. No. No units were rented to a single woman recently. He, for the voice was now clearly male, had read the police instructions and would have notified them if one had. No, certainly no unit had been rented to a nun. The units were well out of their price range. The phone line went dead.

Sal hung up and checked the time. Twenty minutes before deliveries were likely to be made. She could take a few minutes to think.

She sat in her car and concentrated. What else might be different this time? Or, given the compulsive nature the psychiatrist had attributed to her, would she feel she had to stick to the previous MO?

Briefly she considered the possibility that their carefully developed profile could be all wrong. They could, she thought grimly, be emulating the six blind men of Hindustan of whom it was said:

*"Though each was partly in the right,
They all were in the wrong."*

Who could their suspect call for a delivery today? Not only was it a Saturday, but the beginning of the long holiday weekend. But Plainfielders were an accommodating people.

She pulled up the victim profile, studying the list of companies from which the victims had come, then a second list of firms fitting the company profile.

Which of these would be able to deliver on such short notice? Not the lumber company. Flower shops. Bakeries. Drugstores. Restaurants. All these delivered quickly but frequently employed women. Only one produce store, Morton's, still made home deliveries, but they had promised to limit deliveries to old, established customers at their home addresses. So, even if Madeline had obtained the name of a regular customer, which she could have as they were listed in the police case reports, and tried to use that name to request a delivery at a different address, it would be refused.

Office products? Sporting goods? Both were usually delivered by men, but many items were readily handled by a woman, so they might have one or more women drivers on their staff. That left electronics and furniture. No doubt each truckload sent out by an electronics company would include at least one television set, therefore, their trucks would nearly always have two men, a driver and a helper. The same held true for furniture vans. Something flashed through her mind and she hurriedly sought the crime scene profile. It had not mentioned specifically what had been delivered each time. How could they have missed that?

With mounting anxiety, she got Corporal Haines on the phone. Yes, she remembered. The last delivery had been from Van Scover's. An upholstered chair had brought the last victim to his death.

Would she try a furniture store again? If she had planned this at the last minute, she was handicapped more than usual in the available choices. Sal flipped quickly through the book again, searching for other types of businesses fitting the suspect's needs and could come up with none.

She looked at her watch. Five minutes to eight. She told the watchers to keep a particular eye out for a van from a television or electronics firm.

Clicking off her receiver, she considered her next move. It was only then she became aware that sometime during the past twenty minutes, the leaden skies had broken silently, ominously into a steady rain.

CHAPTER 30 In Time for a Wedding

Suppin' is as suppin' does.

Save for the two thin crystal candle holders supporting the long white tapers, everything on the table was white: the fine linen cloth, the two matching napkins, the small, exquisite centerpiece of silk flowers, and, of course, the bride herself. The bride was very pleased. This was far superior to those of the countless co-workers whose weddings she, as the department's senior representative, had been forced to attend. Had it not been for the haunted look, the short, contemptuous snort which summed up the comparison, she would have been much like any other new bride.

But the look *was* there, the gaunt, pale skin refusing to accept the determined application of Ruby Blush, the stark blotch of cheek color against the white face giving the bride an odd mask-like look. The pale blue eyes glittered with anticipation.

Buoyed up by the familiar excitement, she could feel the warmth and something akin to orgasm building inside her.

She felt her cheeks redden at the thought. She reminded herself there was no need to hide her excitement now. Now, should the warmth reach her face, her eyes, it would only add verisimilitude to her story.

For one fleeting moment, she wondered what he would look like this time. The realization that it didn't matter followed swiftly on that thought, squeezing it out of existence. The important thing was that, like the other nine, or was it ten, he would be having his 'last supper.' "Really," she giggled to herself, "when you come right down to it, I am quite democratic."

Stepping back from the table, she examined her preparations, then checked her watch again. Delivery had been promised about 8:30. Twenty minutes to go. She'd better hurry. After all, he could come early.

She straightened the chairs at each end of the table, ready for the bridal toast.

She caught a reflection of her long, thin face in the glass-topped table. She touched the reflection with a gloved finger. "Lady Jane," she whispered. Then she hurriedly rubbed away at the spot, just as Father had rubbed her away.

Nothing to do but wait now. Her thoughts drifted, returning in confused snatches. Thoughts of a small golden sister whose eyes were bluer, hair silkier, smile sweeter, who could do no wrong. These juxtaposed over pictures of a thin formless older sister, competent, capable, dependable, plain, friendless, who, being older, was expected to bear the blame for countless family transgressions, answer for the unclean house, the maid's leaving, the sick baby, the drink soured father, the vague, nervous mother. Then the little girl falling down the wide front staircase, the mute woman in her final imaginary illness-all her fault. Then the final blessing. Father in a drunken dare, crushed between a tractor-trailer and a high concrete wall. All flashed through her mind in seconds.

It was true, she thought. The Lord did work in mysterious ways. Hadn't He rescued her? Hadn't the family insisted she see a doctor after Father's death? Hadn't he suggested she get a job? Hadn't Uncle Rueben, dear, kind Uncle Reuben, gotten her into the district attorney's office? Hadn't she met Warren there? Young, handsome, struggling Assistant District Attorney Warren Watland?

Until she met him, she hadn't any reason to think of herself as someone worth loving, as desirable. Quite the opposite. But Warren changed all that. Grateful that the long wait for a first significant other was over, they had made love with all the fervor of teen-agers. Everything was new, exciting, fun. Gradually exchanging shame and fear for trust, they explored each other's bodies and minds until their nakedness was far more than skin deep. For the first time, each felt connected, bonded, at peace. It was as though two newly hatched birdlings, tossed from their nest by a pirating mynah, had been swept back to safety just at the point of starvation by a generous Providence.

Sometimes she was able to tell Warren about Father and then he would cradle her in his arms. "Never mind. Now you have a new daddy."

And so he was. He bought her first banana split, took her to her first circus. He helped her overcome her phobia about dining out. Each night they went to different restaurants where he would alternate laughing and joking, with tenderly holding her hand. Hidden by long tablecloths, his thigh would press against hers, or he would stroke her foot with his.

With consummate skill, he made love safe, fun, and she rewarded him with the trust she had withheld all her life from others.

Vividly, she recalled the day she told him how Father had bragged about the dress she made for the Senior Prom. Ronald Gages had asked her to go and, though his name was one of those on a long list of undesirables Mother had posted on the refrigerator, she had accepted gladly, relieved that she had been invited at all. But Father said she could go, only if she made her own dress. Why should he buy her a dress when he was paying good tax money for her to learn how to sew in school?

But she sewed badly and the pale citron her mother picked out for her because it looked so pretty in the store, made her look more washed out than ever. At the dance, her escort had held her awkwardly, one moist hot hand holding her icy one, the other burning her waist. They sat out the fast dances, sitting miserably at the darkest end of the room, unthirstily drinking countless cups of punch. No one else asked her to dance. They had been the first couple to leave.

She locked herself in her room when she came home that night and refused to eat the next day. Father angry, perhaps irked, that she was no longer within reach of his vile sarcasm, locked her doors including the one leading to her bathroom. He had kept it locked for three days, the key always on his person.

When Warren heard the story he took her right out to Bronson's where, after watching models parade before her in designer originals, he had made her select her favorite, a long clinging dress of emerald green silk. He had paid for the dress but had made her buy accessories to complete the outfit, again helping her over a hurdle. Before that she had been unable to spend money on herself without looking over her shoulder and buying the cheapest thing available.

She knew she had helped him, too. From her he learned to say, "I love you." The word, "love" had been just as impossible for him to say as it had for her. But he had encouraged her to unlock her talent for mimicry and she, in turn, used her new found freedom to hold nightly 'foreign language classes' in which she was always the teacher and the lesson was always the same.

She recalled them exactly.

"Now, for tonight's lesson, say this: "I love the kind of weather we had today." He would repeat it, laughing. "Good. Now, say this, I love the Verdi we heard tonight." He'd say it, laughing more. "Wonderful! See, it hardly hurts, does it? Now, try this..." and so on until they came to the end of the lesson. "Now here's the last one. Say this and you win the jackpot. Repeat after me, I love you." If he didn't say it quickly enough, she'd tickle him until he did. Then, of course, he got his reward.

He was more than just her love. He was her life. More even than that, her soul.

A loud 'ping' somewhere outside the door pulled her sharply out of her reverie. She moved quickly to the kitchen. There she added the contents of the little paper spill to the punch. The bottle of quinine, so effective in covering any taste that might be noticed, went in next. She watched the punch whirl about, trying to recall how many times she'd seen this before. Nine, or was it ten now, she wasn't quite sure. And always her plans had gone without a hitch.

The sound of the doorbell drew her back. She pushed the old fashioned speaker. "Who is it, please," she asked tremulously.

"Global Television, ma'am. I got yer television here.

"Oh!" She made herself sound surprised. "Oh, well, please bring it right up. I'll unlock for you."

Now the ginger ale, added at the last minute to the drink so it would be nice and bubbly. She heard the elevator stop, approaching footsteps, and then the soft knock.

"Come in! The door's unlocked."

The door inched open as the deliveryman shifted his burden. "Where you want it, Lady?"

This one was just about the right age, about as old as Warren was now, about the age Father had been when he had worked as a delivery man, before marrying the youngest of the Thaxton girls. Yes, this one was just about perfect.

The man stood waiting for her to decide, holding his burden effortlessly. If he was surprised at her bridal finery, he didn't show it. In fact, she thought he seemed to be preoccupied, which was good, and in a hurry, which wasn't. She would have to work fast.

"Oh, just set it anywhere." She sighed, not moving from her study of the punch.

The deliveryman brought his book for her to sign. She ignored it, continuing to stare at the punch, looking bewildered and helpless. "Oh dear, what shall I do?"

"Something the matter, lady? You okay?" It was natural for him to ask.

"Oh, I'm fine I guess." Her tone clearly meaning she wasn't. "I'm just so afraid this punch will not be good and it's so important that everything should be just right! You see," she went on without stopping, "my husband's boss and his wife came to our wedding this morning and *now* they insist on stopping by for another toast before they fly back and we," she wrung her hands, "just moved in and I can't find my recipe book and I don't know *anybody* here and..." She stole a quick glance at the deliveryman, noting he was coming along fine. "And...," she let her voice drop to a whisper, "it has *got* to be just perfect or my husband will... my husband will...." She looked right into the deliveryman's eyes, her own beginning to tear. "Well, he's a good man and all, but he *has* such a terrible temper." This last just audible to her unwitting confidant.

Ernie Maddox looked at her with veiled disgust. God! People do get themselves into the darndest messes, he thought. Here she was, straight from her wedding, and already scared to death of her husband. He thanked God for the millionth time for his Joni, and, full of the milk of human kindness, prepared to be helpful.

He looked into the sparkling punch. "Well, it looks OK to me."

"I wonder," she gently laid her hand on his arm, supplication overlaid with fear, "could... could you possibly taste it and tell me what you think?" She squeezed her eyes shut for a second, as if forcing back tears.

Death On Delivery
A Pennsylvania Dutch Mystery

"Me, lady? What I know about them punches you could put on a pinhead and still have room left over." He shook his head apologetically. "Beer now, there I could be a little help, but punch, forget it!" He held out the book again.

"Oh, but," quickly filling one of the waiting cups, "if you could just tell me if it's too bitter." She held the cup toward him. "You see, the recipe calls for quinine water, my husband hates sweet drinks, but without my recipe book I don't know if I've got the proportions right, and I'm afraid I've gotten it *too* bitter, and then he'll..." She held the cup still closer.

"Okay. I'll try it lady, but don't expect no expert opinion."

"Here. Just sit down a minute." She pulled him down onto the chair. They were so heavy to lift afterwards. A little of the liquid spilled on his jacket, but he didn't seem to notice and she didn't worry about it. It would dry before they found him and once dry it would not be noticed. She hurried to sit across the table from him. "You know," relaxed now that he was settling down to drink, she chattered away, "my father started out as a delivery man, just like you, and he died a very rich man."

Ernie Maddox looked into the cup, and raised it to his lips.

CHAPTER 31 Lady In Waiting

Sometimes you look too close to see.

"Lieutenant! We found her!
"Where?"
"Right downtown. At the Dorchester."
"The *Dorchester*?"
"Yup. Rookie foot patrol officer spotted her car. Heard the APB."

She had her car started before Masters completed the sentence.

"How?"
"It was on his usual patrol of the underground garage there. Thought the car matched the description and called it in. Haines got it."

Racing through the, as yet mercifully thin morning traffic, she concentrated on the quickest route to the Dorchester, normally a ten minute drive from WoodRidge.

"Have they seen her? How sure..."
"Sure. I've got Mechanic on the way to verify, but I'm sure. Can't tell how long it's been there. Parked well back in the darkest part between two of the Dorchester's vans. Only thing is why it's here."

"No sign of her?"
"Nope! What do you think? Think she switched to another car like she did at the store?"

"It's possible. This car switching could be a regular part of her MO for all we know. As for the Dorchester, it's familiar territory for her. The family keeps a suite there. Have you had a look at it?"

"The car? Doing that now." Sal thought he sounded remarkably calm. "It's locked of course. Nothing inside. Car's neat as a pin."

"It would be. Has Mechanic gotten..."

"Lieutenant! Lieutenant!" The calm drained away. "Small van from Global TV just pulled up."

Masters watched as the driver, whistling tunelessly, maneuvered his van expertly past Masters, disappearing from sight down the ramp to the lowest parking level. Masters sprinted for the floor below. Turt and Mechanic followed right behind, Kit, already with bike in hand, quickly overtook them.

Masters gave instructions as he ran. Adamson, still en route from his post, heard too, and quickly called headquarters requesting Chief Warmkessel close the two lanes in Hamilton Circle closest to the Dorchester.

Kit watched the delivery van park just the other side of the elevator. The driver lost no time opening the rear van doors, removing a large portable television set, going to a row of house phones, picking up one, speaking briefly before hanging up.

Fingers arrived next. Faintly visible in the gloom of the underground interior, some twenty yards beyond the van, he slipped out of the shadows, waited until he knew Kit saw him, then nodded toward the service stairs. She answered with a single slow nod, and moved noiselessly to the heavy steel stairway door.

With the ease of long practice, Fingers caught the closing elevator door and slid in beside the deliveryman.

As the elevator door clanged shut, Kit pushed open the steel door and dashed up the service stairs to the first floor.

From there, she stood at the elevator, not pushing either button, merely watching to see where it was headed. The number 16 lit up.

Inside the elevator, Fingers grinned widely at the man. "Mornin'!"

He pressed his thin frame against the rear corner, then stared studiously at the roof. When the deliveryman got off at the sixteenth floor, Fingers continued on up one more flight.

"Okay, I got 'im. He's carrying a 21-inch portable just like we figgered. Got off on sixteen, I'm goin' up one more floor so's I could gat a-hold of you guys. I'll get back down on the stairs. You guys can use the elevators. I'll stay with him. See where he's going. Over."

Half a dozen long jumps of pencil thin legs and Fingers was back down to the floor below. He pulled open the service door just in time to see the man stoop to put his burden down to push the small button next to the door of an apartment midway down the hall, then again assume his burden.

His back toward Fingers, the man's eyes were on whoever opened the door. Quick, light-footed, Fingers ran down the passage keeping his back pressed flat along the wall, praying the man did not turn around. He strained to hear, but the thick carpet swallowed sounds so efficiently only the merest mumble could be heard.

He got to the apartment door just as it was closing. Keeping his thin frame pressed tightly against the wall, he slipped the piece of plastic tape he had ready for that purpose across the door latch with experienced ease. The door closed firmly.

He did not know what to do next. He was accustomed to Main Duke taking over at this point, but there was no sign of Main Duke as yet. He strained to hear what was happening inside the apartment. He could hear nothing, not even a rumble. He moved to the door and put his ear tight against it. Still nothing. Maybe the guy had already bought it. What should he do? Truth to tell, he was scared to tackle a killer by himself. It was one thing to face danger when the gang was with him. Then he was always the first to speak up, to throw out a challenge, but quite another...

He heard the elevator coming up again; they would all be here in a few seconds.

* * * * *

Accompanied by throaty rumbles of thunder, rain splashed angrily against Sal's windshield, mocking the efforts of wipers set uselessly on 'high.' Through the puddled windscreen, everything had an ominous, ribboned look.

Sal struggled to bring her mind back to its familiar order, but her head whirled with uncorrelated thoughts.

She had not really expected another strike so soon. It was frightening to proceed with so little known about how the murders were actually done. How much time elapsed between the deliveryman's arrival and his death? How did the woman manage it? Some kind of punch, they knew that. Burger's grievance surfaced. How *did* she get these men to drink it?

They had simply not had enough time. Lists floated to mind. Had there been a better way to go about it, a better use of the collected information than the subjective construction of profiles, their even more subjective interpretation?

Her brainstorm of using the lists had been woefully inadequate. And useless. Certainly they had not predicted her presence here at this famous downtown hotel. Madeline had out-smarted her.

She sorted through memories more than thirty years old, groping for something, anything, that would help recreate what must be occurring right now, what had occurred eleven times before. Some sort of play-acting inducing the victim to take the fatal drink had been Haines' suggestion, yet she had never known Mad to show any signs of imagination.

Quite the opposite, in fact. Maddie had scorned taking any part in the 'shows' to which the Thaxton cousins frequently subjected the collected adults. She recalled vaguely Maddie was offered the lead in the school production of Glass Menagerie, one for which Sal would have given her eyeteeth, but which her roly-poly form made her laughingly ineligible. Maddie had turned it down cold.

Had she mis-read her cousin entirely? If she was the person they were at this moment trying to trap, she had, on eleven occasions, dressed and acted a part with commendable skill and aplomb. "Where," she asked herself out loud, "was my supposed talent for reading people? Where was my reputed ability to interpret facts without sentiment? Where was my skill in preventing trouble? Where, come to that, were my toes?"

But it was her stomach that now was curled tight and churning. Just one darn physiological symptom after another, she thought.

Then she thought of the Global TV van. Was there another reasonable explanation for its being here on this holiday week-end? She thought not.

Flying through the near empty downtown streets as fast as the pelting rain would permit, she considered her destination. She did not need to wonder long why her cousin had chosen the Dorchester. It was the intelligent thing to do. They both knew this building well. The Thaxtons kept a suite here. As children they had raced up and down the stairs, teased the elevator operator to distraction, sometimes making it the mise-en-scene of one of their homemade plays. Here she would face fewer unknowns than anywhere else. Another thought struck her. Here, in the town's most famous hotel, a delivery on a holiday weekend would not have seemed too unusual.

But surely she would not have the nerve to kill here in the shadow of the police, of her own office, of Warren? But the moment Sal considered it, she knew it was exactly what the woman would do. It fit the brazen way she had charged into her office, it was part and parcel of the unreality of the accusations she had hurled, the faulty conclusions she had drawn.

A call to Burger brought him up to date. Another to Masters to report the familiar apartment number.

She veered sharply, tires clutching the wet road, slick after the long, dry spell. Ahead loomed several school buses. What in the world were...?

The parade! They had forgotten the Labor Day parade! But surely the rain... Yes. That was why they were parked there, no doubt waiting a decision from the parade committee regarding whether or not they would march.

Turning off on a side street to avoid the buses, cost her another half minute. Thirty seconds further away from another tragic, meaningless death. Not very long but time enough to die.

Masters reported in. Fingers had tracked the deliveryman to the sixteenth floor. He was there now too. She had been right, his voice crackled over the instrument.

She felt ill. Now there could be no doubt. The serial killer was indeed her cousin.

She was beyond choices. In an ironic Acschlusian twist, it would be she who would have to drag her in, she, who did not believe that even the state had the right to take a human life, who would be duty bound to provide the documentation necessary to put someone to death. A woman. Her cousin.

Not bad, she thought sardonically. Traitor to my sex, my family and my own beliefs, all in one fell swoop.

Worst of all, she knew that in spite of it all she would do her job to the best of her ability.

She swerved around the final corner on to Hamilton Circle. Officers were just arriving with orange cones and yellow and black roadblocks to close the street. She wondered who had been so quick to order it. The officers were moving silently along, giving no indication of the important events happening on this broad oak-lined thoroughfare.

She pulled up in front of the Dorchester. As she dashed up the three wide steps and across the thirty feet that lay between the steps and the domed entry, her cell-phone beeped again.

"Masters. Outside the door. It's dead quiet here but the deliveryman went in. Fingers saw him. I've been on to the management. Told them to close off this floor. We're keeping everyone off the elevators and stairs. They were pretty hot but I used your name, so they're cooperating for now. I hope to God no other tenant opens their door just now. What do you want us to do?"

"There's only one other suite on that floor and they are in Europe right now. I'm almost there. You're the officer on the scene. Use your judgment."

Kit came running to meet Sal. They ran together to the main door. Kit had the elevator waiting.

* * * * *

Masters examined his choices. If they broke in too soon, they would chance losing their case. The lieutenant had recounted the warnings from chief, commissioner and DA, to bring it in tight or not at all. Still, if they waited too long...

It was too damn quiet in there. On the other hand, how much noise did you make drinking a cup of poison? He had only seen the body of one of the victims himself, but that was plenty.

He decided he could wait no longer. He motioned to the gang to wait outside for instructions.

*****

The elevator door opened with agonizing slowness. Down the hall Masters, gun drawn, was easing the apartment door open.

Sal ran quietly, drawing her own gun. Seldom used outside the required target practice, it felt cold and alien in her hand.

Seeing her, Masters waited three more seconds for her to slide into position behind him. She signaled Haines to go left, Adamson right. Heart thumping, she nodded at Masters and he swung the door open wide.

*****

The scene before them, in those first seconds, would be burned forever into their memories.

From the doorway they could see through the small foyer, passed the newly delivered television set resting haphazardly in the living room, into one end of the dining room. The sight was both incongruous and frightening. A man in dark blue work pants and jacket, stood with his back toward them. His head was bent toward something in his hand. Across from him, facing the three officers as they entered, stood Assistant District Attorney Madeline Grimm, elegantly attired in a long white wedding gown, elbow length gloves, a pearl necklace wrapped fashionably around her upswept hair. Between them, on the white cloth covered table, was a glass punch bowl.

At the expression on the face of his customer, the man turned to see the trio of officers enter, guns drawn.

It was the last to arrive, Sergeant Fourth of July Burger, huffing and puffing from his dash down the hall, who had a clear view of the punch cup in the man's hand. He lunged forward to shove the cup away.

Sal yelled. "Evidence!"

Burger's powerful arm continued to move fast, but now with control. He grasped the shocked man's arm with one strong hand and carefully removed the cup with the other.

In the seconds this took to transpire, Madeline's face flushed bright red with rage. Then, like a piece of cacophonous counterpoint, the two women's voices began, one a high pitched stream of invective, the other low and shaky, automatically mouthing the familiar words, "Madeline Martha Grimm, I arrest you for attempted murder and on suspicion of murder. You have the right to remain silent..."

But silence was not to be had. Screaming abuse, Madeline rushed at Sal, her face contorted beyond recognition, her hands clawing the air as she came. Her eyes, which had not left her cousin's face from the moment she saw her, burned into Sal's.

To the Corrigibles, now gathered around the door, it must have seemed a strange tableau: the delivery man standing rooted to the spot, Sergeant Burger hanging on to the cup holding the crucial evidence, searching about for a safe place to put it down, well away from the flailing arms.

Masters, Adamson and Haines raced toward the wildly careening woman, advancing toward their leader.

Madeline got to Sal first. She grasped her loathed cousin by the neck with the long fingers of both hands and, still screaming, began to shake her back and forth. It was no contest. The taller woman's height, the power of her hatred, the strength of madness, gave her all the leverage she needed. Sal felt the strong hands squeeze. In an instant, everything went black.

They tried to pull the murderer away, but they were only sane men against one soul in torment. Had Sal been able to speak, she could have told them they would not be enough. She knew the incredible strength of the mad, out of control. The last things Sal saw, as she went down, were the dark blue denim legs of Main Duke and Turt's sneakers, untied and holey, opposite Master's neat Reeboks. Then they were joined by Burger's brown oxfords.

Suddenly, the thin hard body swathed in white, fell on top of her, and the three officers, unprepared for the sudden loss of resistance, went down with, and, very nearly on top of the two women.

Burger and Haines were first to right themselves.

Together they grabbed the unconscious suspect, and pulled her off of Sal, laying her on the floor beside her. Masters and Main Duke ran to Sal, pulled her upright, choking and gasping, unable to speak.

Main Duke knelt next to her, fanning her with his cap.

"Give 'er air! Give 'er air," he ordered with the insouciance of an experienced battlefield commander.

When he saw she was recovering, he cast an experienced eye on the other woman, lying there, still as death.

"Didn't do it too hard, did I? I only meant to knock her out."

"Too hard?" Even the tough, experienced Burger was having a hard time understanding. "What are you talking about? Do *what* too hard?"

"You know," Main Duke seemed nettled at this breakdown in communication. "I just pushed that 'whatchamacallit in 'er neck."

He looked from Burger to the other officers. When he saw no dawning light he said, "*You* know. Right here." He moved to Burger to demonstrate.

Sal choked, "No! Vagus nerve," she croaked.

Burger looked at Main Duke with awe, and, Sal thought, a kindred respect. "Where in the hell did you learn to do that?"

"Friend of my Dad's," Main Duke was nonchalant about the whole thing. "I used to do it a lot when I was a kid. But 'Teech' here made me stop it. Said I could kill somebody that way." He looked over at the woman on the floor. "I didn't, did I? I mean, she's not dead, is she?"

Burger, still shaken, replied. "No, I don't think so."

They helped Sal to a chair, where she sat, gasping for air, holding her aching throat. Already huge welts appeared on her neck.

"Cuffs." She heaved asthmatically, motioning with her hands as the unconscious form started to stir. "Before she comes to. Doctor. No paddy wagon. Pictures. Prints. No noise. No black and whites," she croaked. "Cell phone."

Interpreting this correctly, Main Duke and Burger companionably turned the woman over and handcuffed her. Masters used his cell phone to call the necessary troops.

* * * * *

Everyone seemed to arrive at once.

The crime scene officers and the ME had only to drive halfway round Hamilton Circle. Robey, Shari and Mechanic followed a few seconds later. As the new arrivals were being brought up to date, Madeline began to stir. The doctor looked from the assistant district attorney on the floor, to the police lieutenant on the chair. After a terse explanation, he directed Madeline to be held while he gave her an injection putting her out again.

Rasping and coughing, Sal surveyed the crowd. It was too much! The crime scene officers, the ME in his white lab coat, the delivery man in uniform, the Corrigibles, her team, her cousin in bridal finery, and herself, propped against a chair struggling to breathe in this beautifully appointed suite.

She wanted to giggle. It might have been the climax of a particularly energetic dance contest during one of Aunt Victoria's famous masquerade parties, or a dress rehearsal for a little theater play: a bizarre synthesis of Noel Coward, Gilbert and Sullivan and Oliver Twist. All it lacked, was the lead to enter in top hat and tails to whisk away the fainting damsel in the long white dress, and a Cockney gang leader to stride stage center and demand, "Whatcher got here, Mates?"

The uncontrollable giggle was still there, trying to graduate to outright laughter. What actually issued from her adulterated throat was no more than a choked sob.

She struggled up, trying to croak directions, but it was useless. But Masters was there, directing Adamson to take the statement of the almost victim, the calmest of all. All he wanted was to get to the hospital to see his wife and new son.

The crime scene people paid meticulous attention to the proper keeping of the contents of the cup, the punch bowl and the cup itself.

The Corrigibles watched every move of the crime scene officers until they had packed up and moved out. Main Duke looked around and said, "Well, this place certainly looks a mess. I'm hungry. When can we get something to eat around here?"

Adamson looked at the lieutenant, a smile starting in back of his eyes. "Shall I?" She nodded. Together they straggled out, still excited, patting themselves on the back.

Masters, Burger and Sal remained behind waiting for Madeline to come to. Sal preferred to have her walk out, if possible.

Waiting, Sal looked up and saw Masters grinning to himself.

"Some kids," he said when he felt her gaze on his face.

"Yes," she agreed weakly. "They are some kids."

He was silent for a moment. Then he spoke again. "I was just wondering..."

"Wondering what?"

"Did you always go to this much trouble to keep them from getting in hot water? Hell, no wonder you quit teaching!"

Her croaked laughter sounded only a little less hysterical than had her cousin's.

* * * * *

Finally, the drugged woman stirred enough to be moved. Burger, in response to the beseeching expression on Sal's face, cleared the way to take Madeline down through the Dorchester's underground garage, across Hamilton Circle in a police car with deeply tinted windows, and thence to the underground garage in the Community Building. Sal, herself, would take the wheel.

The basement passage was a godsend. If she could help it, photos of two policemen firmly holding this tall, subdued woman in the long, white gown, now torn and disheveled, the family pearls hanging crazily from the forsaken hair-do, were not going to be plastered all over the country.

So Madeline was kept in her car until Chief Warmkessel reported the way clear. At the booking room, he personally took the desk sergeant's place, formally charging Madeline Ruth Thaxton Grimm with the murder of eleven men, and the attempted murder of Ernest R. Maddox.

* * * * *

The prisoner woke long enough to demand to see Warren Watland and permit herself to be changed into a grey prison dress.

But the district attorney responded only to say he would be sending someone to "handle" things.

Sal sought him out, speaking to him as candidly as possible. Madeline's tentative grasp of sanity, she insisted, could not withstand his desertion. If he could just come by and see her, assure her he would not desert her, that he would always care for her, that sometimes love died, even when you didn't want it to.

The suggestion outraged him. "Thank God I'm not marrying into the Thaxton family! You must be as crazy as your cousin if you think I'm going to get mixed up with that mess! If, as you say, I'm personally involved, it wouldn't be right. I'm putting my best man on it. I understand it's an open and shut case. Maddie'll be the first to understand. Maddie *always*..."

* * * * *

The prisoner was bound over for trial as soon as she was able to understand the charges against her, but that happy event never came to pass.

DAY FOUR

CHAPTER 32 End of Story

Home is where the heart iss.

Once again Warmkessel had advised her to go home and get some rest. Once again sleep evaded her. She had spent what was left of the night staring, dry eyed, into space, seeing the rage ravaged face of one with whom she had played so reluctantly, whom she had invited to parties so desultorily, who had been so perfunctory an attendant in her wedding. Perhaps if she had treated her better.... Perhaps if she had seen, early on, the depths of her cousin's despair....

When she closed her eyes she saw only the hands like thin, white, iron tentacles, clenching the car door, hands which had meted out fatal doses of poison to twelve strangers, whose only contact with her was one of innocent charity. Her silent bedroom rang with her cousin's screams. Over and over she saw the thin, tortured body shrink away from her whenever she made the slightest move toward her. Over and over she heard Todd Brookings, his handsome face twisted in a childish smirk, his deep beautifully modulated newscaster's voice seething with barely concealed malice over his frustrated efforts to get the story first, ask, "Lieutenant, how does it feel to arrest your own cousin for murder?"

Death On Delivery
A Pennsylvania Dutch Mystery

Sometime after midnight, the storm, which had provided a fitting accompaniment to the capture, returned. Its energy still unspent, it smothered the whole of Plainfield with rain, deafening thunder, and long stabs of jagged lightening. While the storm tossed the oaks and sycamores, the lindens and maples outside her bedroom windows, she tossed and turned in the big, old-fashioned bed that had been her parents' and grandparents'. Had they, too, spent tortuous nights between the intricately carved roses of the cherry head and footboard?

Finally, she gave it up. Barefooted, bare everything, she crossed the darkened room to stand at the window, looking out on the scene below. It looked as if some giant, unruly child had had a temper tantrum, tossing tree limbs about in noisy vengeance, smashing tall marigolds flat, their gold, orange and white faces drunkenly touching the ground, the colors still faintly luminous in the glare of the lightning. The lawn, spread out in a neat apron of green just that morning, now was carpeted with a thin layer of pale yellow and brown leaves, the first of many to fall. Farther down to the right, a thick limb had fallen, one end resting on the ground, the other on the top of the small gazebo Uncle Charles had made for them, its roof specially built for climbing on and over. Surely the next gust of wind would cause it to come crashing down, demolishing the delicate woodwork. Another blow to childhood memories. It was the last straw.

Glad for something to do, she quickly drew on jeans and sneakers, added a long sleeved cotton jersey, and headed for the back door.

She ignored the line of slickers hanging handily on the mudroom wall. A battle with the elements, a chance to deal with a problem which could not possibly be laid at her feet, might release her thoughts from the depressing vortex into which they had sunk.

She ran through the wet matted leaves avoiding the fallen branches barring the way. Within the space of a few seconds she was deliciously soaked, the rain plastering her hair around her face, her clothes to her body.

The lightning had halted for the moment, and the sky seemed blacker now. She wished she had thought to bring a flashlight.

She walked around the limb, pushing it gently to see if it was caught at the top. The branch was twice as big as it had appeared from her window, and she was too short to simply lift it away. She considered alternatives. A rope, perhaps? A ladder?

A faint light seemed to be moving toward her. An oil lantern from the way it moved, one of several kept ready on each of the outside buildings.

Benjam of course! He would have been awake much of the night, checking for damage.

"Miz McKnight?" The old voice quavered, incredulous. Not waiting for an answer, he hung his lantern on a low branch and came to help. "I'll get under it and push the top part offa the top vunce, you chust guide it ovah the site and let it drop to the grawnt."

He was quick and efficient, taking only a minute or two in spite of the rain pelting down on his upturned face.

"Naw watch awt youse doan get your feets unter it. Bist du fertig?"

She shouted above the wind that she was indeed ready, and, with a great heave, he pushed the huge branch up, freeing it from the trellis. Relieved of its intrusion, the trellis house rocked slightly. Keeping her feet well clear as instructed, she shoved the heavy limb hard, guiding it toward a space clear of other plantings.

He nodded approval at her. She shouted thanks. "Any other problems?"

"Ach no," he shouted back. "Ve knew it vas comin, so ve hat plenty a time to make ready. You chust get back to your haws, or your brudder will kill me yet." He shooed her towards the house as if she were one of his brood of recalcitrant chickens. Already unbelievably cold, she went willingly enough.

In the mud room she dropped her wet clothes, wrapped her body in a thick terry robe taken from a peg, wrapped her dripping hair in a huge towel from a waiting pile and made her way back to her rooms.

Wide awake now, she showered, rubbed herself briskly, toweled most of the water out of her hair, combed it while still damp, leaving it to dry of its own.

As sleep was now totally out of the question, she decided she might as well go to work, face the music, get it over with.

She chose a comfortable, softly flowing grey cotton with a white band at the neckline and a wide full skirt. Match the day, she thought. A pair of grey and white sandals, also comfortable, came next. A switch to a grey leather shoulder bag followed, then she went down, making no noise on the thickly carpeted stairs.

The rain splashed in the open door, sending her back for the white burberry with the wide, yellow windowpane checks. Deciding she'd been wet enough, she pulled the hood well up over her head. The extra half cape reaching almost to the waist, Sherlock fashion, would be just the thing to keep her dry in the still pelting rain. She got her car from the garage.

But once on the road, her determination wavered. It was still dark, the luminous dial on the dashboard clock indicating it was lacking twenty minutes to four. Suddenly she felt ravenous and in need of coffee.

But where? Unlike the bigger cities, Plainfield did not run to all night restaurants, but for one or two truck stops.

Their pallid coffee, served in thin plastic dark brown mugs that did everything possible to make the drink even more unpalatable, would only add to her depression. Not there, then. Where?

She could return home, of course, but her movements in the kitchen would waken the Honeycutts.

The streetlights on Applebutter Road drew her toward Uncle Peter's printing plant. They worked around the clock and had a cafeteria. No. They would have cleaned after the third shift lunch and would not have started breakfast.

"This," she told herself, "is ridiculous. I own over a thousand eating establishments. I should be able to find someplace for coffee"!

Plainfield's two Pleasant Company restaurants opened at six. The staff would be there, but they would be especially busy preparing for the expected holiday Sunday crowd, and she would be in the way.

Then she remembered Don Slogan, who managed the P.C. Jr. north of town. She seemed to remember he was, like her, an early riser. On the off chance he would be at work, she turned her car and headed north.

In the empty streets it took only a few minutes to reach her destination. The rain was slower now, falling as gently and quietly as tears after the first intense acquaintance with grief. Beyond a fine mist, the eastern sky was beginning to lighten. She parked under the sign depicting a peasant couple at tea, the company logo, not yet turned on.

At the back door, she rang the bell marked DELIVERIES. If he was surprised to see her at that place and at that time, he didn't show it.

"Mornin', Dr. McKnight. Come on in! Come on in! Isn't this a stinker?" He looked out the door as she came in. "Looks like it's finally clearing up, though. Good! Good! That'll mean a good breakfast crowd."

Yes, she thought. For him everything would be measured in terms of customer volume. His idea of a 'good breakfast crowd' would be twice that of other managers

His flour spattered face and hair, the white powder obvious against dark skin and crisp curls, could not conceal the honest-to-God smile which telegraphed his pleasure in his work.

The wide, marble topped worktable was already dusted with a light film of flour in preparation for rolling crusts for rhubarb or strawberry, raisin or pecan pies. But more to the point, at least as far as she was concerned at this moment, he had the coffee on.

She breathed in the tantalizing aroma clinging to the damp morning air and felt the first faint return from the depths of intolerable gloom.

"Mind if I help myself?"

"Of course not. *Your* coffee," he grinned in return.

She filled a cup, took a cautious sip from the piping hot brew. Welcome to the real world, she thought as the scalding brew made it's way down.

"I'm just putting a couple of crullers in the fryer. Could you use a couple?" He turned a wide smile to her, halted his swooping arm in front of him, not rushing, waiting her answer. He would only fry as many of the scone-like concoctions as would be eaten within thirty minutes or so.

She nodded thanks. Just what she wanted. While they bubbled away, he took several chilled balls of dough from the refrigerator, ready for pie making. From the boxes of waiting fruit, it looked like, in addition to the apple dumplings and the lemon meringue tarts which were a daily feature, today there would be strawberry tarts, made from berries large, red and ripe.

He worked quickly on, the quiet between them companionable. While the crullers browned, she'd finished her first cup, leaning against the spotless front counter out of Slogan's way, but where she could watch him working, effortless but with a thick grace. As she worked on her second cup, Slogan rolled out the first twelve slabs of dough circles, thin as shirt patches. Next he deftly rolled them one at a time around the rolling pin, set the dough-covered roller on a pie tin, unrolled the dough again, the dough falling accurately into the pan, like an exuberant youth dropping unerringly into a beanbag chair. He moved back and forth at the line of pies, three times, the first using the fingers of both hands in unison as if he were playing the piano, pushing the dough firmly into the bottom of the pans, the second picking up a small sharp knife to trim off the extra crust from the pan's lip, and finally making the decorative edges, pinching the dough by pushing out a bit of dough with the forefinger of one hand and squeezing it together with the other. Finally he pricked the bottom of each crust several times with a fork to prevent bubbles from forming and slid them into the oven, setting the timer.

By the time he pulled up the basket, dropping the four hot crullers into a paper bag with confectioner's sugar, the second cup was empty. Again throwing his wide grin her way, he shook the bag briskly, thoroughly coating the balls with the powdered sugar. With a pair of tongs, he took two out and put them in a small paper bag depicting the same peasant couple at tea.

Handing her the bag, the concern in his eyes, genuine, unspoken, warmed the half smile she had dredged up for him making her feel sheepish. She said awkwardly, "Can't thank you enough. This has been a lifesaver."

He shook away her gratitude. "It's always nice to see you, Dr. McKnight." He raised his coffee to her, nodding briefly. He took a sip and returned to his work. Now he lightly dusted the marble counter with flour, ready for the second batch of pies. Funny, she thought, that after listening untouched through countless hours of speeches expressing gratitude from heads of organizations, heads of state, this spontaneous toast made her feel shy.

He paid no attention to her tongue-tied condition, going on to collect another armful of the 'resting' dough. His voice came, muffled by the large walk-in unit, "I suppose you know how much we all think of you." Enjoying her embarrassed look, he grinned at her again, and went on. "Gives us quite a standing in the comm-u-ni-ty," he pronounced each syllable separately, making the word sound important, as perhaps it was meant to be.

"Really? Well, that's good I guess," she said, still at a loss for words. Faintly, she repeated her thanks and turned to leave.

He came and held the door for her. Several of his crew were there, coming up the short flight of steps as she went down. There was another chorus of cheerful greetings. Noting their delight in finding her, literally on their doorstep, gave her a stab of pleasure.

Warmed by more than the coffee, she slid into her car, settling cup and breakfast in place.

Ahead, a pencil-thin crack in the grey morning sky became visible as she pulled away, a barely perceptible deep rosy line just at the horizon. Another promising sign, she thought. The rains had stopped. The sky was pink, not red.

Red in the morning, sailors take warning.
Red at night, sailors delight."

Still only twenty minutes past five, she decided to drive to the top of the Schnecksville Road hill, a matter of ten minutes drive. There was, after all, no longer any reason to hurry. She could park and watch the sunrise while she ate her breakfast. She shifted into 'drive' and headed east.

CHAPTER 33 Certain Conclusions

Don't look so deep in the river you fall in yourself.

Her first stop was the prison hospital where Madeline was being treated. She arrived just as the shift was changing, was told the prisoner was being washed and could she come back later? No. She had not really said anything, muttering unintelligible sounds from time to time. No, she had not eaten anything. Sal said she would return later in the morning, but would be in her office if needed.

* * * * *

Low voices, a laugh, more voices, then another laugh filtered through the partially open door of her office. Not the team, surely. They had all agreed they should 'sleep in,' drifting in as they chose to complete the necessary paperwork.

Curiously, she opened the door. All four team members rose, attempted to extricate themselves from their chairs, faced her and saluted.

"Reporting for duty sir!"

It was a straggly, unrehearsed chorus, their so dissimilar faces struggling alike to conceal their smiles.

A quick glance at the round table showed they were already busy. As Masters dropped his salute, the others followed, but they remained at attention.

"Never make it on Broadway like that," she muttered faintly. Then to their still erect postures, "At ease, officers."

Rick grinned at her. "Good morning, Lieutenant" he pulled out a chair, motioning her to sit. "Can I get you some coffee?"

She did as bid, looking at them. "I am surprised at seeing you here at this unearthly hour. Aren't you the same fatigued four who insisted you needed to sleep round the clock?"

"Just stealing a page out of your book," Masters grinned innocently. "Nose to the grindstone. Duty before personal convenience. You know." He continued to grin amicably.

"Pay him no mind." Burger's smile was half leer, half impish grin, "I chust came in vunce to give these guys the benefit of my experience and spread around a little integrity." The veteran's face broke into a grin, drawing his lips apart like a stage curtain swept aside to reveal a triumphant cast.

A spontaneous remark from Burger! And humorous too! She was tickled. She supposed he'd had to find a way to suppress any pride he might feel in a job well done. The ploy was very familiar, and she felt an instant kinship for the man.

"Whereas I," a poised Emily Haines darted a quick, comprehending look at Burger, "was right there to pick up the ball and subject it to my analytical skills."

"That's all very well," Adamson's voice came, cool and sardonic, "but where would they be without my crystal ball and fund of knowledge?" Adamson added his smile to the pile, "To say nothing of my synthesizer."

"And of course I am getting ideas and performing my role as leader," his grin widened, "as you can see." Masters indicated the work already on the table.

Both pleased and embarrassed at their precise memory of their first meeting, could it be just four days ago? Her smile flickered and died. "I'm glad you are all here. I haven't had the opportunity to thank you, but I certainly do so now."

She stood up again and went to join them, all four relaxed, towering over her. She smiled ruefully, reaching up rather than out to shake each hand. "I have put in for departmental citations for each of you."

"Shoe's on the other foot, way I see it," Masters said, still smiling. "It's we who should thank you."

Before they could pursue who should be thanking whom, Dolores's face appeared at the connecting door. She too was smiling. "Good morning, Lieutenant."

"You too? What are you doing here so early?"

"Knew it would be a busy day. Thought I'd get a head start. The phone has been ringing incessantly for you."

"Already? It's barely six thirty. I had hoped everybody would be off for the Labor Day weekend. What's the matter with everybody?"

"Lotsa people are down on their knees giving thanks this morning. Plenty relieved they are!"

Sal pushed that aside, nodding at the table. "It looks like everything is well under way here. I may as well get the calls over with."

She looked at the pink phone slips, returning calls to Commissioner Frey, Phyll Dayly, Uncle Rueben, Charlie O'Connell, each offering an invitation of one sort or another to celebrate her success. She cringed at the word, hesitating over Charlie's invite to join him in a steak. Such shared celebratory meals were part and parcel of the co-workers code. Giving up a quiet evening at home was all part of the game. She agreed to the steak.

Chief of Police Warmkessel came in person. Finding a hand shake inadequate, and to the amusement of the assembled team, wrapped his huge arms around her in a dwarfing hug.

* * * * *

For the next few hours they worked steadily, sorting, comparing, deciding. Between tasks, they took turns answering a continuous onslaught of phone calls, sustained by pots of coffee and tea and whatever remained in her refrigerator.

A little after eleven, the Corrigibles arrived, exchanging noisy self-congratulatory remarks with the officers, each reminding the other for the first of what would prove to be many times down the years, of the specific parts he or she had played. This time there was no need to exaggerate, no need to brag. They had done a credible job and it was well appreciated.

She took the entire ensemble off to Ringside Seat for lunch, after which the Corrigibles, begging not to be forgotten, to be called on again, piled back into Main Duke's car and headed back up Hawk Mountain. The officers went back to work.

Suddenly she was seized with an overwhelming urge to see her cousin. She told the team to leave as soon as they had finished their various tasks, sent Dolores home to her family, and headed for the hospital.

Even in a drugged sleep, her cousin looked tense. She lay perfectly straight under the white hospital sheets. Her closed eyes, pulled down at the corners, were shadowed with dark smudges. Long, etched lines were visible under the make-upless face.

The doctor assured her the shallow breathing was natural, that it was best for her to remain sedated for a few days while they filled her veins with nutrients and vitamins. She had, he said, apparently been anemic and very near emaciation for some time. She would be in better shape to face her difficulties when she had been 'fed,' he said, pointing to the dripping intravenous feeding. They had given her some blood, and would give her more. She asked to be notified before the next transfusion.

A primly starched nurse was waiting as she left Madeline's room. She held out a plastic grocery bag, looking from it to Sal with equal distaste.

"You're with the police, I believe?" She said it as though it was a white slavery operation. Sal admitted it. "*And* a member of this poor lady's family too, I've been told." She confessed to that too. "Then perhaps you would be so kind as to take Miss Grimm's clothing along and bring us something more *appropriate*," it was impossible to miss the slight emphasis, "for her to wear when she leaves here?" She continued to hold the bag out to Sal.

Sal took the proffered bag containing her cousin's wet and torn white wedding gown, and fled.

CHAPTER 34 Madeline at Home

Mirrors don't show you nothin' that's not there

Somewhat dazed, she drove to Edgewood Close. She could, at the very least, take Mad's personal effects home and check the house.

She had not been in her cousin's home for, she tried to remember, at least four years. She unlocked the door, stopping just inside in the large square entry hall, regretting she could not simply leave the bag for the live-out housekeeper to find. She moved on to the stairs. Where *should* she leave it?

There seemed to be something very different about the house. She wandered slowly about the high ceilinged rooms, with their original carved moldings at ceiling and floor. These beautiful moldings had, along with the carved chair rails, been preserved by Maddie's mother against her husband's ridicule only by the serendipitous and unexpected visit of Uncle Charlie. He had arrived just as the workmen prepared to tear them out. He had sent the men packing, scolding Aunt Nora in no nonsense tones. When she admitted, in her typical weak, timorous manner, the order had been issued by her husband, Uncle Charlie merely settled down in the living room to wait. When Harold returned home for lunch, he was greeted at his own front door by his wife's brother-in-law, and invited to sit in his own chair.

There he had the law read to him. Great Grandfather Henry Harrison had left his house to Nora as the youngest of his daughters. It was to be cared for and handed on to her children and then to their children and so forth and so forth. It was not, therefore, to be destroyed. If Nora and her husband wanted a home without such things as ceiling moldings, parquet floors, paneled doors, sixteen over twelve light windows and wood burning fieldstone fireplaces in each room, they were free to buy such a place. Charlie would be glad to buy another house for them.

So the cherry, walnut, and oak woodwork remained intact, and Madeline had continued to care for it, giving it the annual treatment which preserved the moisture in the wood and kept it glowing.

Still, in spite of the cheer of its basic design, the house was somehow uninviting. But then it had been so during most of Aunt Nora's tenure. Quite unlike G.G.H.H.'s tenure when his booming accent filled it.

"Gott in himmel nochenmal, but you iss getting bik!" was his usual greeting to each of his grandchildren. Except, Sal thought, for her, the family shrimp and pudge. "Kum in vunce, Lady Salome Chane," he'd say to her. "Here, I'll help you awta that hole! Ain't chu growin' awt insteat off up?"

What would happen to the lovely old home now?

She made her way to the large, airy suite that had been Maddie's. There the sitting room had a virginal, unused look, save for some scrapbooks piled on her school desk. In the bedroom, the closets were empty, a quilt the only bedding on the bed.

Where was Maddie sleeping? She must have moved into another part of the house. The master suite?

Sure enough, here the closets were full of clothes, beautifully tailored, elegant, expensive. She started to leave the bag in the closet, but thought better of it. Wasn't it evidence now? Ought she have taken it to the evidence room?

But no. She could not risk photos of the torn garment finding their way to the front page. This was one thing she could still do for her cousin.

Passing past Maddie's old room on her way back downstairs, some impulse led her to stop in the childhood room again. There was not much to see. She went to the windows which looked on to the back part of the property. There, too, everything was neat and trim, but without the massed flower gardens Grandmother had loved. As she turned to leave, her eyes lighted on the scrapbooks on her cousin's desk. There was something familiar about the edge of a news clipping left protruding from between the pages.

She opened the book and stared. It was a picture of Warren, his jaw dropped unbecomingly as he was told of the Thurston murder. Shocked, she turned the page. The entire book was filled with the same society page clippings Phyll Dayly had provided her team! But here the history was more complete. And it was edited. Wherever a photo included Warren's fiancée, the girl's likeness had been neatly cut out and replaced by one of Madeline.

Stunned, Sal sank weakly into a chair. My God! What was she to do with all of this? Obviously it was police business, but she knew she could not bring herself to take it away. She reminded herself gratefully, that she had no search warrant.

Her mind churned with a histrionic kaleidoscope of "I-should-haves," until she could no longer stand it. She headed back down the beautiful staircase toward the front door.

The library door, opening off the entry hall, stood ajar, a swath of gold light splashing on the brick floor. She had not looked in there, once her favorite room. Here, would be the books she had smuggled into the bathroom to read when she was supposed to be doing her share of the daily chores.

Even then, mysteries were an escape into a world where things were *happening*. She could usually get ten or fifteen minutes of good solid reading in, sitting innocently on the toilet, before someone would bellow for her. "Can't a person even go to the *bathroom* in peace?" Her complaint, uttered in the most injured tones possible, never seemed to conjure up the desired guilt or pity however, so the book would be pushed under the huge, claw foot tub, to be rescued later.

Then she remembered the other thing she had loved about the library. In addition to the books, Grandfather had kept his unique family album, not closed between covers, but hung up, filling one long wall in four, neat rows. The top row had been reserved for two large gold oval frames with formal poses of Grandfather and Grandmother. Below them, in eight equal frames, made by Grandfather himself, and spread equally apart, were those of the eight Thaxton offspring.

Likewise, the third row had held likenesses of the grandchildren, including Sam and her. The fourth reserved for great grandchildren, including Joe, Walt and Lucy.

She debated whether to look at them once more. A slab of light from under the door decided for her. She gathered her last drop of energy and went to check.

The light came from the sun, shining through the long windows, laying golden fingers on the soft grey carpet. She looked at the photo album wall and received another shock.

She stared. The neat, pristine frames did not hold the familiar pictures of the family. Instead, one of the two oval frames in the top row, where once her Grandmother's hung, was a beautifully composed professional photograph of her cousin Madeline. In Grandfather's place was a familiar likeness of Warren Watland, familiar because it was the same one she had seen on his office wall. But it was the three remaining rows that shocked her into stunned silence.

Eight larger frames and two rows of smaller ones hung, as though children and grandchildren belonged there. But the frames were empty!

Here was the heart, the dream that was the key to her cousin. A longing for a family just like the one she had seemed to despise. A longing she had never felt safe to share with anyone. A longing, so far beyond enduring, she had to kill to get relief.

Sal sank into a chair, covered her face with her hands, and wept.

CHAPTER 35 A Surrender of Sorts

In the end, the right deed mends the heart.

She returned to her office, empty now, the companionable warmth gone. "Fitting." she thought. The very idea of going home, of going anywhere where kindness and sanity reined, was impossible now.

She stood at the window, resting her forehead against the cool glass, looking out on Hamilton Circle. The room was dark and quiet, lit only by the last rays of apricot and mauve sunset, and the blinking of a traffic light.

She wished Sam would call. She needed to hear his common sensical voice before her heart broke. She had approved the doctor's decision to keep Madeline heavily sedated. Sam's assurance she had done the right thing would be welcome.

The telephone rang, insistent. Another citizen venting anger or praise? She wanted neither. A family member seeking clarification? She was not ready to give it. A friend offering sympathy? She did not deserve that. Wearily she picked up the receiver.

"Salome?" Pete's voice, low, husky, uncertain.

She was flooded with relief. "Yes, Pete. I am here."

He spoke hesitantly, as if listening intently for some clue to his welcome. "I tried to get through earlier to warn you that young Theodore and his gang were headed down your way." He paused again. "They were higher than a kite, S.J. You certainly gave them the right kind of medicine. They are 'cock of the walk' up here. You would swear they caught the woman single handedly!"

"Well," she said slowly, "Main Duke *did* save my life, and they all had a real part in preventing one more death-that is certainly true. They have a right to be cocky." She could almost feel his arms around her, wrapping her in comfort. Was he going to tell her again, as he had once before, that he loved her, would love her always?

She said quickly, "I'm sure they'll settle down. They were here and had a bang-up lunch with all of us. They'll be fine now."

"Yes. Well, they were whooping it up around town this morning. I stopped and talked to them when I saw them downtown." He seemed to be searching for something to say. "They agreed to stop their harassment of Mr. Soroka too. Acted like it was the farthest thing from their minds. Good idea, too. The last four are due to graduate this year. I reminded them that they need his endorsement. They took it, too. I remember a time when that wouldn't have cut any ice with this gang."

"Yes, I know." She thought back to those first days when they would have jeered at the thought of graduation. "Perhaps they are getting wiser as they get older."

"Perhaps. As you are fond of saying, "'tis a consummation devoutly to be wished.'" He was silent for a moment. Then he said huskily, "Wish to God I could say the same." He sounded as battered as she felt. Some pair we'd make, she thought.

Before he could go on, she said, "Yes. For all of us, I guess. It is so hard to be wise during the fact, isn't it? Much easier afterwards."

He seemed to sense she was getting ready to say good-bye. He spoke quickly, "Salome. I want to know how you *really* are. I can imagine how this is for you. How are you holding up?"

"Oh, fine, just fine." She smothered the impulse to tell him what she'd found at her cousin's house. Had he been here, rather than on the phone, miles away, she would have.

He grunted. "I doubt that. I know you. I'd put money on you're taking the whole responsibility on your shoulders. Isn't that so?"

There is no need to pretend or defend yourself to someone who is convinced you can do no wrong. She told him the truth. "I'd say I've been putting the responsibility where it belongs."

"Surely you can't feel responsible for the behavior of a mad woman. Even if she was..."

"My cousin? Why ever not? I seem to recall your rather frequent praise for what you called my 'radar' in spotting the early signs of trouble in adolescents. As I recall, you had bragged I needed only a half hour with a student to recognize the signs."

She sounded bitter, and why not? Hadn't he been right? Hadn't she been uncannily accurate and prophetic?

"Salome, for the love of Mike, go easy on yourself. What would you tell your students?" He didn't wait for an answer. "You are not responsible for everyone who crosses your path."

"Depends on what you mean by responsibility, doesn't it? Besides, she isn't exactly *anybody*, is she? You forget that I not only didn't help her when she needed it, I'm the one who dragged her..." Her voice caught.

He was silent for a bit. Then he said, "Well, I seem to be making you feel worse, rather than better." There was another silence. Then, "look S.J., just try to let the rest of us take part of the load, eh? And take it easy on yourself. Has your brother returned?"

"No, At least I haven't seen him. He ought to be here soon."

"Good. Good." Another pause. "Will I see you again?"

"I don't know Pete. I suppose so. Right now..."

"I know. I know. Well, I'm sorry I didn't get hold of you to warn you to expect company. I'd better let you go. But Salome, please take care of yourself."

"I will, Pete. You too. And Pete?"

"Yes?"

"Thank you for calling. I do feel better. Really." It was not much but it would have to do.

"Great. That's great." Relief and something else in his voice. Joy?

"'Bye then, Peter"

"'Bye Salome." The line went dead.

She went back to her post at the window again. What she needed was to go home to business as usual. She closed her eyes and instantly saw fields of wild aster, purple, pink, blues as pale navy as a new sky. She longed for a ramble in the woods. But between her office and the woods were perhaps a dozen reporters and photographers. She was not ready for another session with them. Why didn't they go about their business?

"You *are* their business right now," a small voice said. "C'mon. You're the tough one, remember? Just go, and in a few minutes it will all be over."

A whiff of cigarette smoke, drifting up through the open window, brought back the memory of Pete's big warm hand clasping hers to his breast. Desire engulfed her like a tidal wave. What am I going to do about him? Why do I feel this way, now, at my age? I am too *old* for this to be happening to me. How can he arouse a passion I never felt before?

It is clear that keeping away from him hasn't helped much. My God! No wonder they call it a fire!

My, my, she derided herself, we certainly are trotting out all the platitudes, aren't we? Is this how Madeline felt about Warren? Madeline is right. I am lucky. Maddie desperately wanted a man who didn't want her. She had a man who desperately wanted her while she... She stopped. Therein, she thought, was the difference. Pete's love *was* requited. Admit it, she told herself and move on.

She did not hear the familiar tattoo on her door, but turned instinctively when it opened. As always, he knew what to say.

"You rang, Madam?" Uttered in the deep, sepulchral voice that was their shared greeting ever since the days they had parodied the Adams Family. Her twin's arm came up around her shoulder and he drew her away from the window, away from the memories, across the office and back out into the world. "Gosh it's good to see your old puss again, baby sister." He squeezed her again. "Done anything interesting while I was away? I have. I've got a lot to tell you about my trip, and some good news too. The trip turned out to be even more profitable than we anticipated. Got new contracts galore. And they are tickled with the results we've gotten from those Chinese pigs. Gotten so I'm beginning to think the damn things are cute!"

He pulled her along briskly toward the elevators. He went on without giving her a chance to put in an oar. "Got the car waiting and I'm hungry. Are you? Anyway you can come and watch me eat. Although that'll probably put five pounds on you." He grinned and squeezed her again. "Golly, I missed your funny face. I decided I'm taking you along next time, protect me from those Geisha girls they insist on throwing at me."

They were at the big front door, Sam's driver waiting at the curb. A handful of waiting reporters rushed them. Sam pulled her closer, pushing them aside while cameras flashed. He spoke above their prattle. "Okay, fellows. Beat it now. My sister and I have a lot to talk about, and she's tired, and I'm hungry. You already have it all. There's nothing new. Thank you," and he handed her into the car.

He grinned as they sped off. "Apparently you just can't keep out of trouble when I'm gone. Haven't changed a bit in forty-seven years, have you?" He squeezed her again. "Anyway, speaking of how old we are, I'm thinking we should have something really special for our birthday this year. What do you think?" He squeezed her shoulder again.

She looked up at him, seeing him objectively, as one does sometimes, those to whom we are closest. He had, she thought, gotten even better looking. More like Sean Connery than ever. More than handsome, he was intelligent, strong and kind, everything one could wish in a brother.

"Sure, Ugly," she said faintly. "Since you have finally deigned to let me get a word in edgewise. I suppose, being the *elder*, you think you know what's best for us. What do you have in mind?"

"Well, how about a baseball team? I hear the Phillies might consider an offer, and if you could get a couple of days free I thought we'd fly over there and..."

She dissolved into somewhat delirious laughter.

GLOSSARY OF PENNSYLVANIA DUTCH PHRASES

As in all folk languages, spelling and definitions vary. Below are those used in this book.

Mach's Gut – (We) Make it good.
Vas gibt? – What gives?
Nicht wahr? – Is that not so?
Sie ruhic. – Be quiet.
Freundschaft – the entire family
Ich weiss. – I know.
Mach schnell! – Hurry up!
Versteh? – Understand?
Danke. – Thank you.
Denkst du nicht – Don't you think so?
Denkst du? – Do you think so?
Verstehen sie? – Do you understand?
Ya gawiss. – Yes it is.
Vunce – once
Bist du fertig? – Are you ready?
Gott in himmel nochenmal! – God in heaven!

About the Author

Ms. Fairchild is new to fiction writing. A lifelong educator and business woman, Hannah Fairchild's emergence as a writer came about when vision problems caused her to retire from her much loved work as student teacher supervisor.

No longer able to roam country roads in search of wild flowers, Ms. Fairchild saw an opportunity to write the mysteries she'd always wanted to write.

Drawing on her Pennsylvania Dutch heritage for inspiration, ("Throw papa down the stairs his hat," "Ve grow too soon old und too late smart,") her series, "The Pennsylvania Dutch Mysteries," is set in quiet Plainfield, a town still populated by the same hard working, phlegmatic Pennsylvania Dutch who built the town.

The main characters, Sam Thaxton and Salome Thaxton McKnight, twin heirs to the vast Thaxton fortune, are forty-five in the first book. *"If It's Monday it Must Be Murder"* is drawn from her experiences as a teacher of adolescents with behavioral problems, experiences at once so frustrating, mystifying and delightful, there was nothing for it but to record that adventure. Once given life, the "Corrigibles" insisted on having a part in each of the "Pennsylvania Dutch Mysteries" as well.

The second, *"Dead in Pleasant Company,"* features a unique killer who murders via the Internet.

"In Death on Delivery," her third "Pennsylvania Dutch Mystery", the Corrigibles are once again instrumental in saving the day.

Ms. Fairchild writes the sort of mysteries she likes to read, with believable characters that matter, low on commonality and contrivance, high on humanity and humor. Her stories are literate and occasionally even a bit alliterate, each offering something unique to the reader.

A fourth book in the series, *"So Long At The Fair,"* is in the works.

Printed in the United States
41236LVS00001B/41